The Priest Wonho's Memories of Admiral Yi

Other Books by M. F. Sawyer

Married To Islam
cowritten with Dalia Shah

Temple Cook's Guide To (Almost) Enlightenment

More information about these books
is at the end of this one
and may be found at:
www.mfsawyer.com

The Priest Wonho's Memories of Admiral Yi

English Language Edition Compiled by
M. F. Sawyer

iUniverse, Inc.
New York Lincoln Shanghai

The Priest Wonho's Memories of Admiral Yi

Copyright © 2007 by M. F. Sawyer

All rights reserved. No part of this book may be used or reproduced by any means, graphic, electronic, or mechanical, including photocopying, recording, taping or by any information storage retrieval system without the written permission of the publisher except in the case of brief quotations embodied in critical articles and reviews.

iUniverse books may be ordered through booksellers or by contacting:

iUniverse
2021 Pine Lake Road, Suite 100
Lincoln, NE 68512
www.iuniverse.com
1-800-Authors (1-800-288-4677)

Certain characters in this work are historical figures, and certain events portrayed did take place. The locations are largely historical. However, this is a work of fiction. All of the other characters, names, places, and events as well as all incidents, organizations, and dialogue in this novel are either the products of the author's imagination or are used fictitiously.

Cover Design by Chris Smith (smithchris.com)
Edited by Gloria Campbell

ISBN: 978-0-595-42326-2 (pbk)
ISBN: 978-0-595-86663-2 (ebk)

Printed in the United States of America

The Priest Wonho, a wandering Buddhist Monk, nearing his death recalls the horrible Imjin War between Japan and Korea (and China) and tells of his amazing experiences as a helper to Admiral Yi Sun-sin, Korea's greatest hero, and perhaps the greatest admiral the world has ever seen.

This book is dedicated to my mother, Ruth Sawyer, a Language Arts teacher of unsurpassed excellence whose love of literature happily infected me while I was young.

It is also dedicated to Linda Sawyer, whose steady support since the 1980s has been more appreciated than she might ever know, and to George Brooks, the original "Gaijin Samurai." In 1984 George told me the story of this fantastic Korean admiral after a hike to the top of an old Buddhist mountain in Kagoshima-ken, Japan.

Acknowledgments

I have acknowledged many persons in the Compiler's Notes already, but I must again mention George Brooks, "The Gaijin Samurai," for the inspiration his admiration for Admiral Yi passed on to me back in 1984. (He had earned this title long before Tom Cruise tried to steal it.) My father, Hal, passed along a love of history to all of his children. He also gave us an appreciation of Japan based upon his time there in the Korean War, which was further augmented by our wonderful Nisei neighbors, Henry and Minnie Itoi, and their son, Victor. Thanks to Rebecca McDonald for early reading and comments about the manuscript. Chris Smith (www.smithchris.com) put together the original cover and graphics for this book. I'd recommend him to anybody. At iUniverse, Joy Elliot was happy and enthusiastic, and Mike Fielder always organized and professional.

Two books, containing three primary sources, were of key importance in writing this book. These were the highly regarded translations by Ha Tae Hung of *Nanjung Ilgi War Diary of Admiral Yi Sun-Sin* and *Imjin Changch'o Admiral Yi Sun-Sin's Memorials to Court,* which were published by Yonsei University Press in 1977 and 1981. In the second book, there was also a translation of the *Biography of Admiral Yi* by Yi Pun, his nephew. As is repeated in the Compiler's Notes at the back of the book, these were the key sources that made this book possible. They are an utterly essential tool for the English langrage researcher into the life and times of Admiral Yi Sun-sin.

Gloria Campbell, in my highly biased view, is the best editor in the world. I am very lucky to have her. Two professors from Hanseo University in South Korea, Kim Wonho, PhD, and Kim Taejin, PhD, were also very helpful and encouraging both as I wrote and in reading the early manuscripts. The kind patience of Admiral Yi's descendants in answering my questions during my visits to the Admiral's tomb and to nearby Hyonchung Shrine (Hyonghungsa) is also much appreciated.

M. F. Sawyer
Shoreline, Washington
March 2007

Note to the Reader

The manuscripts of the Priest Wonho are still waiting to be found. They are in a sealed jar somewhere within a cave on Mount Tansung near the hermitages and cliff-side carved Buddhas at the temple of Sudok. Until the documents are officially discovered, this book must be called a work of historical fiction.

However, all of the main historical events depicted here are real, and the experiences of Admiral Yi are historically accurate. The facts and interpretations regarding Admiral Yi as given by the Priest Wonho are as authentic as I can make them. All persons named in the book and the events regarding them are true except for those singled out in the Compiler's Notes at the end of the book as "not verified."

Otherwise, the book truthfully reflects what has come down to us except for events and words specific to the Priest Wonho or other not-verified characters.

All military, martial, religious, linguistic, and cultural assertions are as factual as can be ascertained. The battles and deeds of Admiral Yi are recounted from the best of primary sources, these being the written words of Admiral Yi himself and his biography by Yi Pun, his nephew. Yi Pun survived the Admiral after having been his companion for part of the war. These, as well as all other sources for the historical facts, information, and conclusions, are detailed in the Compiler's Notes at the end of the book.

Perhaps sadly, the information about the founding of Japan by the Priest Wonho still needs to be documented. To an objective observer, it now seems proved beyond a reasonable doubt that the land that we now know as Japan was formed by Koreans in the fourth century AD, and most likely by the Kingdom of Paekche. This kingdom, famous for the gently smiling faces of its Buddha images, ruled the southwest part of the Korean peninsula until past the middle of the seventh century AD.

From here forward, we move through the life and times of Korea, Japan, and China during a terrible war. We proceed through a maze of battles, espionage, and court intrigue as seen through the eyes of a man who was in the service of one of the greatest warriors the world has ever known.

Let us begin *The Priest Wonho's Memories of Admiral Yi*. To do so we travel with the writer himself, Wonho, the humble and ever-wandering Buddhist monk.

May we have a good journey.

Foreword

The *Priest Wonho's Memories of Admiral Yi* by the Buddhist Priest Wonho are believed by many Koreans to be the most important medieval manuscripts found in East Asia since the end of World War II. Some Chinese and Japanese would dispute this, but even their historical authorities have agreed that they are a significant find that brings new perspectives about their own countries' histories as well as being of incalculable value to the people of Korea.

Any new insights into the character and ways of Admiral Yi Sun-Sin are of extraordinary importance to all Koreans. He is a man held in high esteem by South Koreans; North Koreans; Koreans living in the central Asian republics, due to Stalin's deportations; and the large Korean-American communities in the United States and Canada. Any new information about Admiral Yi is also of much interest to the Japanese to whom he was the ultimate foe. And for military people and historians everywhere these manuscripts will be extremely valuable. To them, Admiral Yi is arguably the best and the most successful admiral of all time.

These manuscripts also reveal that he was more than just a fantastic warrior. Admiral Yi is a man who makes sure homeless refugees are fed, finds and opens new farmlands for the displaced, and is a man of letters. He is as well read and as skilled a writer as the best of the literati of his time.

Admiral Yi lived during the time of King Henry VIII and Queen Elizabeth I. It was also the time of two of the greatest naval battles in Western history. The first was the Battle of Lepanto in 1571 when the seemingly unbeatable Moslems were defeated off the coast of Cyprus and turned back from Christian Europe. The second battle, in 1588, was the defense of Queen and country by Sir Francis Drake against the Spanish Armada. Admiral Yi was a compatriot in time of Cervantes (who fought at Lepanto) and Don Quixote. He also lived during some Shakespeare's lifetime. Sadly, Admiral Yi would have been all too familiar with some of the characters and events in *Richard III*, *Hamlet*, and *MacBeth*. These plays are very close in spirit to the Korean-Choson court politics of Yi's time.

Admiral Yi, however, knew nothing of doings in the West. He had his own concerns. Among these was that Japan, with tens of thousands of the best swordsman in the world, was coming to Korea.

Only Sir Francis Drake, among naval legends of the time, could be compared to Yi. In any objective assessment, Yi would come out ahead. He did more with less, and repeatedly. His four victories in 1592 alone were enough to make him a military immortal. Militarily, Drake gained at best a draw in his biggest fight, the battle against the Spanish Armada.

Drake was good, no doubt, and a wonderful navigator. However, he never had a Hansando or a Myongnyang.

Of admirals in the West, perhaps only Nelson could compare to Yi. Both won great victories in a wide variety of circumstances against very strong enemies. Both are still among the most revered of military heroes in their respective countries and among military persons everywhere. And both died in their final battles against their most formidable foes.

Some argue that Yi is superior because he did not start out with the world's greatest navy, as did Nelson. They point out that Nelson did not have to design his major warship (or at least greatly improve its design) or to create new types of cannon and hand weapons, particularly at the start of a major war. Nor, they might add, did Nelson have to feed thousands of starving refugees or attempt to keep typhoid fever from killing the crews of his squadrons. And there is no doubt that Nelson did not have intriguers at the royal court who were trying to have him arrested and executed based on the reports of a "patriot" who turned out to be an enemy spy.

The Priest Wonho tells us of Admiral Yi's victories and of other important battles in this war. However, it is not what Wonho tells us of Yi's military exploits that stand out. These have been well known for hundreds of years. What makes *Wonho's Memories* so important is that they show us more of Admiral Yi than anyone, except historians, has previously known. His great scholarship has been neglected. His knowledge of the seven classics of Chinese warfare and his use of their best and most applicable sections have been largely ignored. His great care for the common people; his respect and appreciation for all, Confucianist or Buddhist; his willingness to drink a few too many with his friends; his love for his mother, sons, and the offspring of his two elder brothers who had died; all of this and more comes out clearly in *The Priest Wonho's Memories of Admiral Yi*.

Regarding the Priest Wonho himself, we know next to nothing beyond what is written here. He says that he is good at three things: he learns languages easily, he travels well, and people seem to know they can trust him (and they are right). We know that his mother was Korean and his father Japanese/Korean. We find out about a family tragedy when he was very young, about some of his experiences while traveling in China and Japan, and, of course, about his times with Admiral Yi and in the Imjin War.

We also learn that, as a good Buddhist, he felt his own life to be ephemeral and of no interest, perhaps even to himself. He seems to enjoy laughing at the priest named Wonho. At the same time, he takes his subject most seriously. It seems unlikely that he would ever have made light of Admiral Yi.

Also, Wonho was asked to write these *Memories* late in life at a period when a terrible enemy again threatened his country. This time, the invader was not Japan. The opponent this time was China.

It seems as if the aged Wonho was spending his last days meditating and waiting for death. He may have been a wandering monk who settled at Sudok Temple, perhaps at the request of the abbot. It seems that the abbot of Sudok Temple, on hearing Priest Wonho's life story, asked him to stay. "Remain with us," one can hear him saying, "Stay with us and write what you remember of the old days. Especially, write of your times with Admiral Yi."

We can imagine the old Buddhist thinking about this and perhaps saying that all of these worldly things were of no consequence. Why should such impermanent things be written about? And, maybe, for we will never know for sure, the abbot of the Temple said, "Exactly. These things of the world are not important. Admiral Yi knew this, which is why he lived how he did. He was fearless. He did and said what he believed to be right, even unto death. It is this example that might inspire others."

Then, old Wonho, perhaps with a wizened grin or maybe only a nod, agreed. His pages follow.

Foreword   xvii

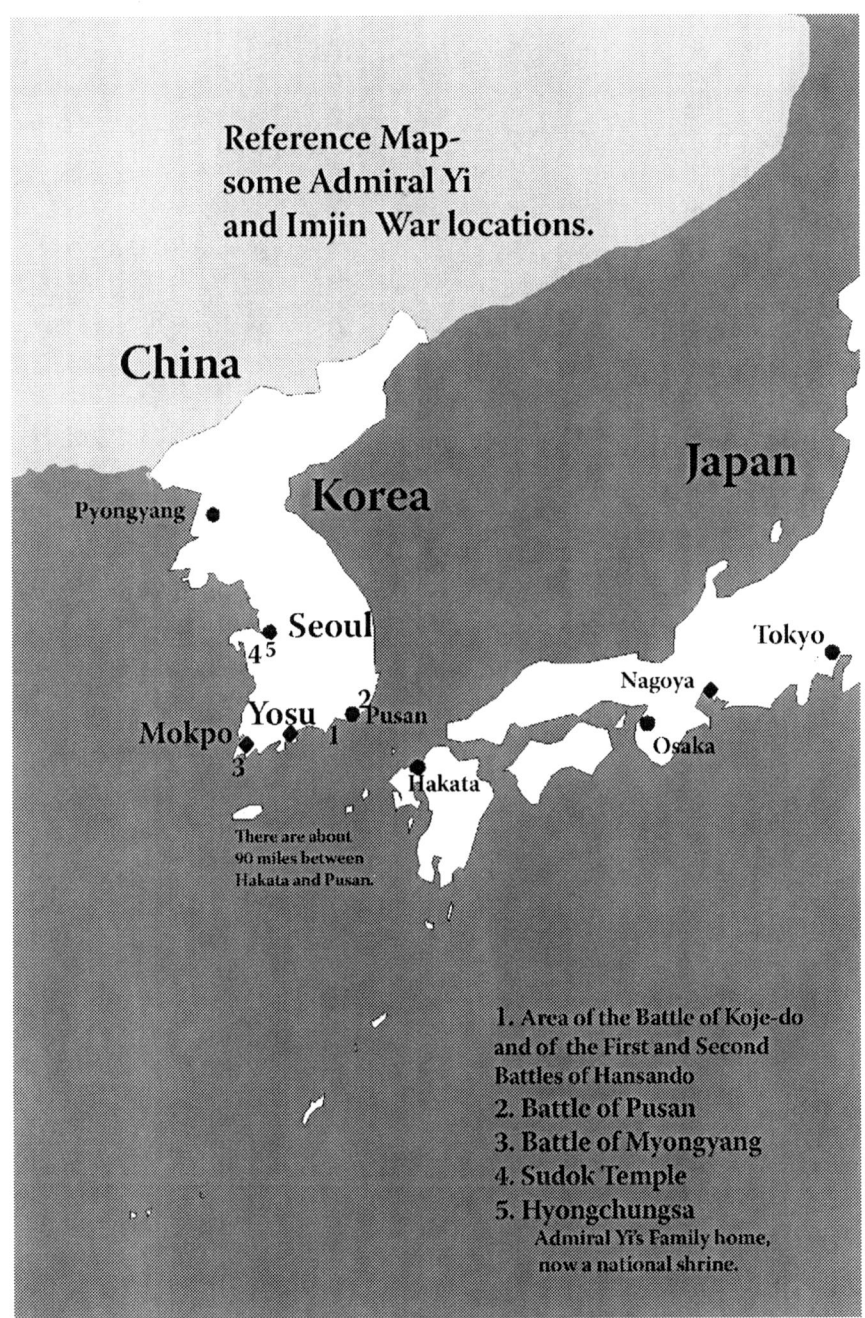

Map of Korea

Chronology of Major Events

This chronology includes the book's major historical events and some important dates and facts regarding Admiral Yi's life, some of which are not otherwise mentioned. The chapters that feature those events and facts mentioned are in parentheses at the end of the respective notation. Chapter 1 begins the book in 1592. Much of the information given here may be found in the two books by Ha Tae-hung mentioned in the Compiler's Notes at the end of the book.

1545—On the 8th day of the third moon (April 28), the baby who would grow up to be his country's greatest military hero was born to the Yi family in Seoul. The story is told that his mother had a dream foretelling greatness for the child, and that he should be named Sun-sin after a legendary Chinese. And it is said that an astrologer prophesied that the boy would be a great military commander when he was 50.

1552—The boy and his family move to Asan, where his tomb is now located as is Hyongchungsa, a monumental shrine dedicated to him at the site of his family home. Here the boy practiced archery, a skill that earned him early renown even in a country of skilled archers who routinely put huge arrows into enemy-sized targets three hundred meters away.

1564–1576—Married in 1564, Yi fathers two sons and, encouraged by his father-in-law, prepares to take the exams for becoming a military officer. The exams feature a variety of tests, including shooting arrows at distant targets from the back of a galloping horse. In his first try, the young man falls from his horse and breaks his leg, impressing the onlookers by bandaging his severely broken limb himself. In his next attempt, four years later in 1576, he passes the exam and is sent to protect the cold northern areas from the Manchurian bandits who are an ever-present problem.

1577—His third son, Myon, is born.

1578–1590—He holds various military posts, mostly in the north. He distinguishes himself for valiant behavior in combat and for maintaining the highest and most proper Confucianist standards of decorum and behavior. His success on the battlefield combined with his highly ethical behavior often leads to conflicts with superior officers and officials because they are jealous of his skill and fear his impeccable honesty. They do not hold to his standards and resent him.

These jealous, petty, and powerful types cause problems. Also, his career is interrupted by the death of his father. In this era, it was the normal procedure to mourn for two years while holding no official post, and Yi did as custom required. However, his skills and abilities are so pronounced that, as the threat of a Japanese invasion became more evident, he is promoted to an important post.

1591—Yi is appointed to naval command (Left Naval Commander) of Cholla Province. The Choson Dynasty had no separate army and navy. All military officers and personnel could be on land one week and at sea the next or vice versa. This why when Koreans translate his rank into English they often call him "General Yi" rather than "Admiral Yi." This is accurate. During his lifetime, there was no difference between a land general and a sea general. One used or maneuvered between fortresses, and the other attacked or defended with ships.

Upon assuming a naval command, Yi Sun-sin immediately began preparations for the worst that could happen. He designed and tested better cannon (Heaven, Earth, Black, and Yellow), trained his almost totally inexperienced officers and sailors as well as possible, and, most famously, began to improve upon the kobukson, the turtle ship, claimed by some to be the world's first true ironclad.

1592—He finishes the kobukson just in time (Ch.1).

These almost impermeable battleships were never huge in number compared with the multi-decked panoekson ships. The latter were good ships, matching any vessel the Japanese had to offer. They were double masted, had a high vantage point for firing at the Japanese, and good protection for non-combatant crewmembers. However, the kobukson provided the psychological edge that gave Admiral Yi what he needed to perform unmatched military sea miracles in what came to be known as the Imjin War.

This War was the brainchild of Hideyoshi, the Japanese ruler. He could not take the title shogun because he lacked the correct ancestry, but as the Taiko he was essentially the same thing. Hideyoshi gave the word and the Japanese invaded Korea landing in Pusan. Their stated goal was to march up the peninsula and invade China.

The invasion commences in the late spring on the 13th day of the 4th Moon. The samurai seem unstoppable, cutting north through the Korean Peninsula like hungry tigers through a flock of sheep. It is one of the most successful pre-panzer "blitzkriegs" ever. The only victory for the Korean Army, or, more accurately land forces in this first year of the war, is at Chinju. The Japanese fail to take the city. They are foiled by the obstinate defenders led by Hwang Chin and by the coming of foul winter weather.

Thanks to the leadership of Admiral Yi, the naval forces of Korea keep the Choson Dynasty afloat. His victories in this year, unmatched in the annals of military history by any other commander at sea, include:

Okpo, 5th Moon. The first significant Korean victory of the war is won. (Ch. 3).

Tangpo, 6th Moon. Yi is shot through and keeps fighting (Ch. 5).

Hansando, 7th Moon. The most significant naval battle of the war is fought. From here on, the wisest of the Japanese know that Hideyoshi's plan to dispose of Korea en route to conquering Ming China is impossible (Ch. 6).

Pusan, 9th Moon. Admiral Yi sails into the lair of the tiger and breathes the fire of the dragon. He attacks the Japanese in their greatest Korean stronghold, killing many and destroying over a hundred of their ships while losing only a few men and no ships (Ch. 12).

Though not a triumph of Admiral Yi, the heroic defense of Chinju led by Hwang Chin (whom the Priest Wonho calls, next to Admiral Yi, his favorite military commander) occurs in the 10th month. This, along with Hansando and Haengju, is often called one of the three great victories of the war (Ch. 12).

1593, 2nd Moon. A victory for Admiral Yi at Ungchon is marred by the collision of two of his ships caused by over-confident and careless captains. One ship is lost (Ch. 13).

6th Moon. Chinju falls, though there is a ray of hope in the defeat (Ch. 14, end of Part One).

1594–1598—Chapters 15–32 cover the rest of the Imjin War, which is also the remainder of Admiral Yi's life. The best and the worst of times are recounted here—love, laughter, slaughter, death, and betrayal with Chinese betraying Koreans to the Japanese, the Japanese as murderous as ever, and the Korean court seemingly hapless and woefully corrupt. These years also include many surprising developments for the Priest Wonho.

1617—The Priest Wonho meets a veteran of the Imjin War, a young sailor who has risen to port commander. Together they recount their years with Admiral Yi and other tales of wonderful heroism and of betrayal. These conversations correspond with the time in which the actual events occurred.

1628—As far as we know, the manuscripts that have become *The Priest Wonho's Memories of Admiral Yi* were started in the late cold months of 1627 and finished by the end of the following spring. Chapter 33 is his epilogue recounting events after Admiral Yi died. It is also his goodbye to his life and, though he did not know it, his farewell to us.

1629 or soon after—The manuscripts of the presumably deceased Priest Wonho are hidden away in a small cave behind the main building of Sudok Temple. One of the two main theories about why they were hidden is that the abbot who commissioned them had died and his successor said, "Put these somewhere safe," or "What are these? Toss them in the cave." The second theory is that a rumor was circulating that the Chinese forces were heading south. If this were true, and if their behavior would be anything like that of the Japanese in 1592, the temple might be burned. The abbot therefore made sure that the Priest Wonho's manuscripts were safe by putting them into jars and storing them in the cave.

I prefer the second theory and can only guess that the abbot had meant to bring them back to a more honorable place once the war ended. Something happened, though. Perhaps the abbot died, and his successor was not aware of the jars in the cave with a collapsed entryway. Why dig it out? It would just fall in again.

1993—A young child playing in the forest behind the main part of Sudok Temple steps into a hole and moves some rocks, and finds an opening. His parents tell a priest, and some jars are discovered. They seem very old. Suspecting there might be valuable items in them, trained archaeologists, observed by government and Buddhist officials, open them very carefully. To everyone's surprise, there are manuscripts that, if real, are about Korea's greatest hero. The controversy begins. This book is one of the results.

Author's Choices on Spelling, Place Names, Dates, and More

Korea keeps changing how it spells things. Kobukson is now supposed to be geobeukseon. Paekche has become Baekche. Sudoksa is now Sudeoksa and Pusan is now Busan. Most history books were printed before the most recent changes and retain the old spellings.

This presented a nightmare for this compiler: Which spellings to use? I chose those in my main sources that are easier for the English language reader to pronounce. Many of the place names have also changed. Many towns, islands, and other places—even provinces—have different names now. In these instances, I have used the name most commonly used by modern Koreans and history books. For example, the battle on Myongnyang in 1597 will be called that and not by its original title: the Battle of Uldolmok. (Both the spellings and the place names were my call, and I apologize in advance to any whom I might have bothered by making the "wrong" choice.)

Regarding dates: In my English translation of the Priest Wonho's pages, I have him and others saying things like *January* and *376 AD.* In fact, Korea used (and in many cases still uses) the lunar calendar, and no

Korean of Admiral Yi's time would have given dates in this way. They are translated solely for the convenience of the modern reader.

In compiling this book, I made other considerations that should also be mentioned.

Some readers will find parts of this book controversial. This compiler has researched all of the statements of the Priest Wonho and the results are at the end of the book in the Compiler's Notes. These Notes are organized chapter by chapter and give references for the information sources and assertions of the Priest Wonho, as far as these can be proven. Of course, some of his statements may never be verified; without a time machine, they cannot be proven.

Happily, everything that was verifiable shows Wonho to have been very accurate. To see how and why, again please refer to the Compiler's Notes.

The Priest Wonho wrote very well, but not chronologically. He wrote, as would an old man given an unexpected task, about a subject sometimes thirty-five years in the past. He recalled things and wrote them in the order they came to mind.

His *Memories of Admiral Yi* in the original Korean-Chinese begin almost with the Battle of Hansando. His first meeting with Admiral Yi, the joke-test played on him, comes in the middle of his writings. The arrest and transport of Admiral Yi to Seoul, when he was tied with the red rope and displayed in a cage, come near the end. Wonho wouldn't have written about this unless pressed by the abbot to do so.

He adds little snippets of facts and memories, many undated, throughout his *Memories*. Many can be approximately dated by comparing them to the Admiral's own diary, his notes to the Court, and by established dates of events and battles, but others must remain uncertain. Still others, like his recollections of conversations with the officer he calls the Young Captain, which occurred about two decades after Admiral Yi's death, can only be approximately dated.

With all of this in mind, *The Priest Wonho's Memories of Admiral Yi* has been put into chronological order as well as can be established. The conversations with the Young Captain have been inserted to give a fuller understanding of Admiral Yi and the events in question.

In the actual conversations and events, Wonho uses what would be the present tense in English as if he is reliving the events of three decades gone by as he wrote. This tense is continued throughout the book.

Certain suffixes are used very often in the Korean and are part of the name. For instance, the *sa* in Sudok means temple. Therefore, to write "The manuscripts of the Priest Wonho were found at Sudoksa Temple" is really to write "The manuscripts of the Priest Wonho were found at Sudok Temple Temple." With *sa* meaning temple, *song* meaning fortress, and *san* meaning mountain, this duplication will be avoided as much as possible.

Proper names are given as in Korean, so Yi (the family name) comes first, as in Yi Sun-Sin. Yi rhymes with Lee, Sun with soon, and Sin sounds more like sheen. Some terms are westernized to help the English reader. For instance, in Korean, Admiral Yi is called General Yi or Navy General Yi. It seemed wiser to stay with Admiral in English. When Wonho refers to Admiral Yi as the Admiral, Admiral is capitalized, as is the word Sir. This seems closest to Wonho's intent.

Sections of the *Nanjung Ilgi War Diary of Admiral Yi Sun-sin* and *Imjin Changch'o Admiral Yi Sun-Sin's Memorials to Court* are included throughout the book. These texts are used to clarify, support, and otherwise expand upon *Wonho's Memories*. It is most certain Wonho himself never had access to these volumes in his lifetime, though, of course, his writings show that he had firsthand knowledge of many of the events described in their contents.

The English translations of these two books written by Ha Tae-hung and published by Yonsei University Press are mentioned in the Compiler's Notes along with other verification sources, but they must be singled out here for special praise. I cannot overemphasize their usefulness to an

English-language-based researcher regarding the life of Admiral Yi and the Imjin War. Also, I owe a large debt of gratitude to Professor Kim Wonho of Hanseo University. Professor Kim verified the accuracy of my English versions of the translations of the works by Admiral Yi and Yi Pun, all of which had the work of Ha Tae-hung as their inspiration.

    I cannot begin to extend enough thanks to those who helped with the translation of *The Priest Wonho's Memories of Admiral Yi* from the original manuscripts. And I am not sure that my Compiler's Notes, with their sparse comments, are enough in way of showing appreciation to the many sources I have used to research the Priest Wonho's accuracy, the life of Admiral Yi, the truth regarding Korean and Japanese history, and more. Thanks to you all.

Part I

▼

Fourth Moon, 1592–Sixth Moon, 1593

Includes:

- *The Priest Wonho meets Admiral Yi.*
- *Admiral Yi finishes the building of the kobukson, the strongest fighting ship in Asia.*
- *The Japanese invade the Kingdom of Choson—the land of Korea.*
- *The Japanese army marches through Korea as if the Korean army does not exist.*
- *Admiral Yi saves Korea with a series of naval victories unmatched in all of recorded history.*
- *The Priest Wonho shares his insights into the Japanese—their history, their leaders, and their language.*
- *A fantastic victory, and then a terrible defeat at Chinju and sad events at Ungchon.*

One could argue that Admiral Yi is the greatest military leader of all time. This might be going too far. Might be. There is always Alexander the Great and, perhaps, Genghis Khan.

Then one may contend that Admiral Yi is most certainly the most fantastic naval commander of all time. And here there would be less of an argument. Except for Admiral Nelson, there are virtually no other contenders for this honor.

But, between Admiral Nelson and Admiral Yi, who is the greater?

We will likely never know, for they came from different times, cultures, and kingdoms and had very different support and resources. However, those responsible for having the lost manuscripts of the Priest Wonho translated into English hope that this book helps shed light upon many points in the Nelson versus Yi argument.

Plus, there is much more to Admiral Yi than the heroic, victorious naval commander. The words of the modest Priest Wonho help us to see this, too.

Chapter 1

My First Meeting with Admiral Yi

The 13th day of the 4th moon, 1592

To satisfactorily fulfill a request from the Left Navy Commander of Cholla Province was not an opportunity to be turned away lightly, especially when one lost nothing in the attempt. I was there, I was available, and I was expendable, so the abbot of the temple sent me to Admiral Yi Sun-Sin.

I had spent years in the country of the likely enemy, Japan. I had traveled to our problematic ally, China, and knew its language, both written and spoken. Of course, I also had been to all parts of Korea, that is, to all corners of our own Kingdom of Choson. I had studied the beliefs, practices, and philosophies of Buddhism in all three of those countries and had read their literature and histories.

In short, I could speak, read, and write the languages that Yi Sun-sin, the soon-to-be legendary figure, needed. I had the knowledge, the abilities, and the experiences that the military man who would become the savior of his country was quietly looking for. And when the abbot of the temple heard of this, he thought of me. I was but a wandering priest who had dropped by and asked for little and ate less, but who could now be put into service and be made useful.

The man that the abbot sent me to was the Left Navy Commander of Cholla Province, a man in his late forties, obviously strong and intelligent, a man who would be noticed even without the trappings of his high office. The abbot had sent me to Yi Sun-Sin who was not yet hailed as the ultimate hero, who was not yet the greatest military leader of our times, and, possibly, of all times, and who had not yet been awarded the title Chungmu: "Loyal Valor."

I knew nothing then of this officer's great achievements. No one did. All I knew was that I was to see the Admiral the first day he was available. Later, I heard that this had meant waiting until after he had observed the "Earth" and "Black" cannons being tested from on board the first of his newly designed iron-plated kobukson (turtle ships).

"The Admiral will see you now." With these words, I am first ushered into his presence. He looks up, totally at ease and relaxed, but still I feel as if I am in the presence of a hunting eagle.

I make polite gestures and give the proper words, his status already infinitely above mine. He responds appropriately, exactly as would be required, but with a style many never possess. Certainly, I know that I do not.

"You are Wonho, a traveling Buddhist monk."

Traveling, yes. I am actually unattached to any temple, though I have one I do officially call home even though it isn't. A few months in any place are enough. But he is waiting for a response.

"Yes, Sir," I say.

"Your father was Japanese?" His eyes are steady on me. I know the rumors that Hideyoshi, the Taiko, the ruler of Japan, is threatening to send his Japanese troops, his samurai, to invade Korea. I remember these ferocious armored fighters all too well. When there is an execution, young samurai bring their swords to test their sharpness on the corpse. This is likely to be their best pre-duel or pre-battle chance to hew into human flesh. The sound of this is as bad as the sight.

Their reputation for deadly, finely-honed skill is well earned. And lately, they are using their firearms as dangerously as they use their razor-sharp blades. I think of them with both weapons. But this is only a passing thought, a wispy memory, as I focus on the more important matter. This man, this military commander named Yi Sun-sin, is asking me about my Japanese blood. I know that I am Korean, loyal to Choson, but he needs to know this, too. I promptly and steadily answer his questions.

"My father was born in Japan and raised there for eight years, but his parents were Korean, as was my mother."

"And you?"

"I am Korean, loyal to Choson." As I speak, the Admiral looks even more closely at me. He has the eyes of one who can spot lies like a snake sees the eggs of a bird's nest.

"Your father.... He was a priest, too?"

"No, Sir. My family were merchants."

"How did it happen that you became a priest?"

His eyes are still on me, but there is less of the hawk and more of the compassionate man. I begin to see the man who later, during the war, sends memorandums to court to try to gain help for the refugees, who got them land to farm, food to eat, and treatment for the horrible typhoid from which he himself would suffer. He knows that for a merchant's son to become a Buddhist priest in this day and age probably means bad things had happened. And, of course, he is right. "That is a long story, Sir." And extremely personal, though I do not say this out loud.

"Just tell what you can of it," he says, most politely. "Focus on how you learned to speak, read, and write Japanese and Chinese, as well as Korean."

Thoughts swirl. Memories. Happiness, then anguish, the agony of my father crying at night and me helpless. I remember the words of the Buddha, the Four Supreme Truths, and know that only what I hang onto can hurt me, that only the memories that I let have power over me can and do. I draw upon my months of solitary meditations, bring in my best sense of detachment, and speak.

"There was a little boy. He had a prosperous father and a beautiful mother. The father loved the mother more than life, and the little boy, his only son, was to his eyes the sun on a clear spring day."

I see my body from above, sitting in the offices of the Admiral, mouth moving, telling the story of how my life came to be as it is. The words continue. "One day the father took the boy to another town, but the road was blocked, impassable for the cart, so they turned around. They came home, and the little boy went running to his house, to his mother's room, happily and quietly to surprise her."

The body in monk's robes stops talking for a moment. It breathes deeply and continues speaking.

"The boy threw open the door only to find his mother with two men. She was on her hands and knees and she was … exposed. One was in front and one behind her. She was not protesting.

"The three of them started, turned toward me, the boy's mother's eyes became wide with surprise, and then shame, fear, and then … the boy's father was there."

The voice stops for a moment. With a different tone, the voice says, "The boy does not remember much else of that day, not exactly."

Admiral Yi does not need to hear the rest. He says, "So your … the father took the boy to a temple?"

"Yes. He had donated a lot over the years, and he only asked that I be well educated as well as worked hard and fairly."

"And they did this."

"Yes. They taught me both Hangul and Chinese Korean, as well as the original Chinese. Then, as a youth, I was sent to China as a helper, a carrier of bags for the main priests as they visited Buddhist sites and temples."

"And you learned a lot."

"I am, of course, a man of meager standing and accomplishments, but for languages I have been told I have some facility."

The Admiral nods. "Thank you for telling me of your education. Please read this." (I will never forget how he so smoothly let go the horror of my mother and father. Of course, it was never directly mentioned again.) The Admiral opens a compartment in his desk and takes out some papers. He hands one of them to me, and I bow as I move to receive it. The calligraphy is excellent, a strong but artistic hand. The Admiral's own—it must be. But his writing is that of a literati, or could be.

I read to him, from what I surmise to be his diary:

The 20th day of the 2nd moon, 1592. Sin-hae, Clear. While conducting the morning inspection, I found the defense lines to be in perfect condition and the freshly outfitted warships to be in proper battle line and with adequate weaponry. Late in the afternoon when I arrived in Yongju, my eyes were welcomed by the red flowers and green leaves in the hills and fields on both sides of the sea. I wondered whether this was not the fabled fairyland of Yongju, the land of perpetual youth.

I finish reading the passage and hand him back his diary.

"All right," he says and hands me another paper. "What about this?"

At first glance, the second document looks to be official. It is. "This appears to be a dispatch from the Traveling High Commissioner," I begin.

"It reads: The Governor of Kyongsang Province, Kim Su, wrote, *So Yoshimoto, the Lord of Tsushima, remarked in his official letter that he had sent a tribute boat to Korea and that if it had not arrived that it must have been sunk in a terrible storm.*"

I stopped. It was strange to read important official documents.

"Yes. You read it well. What do you make of this?"

"Sir, it is not for me to judge the affairs of the government officials and …"

"I know that. I only ask your interpretation."

The Admiral does not have a duplicitous look or that reputation. Plus, it is obvious.

"Sir, the island of Tsushima, as the Japanese call it, is within sight of Yond-do on a clear day. It is a very short sail. Some claim that it has been, or at least can be, swum, though I myself think it too cold and the tides too treacherous for any person. But, Sir, for a ship, Sir, a sinking in a storm in such a short time and distance, let alone one unknown to the master of the island who has just sent tribute, seems questionable."

Admiral Yi sits still, his arms folded, his robes impeccable, his beard perfectly styled. His eyes betray nothing; nor does his voice.

"So you would question the veracity of the Lord of Tsushima?"

"Certainly not, My Lord. It is not for me to question someone of such rank. I was merely asked for my humble interpretation."

For the first time since I met him, Admiral Yi smiles. If I have not trusted him before, now I know that this is a man of honor. I feel it deep inside. A man to whom loyalty may be given, and who likewise deserves and expects it, but a man who rewards it fully, too.

"Let us leave the Korean," he says. "What about this?"

I look at the book. It is Chinese, I see instantly. Sun Tzu is the author, I read. Before seeing the title I know that it is *The Art of War*, one of the seven military classics.

I say this to Admiral Yi.

"Yes. Now read it to me. Read it in Chinese, and then tell it to me in Korean."

"Yes, Sir."

I pause and stop to swallow. He looks at me for a second.

"My apologies. You must be thirsty. We have talked long, and you had been waiting for some time when I returned from shooting my fifteen sets of arrows."

Without waiting for a reply, he calls out. The manner in which the husky attendant quickly responds and then moves so promptly to supply wine for master and guest shows me a lot. It gives me an early hint of how truly respected the Admiral is by his people. I am already beginning to understand why.

"I trust wine is not against your vows?" he asks.

"No, Sir, but drunkenness is and to read Chinese and translate it accurately requires me to be clear."

"I understand. If you would like water instead ..."

"Thank you, Sir, but no. This will do. I will just drink slowly."

With a salutation, following him, I take a sip.

"Good. Now to *The Art of War*." He sits back as if prepared to hear the story of an old friend, the companion of long, interesting hours.

I read to him passages which time will prove he already knows very well. Among them are:

"Pretended weakness is given birth from strength."

"If you besiege an enemy, you must leave them an escape route—though not a real one."

"A victorious battle strategy is not tried again; the ways of successful response against the foe are without end."

As I read to Admiral Yi from *The Art of War*, a voice from outside begins calling loudly. As it enters my consciousness, the voice seems to be nothing but a fruit peddler.

"Fruit for sale," it sings melodically. "Fruit for sale."

I continue to read, but suddenly the words from outside come to me. Some of them are in Japanese!

"Choson wa warui desu, Yi—sama wa hentai. Fruit for sale. Fruit for sale. Taiko wa daiichi desu, to Choson oodasai. Fruit for sale."

All of this is sung in the silly rhythms of the street seller, but these words in Japanese! It is bad Japanese, terribly accented, but unmistakable.

Stopping reading, I look at Admiral Yi. "Sir, this is horrible!"

"Sun Tzu?"

"No, Sir. Of course not. But, outside, do you hear that voice?"

The Admiral pauses. "The fruit seller?"

"Yes, Sir. Sir, that song, it is partly in Japanese, and, it is … insulting!"

"What? What is he saying?"

The words pour out of me. I am surprised by my passion and that I can say these words so bluntly to such a powerful figure.

"Sir, he sings that our kingdom is bad and rude. That you are strange in an unseemly way and that Hideyoshi is great!"

Instantly Admiral Yi shouts, his attendants burst in, and he loudly says to bring him the "big-mouthed fruit peddler immediately."

It is done so quickly that it seems no time has passed. Suddenly a young man is thrown on the floor in front of the Admiral. The two strong attendants stand to each side, glaring belligerently at the man sprawled at their feet. Admiral Yi, of course, does not deign to stand for such a person, but dominates the room even while seated.

"I am told you have been insulting my king, my country, and myself in the language of the island robbers." His voice is like quiet, sharp steel.

"Yes, I have been. And do you know what else?"

And the lout goes on to say in Japanese that Koreans are the sons of Chinese monkeys and Puyo apes!

Aghast, I open my mouth to speak, to report these further blasphemous slanders, but Admiral Yi raises a hand.

I stop, mouth agape. The Admiral says, "Did he just tell you of our simian Chinese and Puyo ancestry?"

Speechless, I nod.

"How was his accent?"

"What?" I forgot even to add Sir.

"Did he sound Japanese?"

"Not at all."

It is hard to speak, but I get the words out.

"Sounded like a Taegu man trying to sound like a Hakata-jin."

I pause.

"Sir."

Admiral Yi looks at me. The man on the floor looks at me. The two husky attendants look at me. Admiral Yi laughs first, permitting the other three to crack up. (I too might have been laughing had I been able to see the expression on my face. Certainly, I have enjoyed recollecting this scene many times since.)

Laughing still, the Admiral says to the man on the floor, "Good job."

He nods at the two attendants. The three leave after being told to enjoy a bottle of wine together when the next shift of attendants comes on duty. This brings thanks as the door closes.

"So," he is still smiling, "you do understand Japanese."

Now the smile is finished.

"Do you sound better than that rude fruit peddler?"

"I have been told, Sir, that for a Korean, I speak that language very well."

"But not like a Japanese?"

"No, Sir. I could fool no Japanese in that regard."

Admiral Yi pauses. Then his eyes look up, above and past me, as if into the distance. I say nothing, as I wait for his thoughts to come back. Minutes pass. I choose not to sip the wine. Then he moves his head and spoken words again come.

"Each of the *Seven Military Classics* of Ancient China mentions the value of surprise."

I nod a small bow.

"You can read and write the languages. And, when you were surprised today, you reacted as I would have hoped. Therefore, I will send for you again."

Again I bow.

"You have heard the rumors of war coming with Hideyoshi's, the Taiko's, Japan?"

"Of course, Sir. We all have."

I do not say that the ship Admiral Yi himself has been developing has been adding to these rumors. There is likely no need to say that the kobukson, the turtle ship, with its armored spiked roofs, iron-plated sides, multiple cannon, and smoking dragon's head, has been adding some weight to this possibility in many minds.

"It seems this war will occur. I must prepare as if it were."

"Yes, Sir."

"I will report to the abbot your appreciated service, and my wish to have you attend me again. This should make sure you are well fed and have a place to sleep."

"Thank you very much, Sir."

He looks around, as if about to dismiss me, but I have to ask, "Sir, if I may be so bold, what is it you wish of me? I am but a Buddhist priest."

I do not add, "in a land ruled by Confucianists where Buddhism has sunk to being largely a religion of the poor, the countryside, and of women."

The Admiral looks at me.

"It is simple. You are a priest, a Buddhist, yes. But you have lived in Japan, studied its history and literature, and from an interesting perspective—one I cannot get from one of my military people or from one of our Confucianist literati. You have a good memory," and he keeps talking to cut off my disclaimer, "… and you have read their books and studied their history."

"Yes, Sir. I have read their books. I have read their histories. As a guest, especially one willing to work as well as to study and with a letter from the abbot who was my father's friend as an introduction, I was given access …"

He cuts me off. "Plus, you have been to China and can read and speak Chinese." He looks at me. "Can you guess now what I want from you?"

I begin to surmise, but cannot put it into words.

Admiral Yi says quietly, "'Know yourself and know the enemy; this is the surest way to be victorious in a hundred battles.' I need to know my enemy. There are some things of which I might not be aware. I do already know of their war skills, of their samurai, of the waegu, their wako—their pirates who have plagued us for centuries, and of how their navy fights, or, at least, has fought until now. These things I do know.

"But, what of the rest? Who are the Japanese? What do they believe? Why do they fight like such demons? Why do they obey Hideyoshi, and how did he come to power?

"Every little thing I can learn about them could be important. 'The sparrow's turn in flight at the proper moment can knock the eagle from the sky.' I want to know all I can of these island barbarians, these people of Wa, these Japanese, that I might beat them; that, if they do attack us, they will be repelled in ways which will convince them never to return.

"I need every weapon I can get. Knowledge of your foe can be a weapon. Knowledge of your allies can be a valuable tool. If the samurai come, they are heading for Ming China, and the Ming know this. They will help us, because it helps them to do so. But their assistance is a two-edged sword or can be. Look what happened with Silla and the Tang."

He pauses and says, "It also helps that you also know of the Chinese.

"To know is to have power. You have knowledge I do not have. Some of this could help me. I want that. I desire any knowledge that can help in a war to save Choson."

His eyes refocus on me. For a few moments, it had been as if he had only been speaking to himself.

"No need to tell you to be quiet about this. If anyone asks, and the abbot will, just say that I wanted you to read some Chinese for me, to confirm my interpretations, and whatever else makes sense."

I nod, and he signals for me to be gone. His mind is already moving to its next project. I give my respects at the door, to which he responds automatically, but still gracefully. Then he surprises me. He speaks a last message, a reminder.

"Next time, I want your answer to 'Who are these Japanese?'"

Chapter 2

▼

Who are the Japanese?

Fourth Moon, 1592 (one of days 23–30)

I have been called for so, despite the storm, the rain, and the wind, I go immediately. As a Buddhist priest, supposedly I am immune to physical unpleasantness. Cold, wet, wind—all of these are meaningless. Would that this were always true.

The attendant who answers the door has been told of my expected arrival. He is one of the big men who had been in on the fruit peddler joke the first time I had come. I am asked in, given towels with which to dry, some hot tea, and, when I am presentable, am ushered in to Admiral Yi.

As before, he greets me with exactly the proper etiquette due someone of my status. However, he looks more serious than before. No wonder—the war had only been a possibility when we first met. Now, it has started, and very badly for us. Our soldiers run away at every opportunity. Or so it seems.

Polite ritualistic greetings completed, the Admiral looks at me and asks, "Who are these Japanese then?"

"Paekche," I answer.

"They are Paekche? We are Paekche," says the Admiral. "We stand on the land of that ancient kingdom. Paekche is one of the three old kingdoms which were combined to form unified Korea." He stops for a moment as if recalling old lessons. "Paekche, Koguryo, and Silla, combined over 900 years ago, are Korea, whether it was as Silla or Koryo or, as now, Choson." He pauses and raises an eyebrow.

"But you know all that."

He motions for a family servant to pour a drink of wine for him and one for me. While it is being served, I notice the perfect cleanliness of the Admiral's office, its elegant simplicity. I am reminded of the ideal of the tea ceremony so revered by Hideyoshi in Japan.

The Admiral is speaking. "It is raining today. The winds certainly prevent any voyages. It is not even pleasant to shoot a few sets of arrows." Another pause. "And there are no traveling officials from his majesty's court upon whom to pay my respects."

He takes a sip of wine. He has decided he really does have some time. He had thought he would, or he would not have sent for me. "Tell it to me like a story. Explain."

I gulp, and, wanting something to drink, instinctively reach for the glass in front of me. I drink from it and then realize it is wine. It is not against my vows to drink alcohol, but this was a complicated tale to tell, and from at least two languages. To fog my mind and words while sharing knowledge with the Admiral—unthinkable!

At least it is a very good wine.

I say, "It is a long tale, Sir."

"Just start at the beginning."

"In 369 AD, the Paekche prince the Japanese call 'Homuda Wake' used a port of Kaya to travel to Kyushu. He brought with him iron weapons, and, most important, horses. There had been no horses in Japan before.

"For a while, he stayed in Kyushu, but Koreans were already there and others from the south, and there were better lands to the east on Honshu.

Within decades he and his followers moved east to Honshu, the big island, where they fought the hairy barbarians, chasing them into the wilderness, and setting about unifying the islands. With their better weapons and cavalry, they were able to do this fairly easily."

The Admiral interjects, "Wa-ke. Wake is an ancient Korean word for prince. It comes from Puyo."

"Yes, Sir," I agree. "As did the founders of Paekche."

"So Homuda Wake of Paekche went to Japan from Korea and, being of a superior civilization, unified the lands."

I nod. I feel safe to take another sip of wine. It would be wonderful, I think, if all the wine offered a wandering priest were so good.

"What was this Homuda Wake's real Korean name? Do we know?" The Admiral, I noted, had taken another sip, too. That he could and sometimes did drink like a sailor was, to my experience, quite true.

"Chin. That was his family name. Even the Japanese records indicate this."

"Chin. Yes. Another name used by the royal family of Paekche."

The Admiral takes a drink of his wine. Outside, the wind picks up. In the distance, there is thunder.

"The Japanese records seem to have split up the life of the person they call 'Homuda Wake' into two. One is *Jimmu* and the other is *O-jin*. The *Jim* in *Jimmu* and the *jin* in *O-jin* seem an obvious reference to *Chin*."

"Is that your only evidence for *Chin* as this Homuda Wake's name?" His eyes, and something in his tone, tell me that I better have more evidence than that. This man only wants information he can rely upon. As a military commander, he knows that imprecise information can result in defeat, death, and dishonor. This is not a military matter, but his need for accuracy is too ingrained to be ignored. It is part of him.

"No, Sir. There is evidence for it in an official Japanese document." I pause, and the eyes of the great warrior tell me to go on. "In the *New Compilation of the Register of Families*, completed for the Emperor Saga in 815

AD, the name Chin as the family name of O-jin's line of emperors is mentioned."

The eyes upon me relax. "So, you say, this Paekche prince went to Japan in 369 AD."

"Yes."

"How do you know this was the year?"

"There is much evidence, but mainly it is because the Japanese records say so."

"This *Register of Families* again?"

"No, Sir. What the Japanese call the *Kojiki* and the *Nihon Shoki*."

"So these Japanese documents, the *Kojiki* and the *Nihon Shoki*, tell of the forming of the empire of the Wa by a Korean Prince and his followers in the year 369 AD."

"Well, yes ... and no...." I already know the reaction this will bring from the Admiral. Now his eyes are even more strongly upon me. He says it, even though he doesn't need to.

"What do you mean?" His voice is quiet, but there is something that tells me to hope that it is never directed at me loudly.

"Well, the documents were written after 668 AD."

"Yes ..."

"And Paekche had just been conquered by Silla ..."

"Of course ..."

"And so the Wa, the Japanese, the cousins of the Paekche, rewrote their history. They were very afraid of Silla. They hated Silla. From the time of Homuda Wake and until the times of the Mongols, the greatest threat from the seas felt by those of Wa was at this time."

The Admiral's voice is very quiet. "Paekche had fallen. Their fatherland, their homeland ..." He is imagining this for himself. I could see there is nothing he would want less; that a tortured death would for him be much better.

I begin, "Yamato Wa, Japan, had sent 10,000 troops to try to help Paekche. However …"

"… in AD 663, at the Paekchon River, 170 T'ang Chinese fighting ships, allies of Silla, annihilated them," finishes the Admiral. He will not be told naval history by me. I nod and go on.

"A scholar of Paekche wrote in the *Nihon Shoki*, 'Then the people of the country said to one another: "Chyu-yu has fallen; there is nothing more to be done; this day the name of Paekche has become extinct. Shall we ever visit again the place where the tombs of our ancestors are?"'

"And the Japanese, the Yamato Wa, they were afraid they were next," he murmurs.

"Yes. They went on to build huge walls on their coasts and to train the people in the fighting arts."

"But Silla and T'ang did not come."

"No, they did not. Silla had its own problems with T'ang by that time or it might have."

Admiral Yi considers this. Then he says, "But those of Wa, the Japanese, they did not know this. And they were scared, and they had lost their homeland. What of these documents they wrote, these revised histories?"

I took another quick sip and continued, "They created new histories, stories which combined the founding myths with some they had already found in Wa with what had really happened. Except, they changed everything to make their dynasty look divine and ancient. In these histories, they honored Paekche and dishonored Silla, but they made themselves the older country, the fatherland and gave their emperors an honorable and distant past. They made up emperors to make their history longer and gave many of them lives of over 100 years. Indeed, their emperors became descendants of the gods."

"So were the Kings of Paekche …"

"Yes. The founding myths of Wa and of Paekche are virtually identical."

"What do they say about 369 AD?"

"According to the *Nihon Shoki*, in the year 369 AD, the very pregnant mother of Homuda Wake, came with many Japanese troops, landed in the south of Korea, went peacefully north through Silla and Paekche, and then, with her troops led by three Paekche generals, turned south again, and conquered Silla and Paekche on her way back to Japan.

"Using magic, she kept herself from having her baby, Homuda Wake, until she was back in Japan."

Laughingly, which helps my mood, too, Admiral Yi says, "All that is preposterous."

"Yes, as written. But the truth is obvious. Silla was only conquered in wishes. And Paekche generals did go to Japan with an army."

"And," concludes the Admiral, "in order to make the Paekche Prince Chin or Homuda Wake a man of the islands and not Korea, by magic he is not born until his mother has gotten back to shore there."

The wind whistles. Rain can still be heard on the roof. I realize that I am no longer chilled, and that a bit more wine would taste good.

"Interesting about the princess," says the Admiral. "More evidence for the name Chin. Chin was the maternal name of the Paekche royal family."

"Yes, Sir. For a while in Paekche, it was the woman who produced the child who mattered, not whose family the father was from."

There is nothing but the sound of the hard weather for a few moments. Then, "Paekche ..." he says. "That kingdom is only a memory now. Is it their revenge then, sending their descendants to reap a hard crop, these invaders from the land they created?"

Chapter 3

The First Victory at Sea—Okpo

Ninth day of the Fifth Moon, 1592

Word came to Yosu that the navy had fought and won. At first, no one could believe it. It was too good to be real. The Japanese had won all the battles until now. All it seemed the Korean military had been good for was to run away. The Japanese armies had gone up and through our huge peninsula from the southeast to the north like a giant tsunami. Even the King had to flee from Seoul. He was with the Ming armies, the Chinese, who had come to help only because the Japanese had announced that their goal was to take Korea en route to conquering China.

Of Korea, only our small part of the southwest of Choson had not been overrun. When the Japanese had first invaded, our area had not been considered important. It was not politically significant, was not on the land routes to China, and was hidden behind difficult mountain passes in the southwest of our country. They probably thought they could rather easily deal with us later.

And no wonder they thought so. They had won victories at every turn. Their military seemed impossibly strong. Yet the word was that our navy had beaten them, and not just beaten them but thrashed them. Led by Admiral Yi, the Korean Navy had sunk forty Japanese vessels without itself losing one. Many Japanese had been killed, and not one Korean ship or boat had been lost. Only one Korean, in fact, had even been injured, and that was a minor arrow wound to the arm.

Admiral Yi had caught them by surprise. The Japanese had grown very confident, perhaps overconfident. Sadly, they had good reason to be overconfident, at least until then. But that was before they faced Admiral Yi. He had spoken to his officers and men before this first naval battle under his command. And as only he could do, he had his commanders and crews all pledge their lives to destroy the enemy.

Japanese ships were plundering the port of Okpo when Admiral Yi and the squadrons of the two southern provinces appeared. The Japanese could not even put out to sea before they were being shot at by cannon and our sharpshooters with their arrows. Many of their ships were destroyed during the first hour.

The next day, our squadrons found other Japanese ships at Chok-jinpo, their crews again ashore looting and plundering. This time, the Japanese did not even try to fight. They ran into the hills, leaving their ships unmanned and helpless. Of course, the Korean navy destroyed them after having captured what supplies it could and after releasing some prisoners found aboard. The prisoners seem to be mostly young women and teenage boys.

Forty Japanese ships! Two victories in two days! The people were shouting and howling with delight. The water of the bays of Yosu never seemed so inviting, the sky never so blue. And the joy with which the navy was received upon its return …

Looking back from thirty-five years, it is amazing how routine it all seems. I have heard the voices, "Of course we won" is how it is looked at.

"Admiral Yi never lost, after all, and this was only his first victory." "Okpo was not that big a battle …," "… was not that exciting," "… is hardly interesting." I have heard these words myself and can mostly understand them. But those who say them were not there.

These first victories gave us renewed hope. The Japanese were defeatable. We had a chance after all. What made it even better was that we had beaten the Japanese without any help from the Chinese. Some had said that only the Ming could save us. Now we saw that we just might be able to look out for ourselves.

A last thought on that first battle. In a way the "ho-hummers" are right. In one way, compared to Admiral Yi's other frays, this was not that notable. Admiral Yi actually fought these battles with more Korean Navy ships present than the Japanese had. He had them outnumbered. That would never happen again.

Chapter 4

Tell Me of Their Leaders

Late in the Fifth Moon, 1592

The Admiral must have sent the abbot of this temple a good message. I sleep in a fine room and I eat well. Also, from this temple the view is outstanding. It is high above the port of Yosu. To be here, to eat, to sleep, to wash, and to meditate in such a place is wonderful. The steep climb from town is worth the strain on my legs and lungs no matter how many times I must make the climb.

From the temple, I look out and down toward the port and the town wrapped around it. While the town surrounds the bay, the mountains and fertile, blooming, terraced valleys flow like green waves around the buildings and wharves. To the east and to the north, these ranges are framed by blue sky, white clouds, and the cooling sea and bays. It is hard to look out hundreds of miles and imagine that the Japanese robbers are out there looting, plundering, kidnapping, raping, and murdering. It is even harder to believe that, should Admiral Yi lose even one big battle, these invaders could be here, and the bustling town below burning and its people enslaved or dead.

Yes, from atop this mountain, it is hard to conceive that should the navy of Admiral Yi be defeated, the Japanese will be able to bring supplies and reinforcements around our peninsula and then north to where the Japanese army has already forced the King to flee and has already captured two princes. Only Admiral Yi has stopped the Japanese so far, Admiral Yi, and distance. The Japanese armies have won so much so fast they have had to stop and wait for supplies to arrive before continuing onwards over the rest of Korea and into China.

Only we here in Cholla, in the southwest part of our Korean peninsula, in what was the southern part of Paekche, have held out. On land, we are protected by horrendous mountain passes with great fortresses strategically placed—fortresses so strong even the Japanese should not be able to break through them. At sea, we have Admiral Yi and his forces. And, in the beginning of the war, we had a kind of luck in that the enemy bypassed us.

They had reckoned without Admiral Yi in their calculations. And if anything were to happen to Admiral Yi, this initial assessment might still be proved correct.

Sometimes I consider all these things as I prepare to meditate on the hillside up from the temple. Here one can meditate with a view to the south and to the west as well as to the dangerous east and the hazardous north. The hike up is on a forested path, and for the view, the air, and the peace, it is a worthwhile climb. Many times I come here for meditation at sunrise and sunset. At times, I sit here all night or all day.

It is here that the messenger from the temple finds me sitting at my favorite spot. I am cross-legged with legs intertwined, head up, back straight, eyes slightly open, thumb and first finger of each hand together, thoughtless. I, the part of me, the true part of me; what is beyond this little I, this part is connected to what is beyond the body, is connected to that which is both not part of and is yet all of this world.

It is one of those moments that for me do not come often enough, or so I keep telling myself. But there is a voice and a hand touching my shoulder. I am brought back to the body. I return to seeing and hearing and to needing to urinate. The messenger is very respectful and apologizes for interrupting me, but with a salutation tells me that Admiral Yi desires my presence at his headquarters' office.

There is another good thing about the temple being on the mountain above the town. Moving downhill, I can travel quickly to Admiral Yi.

And I do move quickly, but still the attendant's expression says, "It's about time you got here," when I arrive. He says nothing out loud, but I wonder how long it had been since the Admiral sent the request for me to the temple. As I wait for the Admiral to be informed of my arrival, I decide to take some quiet steps to make sure there are no delays of this kind in the future. I am considering these when I am quickly shown in.

As we go through the usual greeting courtesies, the Admiral does not talk of his victory in his first series of battles. I acknowledge his successes with appropriate and sincere congratulations and he nods. That is all.

He is busy. Very busy. I know this. A few times, he mentions that Cholla, the southern part of what used to be Paekche, is now holding out against that which it created. He mentions that this land of old Paekche is the one part of Korea that the forgetful and ungrateful island Paekche cousins, the Japanese, have not been able to successfully invade.

He never says so directly, but this parent/child analogy seems to appeal to his Confucianist side. Japan, the child, is showing no respect to the parent, Paekche-Korea. This is very wrong. It is only correct that the parent should teach the child a lesson in manners, in decorum, in what is proper.

Indeed, in teaching the Japanese a lesson, no one will end up doing a more efficient job than the Admiral.

On this day, he says, "Tell me of Japan's leaders."

"Which, Sir? I will tell you whatever I know, of course."

"I will want to know of Hideyoshi, naturally, but what of his predecessors? Who are his models? And who are the heroes, the best generals and admirals to emulate for the Japanese commanders who are here?"

This is something I have given thought to. I had warning this question might be asked. Therefore, I can answer quickly. "Most directly, of course, is Oda Nobunaga. It was he who recognized the skills and abilities of Hideyoshi and who raised him, a mere commoner, to be his Chief of Staff. And it was from this position that Hideyoshi avenged the death of Oda when he was killed by the forces of a traitor general, and who then consolidated his own leadership of Japan." And, it goes without saying it was Hideyoshi who then ordered the invasion of Korea and (if that part of the plan succeeded) Ming China.

Oda was alive and beginning to take over all of Japan when I was there. I heard much of him.

"Tell me of Oda Nobunaga." The Admiral looks comfortable. He has finished eating and has his customary glass of wine in front of him. I, too, have been supplied with drink. This seems to be becoming the habit. The sun bearing in from outside has been shaded by a bamboo curtain, and the room is cooled by a gentle sea breeze.

"He was ruthless," I begin. "As an enemy, he was implacable. And as a friend, you needed to hold to your word exactly. He mastered the use of the firearm with the Japanese soldiers. Firing together, his troops, lined up behind a fortification or even a fence line, consistently annihilated the best sword-wielding armies of Japan.

"One battle, the final one against his family's old enemy, the Takeda clan, was a great, or a terrible, example of this type of warfare."

"So have our armies discovered," murmurs Admiral Yi. "But with our fortresses properly defended at the steep mountain passes and with our excellent archers, they never should have been able to get so far north, and certainly not so quickly."

To this, I can say nothing. I remain silent until I hear, "Please, Priest Wonho, continue about Oda Nobunaga."

Nodding a bow, I begin again. "Oda did not like the Buddhist monasteries. In Japan, many of them had extensive holdings in land and serf farmers and literally thousands of warrior monks. They were not friendly towards him and his aims. He meant to conquer and control all of Japan, and these monasteries did not want any one person to have that much power. They could maintain their power with feuding daimyo, the local aristocrats who are always squabbling with each other, but likely not with a shogun."

"Shogun?"

"A shogun is, or would be, a military commander of all Japan. He would be, technically, second only to the emperor in power."

"The emperor?" said the Admiral. "Hideyoshi has the power, not the emperor. Hideyoshi is the one who ordered Japan to attack us."

"Yes, this is true, but still, the forms must be maintained. Since the imperial line is descended from the gods and has a history of over 1500 years …"

"Yes, of course. Just like the *Kojiki* and *Nihon Shoki* say," smiles the Admiral, who reaches for his wine.

"Yes, with such a divine imperial line in place, thanks to Paekche, it is wise to govern with their approval."

"So, Hideyoshi is Japan's shogun?"

"No, actually. He is not related by blood to Minamoto Yoritomo, the first shogun of Japan. To be a true shogun, one must be. There actually has not been a shogun in Japan for many years. They call Hideyoshi the Taiko instead. It has a similar meaning to shogun."

The Admiral has an interesting look on his face. "You are definitely not a military man."

"Excuse me, Sir?"

"A soldier or sailor is trained to stay on the topic, and you don't."

I am unsure what to say. Admiral Yi goes on. "I was supposed to be hearing about Oda Nobunaga, and, instead, you have already talked about Hideyoshi and Minamoto Yoritomo from centuries ago."

"I am sorry, Sir. Actually, it is all related, but I will try to …"

The Admiral smiles. "No, it is interesting. And everything does relate. But today tell me of Oda. Then Hideyoshi. And perhaps, if we have time, this Minamoto Yoritomo." He pauses and then says, "These three are the most important military figures among the Japanese?"

"Likely, yes." I ponder a few moments. "Certainly no one more so, Sir."

"Good. Then go on. Oda. And the Buddhist monasteries." The Admiral considers. "He sounds like a Japanese version of our own King Taejong."

King Taejong. Yes, he, too, persecuted the Buddhist monasteries and temples. He closed many of them and took their lands and confiscated their slaves, seventy thousand of them. But no, I shake my head.

"Oda was worse," I say.

The Admiral's eyebrows rise. He knows this cannot be good, especially not for a Buddhist priest.

I go on. "I had visited there. If I had happened to visit a year and a half later, I would have died there.

"Oda made an example of the Tendai sect at Enryakuji Monastery on Hiei Mountain. They would not do as he wished so one night he encircled the mountain with his army and commanded them to march to the top. His orders were that everyone found on the mountain was to die. Immediately. Without question. No matter how old, no matter what gender or position. The abbot, babies, grandmothers, fighting monks, or stable keepers—all were to be put to the sword.

"His order was carried out. The example was made." Now it is my turn to reach for the wine. A thought comes to mind, not a new one, but one I had never spoken to the Admiral. "Sir, it was veterans of wars like these which Hideyoshi sent to attack us."

No words. Admiral Yi is looking up at the far wall or ceiling behind me. It is as if he is seeing something I cannot.

"Tell me more of Oda Nobunaga."

"I heard it told that, while he had wives and women, his favorite lover was a young man, a samurai."

"This is not a surprise." Perhaps he is thinking of the teenage Korean boys held captive below deck on Japanese ships who had recently been rescued by his men.

I say, "Oda's lover is said to have died fighting at his side when he died. Oda's body was never found, the house in which he was attacked having been set afire.

"However, there is one tale of Oda with his first wife …"

The Admiral's eyes are upon me.

"Oda did not have faith in her. She was a peace offering from a neighboring clan, the Saitoh. Her name was Nohime or Kicho. Her father, Saitoh Michizane, was one of Oda's first great enemies. Supposedly their marriage meant peace between the feuding families. But Oda did not trust this, or her.

"Yet, for a few months, he did his husbandly duties and slept with her, and, gradually, he appeared to relax. He even told her some personal things and then some little secrets. Still later, he began to get up early, before dawn and sit facing out a window toward the hills.

"His young wife wondered what he was doing and, finally, after much cajoling, he admitted that he was watching for signal fires in the hills from two of the generals who served her father. They had agreed to come to his side and to signal him when the time was ripe for an attack on her family, the Saitoh clan.

"As his wife, she, of course, swore to say nothing, but about a week later, the whole region was mystified by the executions of a great lord's finest two generals. Then a few months later, Oda attacked the neighboring lord and won an easy victory. Without their two best generals, his enemy's forces were weak and demoralized."

The Admiral nods. He looks at me and then, with that far away gaze, looks above me as if to heavens or places I cannot discern.

* * * *

Now, some thirty-five years later, I wonder if he had sensed his own future.

When I told this story to Admiral Yi, I had no idea that the Japanese would try to get rid of the Admiral himself in a similar fashion. No one did.

How sweet and convenient to convince one's enemies to kill their own top commander rather than having to do it yourself. I did not realize the similarity between Oda's trick and what happened with the Admiral until after his arrest.

I wonder if, after having heard the story, the Admiral sensed what was coming. Or if, after his arrest, whether he remembered this story and understood the similarity.

Most likely he did. I never knew him to forget anything. And, just like him, he never bothered to mention it. He always seemed to believe that he had more important matters at hand than worrying about himself.

Chapter 5

"The Bullet Went Through Me"

Sixth Moon, 1592

What have I done, turned off my ears only to stare? The formalities are complete, the proper greetings exchanged, and I have not even heard what he has said.

Admiral Yi stands in front of me, as solid, as whole, as formidable as ever.

"What is wrong, Priest Wonho?" he says for what must be the second time. "You are looking at me very strangely."

"They say ... I have heard, that, at Sachon, in the first of your five victories in eight days that you were shot."

I am almost embarrassed by my words. What I had heard must have been lies. I feel a need to explain.

"I heard that you were hit by a bullet, that it went through you, and yet you stood as if nothing had happened, bleeding down to your feet, holding your bow, and continuing to lead the fight. Then for a solid week after being shot through, you won more battles, sinking and destroying ships, and killing the Japanese robbers at Tangpo, Chinhae, Tanghangpo, and Yulpo."

The Admiral just looks at me.

"I apologize. People on the street tell many stories and, I must admit, I heard some of your sailors telling these tales, too." I breathe deeply. "It is only that I was very concerned when I heard you had been shot. And what I heard was very difficult to believe.

"I am thankful for your health." Finally, I feel I can stop talking.

Admiral Yi still studies me, but then he says, "What you heard was true. I was shot. The bullet went through me. It hit my left shoulder," he gestures with his right hand, "and went out the back, but it did not touch spine, heart, or lungs nor did it crush any bones nor severely mangle any muscles.

"Actually, it did not go totally through by itself. I could feel where it lodged just inside the skin of my back, and, after the battle was over, I had my men cut it out."

I am speechless. This scene is from the battles of the gods in myths, not of real life.

"But, as you can see, I am all right. The physicians say I should take it easy from shooting sets of arrows for a while, and I do not know when I shall again sleep on my left side, but other than that, I am fine."

Nodding and still with little to say, I again express my happiness at his good health.

"Thank you," says Admiral Yi. "Now, please tell me what you know about …"

* * * *

This was the second of his great victories. Again, compared to those still to come, they are now rarely mentioned. It is much grander to speak of the glories of Hansando, Pusan, Myongnyang, and then of Noryang, the final battle as the Japanese barbarians at last left. In comparison to these, this second week of continuous victories seems unimportant.

Except we almost lost him. And at least six years too soon. This is too horrible to be imagined. What would have become of our land, or of China, or, eventually, even of Japan if that first bullet to reach him had hit him just a little bit lower?

Chapter 6

The Young Captain—Scholar Captain

(About 1618 AD)

It is nice for an old man to make a new friend. It was about twenty years after the Japanese had left that I met the Young Captain. That was ten years ago now, and even then I felt myself to be very old.

Now, in an age where most of the people born in my year or even in the next few decades did not even make it to forty, I wonder how I managed it. I question how my creaky bones have groaned away for so long. And I also wonder how my friend, the Young Captain, is doing now.

As I said, I met the Young Captain twenty years after Admiral Yi died. It was winter, and in the south it is warmer. Or, at least, it is less cold. So I was in the south of Korea back in Yosu. As I walked along, perhaps I was remembering the war, the Admiral, and the many events, almost as if it was all someone else's life. Could I really have been so active and have assisted such a renowned hero?

I was staying with my old friends—those still alive—at the same mountain temple. I was walking through the port. Walking ... my life has been walking, a series of journeys by foot. I have been moving by foot on many paths until, soon, the paths which have befriended my feet for so long will take my whole body to measure, and I will move this skinny shell no more.

There were many boats, and I was enjoying the taste of the rice offered by a cheerful woman and the feel of the sun on my robes after a cold night. I was not focused, just moving through the happy whirlwind of a robust port having a good month.

"Priest! Priest!"

I turned. A young navy sailor was approaching me.

"Yes?" I certainly did not know this sailor.

"My captain saw you walk by, and he asked me to bring you to him."

"Me?"

"He seems to know you."

"Me?"

"Yes, you. He said something about 'The Priest from the War,' and sent me after you." The youth stood looking at me. I was surprised, my mind awhirl, and my body unmoving.

I just stood there until the young sailor asked again, rather insistently, "Would you come then, please?"

"Yes." I was wondering what it was the sailor's captain remembered. "Of course."

I followed the sailor to his vessel, but moved even more slowly than usual in order to compose myself, to get my thoughts focused on memories of those years. I was wondering if I would remember this captain, and there were some people from that time that I hoped weren't this captain.

Arriving at the ship, I looked down at its main deck. The captain looked up, studied me, and smiled, "Yes, I knew it was you. Please come aboard."

I did not recognize him. He was a very fit, good-looking man. He appeared to be one of those officers who seemed merely by existing to challenge his crew to keep up.

"Thank you, sir," I said and moved gingerly across the plank ladder.

The captain watched until I was safely aboard.

"I am Yi Woo-Si, Port Captain of Yodo. This is my ship. We have stopped here in Yosu for supplies. Welcome."

Yi is indeed a very common name. There was even an excellent captain who had fought for Admiral Yi, whose name, though written with different Chinese characters, was pronounced the same as the Admiral's. But Admiral Yi.... It was hard for me to think of any Yi but him in the navy.

In my mind, Captain Yi Woo-Si became "the Young Captain." Sometimes afterwards, when we had become friends, I even called him this to his face. He would smile and protest, saying something like, "But I am not young. I am thirty five!" To which I would retort, "When you are in your eighth decade, thirty five will seem like a child."

On that day at the time of our first meeting, I say simply, "I am Wonho. Thank you for your kind welcome."

"You were with Admiral Yi."

"What?" Almost no one still alive knows of this, and I rarely speak of it. Yet the Captain's expression is certain.

I say, "I had the privilege of meeting him and even of sharing with him some of my knowledge and experiences, but …

"You rowed for him at Myongnyang! We were totally outnumbered, at least 150 to 12, and everyone else thought we were sunk. I heard the Admiral threaten to cut off a coward's head. Then he attached his battle flag to the mast, along with the signal for full attack, hauled it to the top of the mast, roared 'Attack,' and then, 'Forward! We must save An Wi!' and …"

Captain Yi Woo-Si, the Young Captain, stops speaking. He has become aware of the loudness and enthusiasm of his words. His whole crew has stopped swabbing the decks and checking sails to listen. Indeed, passersby on the docks have stopped to hear. For a few moments, the Captain had become the teenage warrior who had sailed and fought with the Legend. Praiseworthy all would agree, but still, the Young Captain seems to be thinking, this is not proper commander's decorum.

"You see," he finishes much more quietly. "I know. I was a young boy then, and I was rowing three oars behind you."

This is a surprise. I can say nothing for a few moments. I do not recollect what must have been a young teenager back then, but it was a busy time and he had been behind me. Looking at his warm, friendly face is encouraging. Words come. "Well then, may I dare say 'Greetings to an old shipmate.' It is as you say. I was there."

"I knew it." He turns to his steward. "Food and drink. We have an honored guest."

This first meeting lasted all day and into the night. It had been an unseasonably warm day after a cold night, and then, as the stars and strong moon came out over the hills across the bay, it became cold again.

We kept drinking and talking in spite of the cold. By the time the night was finished, I had learned much about the Young Captain. Not only had he fought as a teenager with Admiral Yi at Myongnyang, he had been on the flagship when the Admiral died thirteen months later in the final battle of the war.

I also learned that Yi Woo-Si, the Young Captain, had been so inspired by Admiral Yi and so molded by his wartime experiences that he had gone on to take and pass the military examinations to become an officer. And, similar to his hero, the Young Captain had done very well in galloping his horse, as an archer, and, especially, in the tests of his knowledge of *The Seven Military Classics of Ancient China*. It was through these Chinese military classics that he opened up to me a whole new understanding and appreciation of Admiral Yi.

Indeed, as time went by, I almost changed Yi Woo-Si's name in my mind from the Young Captain to "the Scholar Captain."

Since the sun was still warm overhead that first day, he was delighted to learn of my abilities in Chinese and Japanese, particularly the former. He asked if I had read *The Seven Military Classics of Ancient China*, and I had to admit that I had not read them fully. I mentioned that I had, of course, heard of them and had read and heard excerpts. I did not say that I had seen and read these excerpts to Admiral Yi himself—that seemed too much. (Indeed, until the abbot of Sudoksa, I have mentioned my travels as a youth in Japan and how they led to Admiral Yi, to almost no one. Wine and age, hence loose lips, and now, a brush with which to write....)

"Do you know how important they were to Admiral Yi?"

"The Chinese books?"

"Yes! We all have to study them, every officer, but only Admiral Yi really understood them. He used their secrets and insights against the Japanese in every battle. Going into his first battles ..."

"Okpo," I interject. "I will never forget the joy here when news of his victories was received ..."

"Yes, before Okpo he had many new and untested crews and commanders. No one knew how we would do fighting the Japanese. The Japanese had yet to lose any battle to the Koreans. So Admiral Yi used the words of Wu Tzu, who said, 'If the soldiers are committed to the death they will live; if the soldiers seek to stay alive they will die.'

"Admiral Yi, before this battle, repeatedly talked to his captains. He had them all pledge to fight, to die if necessary, and to commit their crews to the same. His words, his pledges, worked. We won because we did not fear death. The Japanese we encountered sensed we had no fear, and then, since they wanted to live, we won."

"Those words sound like his," I say.

"Yes," agrees the Young Captain. He signals for more wine. This reminds me of twenty plus years before, too. Admiral Yi liked his wine and, occasionally, would make a night of it. However, I sense that, like the Admiral, the Young Captain would never touch a drop if the enemy were anywhere close by, or likely to be. Wine for the real warrior is to relax between battles, not for false courage before or during them.

"And in Tangpo and Tanghapgpo, in the second campaign ..."

"He was shot through by an enemy bullet that week ..." I am interrupting a lot. It is the wine, I think, or could it be age? But the Young Captain does not mind. I am a Buddhist priest and I am old, and, for these reasons, perhaps I can be excused for having some eccentricities. Also, I have no power over him and his career. And, most important, we are old shipmates. We survived victorious at Myongnyang together.

Nodding, he does not miss a word, "the enemy at Sachon was well entrenched on the high ground above the harbor. They were totally out of range of our cannon and our arrows. But they could hit us. The tide was also against us. So what did Admiral Yi do?"

He takes a drink and, rather than trying to answer, I have a swallow, too. I notice that when it is Korea against Japan in the last war he always says "us" or "we," even though neither he nor I was actively involved in the fighting until 1597. These battles he is talking about were in the first year of the Imjin War, 1592, when he would have been ten years old or younger. Much too young to fight then. Which is not to say that he was a graybeard when he volunteered to row at fourteen. But still, it was "us."

"He withdraws since he will not fight where the terrain gives the enemy such an advantage. This was just as Sun Tzu advocated. But he combined this with another strategy also mentioned in the *Art of War*: 'Strength gives birth to feigned weakness.'

"In other words, the strong can pretend to be weak in order to lure the enemy into fighting at a place where the strong wants to fight.

"Admiral Yi had us pretend to withdraw in defeat twice that week in order to get the Japanese where he wanted them and each time it worked."

"Most of what he did worked," I murmur.

This stops the Young Captain's flow of words for a moment. His face changes. "Yes," he says. He looks down at the deck of his ship, at the water easing by, and then up to the winter clouds, gathering against the pure blue sky. "Yes. I wonder if we shall ever have his like again."

Suddenly I feel serious. "We can only pray that, should we again be so attacked, someone with his spirit emerges."

"And his strength and his courage and his genius," says the Young Captain. He pauses again and takes a sip. "What he did with the design and use of the kobukson, in itself, is enough to supply legend makers and storytellers for a century of centuries."

Upon the mention of the kobukson, I remember something from 1592, the first year of the war. It was probably just after the second week of victories, Tangpo and the others. These were the battles in which he was shot through his shoulder with the bullet coming out of his back.

I recalled that it had been a hot summer. I had walked the steep path down from the temple in the early morning. Eating what was offered and drinking from a well, I followed my feet to the headlands of the port. The natural bay of Yosu curved around me. The temple was above behind the town and port, northwest from where I ended up. I had heard that the Admiral was out on a ship for the day, and so I knew that he would not be calling for me.

Stomach filled with plenty of rice and water, the sun hot, the sea smell strong, I decided to meditate next to the waves. Some masters say this is disadvantageous, that being next to calm lake waters, slow rivers, or small streams is better. They are likely correct. However, having somehow ended up as an assistant, a consultant, to a great warrior who was trying to save the land from horrible invaders, and who was on this day saving us by fighting at sea, meditating on the shore next to the waves felt right.

I chose a flat place in the shade of a withered tree above the high tide line. I looked out at the port, the town, the temple above it (how fitting, I thought), and the sky. For a few moments, I gazed at the mountaintop where I so often meditated. I wondered if through a bend in time I might tomorrow or yesterday see the dot which was me up there meditating. I couldn't.

Then I settled into meditation posture. My body was long molded to this position. It was like coming home to cross my legs, to relax my shoulders over my erect spine and head, to make the eternal circle with thumb meeting forefinger, to slit my eyes, and then, to focus upon my deep breathing, beginning by counting my breaths.

The waves hitting the rocks and the rocky beach made lapping, then slapping, sounds. Some of the slaps did not sound like the others. I wanted to open my eyes, to look around, to see what was making those sounds. Could it be robbers or something else nearby that I should know about? Once, I even imagined the irregular sounds were made by Japanese who were creeping towards Yosu and that I was going to have my throat slit to keep their presence unknown.

The reasons for not attempting meditation next to the sea were indeed making themselves very apparent.

Finally, the noises faded. The focus on counting my breaths succeeded, or, perhaps, I fell asleep. (In the temple where I had trained, falling asleep while meditating would have earned me a brisk slap of a wisp or rod. Certainly now as a veteran priest, I would never fall asleep while meditating, but still I am glad the training priest was not watching me that afternoon.)

Worlds, visions, insights, feelings, glimpses—the window of my consciousness was open, and I saw and felt … how to describe it? It must have lasted many hours of partly true meditation and partly dreaming. There had been many vistas and scenes upon which to ponder. But then there came before me a creature from myth.

A giant water dragon, its flaring smoking head raised up from the sea with spikes protruding from its back as it paddled along, serene for the moment but ever alert, looking for prey. It was huge. It came around the point with a brilliant red-orange-gold sunset surrounding it, the dragon dark and commanding in the deep gray-blue sea. I felt awe, a shudder of magnificence, a joy that I had lived to see such a sight. I looked at this wonderful monster and knew how small was my physical self in this fantasy of worlds.

Then I was back in my conscious body, my mind and body of this world. In front of me, was the kobukson, the turtle ship, with its armor plating, its iron-spiked back (to impale enemy sailors who dared try to board her), and its smoking dragon's head. The pride of the Korean navy, the ship that saved us all, was returning to her homeport carrying the man who had created and designed her, and who was, in a way, her father.

Admiral Yi said the fire in the dragon's head (the smoking head was actually a chimney) was to light the fire arrows to send against Japanese ships, but it always seemed to me that was only part of its purpose. The smoking impervious dragon's head approaching the enemy through the waves would have been one of the last things many Japanese ever saw and would hearten any Korean who might be in trouble. Just knowing that there were kobukson in the vicinity and that Admiral Yi was always looking to send aid to those taking the lead against the enemy helped the Korean cause immeasurably.

Yet, the Korean forces never consisted of a majority of kobukson (except at Myongnyang, when a few of them, not yet complete, were all we had). Actually, the most numerous fighting ship that we had was the panoekson. These were two-masted and multi-decked, the rowers and sailors well protected on a middle deck from enemy arrows, firearms, and cannon. From the upper deck, the fighters had a higher vantage point than the Japanese had during the battles, a very important advantage. The panoekson were never as fearsome as the kobukson, lacking the dragon's head and the armor, but they were the equal of the best Japanese ships.

Good as the panoekson were, though, the Imjin War will always be remembered for Admiral Yi and his kobukson. It was this ship that gave Admiral Yi an unbeatable weapon and he used it to perfection. The samurai knew that the coming of the turtle ship meant an ignoble death. They could not hope for a demise in which they heroically took the enemy with them to the other side. Instead, with the kobukson coming upon them in battle, each samurai was facing slaughter as if he were a farmyard pig.

It would be a sharp bleeding, drowning, burning massacre, not the brave end in combat they had been trained to face. This thought put panic and fear into many otherwise strong and valiant warriors. Only on land did Admiral Yi sometimes let the Japanese have an escape route so they would not take to ravaging the local populations. At sea, it was his duty to send every Japanese to the bottom, and he did so with an excellence the gods of the underworld must have appreciated.

The memory of the kobukson at sunset stirs me, and then I realize I am sitting with the Young Captain, and that he is still speaking. (I never cease to wonder of time. I know it is not real, but it still is wonderfully strange how the memory of a whole day can be recalled in only a few seconds.)

"The kobukson were the perfect weapon against the Japanese," he is saying. "The Japanese fought the traditional way, ramming the enemy ship, or grappling a hold and boarding it, taking over through swordsmanship. Of course, they also fired their guns and arrows at the enemy.

"But against a turtle ship, fire arrows, regular arrows, guns, and even their cannon could do nothing! The whole ship had iron plating in all the vulnerable places that make her virtually impregnable. Yet, at the same time, with her rows of ten sets of oars on each side, combined with Admiral Yi's use of the winds and tides, she could not be escaped—not the way the Admiral maneuvered her in the narrow straits and waterways where the Japanese numbers meant so much less than they would have in the open sea.

"And Admiral Yi himself had designed or tested the four types of cannon—mighty Heaven, strong Earth, accurate Black, and man-killing Yellow—himself. It was he who added the spikes to the back of the ship so any enemy soldier crazy enough to jump aboard would step or fall on them. He also made sure that even a stray shot by the enemy could not accidentally hit the stored gunpowder.

"He improved the design of the kobukson."

"What?" The words just came out. This was a big surprise. "Didn't he invent it? This is what was generally said."

For a moment, the Young Captain looked like a teacher who was pleased to be asked a good question and even more pleased to have an excellent answer. "Actually, no, he didn't. Not that he would not have if there hadn't been records of some already having been around. But the records indicate that early kobukson were available to King Taejong in 1414 and were used against the Wako at Tsushima. The kobukson also …"

Then the Young Captain stopped. He looked at me with a funny expression. "I apologize."

"For what?"

"You rowed on the turtle ship. You have known much of what I have said. In my enthusiasm, I talk as if to someone unfamiliar …"

"Kind Captain, there is no reason to apologize. Much of what you have said I did know at one time but have by now forgotten. I am no longer young. And much of what you said was new to me, such as that King Taejong had a type of turtle ship in 1414."

I smiled and said, "Besides, if old shipmates cannot tell tales to each other, who can?" I took a sip, and realized my cup had become empty. I smiled. "How about some more wine?"

He smiled back and called for the ship's steward. Perhaps it was at that moment we became friends.

Chapter 7

▼

"Why Call It a Turtle Ship?"

Of the year of Mu-sul, 1598, the last year of the war

Perhaps it was that first night that I told the Young Captain of a conversation with a Chinese man, a sailor in the Ming navy. The Chinese had come to help. Japan's goal, after all, was to attack China through Korea. (It has always been this way. Things go from China to Japan via Korea, and vice versa. Sometimes, they have been good things, like Buddhism. At other times …)

It was late in the war, 1598, and that old monkey, the Taiko, Hideyoshi, had finally died. The Japanese would be leaving. The final battle was coming soon.

The only question was whether the Japanese could bribe our Ming Chinese allies into not attacking them when the Japanese fleet finally left the area around Pusan for Japan. (They even tried, tentatively, to get Admiral Yi to back off, to let them go quietly. This would have taken an order from the King, and Admiral Yi said as much. He also seemed to make it clear he hoped this order would not come. In this, his wish was granted.)

The Chinese sailor was saying, "Your Admiral Yi is truly admirable. He is a great warrior indeed."

Of course, I agreed. I also wondered what he really wanted. Then he asked me, "His kobukson is truly a horrible fighting machine. Unbeatable in the coastal waters. And his ship has a dragon's head, which is fearsome in itself, but sometimes is used to spout smoke to spoil the vision of the enemy, and, at other times, there is a cannon aimed out of it. Yet he calls it a turtle ship instead of a dragon ship?"

It was a fair question, for a non-Korean. Of course, as a Chinese, he would see the Dragon as more fierce, more warlike. So I explained how we Koreans saw it.

"Well, we all know that the turtle swims wherever it wants and has an unbreakable shell, just like our ship. But the turtle is also an honored part of all of our Korean traditions. It is important to our mudang, that is, our female shaman…."

He nodded. He knew who our red-robed, dancing, singing, future-reading, spell-casting red-robed women were, so I continued.

"And it's significant to our Taoists, to the Confucianists, and to us Buddhists. You will find it in paintings or statues, or both, in every shrine and temple. So, in this way, the turtle touches all Koreans.

"Plus, the turtle is our animal of the north."

At this, the Chinese man nods as I keep speaking.

"And, he is one of our traditional 'good luck' animals."

The Chinese man begins to say something, but I stop him to conclude, "Also, the turtle to us is an animal of longevity. By using the name 'turtle ship,' a message is being sent to the Japanese: you cannot hurt us, not in the long term. We will be here for a long time. We will survive."

Now the Chinese man can speak. "I understand. We honor the turtle in China, too, but you in Korea, perhaps even more." He looks out at the harbor, at the mightiest ship in Asia, and says, "Wise, wise indeed, is your Admiral. A rare man, indeed."

Then, very quietly, as he bows and moves away, he murmurs, "I wish he were ours."

Chapter 8

▼

"Tell Me About What Happened With the Languages"

Sixth Moon, 1592

"Please tell me about what happened with the languages," finished the Admiral.

I was still reacting to his description of the bullet having gone through him. However, I was able to say, "Between Japanese and Korean?"

"Yes, of course. Why are they so different now?"

"Well, they are, and, in some ways, they aren't. The grammar of the two is virtually identical. Some parts of Japanese are very easy for a Korean to learn, and I understand that the same is true for a Japanese of Korean."

"I have heard this, too." He pauses, choosing his words carefully as he so often did. "You have told me of Paekche conquering Japan beginning in 369 AD. The new court in Japan, this illustrious line of Paekche-founded

Japanese emperors, likely spoke as did their Paekche cousins until at least 664 AD. Correct?"

He sees my respectful nod and continues, "Since then, things have changed. How? Why?"

"Sir, it seems that we speak what came from Silla."

It takes him almost no time to see it. He says, "You mean our Korean of today comes from what the unifiers of our peninsula spoke; that we speak here, in Korea, now, in 1592, a language descended from the Silla dialect of Korean, and the Japanese speak a language descended from the Paekche dialect of Korean, since both of these dialects existed in the seventh century AD."

"Yes, Sir. Koguryo and Paekche both came from old Puyo, but Silla had split off some time before. Certainly a person from Paekche and Silla could have communicated, but there were noticeable differences even then."

The Admiral is very still. Perhaps he is pondering my words, or perhaps he is checking, by ear and sixth sense, the weather. For a navy man, especially during wartime, awareness of the wind and rain is as important every day as is a farmer's feel for rain in the middle of a drought.

His voice resumes, "And then, for centuries after Paekche had fallen, there was very little contact between Korea and Japan."

"Certainly compared to before," I agree. "But until then, even the Nihongi tells how visitors from Paekche automatically spoke and read the language of the land of Wa perfectly, and that even visitors from Silla did not need interpreters though they might make a few mistakes. Even after the fall of Paekche there was trade off and on, but there have been more pirates, more wako, from Japan in recent centuries than regular traders."

"Not the best conditions for maintaining a shared language," says the Admiral.

"And," I add, "There were languages on the islands of Wa before Paekche came. These had to have added some words at least to Japanese."

The Admiral nods and then says, "Plus, after the fall, our written languages took different paths, which would have caused even more differences."

"Yes," I say and pause for a moment. Both Korean and Japanese have taken many Chinese characters into their written languages, but both have also added simpler ways of writing to help the common folk to be able to communicate in writing, too. Learning the Japanese symbols had actually not been so difficult for me, but, of course, the hardest part for most people was the Chinese, which I had already known.

I continue speaking. "The great Buddhist saint, Kobo Daishi, is given credit for bringing forth the kana of the Japanese language, just as King Sejong brought hangul into ours."

"How different are kana and hangul, actually?" asks the Admiral. I know that the Admiral himself writes in the Korean/Chinese of the highborn well-educated classes, but I am not surprised he is curious about the simpler ways.

"They are quite different, Sir. They are not similar at all, except that everyone agrees they are easier to learn and use than Chinese characters. And, both kana for the Japanese and hangul for the Koreans were designed to fit the sounds of their language and to make it easier for the poor and for women to read and write."

"Which is better designed?"

"Hangul, of course," I reply. I say it so quickly that Admiral Yi laughs.

"Sir, this is not just a patriotic answer. I believe hangul is better, more logical, more systematic, easier to learn and use."

He stops laughing and changes the subject. He says, "Do you know the Chinese character Hideyoshi uses for his name?"

"Yes."

"Please write it here, and next to it, write it in the Japanese kana and then write it in hangul."

I do as Admiral Yi requests. He looks at the Chinese characters, says some polite things about my calligraphy, glances at the hangul rendering of the enemy leader's name and then at Hideyoshi written in kana (katakana).

"Hi-de-yo-shi." He sounds out each symbol.

"Yes," I say.

"So this is their *shi*?"

"It is."

"*Shi*. In Japanese, does not the sound of this word also mean death?"

I realize I should stop being surprised by the many things Admiral Yi knows.

"Yes. *Shi* can mean death in Japanese. When the Japanese borrowed China's written language, the Chinese way of saying four, which was *shi*, sounded like their word for death. Just like our Korean word for four, *sa*." Both Koreans and Japanese do not like the number four. In at least this way we are similar even now. The Japanese even have kept a different way to say the number four. They often say *yon* for four, instead of *shi*."

I look at the Admiral. I sense that I have spoken too much, but he says nothing regarding my verbosity. What he does say is, "Death. *Shi*. Hideyoshi." The Admiral pauses. "Yes, a man of death. It fits. My officers have told me that some of the Japanese prisoners say that Hideyoshi really did not want to conquer China by invading and marching through Korea. They say that Hideyoshi simply had a land full of too many battle-seasoned soldiers and needed to give them something to do that would keep them too busy to think of rebelling against him."

"I have heard this theory, too." I hesitate. He looks at me, his eyes showing the question. I continue, "And I believe that it is at least partly true, Sir."

He nods. Then, for some reason, I say, "Sir, last night, as I walked through the port, I heard men talking. They were talking of Hideyoshi and of you."

He just looks at me.

"They had been drinking and were saying that they wished the 'god-damned Taiko would get into his biggest and best Japanese ship and try to sail it past Yosu to relieve their armies in the north so Admiral Yi could go out there with his turtle ship.' Their details of what you would do to him were very unsavory."

I had meant to show him the increasing confidence of the people of the port, but he does not smile.

Instead, he asks, "Have you heard of 'The Mound of Ears'?"

I frown. "I had hoped it was only a rumor."

"No, it is true. In Japan, in Kyoto, they have made a mound of over 100,000 ears and noses cut from those killed here in Korea.

"If Hideyoshi did dare to sail here, and I cannot think he would ever be so foolish as to answer my prayers in this way; if he were to sail where I could reach him, there would only be one supreme standing order: 'If at all possible, bring him to Admiral Yi alive. There will be a huge reward for his head, and double for it still attached and him still breathing.'"

As he says these words, his look is what I imagine a dragon revenging the death of its brood would have. I know with a certainty that what the men outside the inn had said last night was far too kind.

One thing for which Admiral Yi was famous was his ability to handle many topics at the same time. He displayed this now. His expression went from one of wishing he could get his hands on Hideyoshi Toyotomi alive to something very different.

"Have you been to Changsaengpo?" he asked.

I hesitated, not shifting as quickly as he and then said, "Yes."

"It is good land, is it not?"

"Absolutely," I concurred. I had walked through these lands, which seemed very rich and fertile and were quite close to Yosu. Then I guessed what he was going to do as he began to explain.

"You have seen the refugees in the town?"

"Of course." They seemed to be everywhere. Some seemed to have nowhere to go inside even when it rained.

"They come to us for safety from the Japanese. They need food and shelter. I have given orders to have them fed and clothed. But there are so many, and there will be more. Every time our fleet goes out against the Japanese this happens. Poor wretches who are starving and hiding in caves come running down to the shore to us. They tell us everything they know about the Japanese, about the crimes they have witnessed or experienced, and they are overjoyed to witness or to hear of our successes.

"Already we have hundreds of refugees here in Yosu. I have decided to do my best to give them the opportunity to live again."

* * * *

Excerpt from *Memorial to Court #8, 14th of Sixth Moon, 20th Year of Wan-li (Imjin, 1592)*

During the recent operations male and female war refugees of all ages from around Ungchon to the west of Namhae have appeared from their hiding places in the mountains after having witnessed the Japanese having been defeated and chased away by our squadrons. They have literally danced with jubilation at our victories. They ran down from their hiding places to the shore, where they told us all they could about enemy movements, encampments, and numbers. Deeply moved by their pitiful condition, with many barely clothed and all near starving, I gave them rice and cloth that had been captured from the enemy vessels.

In addition, here at Navy Headquarters in Yosu many people have come to seek safety. The numbers of farmers, fishermen, parents, children, wives, and relatives increases daily. Though they work as best they can, with increasing numbers soon there will not be enough jobs or food for them in the town. Therefore, I had them settled near Yosu in the broad fertile land in Chang-

saengpo and other villages, where they should be able to live in peace and to farm. Any food they produce will, of course, be helpful in the war effort.

It is a distinguished task equal to beheading the enemy invaders to find our people who have been enslaved by the enemy and to recapture them alive. Therefore, our men have been given special orders to check for captured prisoners before burning captured enemy vessels, and have been reminded that in the heat of battle they should be careful not to accidentally kill Korean captives they find on enemy boats.

Already some of the prisoners whom we have been able to rescue have been able to provide us with useful information. This includes....

Chapter 9

▼

"He Bettered Them"
1618 AD

It was either the second or third time, or maybe it was still the first, with the Young Captain. It was likely in the year 1618 AD. Although it was only nine or ten years ago, it is hard to remember exactly.

And I thought I was old then.

However, the Young Captain did repeat himself. Perhaps I heard this the first, second, and every time I saw him. Some of the stories I was sure to hear almost every time we were together. His enthusiasm for everything about Admiral Yi was so strong that I think he would have done this deliberately even had he been aware of it.

Perhaps this was indeed the case. I could never really tell. Certainly, though, as a polite recipient of his wine and hospitality, I always responded appreciatively and with questions. So, perhaps if he was repeating himself on purpose, it was partly my doing.

I have always enjoyed the company of men who can enjoy the grandeur, the heroism, and the accomplishments of others. It is only those who find fault and complain about everyone and everything that drive me away.

There have been times I have left a warm place which feeds me well to a cold and hungry road if only to escape the carping of a pessimistic, jealous, and fearful innkeeper, landowner, or, even, abbot.

"He bettered them!" exclaims the Young Captain. "The writers of the *Seven Classics* themselves could have done no better than Admiral Yi in following their own advice."

As always, I smile, nod, and take a sip.

"He used the turtle ship, the kobukson, just like Tai Kung in his *Six Secret Teachings* counseled the use of 'Lightning Chariots.' And this is just what Sun Tzu said in *The Art of War*, too. He said to use chariots in lightning attacks to penetrate solid infantry and cavalry formations.

"Admiral Yi did this, except on the sea! His turtle ships became his attack chariots, and with them, he totally disrupted the enemy forces. His armor-plated turtle ships, completely invulnerable to the enemy's puny cannon, could strike like a tiger amidst stray dogs and did, time after time.

"And at Tangpo, even though a bullet had gone through him just a day or two before, he used the trick of pretending defeat and retreat to lure them out. They fell for this trick a few times in the early battles. And then, when he had beaten them, he did not destroy all of their ships. He left some of their vessels untouched and seaworthy. Do you know why?"

As always, I shake my head No. And, likely, I take another sip of wine. The Young Captain's is never quite as good as what I had with Admiral Yi, but it is warming. And the Young Captain is always the best of companions. It is rejuvenating to be with someone so zestful; for a few moments during each visit I feel as if I were in my forties again. My back seems straight and strong, my limbs more powerful, and my eyes sharp and clear.

The Young Captain says, "First, according to Sun Tzu, you always leave a perceived outlet to the enemy. If they think they can get away, they will not fight so hard. If they think they can escape, they will not fight to the death. Thus, they are easier to kill. On the other hand, if you chase them down and corner them, they will probably fight like angry wolves, and you will lose more of your people than necessary.

"Second, Admiral Yi knew that by leaving the survivors what they thought to be an escape route, they would be less likely to panic and terrorize the local people. If he destroyed all their ships, what would the survivors on land do? Admiral Yi knew the answer. He knew that survivors on land who had lost their ships, who were hungry and desperately roaming the hills, would do their worst, that they would terrorize whatever farmers or villagers they came across.

"In this, he beats the Chinese authors! I did not find this reason for leaving the enemy a perceived escape route given in any of the *Seven Military Classics*."

At this point, the Young Captain always focuses on me, and I nod or speak my approval and admiration of Admiral Yi. The Young Captain smiles, takes a big gulp from his cup, and, if he is not too busy and we are indeed to make a day and likely a night of it, he says something like:

"Indeed, after Hansando, the Japanese never wanted to fight him again. They spent the next six years trying to avoid him."

Hansando. The great victory. THE great victory. Sitting with the Young Captain, looking back from more than 25 years, it is clear that this triumph doomed the Japanese. They would never be able to conquer China, which was Hideyoshi's professed goal. They would never even be able to keep what they had already stolen of Korea without control of the seas. And this, after Hansando, was denied them. Every objective military assessment showed this to be true. It was only the fear of their leader, Hideyoshi, which kept the Japanese around Korea for six more years, mostly raiding from their bases around Pusan. Now that the Young Captain has mentioned Hansando, I know it will be a long evening. It is one of his favorite topics. I settle back, feeling warm, good wine at hand, a fine dinner to come, and an enthusiastic host.

"The enemy was safe. They were snug in port. Hansando is a wonderful harbor, or why would Admiral Yi later have used it himself? They felt safe, in part because they were protected by Kyonnaeryang Strait, which is not even 400 meters wide and which has many sunken rocks. There was not enough room for the Korean ships to attack in force without hitting each other or grounding on the rocks.

"So Admiral Yi lured the enemy out. Again, we attacked with a small force and then ran away. The Japanese—seventy ships of them—followed our small attacking force out of the harbor to gain what they must have thought would be an easy victory. Surprise! Admiral Yi and the squadrons of the three provinces were waiting. We moved into crane wing formation and annihilated the Japanese."

Crane wing formation. I knew this well by now. It was called this because it was like a half-circle, like the shape a crane's wings take when both are at the top of their movement. The Japanese ships at Hansando sailed straight into what to them must have seemed like the gaping mouth of a horrible, huge shark—a giant, very hungry Japanese-gobbling maneater complete with cannon, fire-arrows, sharpshooters, expert bowmen, and armor-protected ships ready to ram in their sides.

"Yes, at Hansando Admiral Yi again used the wisdom of Sun Tzu. Sun Tzu said to avoid the substantial and instead to attack the vacuous. Admiral Yi tricked the Japanese into leaving where they had been substantial, and then beat them when they were dispersed, disorganized, and surprised—vacuous."

The Young Captain goes on to recount individual deeds in this battle and tactics used by various ship captains. He tells how Admiral Yi was always looking for brave and commendable actions by those in his command, and how freely he gave credit to those who deserved it in his *Memorials to Court*. "In fact," says the Young Captain, "he wrote a letter to the king simply to request that Kim In-yong, one of my predecessors as captain of the port of Yodo, be rewarded by the court similarly to others who had performed admirably in battle."

Then the Young Captain's face changes. "There was, of course, also no one quicker than Admiral Yi to deal promptly with cowardice or treachery. You know that from close experience, don't you?"

I nod my head. He is studying my face, which is likely showing the memories.

The Young Captain goes on. "This is again how the Chinese masters would have it," he says. "Admiral Yi himself said that the sailor who disobeyed an order in combat was to be killed immediately; that this had to be done. However, he was also the first to reward and commend the brave.

"This is exactly as the Chinese classics maintained that it had to be. In *The Three Strategies,* Huang Shih-kung says, 'Rewards and Punishments must be certain as Heaven and Earth, for only then can the general employ the men.' In *Six Secret Teachings,* Tai Kung writes, 'In general, one values credibility in employing rewards, and values certainty in employing punishments.' Plus, in *The Art of War* it is written by Sun Tzu, 'In general, executions provide the means to accentuate and encourage the martial. If by executing one man the whole army takes notice, execute him.'"

I say, "All of those sound exactly like Admiral Yi."

The Young Captain almost sighs. "Yes. I truly believe what I said—he excelled over them. He bettered the Chinese masters in their own field."

"You heard what the Ming commodore said of Admiral Yi?"

"Chen Lien?"

"Yes." I guess that the Young Captain already knows what I am going to say, but that is all right. Even though a port commander and ship's captain, he is a gracious enough host to let his shipmate from long ago, even a Buddhist priest, add a little to the glorious stories regarding his hero. Chen Lien was the commander of the Ming Chinese naval forces who had come to help in 1598, that is, in the last year of the war with the Japanese. Haughty and arrogant as any Chinese general or admiral, at least Chen

Lien had recognized the truth about Admiral Yi. And, in the end, Chen Lien had fought.

"Chen Lien called Admiral Yi 'Li-yeh,' meaning 'His Excellency Admiral Yi.' He said more than once, 'Li-yeh is too great to live in a small country like Korea. He should come to China, where he could be a great mandarin.'"

"From Chen Lien that is a lot," says the Young Captain.

"From any Chinese that would be a lot," I add.

We both laugh and drink some wine.

Those were good times, between wars, with the Young Captain. It was about ten years ago when we had most of our meetings. We could laugh about China then. The Young Captain never liked the Chinese of his generation. In fact, he hated them. He had hard feelings about their bad behavior as our allies during the war. But, certainly, he admired their history and respected their military writers. Besides, Admiral Yi, even then, had been dead for twenty years, and the Japanese gone for that long, too. He died, and they left, in 1598. I met the Young Captain, or should I say re-met him, in 1618. Once in a while, twenty years later, the Young Captain could laugh about the Chinese.

Now as I write, it is 1628, and the Ming Chinese, our former allies, have been displaced by the Manchu. The Ming, however temperamental, superior-minded, and haughty, had been our ally. Now, the China of the Manchu is our enemy. The Manchu have occupied the northern part of our country. The royal court has to put up with most sad indignities. No one knows where it will end. Perhaps the Manchu Chinese will come here to the south also? The abbot has asked me to write of my life, including Japan, and, in particular, the memories of Admiral Yi. He has never really told me the reason. Is there a connection? Does the abbot know something that is going to happen or might happen? What purpose could my writings of such a great person as Admiral Yi serve? The best literati of China, Japan, and my country know of Admiral Yi and have written about him.

My country sits between two very thorny neighbors. Our cousin, Japan, we had to beat, and now we must somehow hold off huge China. China, which gave us so much in culture, in writing, in philosophy, and even our Buddhism. Yes, even our Buddhism came from India across the huge mountains and around the south lands to China, then to Korea, and from here in Paekche to Japan.

Perhaps the abbot wonders if what the Chinese Commodore Chen Lien once called our "little country" can even survive. Possibly, he feels that only with the inspirational and true stories of men like Admiral Yi can we be inspired to suffer and bravely fight through yet another calamity.

I wonder what my little writings can do in all of this. I wonder what one person can do in any of this at all. Does not the Buddha teach that all here is an illusion?

But it gets so complicated, and even the followers of the Buddha, who said not to harm any living creature, fight as warriors. They reason that if it is all an illusion, then so is death, so why not fight? If it is all an illusion, why bother to live at all? If it is all an illusion …

I am old now, so old. If I write too long, I can barely stand afterwards without help. Winter is especially hard for me. I have heard that the Buddha's India is always warm. Did this help him to live for so long?

Yet I do know that at times in my meditations I have glimpsed something. Once I thought a goddess had come to me in the forest. There have been moments where I caught the scent, have seen a glimpse, of what the Buddha knew.

Yes, I rowed for Admiral Yi, and, in this way, I helped people to be killed and in the final battle … I am not sure that this was correct, really, though I did it.

But there is a reason for life. I know it.

I just hope I see it more clearly, and for a while longer, before this one ends.

Chapter 10

The Priest Wonho, Suspected Criminal

Late in the Eighth Moon, 1592

"You are guilty then." The eyes of the Admiral are steady upon me.

"I am the person you identified." My voice is as steady as his eyes, though my eyes are focused a bit lower than are his, as is appropriate.

"So you admit your guilt?" I can tell he already knows what I believe the truth to be.

"I admit to being there, and to acting. Guilt, or not, is for the Honorable Admiral to decide." For a moment, I look up into his eyes. "Of course."

Admiral Yi considers my words.

"Last night, in the entertainment district, five of my sailors were attacked and beaten by a man in gray robes, an apparent priest. Now you, Wonho, admit to being this man."

"I did interact with five men last night in the lively area of town. I admit to this. It is the truth."

"Interact!" Is that what you call it? Two of my sailors can barely walk, one has a broken nose, and another will not be able to row again for months. The fifth only has a severe headache."

"I regret that these were your sailors, Sir. Certainly I did not know this last night." That is most certain. Whether they were farmers, rich landholders, fishermen, or military men was the last thing on my mind.

"Would it have made any difference if you had known?"

This is an important question. But I have to answer honestly. It is the way of the Buddha, and, besides, I believe the Admiral would know if I were to lie.

I look at the floor and wish very much I had not been the cause of an interruption in the Admiral's schedule. He is now renowned throughout the land and beyond. His victory at Hansando will likely result in his promotion to Chahon Taebu, to senior commander status. Some are already calling him the savior of the kingdom.

And now he has to take time with me, a suspected criminal. How stupid of me not to find another way.

I tell him the truth. "No, it would have made no difference, Sir. One needed to be stopped, and the others attacked me. I did as I have trained to do."

"They say that you attacked them."

"I asked the first two to stop what they were doing. Then when they reacted to this poorly, three of their friends came out of the bar and tried to help their comrades."

"What were the men doing that you asked them to stop?"

I picture the scene. I have already gone over it many times in my mind. Why must I walk so much? Why is it I need so little sleep? Why are midnight wanderings on moonlit nights so soothing to my spirit? What is it that draws me barefoot to the cool wind on a warm night with the clouds made white by the stars going by, enjoying the sensations of the bottoms of my feet on the different types of ground?

Whatever the reasons, nighttime walks are good for me. Usually, that is. And I have excellent sight at night.

I see myself in my memory's eye, looking at myself as I am on my way back to the temple through the festive part of town. It is often enjoyable to see men happy and laughing, and the human experience is always an interesting one. Plus, good eyes or not, it is the most well lit area.

The town of Yosu seems happy. The Japanese have been beaten again. The harvests look to be better than expected. The fishermen have been able to fish unmolested by Japanese raiders and have had a good catch. It seems a joyful time as I move through the nighttime activities of women, music, and drink. I am breathing deeply, easily. Then I hear the scream.

It is a woman. It is a sound of fear. Then I hear a man's voice, angry, loud, and drunk. I hear the sound of a blow. The woman screams again, in pain this time.

My feet are moving to the place. I see two men and one woman. She is on her knees, and one of the men is yelling at her, raising his fist. He is telling her to be a good whore and to do what he and his friend want.

"Stop!" I say. "Please!"

I am not even aware I have spoken. It is as if I am outside myself, looking at the scene.

Surprised, all eyes turn toward me. The woman is still scared, the men startled, then annoyed. The angry one looks me up and down. I know I am only of average height and weight. I certainly do not look imposing or threatening. Nor do I wish to.

"Fuck off, priest! This is none of your business," says the angry one.

"Maybe the whore is Buddhist," says the other man. Now that he has spoken, I can see he will not be a calming influence on his friend.

"I am not a prostitute!" says the woman. "I work in the inn, yes, but our farm was burned, and we need to eat. My husband has been taken to the army to fight, and I have a daughter …"

"Shut up, lying bitch!" says the angry one. He turns and strikes her again, a strong backhand to the face.

I am moving. I come in behind him, take his shoulders, and turn the right backward and the left forward while raising my right knee. With my right foot, I kick the back of his left knee, collapsing it, and then strike him on the jaw with my elbow as he goes down hard on his back. I have turned him and had him fall between his friend and me.

"Please," I say loudly. "Let us not quarrel."

The friend either does not hear or does not care. He charges me around the man on the ground. He is moving fast, arms outstretched to grab me. I move to the side and forward, my hands up. I circle down and forward with both of my arms, whipping his arms down, and then turn toward and past him, pivoting full force counter-clockwise to my front, bringing my right forearm forward horizontally in the "unbreakable position."

My forearm hits his face as he charges forward. His arms having been thrown down, I feel his nose crush as his head jerks back. His feet literally come off the ground, and he lands hard on the back of his head somewhere behind me.

It was then that I hear the shouts behind me. "Hey, stop that!"

"That priest just hurt Doo-hoon."

The third is already running towards me. His two friends follow.

Admiral Yi, in what is now a courtroom, for I am being judged, is looking at me. All of these memories have flashed through my mind. I remember that he is waiting for my answer to his question about what his men had been doing. I simply say, "I asked one of them to stop hitting a woman."

Silence. Admiral Yi's eyes are upon me. I wonder what he will say next. I know that he is one of the few who know of my father and of my mother. Will this matter? Does he even remember? Yes, he remembers. He forgets nothing, I decide. My thoughts shift back to the matter at hand as he speaks.

"And how did these two young gallants react to your request?" The way he says "gallants" gives me hope.

"They expressed a wish that I go elsewhere and perform sexual acts."

"Yes. And what was their complaint with the woman?"

"She said she was not of the type they thought and did not wish to do as they wanted."

"And when did you attack them?"

"One of them struck the woman again. I stopped him from repeating this action. Then his friend charged me." I pause. "That is the one with the broken nose."

Quiet again. "The other three?"

"They came out of the inn and saw me dealing with their friends and tried to help them. I regret that they did not give me a chance to explain. However, many would have reacted just as did they if they came out and saw what they thought was their friends being attacked and beaten."

"You vanquished five of my men, Priest Wonho." There is a different tone in his voice now.

"They only came near me one at a time, Sir."

"Five of them. They were at Hansando. They are not cowards, or, if they were, at least they held out and helped us to win."

"Last night they were unarmed, thankfully, Sir. If it had been a matter of arrows or firearms, the story would likely have been much different."

"What about a knife?" His question is sincerely curious.

"Against one, with a knife, I would have a chance."

"A sword?"

"I would have to be very lucky or to be facing someone totally untrained in its use."

"A staff?"

"The same, but I would prefer this to the sword."

"What about the one with the stick?"

I see this one. The fifth. He saw his two friends go down in front of him, and paused to grab a stick, a hard piece meant for a strong fire and then came at me. He brandished it like a club.

"I believe he is the one with the headache."

"What did you do to him?"

"I took his stick away from him, and then gave it back to him—to his head." By now, I can tell that Admiral Yi has made up his mind, but as often happens he surprises me.

"Could you have killed them all?"

For a moment, I do not know what to say. I had not considered this. "Sir, what I have trained to do is not to kill, but only to injure as much as necessary. As a Buddhist priest …"

"Wonho, do not lie to me!" His voice is thunderous.

"Sir, I …"

"You peaceful Buddhists. Some of the deadliest Japanese are Buddhists. Zen monks. Meditating swordsmen." He is as loud as I have ever heard him. "And here in Korea, you know what our own Buddhists have been doing. Look at Samhye of Sunchon, Uinung of Hungyang, Songhwi of Kwangju, and Chiwon of Koksong!"

"Yes, Sir. I have heard. At your request, they gather warriors, mostly monks, priests, and hermits."

"And their men are better fighters than most members of our Korean army." He says this with a tone that shows that he both appreciates the Buddhists and wishes for better from the regular army. Then he continues, "And you, a peaceful Buddhist, who is against killing … you, who waylays five of my sailors at night and leaves them groaning in the dark. You, who are thinking of joining our Buddhist fighting units who are helping so much against the Japanese!"

He almost snorts, "Do not tell me very much of your peaceful nature, or of how Buddhists are so against killing. Not you, who is thinking of joining the guerilla monks against the Japanese."

My mind is racing. I am trying to guess how Admiral Yi knows this. Of course, I realize. The abbot was probably told to watch me. "I have been asked about this, Sir, at the temple, by …"

"You will not join them."

"Sir?"

"You are in my service."

"Sir?"

"Besides, you are a criminal suspect awaiting judgment and sentence."

Then he does another one of those turns in thinking which always catch me by surprise. He asks, "Priest Wonho, how did you learn this way of fighting?"

I almost say, "What?" but don't. Instead, I collect my thoughts. Memories come, at first slowly and then in a flood. Some of the best times I ever had, and as is so often the case, I did not realize it until they were done.

"On the trip to China as a youth, my party fell in on the road with a Chinese priest."

I can still remember my joy at finding out that I would be allowed to be a baggage carrier for that journey. I was the lowest ranking and the youngest member of the temple to go to China, but still I was going! I remember looking outside at the icicles, the sun reflecting diamonds in them as they melted at midday (I loved the cold winter back then, in my youth) and wishing for spring so the day of the journey would soon be at hand.

When we met the Chinese priest, I could tell that there was something unusual about him. It was not until the bandits accosted us that I knew what this was. Of course, I do not say all of this to Admiral Yi. To him I say, "When bandits waylaid us, I tried to stand up to them, only to get smacked down by the first who came near me. At this, the Chinese monk, with incredible speed and intensity, knocked down, beat, and chased away the whole bandit band. He made it look very easy.

"Admiral, this man, while totally drunk, could beat ten of me as I am now with one hand and one eye. But he liked me and that I had tried, and in the time we had left together he taught me what he thought I could learn."

I remember those lessons. I had never worked so hard. My body stretched and contorted and strained in ways I did not think it could. Simple food never tasted so good, nor water so sweet as after a few hours with him. The monk said he had to do what he could in a short amount of time, so I had to work hard and quickly. However, I think he would have trained me the same way even if I had seven years, which was the minimum at his temple in order to attain the status of a real fighter.

I tell the Admiral, "He said I would never be great at kicking high, but that otherwise, bandits of the sort we had encountered on the road would not be much of a problem again. That is …"

"What?" Admiral Yi asked.

"That is, as long as I kept practicing what he had taught me. He said to practice it in my mind's eye even when I did not practice it with my body, but to practice it physically whenever I could."

"How long were you with him?"

"Two months."

"And you learned so much?"

"Sir, I actually learned very little. I learned about twenty moves. He had to learn at least 264—the number 264 is the holy 88 times the mystical three—plus longer movements, in order to be able to begin to train seriously. He, of course, was also an expert with many weapons. He said that it took seven years of intense training to be considered a proficient fighter, but that in truth the monks there kept learning their whole lives."

I pause, and then hazard to say, "And, Sir, none of the moves in themselves are deadly, by design. At least, the twenty I learned. In fact, the monk said only one of the first 264 was, and that it was not taught until among the last.

"Ideally, Sir, we Buddhists really do not wish to kill."

Admiral Yi does not rise to this bait. Instead, he says, "So, the monk chose twenty moves for you to learn in only two months."

"Yes, Sir. He based them on my physical skills, or lack of them, and on various potential attacks. Man in front grabbing, man punching, man kicking, man charging from the front or side, man with stick, two attackers, one on each side, and so on. He tried to give me something simple and effective for as many situations as he could."

"He did a good job of it apparently."

I look down. I wonder if he is going to change subjects on me again, if he will surprise me with more questions. I notice the grain of the wood, the freshness of the varnish, and how clean everything is. In the distance, I can hear the sea.

He is speaking again.

"Now it is time for me to hear from the victims of your attack. They are waiting outside. Please await my decision." The way he says "victims" gives me more hope.

I nod and am escorted by the husky attendant to a room a few doors away. He has been standing to the side, listening unobserved, the whole time. I notice that the attendant is behaving somewhat differently toward me than he has before. I realize it is because he is seeing me as a man now, as a person worthy of a different type of consideration, as a potential opponent or ally and not just as a priest likely to be found in the market begging for day-old rice from guilt-ridden old ladies. The attendant signals to a servant girl, who brings me some tea and rice crackers.

Sipping the warm tea and chewing the crackers, which are good, I try to hear what is happening down the hall. I can make out sounds, but not the individual words. I am wondering how long the Admiral will take with the five and, particularly, the first two. The possibilities for my sentence are endless. When I was with him, I thought he was seeing things as I had, but had I understood this correctly? And what might the five men be saying? Besides, by injuring fighting men enlisted in the service of Choson, I could be held to have performed traitorously. My life could actually be forfeit. I take a deep breath. What if I had misread Admiral Yi? I look at the wood of the floor edge. Its grain tells me nothing.

Suddenly the door opens. Two men are there. One is the expressionless, unreadable attendant. Next to him is one of the three men from the second group in last night's battle, one of the would-be rescuers of their shipmates.

I look at the rescuer, who looks very different in the day and in the Admiral's headquarters. He bows and says, "Thank you for your gracious display of the benevolent and pacifistic nature of Buddhism last night." He stops, bows, and moves away.

Next come the other two would-be rescuers, who deliver similar messages, again with bows. The attendant stands quietly, watching and listening.

Then next to the attendant is a man with a bandage across his face. This is the friend of the man who struck the woman. He is the one who suggested, "The whore must be Buddhist." This man's message, hard to understand through the bandage and broken flesh, is, "Through your kindly acts toward me last night you have helped me to see the truth of the divine nature of the message of Buddha. My most sincere gratitude."

My mind gives this one a name, Broken Nose. The look in his eyes gives a much different message than that given by his words. I know to watch out for him.

Last, moving with a crutch, is the man who struck the woman. I am surprised. Unlike Broken Nose, this man appears sincere when he bows and says, "Thank you for showing me the evils of too much drink and the value of sincere meditation and practice. You have been a credit to Buddhism."

He pauses and looks directly at me. "Thank you for not killing me or my friends." Then he limps away.

I sit silently, trying to put together what all this means. The attendant just looks at me, but, finally, when the last of the five is well gone he says, "I have been instructed to summarize the decision of Admiral Yi for you. You are to follow it to the letter."

I nod.

"The Admiral also asked me to tell you some of what he said to those five." Now, finally, he shows an expression. It is a smile.

"First, he told the last three that their instincts were generally good. He said that to help a shipmate in need is indeed a wise general policy. He mentioned that their mistake was in helping their shipmates in a fight against an enemy who was not really an enemy." He pauses. "The Admiral called you a potentially deadly enemy.

"He pointed out that you could easily have slit any of their throats while they were down. The Admiral also quoted from the report brought in this morning, 'The priest moved like lightning and hit as hard as a lunging bear.'" The attendant looks at me very intently, as if trying to see this speed and power somewhere inside my robes. I choose to say nothing, to let him imagine what he wishes.

"Then he told them that you were not just any priest, but that you were working for him, and…," he clears his throat, "… that this should be a good lesson; that danger could come in any form at any time and that one should always be ready and that one needed to know when to think, as well as when to react. He pointed out that the Japanese had reacted at Hansando without thinking and look at what had happened to them.

"With the last three, he then said, they would be let go as soon as they had bowed to you and given you their thanks. He, of course, told them the formula for their expression of gratitude." He smiles again.

"It was much appreciated," I venture.

"Yes, I am sure. The Admiral will enjoy hearing of the expression on your face, especially after the first man thanked you." He smiles again. He is actually a handsome man.

"It reminded me of the time the fruit peddler was slandering the Admiral using Japanese, the first time you were called to visit." He is still smiling, but then it goes away. "For the other two, he had different words. These are to remain private, except, rest assured, neither of those two will bother you, or any woman, at any time, at least while Admiral Yi is alive to hear of it."

I nod again. But I still know that I had better keep an eye out for Broken Nose. If he thought he could harm me without Admiral Yi knowing it had been him …

"Now, for your sentence."

My back stiffens at these words.

"There are a few parts to it." He pauses, probably on purpose, enjoying the moment.

"First, you are to stay at Admiral Yi's disposal at all times. You are not to join any guerrilla monk bands or to engage in combat against the Japanese except in the direct service of the Admiral."

"I understand," I answer neutrally.

In a lower voice, the attendant says, "Eventually, the Admiral will let you fight, do not worry. We do not have enough fighting men the way it is. He does everything for a reason."

Part of me almost laughs. The attendant has called me a "fighting man." This is something I have never been. But this is not a humorous moment.

His voice becomes official again. "Second, you are to find this woman who was struck by one of our sailors last night. The sailor said she claimed not to be a prostitute, that she lied and said she was married to a soldier and that she was a mother."

"I also heard her say this."

"Find her, and if she is truly a wife of a soldier and not a prostitute, you are to take her to the village elders of Changsaengpo and, under the authority of Admiral Yi, have her housed, fed, and given sufficient land so that she can eventually support herself and her child until her husband's return."

"She sounded sincere, but if in fact she is a prostitute …?"

"This was not spoken of, but I believe the Admiral wishes you to do as seems best."

"Is there anything else?"

"The Admiral says that if you come across any more of his sailors behaving abominably," the attendant again pauses deliberately, "to please not break their elbows or knees, that these are needed for rowing, firing cannon, and shooting the bow, but that headaches, broken noses, sore groins, and such are quite acceptable."

I can say nothing for a moment, but then bow my head and say, "I understand."

The attendant returns my bow, takes the little grin from his face, and leaves to report back to the Admiral.

* * * *

The incident with the woman and the five sailors happened over thirty-five years ago. If I were to come upon a similar scene in any city now, perhaps they would be able to hear my feeble shouts before laughing at my old bones. Except, of course, I need more sleep now than I could have imagined then, and I would not be out so late nor in such a quarter.

I found the woman. She was telling the truth. She was married to a man who had been drafted and taken away as a soldier, and she was the mother of a young child.

The woman was also lying. She had performed sexually with men for money. It was that, she had believed, or to starve. However, as she confessed to me, she had only done things with her mouth and her hands. Only her husband would ever be permitted to sheathe himself inside her, to father a child by her.

She had been resisting the sailor that night because he wanted her on her back, not on her knees. She seemed to believe that she was not a prostitute as long as no other man got inside of her. She seemed to want to believe this very much. She asked me if I believed it.

Last I heard, she was still in Changsaengpo at the farm.

Chapter 11

▼

Of Warrior Monks and Refugees

First Moon, 1593

Summary of excerpts from *Memorials to Court 19 and 20,* both sent by Admiral Yi to the King on the 26th of the First Moon, 1593

I memorialize the throne for reference on the following matters.

The Japanese invaders probe the defenses of Cholla Province by land and sea. Their desire to invade is clear. Although I am in charge of sea warfare, to ignore the land defenses would be foolhardy. Cholla Province has strong natural defenses at the mountain passes, which must be held. The enemy cannot be allowed to pass the fortresses at these points, lest the navy itself be in danger of losing its home ports, and the farms which are feeding the kingdom also be lost.

With this in mind, beginning in the Eighth Moon last year I sent to neighboring towns to find Buddhist monks and those masquerading as monks to report to fortresses to assist in their defense. Within one month about 400 monks had gladly responded to the call. Among them certain individuals stood out as courageous and intelligent leaders. From these, I commissioned officers and unit commanders.

While planning to recruit more monk and priest warriors, other leaders arose in the country who formed and recruited guerrilla bands. I have assigned these self-arisen and designated leaders to various fortresses, and, in the case of those who were assigned to port cities, have also in some cases given them the command of ships.

The names of all of these leaders, and their various appointments, are included herein. Each of these commanders is to observe enemy movements, to defend the fortresses to the last man, and to participate in other battles on sea and land as the case might be.

Of late, two hundred more families of wandering war refugees have come for aid and safety to the jurisdiction of my Navy Headquarters. They have been given food and temporary accommodations, but until peace is restored they cannot safely return to their native homes. Food is also very limited.

In this regard, the Border Defense Command sent this message, "If there are lands suitable for agriculture on islands safe from the Japanese, you may establish these refugees in new farm villages as you see fit."

The results of a careful survey show Tolsando to be the most preferable choice in this regard. It is protected from the Japanese by high coastlines and my ships, and it is fertile and well watered. The refugees settled there have happily commenced to the spring plowing.

Previously, the Ministry of War had objected to the agricultural use of Tolsando due to the tradition of breeding horses for military use on this island. However, with the emergency of war upon us, and with many people having lost their livelihoods and in danger of starvation, and with their being small likelihood that the tilling of soil by refugees will be of any harm to horse-breeding, it is sincerely hoped that a royal decree be issued to allow and promote both horse-breeding and the relief of these refugees in the manner detailed above.

Yi, Commander

26th of the First Moon in the 21st Year of Wan-li (Kyesa, 1593)

Chapter 12

The Best Month of the War

Of Third Moon, 1593

Was there a best month of the war? This question came to me. How could there be a best month to any war? Wars are to be endured and to be won. Is not the term "best" inappropriate? Perhaps the best month of any war is always its last month.

Do I worry too much of words? Of their nuances and meanings? Why do I write thus, anyway? Does not the Buddha say that words are inadequate for conveying the higher truths, that words are a trap to keep the mind enmeshed in this false world? With him I would, of course, agree. But, until I reach these truths (and when will this be?), what I have, most of the time, is words. And even the Buddha used them with others. For him, too, they were part of what he had to try to let others know, to help them to remember the Truth.

But "hopeful." Here is a word. I can remember a hopeful month. Everything seemed to be going well. It looked like the Japanese would be leaving very soon.

Admiral Yi had won four great victorious naval campaigns. The Japanese could not come close to beating him. The first major defeat dealt to the Japanese by the Koreans in the whole Imjin War was the Admiral's victory at Okpo in May of 1592. Then, only weeks later came the second campaign, and despite being shot, he smashed the enemy again in the seven days of battles that included Tangpo. The kobukson, the turtle ship, totally proves its worth here, if it hadn't already.

Third came Hansando, which broke Japan's navy. From this battle on, as has been pointed out many times to me by the Young Captain, the Japanese were no longer waging an offensive naval war. They steadily lost ground on land and sea (at least while Admiral Yi was in command of the Korean naval forces) for the rest of the war. They went from attacking to defending. The most the Japanese navy could do after Hansando (until, of course, the tragedy of the arrest, and Won Kyun had taken command of the naval forces of the three provinces) was to sneak out to raid at night, and try to avoid Korean naval ships at all costs.

It had taken the Japanese until Hansando to fully realize that they were well advised not to fight Admiral Yi at sea. They succeeded in avoiding him in August. So, on September 1, 1592, he went to them. He sailed into their strongest harbor in Korea, their safest place, and thrashed them again. At Pusan Harbor, he showed them that their navy was not safe even in their most strongly defended port.

At this point, many Japanese defenders began to wonder. They thought things like: with the Japanese ships losing every battle and the accursed Admiral Yi able to sail into Pusan Harbor and triumph, if I survive the battles on land with the Koreans and the Chinese, will I still be sunk on the way home to be dragged down to the bottom of the sea by the weight of my armor, my last breath being an inhalation of cold brine? Or will they take my ship, and the last thing I see is a sword coming for my head to become a trophy while my body becomes shark food?

This was Admiral Yi's fourth great victory. He had 166 ships and the Japanese 470. Plus, the Japanese were entrenched around the harbor with cannon and thousands of troops. Despite these advantages, Admiral Yi's forces destroyed over 130 Japanese vessels while losing none themselves. And it was his choice to stop destroying even more.

He stopped the attack only when he realized that if he destroyed too many vessels, the Japanese would not be able to consider going back to Japan. He also knew that the navy, by itself, could not kill all of the Japanese, and that without all of their ships, the desperate survivors on land would deal most horribly with any Korean civilians they came across.

Of course, the attack was not exactly how the Admiral would have had it. He had wanted the Korean and Chinese armies to attack at the same time as his navy did. With a joint operation like this, the Japanese could have been wiped out. If the armies of Choson and the Ming had been attacking on land when the Admiral sailed into Pusan Harbor, he could have destroyed every ship, and then his forces could have landed and helped to finish off the trapped enemy soldiers.

Naval victories alone truly would not be enough to put an end to the war, at least any time soon. The end result could well be eventual victory, but not quickly. Admiral Yi fully recognized this. The problem was that, in 1592, the first year of the war, the Korean army had won only a single victory. It was at the city of Chinju where we had held in the tenth month against huge odds. This had forced the Japanese back for at least the winter. Chinju was a city between Pusan and Cholla Province, Cholla Province being the home of the town of Yosu and the fleet of Admiral Yi.

Chinju had held. It was the only victory the army managed in 1592, but a very important one. If it had fallen quickly, the Japanese forces might have been able to come upon Yosu by land and overcome Admiral Yi's navy by capturing the ports.

Finally, though, a few more good things began to occur for us on land. Our new Chinese allies (let us not talk of the indignities they forced upon our King in order to be assured their help, nor of how some of their soldiers treated local Koreans. It is enough to say that some Korean farmers and townspeople feared the actions of our Chinese allies as much as they did those of the Japanese invaders).

I am cold. I am writing of things thirty-four and thirty-five years in the past, of a month of hope in a terrible war, and now it is 1627, and these Chinese are back, this time not even pretending to be allies, with troops in the northern half of the kingdom, and I am cold and old. This writing is of the past. Why does the abbot have me write? My hand grows tired, the joints ache. Can my script still be worth reading? I eat, I sleep, and only with difficulty do I trickle and pass dry or greasy turdlets. I meditate, and now, instead of working to help the temple, I write. Perhaps it is just because I am so feeble a worker in the grounds and gardens that the abbot has asked me to write instead? Except, ink and manuscript are not cheap. He must see some value.

I wander. My mind goes here and there now as my feet used to. But this is my lot. I should consider this writing my work. It is what the abbot has assigned me, rather than raking or sweeping or working in the fields. That is all. I shall do the best I can without affectation or expectation. That is all I can do. Back to it.

The new Chinese "allies" beat the Japanese in Pyongyang. This forced the Japanese to pull back toward Seoul. Finally, their armies were headed south, not north. But then the Ming Chinese were beaten in the next major battle. The Japanese looked to be able to hold onto Seoul after all.

Except, finally, down the Han River from Seoul, the Korean Army came through at the steep hill fortress of Haengju.

Haengju. Just the sound of it still brings a smile. The memory of the news brings warmth to my cold, old bones.

In Yosu, we first heard of the battle from a military courier. He had first officially reported it to Admiral Yi, and then, not bound by any oath of secrecy, had gotten thoroughly and happily drunk that night. Loudly, he told everyone within hearing of the news. (Looking back on it, Admiral Yi probably told him to do so and, most likely, gave him the money to buy himself a few bottles of soju.)

"Kwon Yul has beaten the Japanese at Haengju!"

"Really?" came the responses, mostly hopeful, but surprised. The army had done little to cheer about up to now.

"Yes! It is true! Kwon Yul had less than 3,000 soldiers against the enemy's 30,000! The enemy kept coming and coming, climbing the walls, but our men fired arrow after arrow. The bodies of the Japanese were in huge piles beneath the walls.

"Then we ran out of arrows, but we held them off with rocks which had been carried to the parapets by our women who used their skirts to hold them. Then our men threw the rocks down onto the heads of the Japanese.

"Our navy resupplied us with more arrows at great risk, and we kept fighting! But we were running low on water. Very low. And the enemy kept coming and coming. Their arrows and bullets seemed to fall like the monsoon rain, but still, we held on!

"The Japanese troops were becoming despondent. We were fighting too hard and too well. Their generals had a hard time getting them to keep climbing the slopes to attack our tall, deadly walls. To encourage their men, the Japanese generals said, 'Look, the Koreans are very low on water. Keep attacking for a little while longer, and we are sure to win.'

"So what did Kwon Yul do?" The messenger dramatically takes a big gulp. "He had horses taken to where the Japanese could see them and had them washed! The Japanese could see buckets of water poured onto the horses, and then see them brushed down and groomed. Word quickly spread among the Japanese that the Koreans had plenty of water, that they were even washing their horses. The soldiers believed the generals to have been either lying or badly mistaken.

"The Japanese commanders had no choice but to admit defeat. The morale of their men was ruined. They began to pull back, but while they did, Kwon Yul staged a surprise attack from the fortress, the last thing the Japanese could have expected. This attack killed thousands of the Japanese, including three of their generals, and we captured a thousand items of enemy equipment!"

People are cheering in the inn at the news, laughing and slapping each other on the back. Broken Nose might even have smiled at me at this moment, had he been there. However, the best was yet to come. The messenger had finished taking some more gulps of the soju, and he shouted out, "But do you know what Kwon Yul had done?"

There is instant silence. What could be better then the news he had already given us? Yet he looked and sounded as if there was something more.

"There truly was no water in the fortress to be wasted. Kwon Yul's soldiers were indeed near death from lack of water. But still he had had the horses washed—washed with buckets of rice!"

It takes a second to comprehend. Buckets of rice! We each imagine what a bucket of rice being poured over the back of a horse would look like from a long distance away. Then we see it. The Japanese had been totally tricked. What a wonderful thing!

Pandemonium in the inn. Joy.

I wonder if Admiral Yi, lying in his room, listening to the sea, could hear the noise we made. I am betting he could. I am also guessing that this was one night when he slept well and with a smile. It was a happy night early in the third moon of 1593, our time of hope.

It would be the best, or, at least, the most hopeful time that we would have for five more years. It seemed then that the war would end soon. The Korean navy under his leadership had beaten the Japanese, the Japanese armies in the north had finally been stopped by the land forces, first by the Ming Chinese allies at Pyongyang, and now by Koreans at Haengju. And this was after we had already emerged triumphant at the siege of Chinju.

Yes, that night was probably the best night of the most hopeful month of the war.

I would like to think that Admiral Yi was happy that night and slept peacefully. Because, coming up for him, and us, there would be few times such as this again. Events over the next five years were not always so bright. In fact, they usually weren't.

And soon he would take the fleet to Ungchon, and we would hear of the second battle of Chinju.

CHAPTER 13

▼

CARELESSNESS

Of the Fourth Moon, 1593

Soon after news of our army's great victory at Haengju, Admiral Yi took the fleet out to attack the Japanese at Ungchon. Despite the triumph of our land forces near Seoul, the Korean army in the south of our huge peninsula would give no help. So without them, using his special brand of wise aggressiveness, the Admiral mounted an amphibious joint operation of his own.

At Ungchon, he directed the monk bands he had raised (and which I had been forbidden to join) to land on shore to cut off the Japanese retreat. The monks fought very well, as did the navy. The battle should have been considered another great victory. Many Japanese were killed. Plus, the passage to Pusan for the annihilation of the Japanese as they left Korea for good (this looked to be happening soon) was made easier. This had been the primary goal of the attack.

As I said, this should have been another great victory. However, two of Admiral Yi's ship commanders had become much too careless and overconfident. In fact, according to the Young Captain speaking years later, the Port Commander of Palpo and the Port Commander of Karipo had made a bet on who could sink or destroy the most Japanese vessels in this battle. During the fray they both charged ahead and smashed some Japanese ships. However, as they moved back they were not paying attention. Intent on observing the enemy movements, they collided with each other. Then, with Japanese projectiles raining in where the protective shield had been knocked down, one of the ships capsized when the crew all ran for cover to the opposite side of the ship.

Admiral Yi had never lost a ship to the Japanese before. I can only imagine his reaction. It was said that the members of the crew who had escaped the Japanese had deserted to escape the wrath of Admiral Yi, which was understandable, if mistaken. The Admiral knew the ship commanders were responsible for the disaster, not the sailors.

He did not call for me at all in the weeks following this battle. Rumors had it that he had offered his resignation to His Majesty because of this event. There were debates in every inn about this. Some said that such an offer of resignation would have been sincere, while others maintained it was simply proper Confucianist etiquette for the Admiral to make a gesture of that sort and that no one would take it seriously. These people accurately pointed out that no person was more proper in all of his actions than Admiral Yi. Certainly, most insisted, nothing would come of it. The King would be crazy to let his best commander resign over such a thing. They were sure of this.

And if someone had told them what was actually going to happen in a few years, they would not have believed it.

*　　*　　*　　*

Memorial to the Court #23
Awaiting Royal Punishment for the Loss of a Lead Ship

I memorialize the throne.

Since I presumed to assume the command of our military's naval forces, I have been afraid that I might fail to fully live up to the generosity of Your Majesty. By Providence at previous battles, the squadrons I commanded have been victorious at sea over the cruel alien invader who has plundered our country and raped our fair land since the early summer of last year. However, despite my instructions that "Both fear and disdain of the enemy brings defeat," two of my ship commanders, recklessly attacking the enemy in order to attain glory and high honors, did inadvertently collide with each other while in battle, the result being the loss of a lead ship and deaths in high numbers.

As commanding admiral at this battle, such an event can only be construed to show that I have careless control over my sailors and have wrongly commanded my subordinate officers. I am stricken by this unforeseen and tragic event, for which I take upon myself the whole responsibility. I prostrate myself in shame while awaiting your Majesty's punishment.

Yi, Commander

6th of Fourth Moon in the 21st Year of Wan-li (Kyesa, 1593)

Chapter 14

▼

The Second Battle of Chinju

Fifth and Sixth Moon, 1593

I did not know about Ungchon until well after it had happened. I was not in Yosu awaiting news as I had been after previous battles. Admiral Yi had let me know why I was not to join one of the groups of warrior priests and monks. He had sent me on a mission.

* * * *

"Sir, the Japanese are coming here. There will be many of them. Their commanders are angry at the defeat you gave them in the tenth moon last year."

I am speaking to Hwang Chin, the commander of the defenses of the key city of Chinju. He was the primary hero of the first victory Korean land forces had won against the Japanese in the tenth month of 1592. He looks tired, but strong. He also looks as if he is still undecided about me.

To my warning, he replies, "There are those who say you are wrong. Some say the vicious invaders will leave the country. Some say that the defeats your commander, so you say, Admiral Yi, has administered to them, have taken away their spirit. One also hears that the defeat by the Ming at Pyongyang, combined with the great triumph at Haengju by Kwon Yul, has taught them all the lesson they need, that they are now a whipped dog going home with its tail between its legs."

I have heard this, too, but I know the facts. I know them all too directly. "Sir, I wish that were true. It is true that they are not as confident as they used to be and that they do very much fear the Korean Navy and Admiral Yi, but they fear their Taiko, Hideyoshi, even more. They cannot leave until he says, and …"

"Go on, spy-priest," says Hwang Chin.

Spy-priest. That is the only time I was ever called that. Even then, in the urgent situation in which I found myself, it came to my mind that this humble wandering priest was now being called things like "fighting man" and "spy." Two years ago, those titles would have been unimaginable.

However, that had been Admiral Yi's mission. He had sent me out with simple instructions: Try to find out what the Japanese were really doing. Were they actually going back to Japan or were they up to other mischief? Rumors abounded. The Chinese were saying this and doing that while captured Japanese said something else, and escaped Korean prisoners still another thing. The actions of the Japanese themselves were contradictory. Many seemed to have left Korea, but others seemed to be settling in for a long stay. Plus, there were reports that a new shipment of troops had arrived. Meanwhile, the messages from the Royal Court were sometimes (I was never told this directly, of course, and certainly not by Admiral Yi, but I heard things) grievous nonsense and based upon last month's rumors, but still, these were the instructions of the King, so …

Admiral Yi had said basically that I knew how to live off the land, that I knew the Japanese language and had dealt with Japanese, that I was a Buddhist priest, and that at least some Japanese respected that. He knew that I could take care of myself fairly well (he had said, "If you have to kill to save yourself, Wonho, do it. Do not be the rare Buddhist who takes the precepts too seriously"), and, most important, he trusted me.

He said, "If you get any information you really believe to be true, inform the commanders it affects, or me, whoever is closest, immediately. If the other commander is closer, report to me immediately thereafter."

So, after weeks of being away from Admiral Yi, and following some frightening and hungry times, I now stand in Chinju, telling the commander, Hwang Chin, what I know. He has asked me to "go on."

"And Sir, they are angry about the defeats up north and about how they cannot beat Admiral Yi and because they cannot go home, and ..."

"They are going to take all that anger out on us," summarizes Hwang Chin.

"Sir, you beat them eight months ago, and now you are close enough to where they have all gathered, that is, to the Pusan area, to be a good target. Plus ..."

"... if they take Chinju, they might be able to continue on into Cholla Province and defeat Admiral Yi by land since they cannot defeat him by sea."

I note but say nothing about how Admiral Yi is not the only military leader who seems to finish the thoughts of subordinates. I say, "Yes, Sir. They cannot beat him at sea, but if they take Yosu and even Mokpo by land, he will have nowhere for his ships. That, at least, is their strategy."

Commander Hwang Chin looks at me. "You say you were sent out by Admiral Yi, and that reporting to me enroute back to him was part of your assignment."

"Yes, Sir."

"Am I to believe your story?"

"About my mission, Sir, or about the intent of the Japanese to attack Chinju within a few weeks and with great force?"

"Both. Either."

"My mission is the truth, Sir. As for what I have learned of the Japanese plans, I only wish I were wrong."

Hwang Chin says nothing for a moment. He sighs, and then says quietly, "Even were you to be a Japanese spy, I can imagine it would do little service to Japan to tell me to strengthen my defenses and prepare for an attack."

I am responding quickly. My words come before I have thought about them, which is not my usual way. "Sir, if I were a Japanese spy, I would hope you would have me arrested and sent directly to Admiral Yi, who would surely have me torn to pieces before beheading me if I were indeed something so awful." I pause. "He deals with spies like that." I remember the time I witnessed the executions. It had not been intentional and had certainly not been something I would wish to see again.

"Or, you could just send to him for confirmation and keep me here until you get word. Certainly, if you believe I am a Japanese spy, it would not do to let me go. I have seen the inside of the city and of the walls. I would know too much."

Chinju's commander looks at me. "You are correct. However, unfortunately, many good Koreans have been here. They know this place better than you, by far. And how many do you think would sell all they knew for so much gold or silver or could resist telling if tortured? Do you really think I have any secrets here the Japanese commanders do not know of? They probably have copies of my unit rosters!

"The only reason a Japanese spy would tell me what you have would be to keep my immense number of troops bottled up here preparing for defense when we could instead be out attacking the enemy near Pusan, but," here he sighs, "You and I both know that an attack by my 'huge' forces would be like a flea attacking a warhorse, so such a mission would be pointless."

He looks me in the eye. "I must conclude that, if you are a spy, you are the stupidest spy possible. Your mission would be pointless, and you would be risking your life for nothing. And you are not a stupid man, are you?"

Before I can find what might be a proper response, he goes on.

"Thank you, priest, for your warning. Thank your Admiral, too. I, also, have been looking for information, and what you say only confirms what I have already acquired. The Korean army is still only good for defense, and even then, only sometimes. Unless our allies, the Ming, attack the Japanese and really force the issue, the Japanese will come after us here in Chinju. And," he shakes his head, "the Ming are unlikely to do anything. They think the war is already over since they have pushed the Japanese away from the border to China and they are now apparently negotiating with Hideyoshi in Japan.

"So, to the Chinese, what is a Korean city like Chinju? What do we matter?" His voice is not bitter, only realistic.

Next to Admiral Yi, of all the military men I have met, he is perhaps the one I most respect.

"Let Admiral Yi know we will do our best here. Please extend our compliments for his victories and our most sincere wishes for many of the same until the Japanese invaders have finally been driven away." His eyes go somewhere else as he says, "It is my duty to hold Chinju to the death, and I will."

And, of course, Hwang Chin did.

It was 3,000 against 50,000. Later, I would find out from the words of an escaped prisoner that Hideyoshi had personally sent reinforcements from Japan in order to attack Chinju. The Korean victory at Chinju had been taken as a personal affront by the Taiko and had to be avenged.

For a while, days of heavy rains kept the Japanese from being able to attack. It seemed the heavens were protecting the defenders. But then one day the sun rose unobscured by clouds, and, with it, the 50,000 from the land of the rising sun attacked.

The 3,000 defenders shot arrows, dropped boiling water from the walls onto enemy climbers, threw bombs, and chopped with axes, but the enemy kept coming. There were stories of Japanese who charged forward holding bombs, literally suicidal human bombs, trying to break through Chinju's defenses. Against them, inside the walls women cut off their hair to replace worn-out bowstrings.

Finally, when all the arrows had been shot, all the gunpowder used, and no further defense of Chinju was possible, Hwang Chin led the final charge against the attacking enemy. A bullet killed him. The mighty fortress of Chinju had fallen.

I heard that Admiral Yi had expressed disbelief when he heard that Chinju was in danger. It seems that he had not thought it possible that such a fortress could be taken. He said nothing more to me about Chinju, however, until after we had all heard confirmation that the disaster was factual.

Then Admiral Yi himself told me a story that by now probably every Korean has heard. I am guessing he chose to share it with me because I had been there on a mission for him. Regarding my spy mission, he had expressed gratitude at my report and had been interested in some of its other details. Then he left it behind. It was never mentioned again, unless indirectly on the day he asked, "Did you hear of Kiyamura?"

"Excuse me, Sir?"

"Kiyamura Mutsuke, the Japanese commander of the forces which took Chinju."

"What about him, Sir."

"He is dead."

"In the assault?"

"No, in the celebration."

I say nothing, but am certain that I look quite puzzled.

The Admiral continues, "The Japanese held a victory party in a pavilion overlooking the Nam River. A pretty 16-year-old kisaeng named Nongae asked Kiyamura to dance. She must have been quite alluring. Certainly she was wearing many spectacular looking rings."

He waits, looking at me, and then asks, "Can you guess what happened?"

A Japanese warrior, and a general at that, killed by a 16-year-old entertainment girl? I guess. "Did she stab him?"

The Admiral shakes his head. "Apparently, she got him near the edge, put her arms around him and interlocked the huge rings of one hand to those of the other. Kiyamura could not disengage her arms, and it happened too quickly for his friends to help. They both fell off the cliff to their deaths. More correctly, he fell, after she propelled them both off the edge."

I am silent, stunned in admiration of the deed. The Admiral understands my expression, and goes on, "The Japanese treated the people of our land as foreign conquerors. They were arrogant, superior, murderous, and rapacious. If they had come here with benevolent feelings, with kindness and justice, they might have had a chance in the long as well as the short run.

"But they didn't and now the whole country is against them. Everyone from the King to the literati and the highborn, down to the farmer, the servant, the slave, the monk, and even the dancing girls. I am not so stupid, Wonho, as to not know that many of the poor in Korea have little love for our Royal Court. The farmers hate the high taxes, there is too much corruption, and some of the slaves believe they have nothing to lose. The Japanese might not have seemed so bad to some had they behaved differently. But, now, no."

He is looking above and beyond me. It is as if he is talking to more listeners than me.

"No enemy can win against a whole country, Wonho. No enemy can. Not for long. The price of such a victory would be much too high to pay. What this girl did is perhaps more important then the victories at Haengju or at Hansando in the message it sends. The message she sent with her death is one that any sane person could understand if he heard it. I only wonder if the Japanese who matters is listening."

I know he is thinking of Hideyoshi again, but I say, "So, we will win, for sure, Sir?"

His words are definite. "More certainly, Wonho, I would say that Japan will lose. Sooner or later, the price for staying will be too terrible for them to pay. The only question for us Koreans now is how soon this will be and how many and which of us will have to die for this to happen."

Then he said words that I am not sure he was aware that he was speaking out loud. I am not sure they were meant for me. I just happened to be there. He was looking up now, above me, at the heavens through the beams of the roof. What he said was barely audible. "And it is my job to make sure that the price they pay for having come here is so high and horrible that they do not want to come back here for a long, long time."

Part II

Seventh Moon, 1593–First Moon, 1597

Includes:

- *Admiral Yi wants to finish off the Japanese with a united Army/Navy offensive, but the Korean Army balks at taking the offensive without Chinese help.*

- *Meanwhile, Chinese diplomats negotiate nonsense with the Taiko in Japan, as detailed by a brave escapee from the Taiko's headquarters at Nagoya in Japan.*

- *Typhoid decimates the navy.*

- *Won Kyun, with bribes and lies, schemes against Admiral Yi.*

- *A test occurs.*

- *The Priest Wonho successfully fulfills a second mission.*

- *Wonho describes a deadly school for Japanese swordsmen and a superior Buddhist Saint.*

- *The Japanese avoid a major naval confrontation with Admiral Yi because, as the Young Captain says, "They were terrified of him."*

Admiral Yi is said to have always kept two huge swords at his headquarters. Both of these martial monstrosities are now on view at Hyonchungsa. At about six feet long, they were much too unwieldy to be used in actual combat. However, their sense of ominous presence and deadly intent is palpable. On one of these swords is inscribed the Admiral's own words dedicated to his war against the Japanese and his fight against anyone else who would dare to threaten the kingdom to which he was born and foresworn. In English, his words would read:

> *As this sword is pledged to the sky,*
> *The mountains and the waters tremble.*

Chapter 15

"They Were Terrified Of Him"

1618 AD (Remembering 1593–1597 AD.)

We both looked at him. I am certain that our faces showed exactly what we felt about his question, and that in doing this, our expressions said way too much.

The Young Captain and I had just heard a question that had so many implications, which was both so reasonable and so profoundly ignorant, so blissfully confident and so arrogantly presumptive, that, for a moment, we were stunned into silence. I did not know whether to laugh, to feel anger, or simply to answer. I fought to stay detached from words and feelings.

The Young Captain was not a Buddhist priest. I am not sure what he was going through inside, though I sensed it was much the same as I felt. However, he had other considerations. He had a different relationship with the questioner, a military one. The questioner was one of his junior officers. Plus, the skinny young man who had so blithely queried us was a junior officer who had been drinking. In our land, drinkers are, of course, always given some latitude. And he was so very young, so very new, so very fresh.

It was then that I mentally dubbed him "the Fresh Lieutenant." This he remained the rest of the time I knew him. Even the Young Captain came to call him this when we were talking privately.

I had met the lieutenant that evening. The Young Captain's command ship had come into the port of Mokpo. It was a happy coincidence since I had not known he would be there, and he had not expected to find me. Mokpo is to the southwest what Pusan is to the southeast. However, in the war there was one big difference. The Japanese never got to Mokpo. They had tried. They had been stopped by Admiral Yi at Myongnyang, which is near Mokpo.

Myongnyang was a place of many memories for the Young Captain and for me. It was largely these memories we had invited the Fresh Lieutenant to hear about that night. Mokpo is very cold in the winter wind, but this was early autumn, and we sat on deck, enjoying the twilight sky and the smells of the sea mixed with the odors of the coast.

The Young Captain liked the Fresh Lieutenant. I knew this right away. Only people he liked were allowed to hear these memories. Not everyone was invited to sit with us when we drank, including his fellow officers. Plus, in many ways the Fresh Lieutenant was a very likable fellow. He was intelligent in an often surprising way, and he always tried hard and meant well. He also had a humorous way of speaking when he had been drinking, and the expressions on his face could be priceless when something surprised or concerned him.

However, I also knew that the Young Captain sometimes was very exasperated by the Fresh Lieutenant. The question the junior officer had asked was an example of how he could create awkward situations unnecessarily. His questions and blurted-out statements would get him into as much trouble as his behavior. And this was significant, since all too often his actions verged on being scandalous.

"He is the horniest man I have ever known," the Young Captain once said. "He cannot see a pretty lady without wanting to mount her. He will be lucky not to be killed by a father, a brother, a fiancé, or a husband. He needs to marry soon and to a very strong woman."

But, on this evening, we were not staring at him because of his lustful escapades. We had focused our eyes on him because of his question.

"Admiral Yi had kicked their asses," the Fresh Lieutenant had said appreciatively. "He had beaten them four times in 1592. He whipped them at Okpo, Tangpo, Hansando, and then Pusan. So why did it take until 1598 to get those ugly dwarf island robbers out of our country?"

This question was bad enough. We were already silent, shocked, but it still might have been all right if he had just shut up right there. However, of course, he didn't. He went right on, blurting out, "Why didn't Admiral Yi finish the war faster?"

The Young Captain and I were both so amazed that we turned to stare. Our expressions had to have shown our complex feelings. The Fresh Lieutenant looked at each of us, waited, and then looked more closely, trying to wipe away the soju-induced fog over his mind. He knew how we both felt about Admiral Yi.

Too late, he appeared to see what was coming. "I meant no offense …"

"Why wasn't the war finished sooner?" interrupted the Young Captain. Though still a spring sprout when compared to me, the Young Captain was over a decade older than the Fresh Lieutenant. "Do you really think that if Admiral Yi had been able to do anything to end it sooner, that he would not have done it?"

The poor junior officer began to reply, but the Young Captain kept going. "Do you really think the Japanese stayed camped out in the Pusan area, raping and pillaging for five extra years and that the Admiral let them? That he could have gotten them out of there more quickly? That he didn't want to do exactly that?"

The Young Captain was getting louder. "He died getting them out of our country! He …"

"There were many factors at work," I said quietly. The Young Captain stopped and looked at me. I winked, at which he looked questioningly, and I went on, looking again at the Fresh Lieutenant. "We old farts can remember them better than you—you who were barely away from your mommy's breasts when the war ended."

"Factors," said the Young Captain scornfully, but he was no longer focusing so much of his heated energy at his junior officer. Now he was remembering. "Yes. Factors." A look passed over his face that reminded me of Admiral Yi when he had been thinking of getting his hands on the Taiko. "Yes. Things happened." He refocused on the Fresh Lieutenant and began to speak again, this time less heatedly.

"The Ming Chinese army withdrew. They thought the Japanese had been beaten and that the war was over since China now seemed safe. For them, in a way, they were right. The Japanese had really lost any chance of getting much into China, if at all, at least for a while. And do you think the Ming cared if the Japanese occupied the farthermost part of Korea for one or two or four or five years longer?"

His words remind me of those spoken by Hwang Chin in Chinju over two decades before. However, I decide to mention this to him later. Have I told him I met Hwang Chin? Does he know I was at Chinju shortly before the second Japanese siege? Does he even know that I went on that first mission for Admiral Yi? My old mind forgets. Perhaps, I decide, I will mention this later. But now he is still instructing the Fresh Lieutenant.

"They had their negotiator working in Japan. Everyone, except for Admiral Yi, that is, seemed to be happy to wait for the negotiations to take place." Again, my mind wanders. I remember the testimony of an escaped prisoner. Words about what had gone on with the Ming Chinese and Hideyoshi in the Nagoya court mummery while Koreans were captured and killed, and the mountain of ears continued to grow.

The Young Captain pauses, so I add, "The Korean Army did not believe itself strong enough alone to push the Japanese out of the country, though Admiral Yi repeatedly requested a joint land-sea operation to do just that …"

The Young Captain cuts in, "But Field Marshal Kwon Yul, the hero of Haengju, commander of the army and brave fighter that he was, was basically a defensive-minded warrior. If you attacked him, you could not break him. However, he was one to resist, not push. It was as if he thought the other defenders would be as strong as he was, and he felt he did not have a good chance on the offensive."

Then he recounted, "So the Ming had pulled back, the Korean army was hesitant to attack without them, and the Japanese navy had by now become absolutely terrified of Admiral Yi. They did not want to fight him in an open battle. Plus, Admiral Yi knew that the navy by itself could not evict the bastardly trespassers from our land.

"And then, things got even worse." The Young Captain took a long swallow.

The Fresh Lieutenant dared to speak. "Worse? How?"

"Typhoid," I said. "Epidemics of it. Thousands dead. Including our sailors."

"Near-starvation," said the Young Captain. "Where did food come from? Who could farm, and when, during the war? The Admiral did all he could to encourage agriculture and to keep the crops going, but there were so many difficulties …"

"Including more and more refugees to take care of," I added.

"And the army stealing what few sailors we had to fight as soldiers whenever they got a chance. General Kwon Yul always needed more troops, as did Admiral Yi, and sometimes the junior officers for the Field Marshal would forcefully 'recruit' our sailors."

It was my turn. "And all the squabbling at court. All the factions fighting, the Eastern Confucianists against the Western Confucianists, and (so-called) Admiral Won Kyun's constant slander of Admiral Yi. So many lies from Won Kyun, and his unabashed sending of gifts to so many of the royal advisers."

I had to stop there. Speaking of the rest is always hard for me. The Young Captain said it instead. "Then, in the second moon of 1597, Admiral Yi was arrested and taken away for trial."

The Fresh Lieutenant sat silently. Then he said, "So the Chinese pulled back their armies while their negotiator ..."

"His name was Shen Wei-ching." The Young Captain interjected whenever he felt it appropriate.

"... while Shen Wei-ching tried to conclude a peace with Japan ..."

"With the monkey bastard Hideyoshi."

The Fresh Lieutenant started summarizing again, "So while Shen Wei-Ching of Ming China was negotiating with the monkey bastard Hideyoshi of Japan about ending the invasion, the Chinese forces pulled back, letting the Japanese stay in the Pusan area, and our army by itself was not strong enough to kick them out ...

"Even though Admiral Yi proposed a joint army/navy attack time after time. But our royal court was seemingly content with mostly waiting for the Chinese negotiators to finish with Hideyoshi in Japan."

"Yes, plus General Kwon Yul was better at defending than attacking," continued the Fresh Lieutenant.

"Right."

"And the Japanese were scared to fight Admiral Yi."

"They were terrified of him." A smile came to the Young Captain's face. The fear felt by the Japanese was at least a pleasant thought.

Happy to see the smile where just moments before there had been anger directed at him, the Fresh Lieutenant concluded, "And so Admiral Yi had to wait, and while waiting had to endure plagues of typhoid, shortages of food, depleted manpower, refugee problems, harassment by his jealous fellow officer, Admiral Won Kyun, and attacks at court, and then, finally, he was arrested."

The Young Captain nodded. I sat quietly, remembering, feeling it all again.

"I have never understood his arrest." With these words, the Fresh Lieutenant had united with us. He was safe again, on common ground. Now we were looking at him with much different expressions. But the Lieutenant had to ask, "Is it really true they took him to Seoul in a cage mounted on an ox cart and tied with a red rope?"

The Young Captain and I looked at each other. I shook my head, and said, "Some people don't know when to shut up." Then I turned to the Fresh Lieutenant and said, "Yes, it is true."

I cannot say anything more, so the Young Captain begins to speak. But what he says isn't what I expect. "I have heard that the same reasons Admiral Yi became a military man are the same reasons he was arrested."

Both the Fresh Lieutenant and I are now looking at the Young Captain. He takes another surprising turn saying, "It was his father-in-law who strongly recommended a career in the military to Yi Sun-Sin. The young man was still deciding what course to take with his life, and the older man was wise.

"The father-in law looked at his son-in-law carefully. He saw a young, athletic, strong, and highly intelligent man, and he tried to imagine this man moving about in the worlds of the Sowon, the tribute collection bureaus and dealing with the Chuin or the Sajuin, the hereditary bureau masters. The father-in-law tried to imagine his son-in-law happily successful in this world where local district tribute clerks had to borrow money at fifty percent annual interest to pay off crooked bureau masters. He tried to see his son-in-law thriving in a situation where all the extra costs of this corruption were passed down to those who could least afford to pay it, the peasants.

"His father-in-law tried to envision Yi Sun-Sin moving happily about in this world where the bureau masters would charge rent for 'storage' of tribute items, and where the crooked bureaucrats would sell tribute items to merchants, and then buy cheaper, lower-quality items to be forwarded to the court while pocketing the profits. He tried to imagine a happy son-in-law working in a place where only ten to twenty percent of what was taken from the people as tribute actually makes it to the state treasury, and the rest goes to the bastard racketeers.

"The father-in-law couldn't do it. He couldn't picture his son-in-law thriving in this environment. For his son-in-law was very unusual. Not only was he handsome and strong, intelligent and bold, but he was also exceptionally honest and straightforward. To the son-in-law, right was right and wrong was wrong, and he would only agree to be part of what was right."

It is obvious that the Young Captain has thought this through very carefully. He has researched everything he can find out about Admiral Yi Sun-sin. I have known this, but this is new information. Certainly, he has heard these things from a family member or a close friend of the family. I have never really considered Admiral Yi as anything but a superb military commander, although I had known since the first day I met him what a wonderful mind he had and his excellent command of languages and superb knowledge of history.

So, I now find out that his father-in-law recommended that the Admiral's military career not be decided upon until quite late. This is fascinating. And the father-in-law had, of course, been correct. The young son-in-law who became our great Admiral would never have fit in at court with all those sycophants.

I take a sip and note that though the breeze has shifted it is still warm. This is good. Then I realize that the Young Captain has started talking again.

"So the father-in-law saw that the military where there were obvious cases of right versus wrong offered the best chances for his gifted son-in-law. To defend Choson against attackers was a noble pursuit, and in the military his son-in-law's profound honesty and sense of 'doing things the correct way' would be much more appreciated than it would be as a civilian."

He pauses. "Not that it always was, of course." The Young Captain takes a gulp of wine, but this barely slows him down. Does he know his next words will stun both of his listeners?

"He was arrested more than once, you know."

"What?" The Lieutenant and I say at the same time. I had not known this, and the younger officer obviously hadn't either.

"Yes. Early in his career. Before there was any hint of the Japanese being a threat to us." The Captain takes another swig.

"The Admiral refused to kowtow, even as a junior officer. He would not visit the homes of government ministers for the sake of propriety. He did not wish to curry favor in this way, or to appear to do so. He would not offer gifts to those who were in important positions. Once, when he was the chief of personnel, he would not approve a promotion of a junior officer over some others who were senior. Even though the Chief of Military Affairs requested the promotion, he would not approve it!

"Of course Yi Sun-sin was correct. The unusually quick promotion requested for the other officer had not been earned by anything but friendship with the Chief of Military Affairs. Though denying a promotion after repeated requests from the Chief of Military Affairs was certainly not the way to make friends among your superiors."

He looks pointedly at the younger officer. "Is it?"

"No," says the Lieutenant. It seems the young man is trying to imagine himself in the young Yi Sun-sin's position, and standing up on principle and refusing a request of the Chief of Military Affairs. He looks pained.

The Young Captain continues, "Sometimes he even got criticized for winning battles. While stationed up north near the border to Manchuria, he used clever tactics to capture the infamous bandit chieftain Mu Pai-nai and his huge band of merciless bandits, the Orankae. No one had thought this was possible.

"These bandits had been pillaging our northern border areas for years, and he stopped them. So what was his reward?"

We are silent, so he tells us. "His commanding general, unhappy at not being able to claim the victory for himself, complained that the junior officer had acted without properly consulting his superiors in advance."

The Lieutenant makes a face, and, not for the first time, I conclude that his expressive face will likely not always prove helpful to him. It shows too much. However, I, too, am shaking my head. The Young Captain notes our responses and goes on.

"Later, when Yi Sun-sin was first in Cholla, he was a junior naval officer, and he made two successive commanders very angry. The first was vexed when one of his sailors was stopped from cutting down a paulownia tree. The commander was musical. He wanted the wood to make a six-stringed komungo. The axeman was stopped by junior officer Yi Sun-sin, who said, 'This tree is on crown land. Can any commander so lightly choose to cut it down?'

"The next commander was upset because Yi Sun-sin would refuse to act submissive towards him. This commander, whose name was Yong, deliberately planned a surprise inspection to the five ports of Cholla. Yi Sun-sin at that time was in charge of the port of Palpo, which actually was in the best shape of the five. As usual, though, with the Korean military, there was a problem with sailors being absent without leave at that time. Still, Palpo only had three missing, which was much the smallest number. The commander, though, was going to send a memorial to court distorting the facts, making Palpo and Yi Sun-sin, look the worst. But, this liar was informed that Yi Sun-sin had records of the actual numbers and would use this information if questioned, so this did not happen."

This is all so disturbing that I have to say, "Certainly not all of Admiral Yi's superiors penalized him for his honesty, skill, and intelligence."

The Young Captain does not miss a beat. "Of course not. Many commended him. His rise in rank was actually quite fast considering the opposition he engendered and his late start because of the horseriding accident in his first test. It is as you once said, Wonho. You can almost judge the worth of a person by his reaction to greatness in others."

I do not remember having said this to the Young Captain, but I certainly believe it. I nod.

The Fresh Lieutenant interjects, "But you said he was arrested before. When was that? What happened?" He looks very earnest, very concerned. He is emotionally caught up in the injustice of what had happened to Yi Sun-sin, our remarkable Admiral.

"What happened? What do you think? It was up north, with the army. He salvaged a battle against incredible odds, rescuing dozens of our soldiers in the process. He did this without enough troops, after having for months sent request after request to his commander for more soldiers. So what reward did he get for his heroism? He was arrested by his commander who wanted to torture him to make him confess to having lost a battle and to accept the guilt for it. The man who would become our Admiral refused to yield. Admiral Yi maintained that he had not lost the battle, and that the only reason it was even close was that his many requests for more troops had been denied. Plus he mentioned that he had copies of the requests that he had sent.

"Eventually, guess what? Yi Sun-sin was pardoned by the King, but only after having been reduced in rank to private."

The Young Captain stops. His audience is stunned.

"I never knew this," I say. "I did not know that it happened to him twice."

The Fresh Lieutenant says nothing, but he looks as if he could put his fist through the side of a turtle ship.

The Young Captain drains his cup. "Of course, after the first time, he quickly rose in rank again, thankfully in time to have the kobukson ready for Hideyoshi's bastardly fleets." The Young Captain has just about talked himself out. He chooses to pass the baton to me. "That was when you met him, wasn't it, Wonho?"

"Yes, just before the war," I agree. "The first kobukson was being field-tested when I was called to his headquarters." I pause. "I cannot believe he was arrested once before! I had never heard this."

"It is the thanks you get from our royal court for greatness," says the Young Captain. "No, I cannot say that. I would like to think that things are better now than they were then." He winks at me so the Fresh Lieutenant cannot see and turns to the junior officer.

"Don't you think things are better now? These things could not happen in Choson today, could they? The modern Korean military is beyond such petty rivalries, and the court of the present King is one of exalted philosophy and the highest of ethics and morals, wouldn't you say?"

He looks intently at the Fresh Lieutenant who does not know how to respond. I am glad I am not in his shoes at this moment.

Finally, the Lieutenant says, very formally, "I am certain that you are very correct, Sir."

The Young Captain and I burst out laughing. It is funny only because of the reaction of the Fresh Lieutenant and the look on his face and tone of his voice. Even though I am laughing, I realize that it really is not that humorous. Rather, it is actually sad. Nothing really has changed. The court politics and the ways of doing things in our kingdom are just as corrupt now as they were then and nearly always have been.

Chapter 16

▼

The Escaped Prisoner
Eighth Moon, 1593

Admiral Yi had called for me. As usual, I went to him immediately. Just after I had arrived, his husky attendant gave me my instructions. The attendant's name, I knew by now, was Kim Taejin. We had come to be on a familiar basis. Taejin told me, "You are to enter and do nothing but listen. An escaped prisoner has returned to us all the way from Japan. The Admiral wishes you to hear his words."

I nod. Taejin gives a small bow in return and leads me to the main hall. He slides open the door and beckons to a cushion in the corner. I enter and the door quietly slides shut behind me. The Admiral, his officers, the official scribe, the various servants, and the man who seems to be the escaped prisoner are all busy. My quiet entry is not mentioned by anyone. It is taken as household business or as a servant entering.

In a way, that is what I am. I do serve Admiral Yi.

I am seated advantageously. I wonder if the Admiral himself or Taejin had settled upon this seemingly out-of-the-way spot so I can listen to and observe the interview. There is drinking water here, also. It seems this could be a long session. Again, I wonder if this were the Admiral's kind forethought, or Taejin's? It comes to mind that through his actions the attendant is mirroring the feelings of the Admiral. The Admiral is honest, straight-laced, kind, and efficient. He is the best of friends and the most horrible of enemies. The water waiting here for me and the position of the cushion where I can unobtrusively see and hear so well is a reflection of the Admiral. It is his doing even if he did not say the words.

The escaped prisoner is Che Man-chun. He is a lithe man, handsome and well spoken. His intelligence is obvious even before I hear him speak. Then it becomes more so. Almost the first words I hear him say are that he had been a naval officer in the Kyongsang Right Naval Station.

When I hear "Kyongsang Right Naval Station" my eyebrows raise. This man had been an officer for Admiral Won Kyun, the self-appointed enemy of Admiral Yi. Even this early in the war, Won Kyun's ill feelings towards Admiral Yi were obvious. Won Kyun was jealous of Admiral Yi's success. Many, including me, believed Won Kyun was jealous simply because he knew he would never be the man or commander that Admiral Yi was.

We all know how upset Won Kyun is by Admiral Yi's successes and by his obvious greatness. These feelings cannot be hidden. However, at this moment, Admiral Yi and Admiral Won Kyun (I do not like to call him admiral) are equals in rank, however unequal in character, courage, and leadership. Admiral Yi must work with him, and for the sake of King and Korea, does.

However, I know that Admiral Yi does not trust Won Kyun. Who could trust someone who is always plotting against oneself? Who could respect someone who always wants the highest command and loses every battle in which he has it? Who could work happily with someone who is constantly sending presents, more accurately, bribes to officials at court in exchange for their patronage, especially when part of this patronage is to attack you? Who could happily work with someone who is buying friends at court to support his lies, which are constantly being sent to the King, about oneself? Not one of us can guess that the ridiculous plotting of Won Kyun and his powerful friends around the King will have the effect it does less than four years later. If we had known, I am sure someone like the loyal attendant Kim Taejin would have taken steps to preclude it. Won Kyun would have suffered a fatal accident, I am almost certain. But none of us could have imagined what would happen.

Many of the officers and sailors who sail under Won Kyun's command wish they didn't. This is well known. That this escaped prisoner is now with Admiral Yi and not his old commander in itself says much. However, the specter of Won Kyun now hovers over this man and his tale. My interest in his story has already been high. Now the escaped prisoner has my undivided attention.

Che Man-chun had been captured as he was returning to duty from leave in Kimhaegang. He was in a small boat and decided to check out the Japanese positions and vessels in Ungchon on his way back. Many small boats were about, and it was not likely that his would be noticed. Even if he was, it was unlikely he would be pursued, and if that happened, he might still get away.

A good idea turned out to be bad. His small boat met a large number of Japanese vessels. Six of them pursued him. All six were larger than Che Man-chun's boat. He, his crew, and his boat were captured by the Japanese off the island of Kojedo.

The Japanese took Che Man-chun and ten of his crew, bound hand and foot by ropes, to the Japanese camp at Ungchon. There, they were presented to Yasunori, the Japanese Commander. His crewmembers were given to other captains, but Yasunori kept Che Man-chun in his section of camp.

Yasunori seemed to recognize Che Man-chun. "Were you not commanding a boat at Hansando against us? How many guns, swords, and pieces of armor did you capture from us there?" the Japanese commander asked.

Playing it safe, Che denied having been at that battle. He said he had only very recently been ordered to this part of Korea. Yasunori never indicated whether he believed Che or not, but he continued to keep Che around.

Twice in the first few months of his captivity, the Korean officer tried to escape. The Japanese somehow discovered the plan for the first escape attempt. All of the prisoners who had agreed to escape with Che, young uneducated sailors from Changwon, were beheaded. The second attempt, a month later, was revealed to the Japanese by some of the Koreans that Che had asked to help. Perhaps this group, which was from Ungchon, had learned a lesson from the beheadings.

After these escape plots, Che Man-chun was watched even more closely. As a prisoner of the Japanese at Ungchon, he observed the Korean naval attacks at that port. They were great victories for which he was thrilled; they were excellent battles, that was, until the two ships collided.

As Che mentions this collision, I notice a subtle shift in Admiral Yi's expression. For a moment, I wonder if Che is wise to mention such things, but then leave the thought behind. That the ships collided is a fact. All know of it. That Admiral Yi did not order the two captains to behave so carelessly and over-aggressively is also well known. Che has been asked to tell everything he saw and learned, and he is doing so. The truth is simply the truth. This is perhaps one of the things, which Admiral Yi best exemplifies and lives by. Admiral Yi will not hold the truth against this man.

My ears have wandered. I must listen.

More distasteful words, but sadly, again simply the facts. Che is telling of how well entrenched the Japanese are in Pusan, Ulsan, Kijang, Suyong, and Tongnae. Pusan, especially, has large numbers of Japanese persons and vessels. Then he is telling of their other encampments at Ungchon, Kojedo, and Tangpo. He speaks of how, in some places, the Koreans and

Japanese have adjusted to each other and live in mixed residential neighborhoods and even in the same buildings.

There is no happiness at hearing this information, though none of it is a surprise. Then, happily, there are better tidings. It is good to hear confirmation that in some places there are only a few Japanese and ships. It is also nice to find out what some of the Japanese are thinking and even daring to say.

Che quotes one Japanese who in private had said, "Even we Japanese feel Hideyoshi to be a haughty tiger. Many loved ones are dying in a foreign land, parents and children apart, because of him. Thankfully, the old devil is sixty-three and is not healthy. Soon he shall leave the earth. And when he does, do you think it is only the Koreans who will jump for joy? We Japanese will also rejoice to be rid of this foul-scheming demon."

Che Man-chun continues:

"Soon after the attack by the Korean Navy at Ungchon where our two ships collided, the Japanese Commander made me pretend to be an important Korean captain who had been captured. I was given a false identity and a history as a commander of 800 men and a huge ship.

"As this 'great captain' I was put on a vessel to Japan and was sent to Hideyoshi himself. The Taiko first planned to enjoy my execution. He said he was going to burn me at the stake, but he changed his mind. When he discovered I was a person of some literary talent, he sent me instead to his chief scribe, Kishita. Perhaps it was Kishita who asked the Taiko to spare my life. This I found out much later.

"Soon I had to cut my hair and dress in the Japanese way. I was very homesick and felt like a caged bird in the wrong land. I yearned only to escape. I became sick with rheumatism to the point of paralysis. My whole body was bloated. My life was leaving me. I was sure my spirit wanted to return home.

"Kishita called for a monk known for his cures. Perhaps it was seeing a Buddhist monk, albeit a Japanese one, as much as his potions and herbs which saved me. I knew that Buddhism had gone from our land to that of the Japanese many years ago and that Buddhists believed the Buddha was everywhere. Somehow, the idea that Buddhism was in both our lands helped me to believe I could return home. I recovered my health.

"While in Japan working for the scribe Kishita, I had two main goals: to escape and return home and to find out as much useful information as I could while I was so close to the Taiko. I tried to write down much of what I learned on small scraps of paper for when I escaped, but, unfortunately, these were lost at sea on the journey home.

I will tell everything that I can remember. I am sorry to have lost my notes. I fear I may leave something useful or important out due to my poor memory and the rush of so many events in my life. However, here is what I believe are the most important parts of what I learned or witnessed.

"The Taiko has established what are called temporary headquarters in Nagoya. Early in the summer last year, he led 200,000 troops there. He had a six-story pavilion built as part of his great castle within the whole city, which itself is surrounded by three rings of walls. He lives in the pavilion, and big guns are at all key places on the walls around the city. Inside the walls are many palaces and huge warehouses. Many of these warehouses are filled with plunder stolen from us.

"Nagoya is on the southern coast of the main island of Japan. It is a three-week journey on land from Kyushu, the nearest main Japanese island to Korea. From Kyushu to here was a three-day sail, with Tsushima about midway in between.

"As a worker for Kishita, Hideyoshi's chief clerk, I had access to many written records. I also heard many things. Of course, I listened for anything that might have to do with Korea.

"I paid especial attention to the goings-on with the envoys of Ming China. It is the notes of their interactions with the Japanese that I most regret having lost.

"Hideyoshi made the Chinese envoys wait. First, they were kept outside of the city walls in a private inn for three days. Then he sent some monks to converse with them, both in writing and via interpreters. Next, Hideyoshi ordered his entourage to provide a grand banquet for the Ming ambassadors.

"Japanese actors performed; geisha girls sang, danced, and served; sake flowed as the Japanese hosts sat on an eleven-meter-long platform against a wall covered with hanging red brocade tapestries. Hideyoshi himself did not attend.

"After the banquet, the Ming Chinese envoys were conducted to a reception hall west of the castle. Here they met Hideyoshi for the first time. Because of my job working for Kishita, I could see the records of their conversations and of the writings that passed back and forth.

"First, after having formally presented their credentials, the Ming envoys gave the Taiko a memorandum which stated: 'Korea first opened her entrance gates in Kyongsang and Cholla provinces and drew the Japanese troops, then closed them off to intercept the Japanese on their way out. Korea is wrong for not reporting the truth to the Ming Empire. How can the Korean King escape punishment? The Taiko, Hideyoshi, is actually as faithful a vassal to the Ming Emperor as are these two envoys. Should these words not be true, these envoys shall borrow swords to slice their own entrails to die without regret.

"'To conclude peace between our two lands is a happy event for one thousand and ten years. The Japanese commander in Korea will verify our words. For the Taiko to determine upon peace, and to send this message back with these envoys, is a fine idea indeed.'"

There are mutterings in the room at these words. Someone says, "That is such obvious rubbish."

Admiral Yi silences the grumbles. "This is courtier speaking to courtier, the Emperor of the Ming via his messengers to the leader of Japan. Who can expect the truth with such? Our King will know their words for what they are."

He looks at the escaped prisoner and says, "Continue, Captain Che."

That the Admiral has called him by his rank is significant. He has shown he does not see this man as having been totally dishonored and that he values his words.

Captain Che nods and, it seems to me more for the others than for Admiral Yi, says, "Sir, I am only telling what I heard and saw. I am not saying that I believe these words I am reporting, just that these words were communicated by the Ming and the Japanese as I have said."

"Which is what I have asked you to do. Please continue."

Captain Che bows again and goes on.

"Another memorandum was given to the Taiko, again addressed specifically to him by the Ming Emperor. It read: 'The Japanese warlords conceived an ambitious plan to conquer the mainland of China. This is as foolish and reckless as a mosquito that tries to cross the sea on its feet. Even though they have fought a hundred battles and won a hundred victories in the present war; even so, to forebear would be to stabilize a thousand things. So I have said to the King of Korea, and so I say to you.'

"Upon time for the Ming envoys to return to China, the Taiko himself saw them off onto their ship. He gave them ten swords and ten spears as presents and thirty pounds of silver. But nothing of substance ever became clear as to the Taiko's true intent.

"I do know that he was said to have dispatched 30,000 assault troops to avenge the defeat at Chinju. And, that when the Japanese had taken the city, he had the Japanese field commanders send him the heads of the leaders of Chinju's defense as presents. He is said to have responded to this by saying, 'Now there is nothing left to do. Come the Eighth Moon, I will withdraw my soldiers from Korea back to Japan.'

"I had never given up my hopes of escape. I was healthy again, I had what could be valuable information, I missed my homeland, and I know it was my duty to try to return. Late in the winter, I began to plot an escape with my fellow Korean prisoners. These included men from Kimhae, Changwon, Miryang, and Ulsan and the scholar HoYong-myong. However, this plan could not be carried out because we could not meet often enough.

When Che reported the heads of the leaders of Chinju as having been sent to Hideyoshi, no one blinked. By now, such matters are commonplace. I, however, do send a prayer for the valiant commander Hwang Chin. I know that if his spirit were watching his head, he would have been trying to tell his mouth, "Bite him. Bite him!" when it got close to the Taiko.

The escaped prisoner Che goes on to tell of his fourth escape plot, the one that finally succeeded. He and twelve other men, mostly captured slaves, stole a boat and hid on a Japanese island named Ikki. When they began to sail toward home, the wind and weather seemed to be in their favor, but then they met a fleet of 300 Japanese ships coming toward Nagoya, and, therefore, directly at them. They rushed their stolen boat back to Ikki where they waited and gathered supplies by selling what few valuables they had. These items mostly consisted of the stylish clothes Che himself had been given to wear while at work near the court of Hideyoshi.

Finally, with plenty of food and water, they were able to try again. This time they made it through the inland Sea of Japan, between the major islands of Honshu and Kyushu, past many smaller islands and dozens of unsuspecting Japanese fishermen's boats as well as military ships, through the narrow straits, and then into the East Sea and three days more home to Korea. It would have been death if the Japanese had caught them.

He had made it home, but for Che Man-chun, would it be death anyway? He was an officer, and he had surrendered to the enemy without a fight. For this, his life could be forfeit. It would be for the King to decide. I leave with the group of listeners, and Kim Taejin tells me that I should be ready to report to the Admiral the next day.

I wonder at it all as I walk back to the temple. I am a man and, even though a priest, I eat, walk, sleep. I often work, though many claim we are lazy. My life was so routine until the war began. Yes, I had traveled, but that was my way. For me, it was the thing to do. For others, it is farming or fishing and family. But this man, Captain Che, what an adventure he had survived! I hoped the King would let him live.

The next day I am sent for again. When I arrive, the Admiral seems busy. Seems? No, he is always busy. The business of the whole southern part of the kingdom is flowing around him, and the fate of it all rests on his shoulders. Yet, most of the time, he makes it seem easy. He is always busy, though he usually does not seem to be. There is always a sense of balance, of inner depth and repose about him. This is so even during battle, I was told. One day, I would see it for myself.

Yet now he seems busy. I cannot help but wonder why.

"I had you witness the escaped prisoner's telling of his tale yesterday."

"Yes, Sir," I say.

"Your thoughts?"

"Sir?"

"Priest Wonho, you have been to Japan; you have lived there, and you know people. Was he telling the truth about his capture, what he experienced and heard, and about his escape?"

I have thought about little else since hearing the talk the day before, so I can answer quickly. "I believe him, Sir."

The Admiral continues to look at me. He nods and points to part of what must be an official message he has just finished writing. I read it as commanded.

The testimony of Che Man-chun recorded above has been verified as accurate by interviewing his fellow escapees and by the comparison of his account with all other information we have gathered.

The previously excellent record of Che Man-chun has fallen to the lowest levels. Previously, as an officer for the King he was known as a man of superior talent and commendable courage in battle. However, instead of fighting to the death against the Japanese when horribly outnumbered, he allowed himself to be taken prisoner. As a prisoner he even worked for the Japanese in their own country as a clerk and scribe. With such acts, his obligation and loyalty as a subject have fallen to that of a worm.

However, as a talented and clever literary man, he carefully noted all potentially useful facts that he could gather regarding the enemy forces and plans. He did the work of the best of spies in so doing. Then he escaped at the risk of his life, leading home a dozen of his countrymen. Plus, upon arriving back home, he wasted no time in reporting his escape, and all facts he could supply, to the officers of the King's military.

His personal plight is pitiful. He has said that, if he could be so bold, his only wish is to be allowed to again fight the Japanese in the service of his King. The whole transcript of his interview supplements this Memorial to Court. His former commander, Won Kyun, Commander of Kyongsang Right Naval Station, has been informed of the situation.

Yi, Commander

Eighth Moon, in the 21st Year of Wan-li (Kyesa, 1593)

I finish reading and look up. The Admiral has quietly moved to an unread message. He looks up and says nothing, and neither do I. We both know it was all he could do to help Captain Che, and we both know the wisest thing would be to put such an obviously able man back into service in the fleet as soon as possible.

We both also knew that the chances of this being the King's decision is anyone's guess, and that, perhaps sadly, the decision might be left to Che's old commander, Won Kyun. And Won Kyun might be angry that after his escape, Che has gone to Admiral Yi, not directly to him.

But that is the future. What we have is the moment. And for now, there is no need to say anything more about the case of Che Man-chun.

"Is there anything else, Admiral?"

"Not right now, Priest Wonho."

With the usual courtesies, I leave. I want to go to the mountain above the temple. The events of humanity and its transitory lives are becoming too significant to me. I need some time alone to find peace, calm, balance, detachment. I need to breathe deeply the fresh air of the mountain where it meets the breezes of the sea, and I require time to let the calmness of the earth move up my spine to settle my upset mind.

Then I open the door to the outside. It is raining. Only half an hour before there had been clear skies. I wonder at it. Seldom does it rain here this time of year.

Somehow, the rare rain makes me laugh. Or perhaps I laugh simply because I need to, and the weather is the best available excuse. "Stop thinking so much," I say to myself. "Stop analyzing everything." Then the raindrops begin to hit my face and my robes. At least it is a warm rain.

Chapter 17

▼

Assigned to a Second Mission
1618 AD (about 1598)

"Priest, you don't understand about men and women. How could you?" The Fresh Lieutenant burps, his eyes on me. I recognize that look. It tells me that he also sees me as too old to be able to remember the passion of men and women, even if I had lived a more usual life with a wife and children. I also remember what the Young Captain has said about him, that he is the most physically lustful man he has ever met. The Fresh Lieutenant burps again and then continues, "You couldn't understand."

How could I understand about love and sex and relationships, he is thinking, being as old as I am, and having never been married?

Husband and wife. I saw enough of husband and wife with my parents.

Perhaps because of my experiences as a child, I have reflected a lot about the situation of women in my country. That I am a Buddhist has influenced this, too. Many women of Korea have become Buddhists. It is no wonder. Buddhism is kinder to women than is Confucianism.

Confucianism maintains five tenets upon which all Confucianists agree, no matter what sect they belong to. These tenets are: absolute loyalty to one's sovereign; filial piety, especially toward one's father; love between husband and wife; respect for elders; and trustworthiness between friends. Within these beliefs are others, especially regarding women.

Women are taught that it is their supreme virtue to be submissive. They are taught that to be called a "wise mother and good wife" is the highest of compliments, and that they have three primary obediences in life. These are to father, then to husband, and then, if widowed, to the oldest son. The male is to be obeyed, the female to be servile and unargumentative.

Under Buddhism, women had it better. They could inherit property. They had some areas in life in which they were free to make choices. Now, all of this is gone for them. Under Confucianism, they are owned by father and, later, husband. They may possess no land in their own name. Women have almost no choice in the major events in their lives. They are always subject to the whims of the men in their lives—father, husband, and sons, and pity the poor woman who bears no male offspring. I have wondered if this lack of freedom, of the ability to choose for herself, influenced my mother. If she had not felt she had to love my father and that she was required to be totally loyal, would she have felt free to love him and to be true to him? I have thought about this perhaps too many times.

I have wondered if this lack of choice in our land has influenced many of the people I have known, especially the females.

For me, being a Buddhist priest has given me a great excuse to keep away from emotional involvement with ladies. Certainly I was not expected to marry. But I have not been able to forget about male and female matters. I have not been without the feelings and longings which all men experience.

Admiral Yi, without having meant to, sent me on a mission where I experienced more regarding women than I had ever thought I would. The Admiral, who fathered children by two women, was not a stranger to the bedroom. However, he never let himself be distracted by the fair sex while in camp or at sea. (This was unlike some others. Won Kyun's carrying on was well known, and, of course, many of his subordinates imitated him.)

I, though, was nothing but a simple and very unmarried priest. Little could the Admiral have guessed what he sent me to. And he would never know.

My mission seemed much less dangerous than the one that had me end up in Chinju. This was a much more simple thing, being an investigation regarding Koreans far from the Japanese and potential battles. The Admiral had heard stories regarding what was happening in some of the refugee farming areas he had set up and wanted me to find out the truth.

"These farms are important. They feed the navy. They help to feed the army. We might even need to send more supplies to the King should this be needed," said the Admiral.

"Yes, Sir," I replied.

"They must be productive. We need the supplies they give us."

I did not add, nor of course did Admiral Yi say, that he had taken a chance starting these farms in the first place. The Admiral had given refugees and sailors and soldiers too old to be on active duty a safe place to live and farm while, at the same time, performing valuable service for the war effort. However, he had done so by stretching the limits of his authority. He had broadly interpreted instructions from the Defense Command, and, only after doing so, had informed the King that lands previously reserved for the royal horse herds were now being used by refugees for farming.

He had gotten away with it, at least so far. But these farms needed to succeed. Any problems on these farms would be branded as his personal failures by his enemies at court and would be used as more reasons to have him removed. The court was already full of Won Kyun's lies about him.

Now, in retrospect, I can see more clearly the danger that Admiral Yi was in at every moment. The Japanese in some ways were a more honest enemy than were some of his own countrymen. The Japanese quite openly wanted him dead. They wanted to kill him, to sink his ships, and to take over his country. In his own country, the other faction at our own court cloaked their loathing of him in fine words and seemed to resent his success against the Japanese as much as they hated the invaders.

It is clearer now. Back then, I could not have seen it. I would not have wanted to believe it, anyway. But he knew. The Admiral faced it every minute of every day. One group of Confucianists, the Eastern, believed that *li*, the mind, was paramount. The other group, the Western Confucianists, believed the life force of *ki* was more important. The two groups hated each other, and the King was in the middle of these schemers. His advisors were split between the Eastern and Western groups. The Minister of the Left, Ryu Seong-Ryong, of the Eastern group, had rightly championed Admiral Yi as the man of the hour.

This was ironic, for this leader certainly had not chosen correctly before. Just before the Japanese had invaded in 1592, the Eastern group had declared that Hideyoshi would never actually be so foolish as to send his armies across the sea.

Being so absolutely wrong had not been their proudest moment.

However, they got it very right in championing Admiral Yi as the man to save Korea. The downside though for Admiral Yi was that the support of the Eastern group automatically made him the enemy of the other side. The Western Confucianists began to support Admiral Won Kyun simply because he was against the other side's choice. This quickly proved to be quite a wonderful thing for them in other ways. Won Kyun began to send his supporters many 'gifts,' as well as slanderous lies regarding Admiral Yi.

Sadly and ridiculously, these members of our own King's court wanted to take the southern navy, the fleets of the three provinces, away from Admiral Yi, our greatest commander. These highly-educated worthies, because of their differences in belief with their opponents regarding the priority of *li* versus *ki* wanted the man who had saved our country to be removed and, perhaps, even to be executed.

It didn't matter that he had saved our kingdom from the Japanese. It didn't matter that he had been the only leader who put fear into the hearts of the island barbarians. The Western Confucianists still believed it would be better to be rid of Admiral Yi because the Minister of the Left, Ryu Seong-Ryong, of the Eastern group, championed him. Nothing else was as important to them.

As a Buddhist, I am, hopefully, beyond the Confucianist bickering. I can call it stupid, even though I am aware of some Buddhists who have behaved just as stubbornly and foolishly over points of doctrine. In particular, I saw such behavior in Japan.

Now, as an old man who is a Buddhist, I can call this for what it was and is. Sheer idiocy. It is humanity and our court politics at their worst.

However, back in 1594, when Admiral Yi sent me to the farms to see what was really going on, I did not know of all this intrigue. I had only heard hints of it. Certainly, I knew that Won Kyun was Admiral Yi's jealous opponent. (Thankfully, not all persons of high rank in our kingdom are jealous of the success of others. General Kwon Yul always had the highest respect for Admiral Yi, and I personally felt the regard Hwang Chin of Chinju had for him. Except, they were heroes, too. Won Kyun proved to be far from that.) But, I would not rate Won Kyun as a true rival to the Admiral. The difference in ability between the two was always so great and so obvious that I never, at that time, took Won Kyun as a serious threat to Admiral Yi.

If I had been able to foresee the future, I wonder what I would have done. Would Won Kyun have had an "accident" for the good of the country? I cannot say. I did not know then, so I do not know now. I did not actually face that decision.

As I traveled to the farms, I was unaware of the slander spreading around the royal palace about the wonderful man I was fortunate to be assisting. This was likely a good thing. It is possible I did better not knowing so much was at stake. Plus, I might not have stopped in the forest to play the flute that one day if I had known. And what would the rest of this little life have been without the memory of that day?

The Admiral had said, "My official inspectors are sometimes shown only what they are wanted to see. They get some of, but not all of, the truth. Go, Priest Wonho, and find out what is really happening there. I hear rumors, but I cannot act on rumors. The complaints involve a royal appointee. Bring me the facts."

"I will do my best, Sir," I said to the Admiral.

Then he said words that he repeated only one other time to me. "I know you will. And it is a good best. Travel well, priest."

It is such words, from such a man, that inspire a person. They were simple statements that transformed normal fishermen and farmers and inexperienced commanders into squadrons and crews that beat back some of the most ferocious, experienced, and deadly forces one could ever encounter. It was such words from this man that saved King and land, even though King and land at times seemed not to want to be rescued or to be worth rescuing.

So I traveled to the farms on another mission for Admiral Yi and to days and nights I would not have believed possible for me.

At least this time, I was a Korean traveling about in Korea amongst Koreans. This time I could not be called a spy. Not really.

Chapter 18

The Love of the Goddess

Eighth Moon, 1593

Except for the war years, I have lived my adult life on the road between temples. And sometimes they seem a long way apart. However, occasionally I make the time between the stone pagodas and sunset gongs even longer than it has to be. I pause in my wanderings to meditate. There are moments when I find myself in the mountains and hills between villages or near the sea, with only my staff, my bowl, and the robes I wear. There are times during these solitary spans when I stop to sit and feel the oneness and nothingness in the shadows of a peaceful meadow or a cleft in a strong hillside rock.

I stop to meditate or, sometimes, I have a flute with me. I play it as I let my mind go, thoughts leave, wants and worries and concerns evaporate.

Usually the flute I play is a simple instrument, perhaps one of bamboo. Merely a humble, cheap thing someone has offered to me as I walked by, or that I have found discarded along the road. A few times, I have actually found fallen bamboo of the right type and have done my best to carve a flute of my own making.

I have no special skill in making or in playing. I have never been trained. At the temples, for the chanting and rituals, I was a drummer at times. But I never had instruction in the flute.

Yet there is strength and fragility in the sound of the flute. Its music has power yet is delicate, just like our existence here in these weak, temporary, and yet sometimes wonderful human forms. Yes, I know our bodies can be wonderful; just as well as I know they can be awful. Buddhism often seems to emphasize the worst of the physical, but in truth we are here in them for a reason. Even the life of the Buddha himself shows this. Our bodies teach us. We learn despite them and because of them.

In this life, from my body I have definitely learned.

The weather is beautiful as I begin my second mission for Admiral Yi. It is a thing of joy to again be on the trails and roads of my green and scenic land. I am away from the many occurrences and busynesses of the military camp and back in the green forest and the fields, the sun shining, the moving air cool. Perhaps it is the wind in the branches, or the birds, or some pre-war memory, but something brings to my consciousness the music of the temples.

It is as if I can hear the cold, crisp, predawn gong on Homan-san near Dazaifu in Japan. The notes of the music of the morning procession at Chongnieu in China flow again. The chanting to drums and flute of my own temple, where my father had left me so many years before, fills me. The feeling of the music comes to me, the knowingness of a connection to something more than what we simply feel and hear and touch in these, our bodies.

My legs and lungs feel strong, my heart immortal, my spirit glad, and, as I sometimes do, I step off the road and walk to a private place. Years alone on foot have taught me well how to read the land. Many seasons of listening and watching have taught me the mating songs and flights of the birds, the sounds of our insects, and the habits of many of our animals. If you can read them, there are signs that a hawk is flying close by and hints that a tiger might be stalking somewhere near if you can see or hear them. The land itself can also be understood if one takes the time to learn.

And I have had much time and have taken it. Sure enough, off the road I soon find the spot that I had imagined to be waiting. A glade, next to the small stream, the sound of its small waterfall barely heard in the distance. A private place, cool in the shade for a warm day. Water to drink and far enough from the road to make music without being heard.

I take out the flute that I am carrying. A whimsical thing, not made to last. Like everything here, just more obviously so. I wipe it clean, check to make sure nothing has lodged inside and blow into it. The sound is fine. As I play it a bit more, I know that this little piece of plant produces music that is better than usual. I smile to myself. Even I can use this flute fairly well.

And so I play.

I play without thought, without consciousness, without foresight, without care. I blow into the flute and my fingers move with only vague feelings of the memories of the music of the temples in my spirit's ear, with merely a wispy memory of the fabled songs of the celestial harps. The sun moves across the sky, the breezes shift, the sun begins to move down toward the golden goodbye to the day.

The goddess appears. She comes in red robes, and she dances. She is young and timelessly gorgeous, and she dances to the music—music that is not of me, by me, but is of all time and truth and joy and life and that which is beyond life. Her robes come off, and she dances naked and perfect. She dances, and then she is next to me, then on me, telling me to keep playing, and I do, even as she sits astride me and moves as a woman does, rides me, telling me to play, and I do. And I play, and she moves, and she sighs, and she says words and phrases I do not know, and her hands on my chest inside my opened robes squeeze and scratch at my chest as she cries out and cries out again, and then my music changes to a plaintive wail as I too shout, let out, let go. I feel as a man feels inside a woman, but she is a goddess, and ... and I have never dreamed of such a thing.

Well, perhaps I have dreamed, but ...

The goddess falls across my chest, limp, my arms going around her. I lie there on my back, wondering if this was how it felt to be divine, or to be touched by divinity. Her breathing reaches into my heart. The music, the goddess, the feelings, and now the sunset over it all, the sky turning its full collection of colors as if in honor of the perfect day.

I think that if the goddess had come here to gather my spirit, that if it is my time to die, then indeed, let me die like this, with this feeling, in this way.

I lie there, beyond words, almost beyond this life. I don't know how long. It is almost dark with only the barest sights still left of the sky's celebration when normalcy begins to return. I feel a twig lodged beneath my bottom. A mosquito or two is somewhere around. The goddess begins to feel a bit heavy.

A voice says, "I feel cold." It is she.

Quickly and gently, I wrap my robes over her back, rear, and legs.

"Thank you," she says. She shifts her body, moving as if to prevent stiffness.

There is a silence. The wind blows. It is no longer a breeze. She is correct. In comparison to the day, it feels cold. I hold her, and she burrows against me.

"Where were you spending the night tonight?" she asks.

"Wherever I found myself."

"What is your name?"

"Wonho."

I am speaking naturally. It is as if loving a goddess in the forest as sunset approaches is the most natural thing in the world for me. Never have I cared less about the past or the future, except while in the best and deepest of meditations, then during these moments.

"My name is Sugyong," she says.

I lie quietly. It is as if answering questions is all right but initiating speech is beyond me.

Her voice begins again. "My shin eomeoni told me to leave and not to come back until I had found the music and had merged with it."

Then I realize it. "You are a mudang!" I say.

Her shin eomeoni. Her spiritual mother. The red robes. Her otherworldliness. She is a mudang, a shaman; some would call her a sorceress. She reads fortunes, foretells the future, creates herbal potions, and makes magic.

"Not yet. I am still a shin ddal. Likely soon, though, I will be on my own."

A shin ddal. A spirit daughter. A female shin aegi—a spirit child.

My mind whirls. I, Wonho, a Buddhist priest, have just been as a man with a female, and not just a regular woman, but a mudang. Never would I, never could I, have dreamed of such a thing.

She speaks again. "I was sent out today by my spirit mother. She said I could find music today." She looks at me. Her eyes are beautiful, but very strong. It seems she is making up her mind about me, whether to talk to me from her heart, to share herself fully in words as she has shared herself so wonderfully with her body. The look softens, and she turns back toward the sound of the water and goes on.

"Music has been my problem. I am fine for the making of costumes and of paper flowers for the rituals. I am very good at preparing and maintaining the location of the rituals, be it in a shrine or elsewhere. I prepare the food for the rituals properly and was correct in kutcheoilja. I never did the rituals except in proper sequence. I was even all right at chaedam. I could nicely entertain the audience with my repartee with the musicians. However, my cheongbae was not good enough. At times, my chanting to bring forth and charm the spirits was full of power and, at other times I missed. The same was true of my own playing of instruments. But my dancing has never been right. I was always off."

"Your dancing!" I say. "You danced today like a goddess!"

I know even as it is happening that I will never forget the look she gives me before she says, "That was before today. My spirit mother said I would find the music, the dance. And I did. It came from you."

I am speechless. I want to say that I am not even a proper musician, that I really don't play that well, but something stays my words. I can't say this. (Now, so many years later, I know that it was not me playing that day at all, but some musical spirit or some melodic rhythmic breath of a god that happened to fill me for one afternoon and evening. It has never happened like that to me again. Perhaps it only happens often to the great musicians, which is why they are great.)

She goes on, "Now I will be able to do the three main tasks of the mudang. Now I will be able to do jeom, kusa, and kut." She pauses and looks up. Breathing deeply, she says, "The kongsu will be with me. My time has come."

Jeom, I remember. Fortune-telling. Divination. Often followed by a kusa or a kut. The kut is the easy one. It is a series of large rituals. It is to change something that could happen or to repair something that has happened. The kut might be used to keep misfortune away or to restore one's health. There are chants, music, bangool bells, and dancing. Of course, there is kongsu where the gods or spirits speak through the mouth of the mudang to the client. The words to some of the chants are so old no one except the mudang even knows what they mean. In the oldest of languages they call forth the spirits and the gods. And the dancing is shin chum, god dancing. It cannot be taught.

God dancing. I realize it. No wonder I thought she was a goddess. A goddess was in her. And the words I did not know that she was saying. Of course. They are from the ancient tongues, the elder gods.

And she believes she has come to her true music, to her inspired dancing, because of my music. And this is what she had been missing. Music. Rhythm in speech and dancing.

She sits up, but I do not move. It isn't that I can't. Then, slowly, I move my feet and stretch my legs. The sound of the stream seems louder as night approaches. The insects and frogs have awakened, too.

"I know of a place," she says. "An abandoned herder's hut. It would be out of the wind."

Following her, I am amazed by the perfection of her shape. Even through her re-donned robes, it is obvious. I can see why I believed she was actually a goddess. She moves gracefully, smoothly, and quickly. She knows the wisdom of arriving before dark.

Inside the hut, we keep each other warm. And she leads in various repeats of what we had done in the afternoon. Something stills any sense of hesitancy or impropriety I might normally have felt. All of my being says it is right to be with her on this day and night. My only apprehension during this night is that she will ask me to play the flute again, for I sense that I will not be able to achieve or again be granted the magical musical inspiration of the afternoon. But she is a mudang, after all. Perhaps she senses this, knows this. She does not ask.

She tells me of her life. Unlike most mudang of the south, she was not born into a family of mudang. Hers is not a hereditary calling. Instead, she is a charismatic mudang. These are more usual in the north.

"My spirit mother was born late to her parents. She was barely trained when they died. She lost her one child. Not to the Japanese, but to illness. Her mate she lost to the Japanese." It is an all too familiar story these days. No comment is necessary.

"But she had heard of a strange child. This child was sick with unexplained illnesses. She could not eat, became physically and mentally weak, began to see spirits and things no one else could and predicted things that came true. This happened once, and then again.

"My spirit mother heard of my illnesses, and she came to see me. She believed the illnesses she had heard of to be signs of shingyung, to be signs that a child was possessed, was in communication with the spirits and gods that control the earth.

"I was only twelve, and I was scared of her at first. However, my parents were poor, and her reputation was great, so they did not hesitate long before agreeing that I should become her spirit child. They agreed that I would become her shin aegi."

"How many years ago was that?"

"Ten."

She is twenty-two years old. I marvel at this. I am close to fifty. And I sense a wisdom in her I may never achieve, except for scattered, non-maintainable moments. And this wisdom is in a young body indeed fit for a goddess come to earth.

In the morning, I feel surprisingly fit. I have not had much sleep. She has gathered food from the forest for us, which she prepared with some barley and a bit of rice she had with her already. With cool water, it is the best meal I have ever had.

She asks, "What brings you here?"

I do not answer, surprised by the question. She asks again, "Why are you walking here? There are few Buddhist priests on the roads these days."

I can hardly tell her that I am on a mission for Admiral Yi, that I have just finished checking on some mainland farms, where everything was going well, and that now I am on my way to where a boat will take me to Tolsando. Instead, I use the name of a person I knew of on the farms of Tolsando, saying I am going to visit him.

"Oh," she answers. "There are problems there."

This is what I was going there to find out about. I ask her what problems she means. She tells me that the man who was originally simply a very bad horse farm supervisor had also been given authority over the new farmers there. No one likes him or trusts him. He acts in an extremely small-minded and arbitrary fashion, and it would be better for all concerned if the Japanese captured him and took him away.

"Really?" I say. "How do you know this?"

"Mudang talk, of course." She sees me smile at this and hesitates, so I explain.

"I was thinking, 'just like some priests.'"

She grins and nods. "The Tangol of Tolsando is a friend of my spirit mother."

* * * *

(*There is a gap in the manuscripts at this point. The discovered writings that describe the events closest in time to the Priest Wonho's encounter with the mudang continue below.*)

Everything on Tolsando was as bad as she described. My report to Admiral Yi upon my return concluded that the supervision of the island's horse breeding and of the farms was deplorable. I gave him exact details as I had witnessed them and said that various persons on the mainland had even heard of the man's poor reputation. The Admiral thanked me for the report and that he appreciated the confirmation. He left unsaid the fact that he would not criticize a person to the royal court without being very sure of the facts, which was very unlike what many were doing to him.

Then he asked me something unrelated to my mission. As always, his abrupt change of subjects startled me. It is especially startling because part of me is still distracted by the time I had spent with Sugyong, and my focus is not what it normally is when I am with him. Part of me is still savoring the memory of having been playing the flute in the forest on a beautiful day when something divine came into my life.

I have been told that I am a person who can only do one thing at a time compared to others who have ten things going at once. Admiral Yi was one of the latter. He could focus on more things at one time than any person I have ever met.

"Priest Wonho, what of the conflicting requisitions?"

"Sir?"

"You have heard, have you not, of how the army tells the magistrates of a town to do one thing, and the instructions of the navy tell them to do something else?"

"Yes, Sir."

"Tell me what you have heard."

I consider my words before answering. I always speak carefully when asked questions by the Admiral, for he values accuracy as much as or more than any person I have ever spoken to. And I know that I am still a bit distracted. Yet on this matter, I am sure I can offer him nothing that he has not already heard or surmised.

"There is some confusion, Sir. I have heard that your orders came to build a ship and to supply a crew for it, and then, a month or two later, an official came who says, 'No, this is no longer a naval area. You are under army command. We need all your able-bodied men as foot soldiers.'"

"And the results, Priest Wonho?"

"Few good, Sir. You do not get needed ships or full crews for the few that are built. The army does not get so many men because many refuse to go saying they are under orders from the navy. Then some of the same men refuse to join the naval forces because they can say that the army has ordered them not to. And any city official who is weak, lazy, or cowardly can stall before doing anything while waiting for the situation to be resolved."

"You have seen this happening during your travels, Priest Wonho?"

For a moment, I am almost tempted to say that I have seen and experienced a whole lot during my recent travels, but as I question the inclinations of my mind, I answer seriously, "Sir, I have seen it, and heard of it.

The confusion, the sets of different orders, they are not, they cannot be, helpful."

The Admiral nods. Then, in my mind, more active than ever before as if inflamed by my time with Sugyong, I try to imagine his thoughts. I imagine they are: "Everyone sees it—the common people, this priest, every fisherman, and farmer. Why can't the royal court and their appointed officials stop making it so much harder for me to go out and do my job? Why can't they support me as I do what the land forces hesitate to do—to fight the Japanese and make them know that going back to their islands is the best thing for them, indeed, that the Japanese either go home or they leave their bones here."

I imagine these to be his thoughts, but I could be wrong. And even if I were correct, or especially if I were correct, in this case, he could not say them. Not to me. A criticism of the royal way of doing business would be highly inappropriate, and the Admiral is the most appropriate of men. He could no more complain to me of the doings of the royal court than I could share with him that I had enjoyed wonderful times with a fantastic woman during my journey. All the Admiral does instead is to think for a few moments, looking up at the ceiling and breathing deeply, as is his way. Then he says, "Thank you, Priest Wonho," and I know it is time for me to go.

*   *   *   *

Summary and excerpts from *Memorials to Court 53 and 54,* both sent by Admiral Yi to the King during the First Moon, 1594.

The Traveling High Commissioner, Lee Chong-am, has informed me by official letter that the Ministry of Finance has notified him that the horse-farm inspector of Tolsando has been appointed to be concurrent supervisor of the new farms on the island. The current holder of this dual position, Cha Tok-nyong, has gained a (upon investigation deserved) reputation for treating his herdsmen very badly. The grievances have reached the point to where even the daily livelihood of the people has been threatened. Now he has begun treating the new farmers on Tolsando in a similar manner, which could adversely affect the agricultural affairs of the whole province. A poor harvest on Tolsando might result in my crews not having sufficient food for survival, let alone for strength to fight and beat the Japanese. For the benefit of the people and of the navy, I therefore request that Cha Tok-nyong be transferred immediately, and that a goodhearted manager be appointed and sent to Tolsando as soon as possible.

*   *   *   *

The enemy has moved forces toward Cholla Province, with the obvious intent of attacking the southeast part of the Kingdom and wiping out the homeports of the royal naval squadrons. The enemy is specifically concentrated at this time on the island of Koje.

Naturally, it is my highest desire to lead out an amply equipped, fully crewed fleet of warships against the enemy. However, at a time when even one ship is precious, the planned building of twenty new ships in the nine coastal counties has been suspended.

Unfortunately, the Traveling High Commissioner, Lee Chong-am, has reduced the number of coastal counties that are to supply ships and sailors to our naval forces. This is despite the King's own gracious decree that calls for no administrative changes in the coastal areas assigned to the navy.

Without the new warships, our naval situation would of course be more vulnerable. With this in mind, I request most earnestly that the counties that had been under naval administration be returned to it, and that the ships that had been ordered to be constructed be completed forthwith.

It would be a good thing to free the administration of the court, the military, and the minds of the people from multiple and conflicting demands and drafts by the commanders of the naval forces and of the land forces. With this view in my mind, I propose to memorialize the throne with my vacuous thoughts.

Yi, Commander
First Moon in the 22nd Year of
Wanli (Kab-o, 1594)

Chapter 19

▼

The Test

Of Fourth Moon, 1594

"You were there for the special officer's examinations?" asks the Young Captain.

"Yes," I admit. "It was early in 1594."

The Young Captain nods. "It was just like the Admiral to hold those. He was always wanting a good man to be rewarded." He pauses, thinking about something.

I wonder if he is going to comment on the fact that the Admiral himself had broken his leg falling off his horse during the kisa section of his own first military exam. Everyone knows how the man who would become our great Admiral was almost killed at the age of 27 by that accident. He was galloping along, firing his dan kong short arrows from his bo-sa at the round-shaped juk, and then his horse stumbled. He fell off in a horrible way. Many thought he had been killed. However, he surprised everyone by getting up and wrapping up his badly broken left leg with the bark of a nearby willow tree. To no one's surprise, he handily passed the next set of military exams with high scores.

However, for his career this produced some untoward effects. By the time he entered the military he was older chronologically than many officers who were senior to him in rank. He might be the same age as a captain or major while he was still a lieutenant. In a land where a person's age is respected, and where the language itself shifts depending upon the age of the person with whom one is speaking, his relatively old age for his rank caused some uneasiness.

But the Young Captain does not mention any of this. Instead, he goes on about the tests that the Admiral had arranged for his men during the war.

"Admiral Yi had heard about the test for officers the army was giving in Chonju, but he could not let his men attend it. He could not man the fleet in the absence of so many. So he asked the King to give a special examination at the naval headquarters, right?" His question is not really a question, but I nod anyway.

"What has always amused me about this is how he got around having to give his men the part of the test involving shooting from the galloping horse."

"Why is that?"

"What was the real reason? Was it really because there was no appropriate test of the ground on which to gallop a horse and fire at the targets, or was it because he knew that most of his bunch of ship-trained naval fighters could not ride a horse very well, if at all, let alone shoot accurately while galloping!"

I smile, being sure there is some truth to his suspicion. "I could not know the whole truth," I begin. "I was not privy to all of the details of how the official examinations were set up. My part was small in it indeed."

"What part was this?" The Young Captain's question really seems to be "You weren't part of the navy yet. How could you participate at all?"

"It was my job to bang the drum if the man shooting hit the target."

"You were a judge?"

"No. There were three of us at the end of the shooting range, and an officer made the final decision although there were more judges than him to see the truth. He would signal to me to bang the drum if the arrow hit the target and to another man to strike a gong and wave a white flag if it missed."

It had seemed to be a good thing to offer to be of whatever assistance I could, and I had been glad to be told I could assist on the firing course. But, with over a hundred examinees with each firing at least fifteen arrows, it had turned into a long day. It also did not help that we were so far away that most of the time we could not even see who was shooting. Knowing who was shooting and being able to wish those I knew well as they fired would have made the day more interesting, at least for me.

Yet, again, it was good to be of assistance in such an important event, and at least that day the weather was warm. There was some sun, a few clouds, no rain, and only a gentle wind. The officer with us told us that this was a good thing. He said that only once had he heard of people in our position on a windier day during the archery tests being hit by a stray arrow. Then I thought about the realities of the skill that some of these men displayed and again marveled at what some could accomplish.

"I have never been an archer. It is still hard for me to see how any person can reach a target over 250 meters away from where they stand, let alone hit it." Then I realize it. "But you did in your test, didn't you?"

The Young Captain nods. "I just wish I could have had Admiral Yi as one of my judges, whether I had to do it on horseback or not."

To this, it is my turn to nod. Then to get back to his original question, "You are probably right to suspect a mixture of motives in Admiral Yi's keeping his men off of horseback during the special examinations, but I can see why he did. We would have done very well compared to the army if we could have done a test based on firing at targets from a rocking ship at sea!"

"True enough," says my friend. "More wine, Wonho?"

* * * *

Memorial to the Court #63
Regarding the Conducting of Special Examinations for Military Service

I memorialize the throne.

All sailors rejoiced upon hearing of the news of the official communication from Yi Chong-am, Traveling Higher Commissioner, who relayed the Military Education Command's instructions regarding the visit of the Crown Prince to Chonju to attend the special examinations for military service, the date for which was set at the 27th of the Twelfth Moon last year.

However, as commander of our naval forces, to my regret I was unable to allow so many brave men leave to attend the tests due to the distance they would have had to travel and to the proximity of a strong and dastardly enemy who could attack at any time. Due to this, I humbly recommended to the throne that a similar special examination be granted our naval forces here in our naval headquarters. This examination would be fitted to local conditions, as following the precedent of Kyongsang Province, by allowing for the testing of shooting short fire arrows on foot rather than shooting from horseback, as on the small islands used for bases by our navy we are ill-afforded the flat spacious grounds necessary for the galloping of horses.

In response to my request an official letter from the Ministry of War arrived, which read as follows:

Your memorial to the throne regarding a special examination for naval personnel has been considered by the Ministry and in accordance with the views of His Majesty, the following is recommended:

"It is not the usual procedure to allow for an examination in continuation of one for which the successful civil and military service candidates have already been announced. However, it would also be unfortunate not to give an equal opportunity for recognition and promotion to the members of our navy, who have fought well and have bravely endured many difficulties. Therefore,

although the results of the examinations be not published simultaneously, it is still fair to use examinations to single out worthy talents even at separate places and at different times. However, testing the candidates by short fire-arrow on foot rather than by long arrow shooting on horseback, as Admiral Yi has requested be allowed, would likely result in too many persons passing the test who would not otherwise be able to achieve the minimum required high standard of marksmanship. Accordingly, let us limit the number of men who may pass this test to one hundred."

In accordance with the above, His Majesty on the 7th of the Second Moon of this, the 22nd year of Wan-li, decreed that the proposed special examinations take place according to the memorial, with the Chief Judge to be Yi Kwang, Right Deputy Transmitter Secretary of the Privy Council.

In accordance with the official letter as transcribed above, I sent an official letter to the Field Marshal requesting that he send an experienced civilian observer to watch the special examinations. The Field Marshal nominated the Magistrate of Samga, Ko Sang-am, for this position.

Accordingly, on the 6th of the Fourth Moon the special examination grounds were opened. I, as commander, Yi Ok-ki, and Ku Sa-chik served as examiners, with the said Ko Sang-am and the Magistrates of Changhung, Hohung, and Ungchon as civilian observers.

In line with the usual rule in their shooting practice, all candidates taking part in this special contest were awarded two points for each direct hit when shooting two sets of five long iron-tipped arrows, and one point for each direct hit when shooting one set of five short fire-arrows.

I hereby send the results of these examinations. As stipulated, the list contains no more than the one hundred successful candidates, each marked with highest, second, or third grades, and detailing their names, fathers' names, and their ages, addresses, and previous positions.

Yi, Commander
11th of Fourth Moon in the 22nd
Year of Wan-li (Kab-o, 1594)

Chapter 20

▼

The Saint and the Sword

Summer of 1594

It is a grand morning. There is no enemy attack threatening, and the weather is perfect. The day looks to become hot, but there is a cool dawn breeze. The sea is a beautiful blue, and white clouds dance merrily above the green hills and peaks. The water birds are out in large numbers, and even they seem more colorful and vibrant than usual. Usually it is the sky of autumn that is the most beautiful in Korea. Even the Chinese poets extol the colorful fame of our fall skies. Yet, on this summer day, no sight above could surpass what I am seeing.

Even so, I have an unhappy feeling, almost a darkness, as I stride toward Admiral Yi's headquarters. I wonder about this negativity I am sensing. I worry that what I might be sensing is what Admiral Yi is feeling. Now he is stuck waiting. He cannot do as he wishes and launch a full army/navy offensive to rid Choson of the last of Hideyoshi's troops. He has time on his hands, much more than he has had. And the Japanese still occupy the southeast tip of the kingdom. He will not be content while they are still here.

I remember how he felt in the Third Moon after he received a message from the Chinese Commanding General Tan Tsung-jen instructing him not to attack the Japanese for the time being since they had just had a truce talk with the Japanese in Ungchon. The Admiral had, to say the least, been terribly annoyed by this message. The next day, he had been sick with an acute pain in his stomach.

Now, with the Admiral in a similar mood, or so it seems, he has asked for me. And there are a couple of questions he might have in store for me that I really do not want to answer.

Sure enough, when I arrive and have been sent to him, he asks me one of the questions I had been hoping not to be asked.

"You told me some things of the Japanese leaders, Priest Wonho. You told me much of their language and of their history. And I learned unexpectedly that you know of some of the fighting ways of China."

I nod. He does not look upset. This, at least, is good. Then comes the question.

"While you were in Japan, did you ever learn anything of Japan's fighting arts?"

Admiral Yi's question is a logical one, a good one. I have even thought about bringing up what I knew about this before. However, it didn't seem likely to be that useful. The terrible sword skill of the Japanese samurai was well known to all, even before the Taiko had sent over two hundred thousand of them to Korea in 1592, the year of Imjin.

For centuries before the Imjin War, we had been plagued by the Japanese pirates, the waegu, called *wako* in Japanese. These pirates were often samurai whose masters had died. For these master-less samurai, called ronin, to choose to become pirates made much sense. For one, there was a high potential reward in plunder and pay. Being a pirate could also offer the thrill of battle for which the samurai had been trained since childhood.

Unemployed samurai could join with a wako group, gear up for battle, go out on a raid to Korea, and get paid well for chopping up some poorly-trained local militia forces. And when, as often happened, there would be no fighting because the local forces would be so scared of them they would run away, there would be the loot. The town was still there to be plundered, and the women and children to be enjoyed and kidnapped. It was especially popular to raid the nearby southern Korean cities, but some of the more adventurous samurai had even done some plundering in China, which was a much more dangerous journey by sea from Japan.

So I had felt no need to point out what I know about their swordsmanship. We Koreans had known about it for centuries. Besides, Admiral Yi's battles are naval, and usually it is the long-range weapons and maybe ramming, not swords, which decide them. Swords are mostly for mopping-up work, like cutting off heads.

But now the Admiral has asked me. I consider my answer, even though I have rehearsed it many times. I decide to just tell it all as I had already played it out in my mind.

"I was very fortunate. I traveled over much of Japan, as you know, and, for part of my time there, I was lucky enough to be able to stay at Tenshin Shoden Katori Shinto Ryu." I pause, wondering if the Admiral is going to surprise me by saying something that proves he knows everything about this school already. But he says nothing, so I go on.

"It is a relatively new school, only a century old, but I believe it is one of the best schools of swordsmanship in Japan. It is far to the east of Honshu, a day's journey past Edo. It is not big, but it is excellent."

"What brought you to this school of swordsmanship?" asks the Admiral.

"The Daishi, Sir," I answer. "Kobo Daishi."

"He is your favorite Japanese Buddhist, is he not? He is the one you mentioned who developed their writing system?" Yes, the Admiral has done it again. He has surprised me. How could he have remembered that? I mentioned that to him over two years ago.

"Yes, Sir. I believe that Kobo Daishi might be the most inspiring Japanese who ever lived."

"I wish he were around today. They could use some holy inspiration," muses the Admiral. "Tell me of this Daishi, of how he lured you to this Tenshin Shoden Katori Shinto Ryu, and of the swordsmen there and what they learn." I note that he has only heard the name of the school once, but that he repeats it perfectly.

"The Daishi first, Sir?"

"Today, Priest Wonho, I have time to listen." He takes a deep breath, as if making sure that he really does have a whole morning for the luxury of not making life or death decisions, even if it is a luxury he would prefer not to have. "Just tell it all."

"Yes, Sir." It is my turn to take a deep breath. As I begin to tell Admiral Yi of Kobo Daishi, I realize that I must summarize a lot, or it could take days. Kobo Daishi was truly an amazing man. Born to a well-to-do aristocratic family, he gave up public life for the robes of the wandering monk. Only later, would he become an ordained Buddhist priest. After hard travels and long effort, he finally achieved enlightenment at sunrise in a rocky cave at the far-off, storm-swept coastline of Cape Muroto in Shikoku. He traveled to China where the master of an esoteric order who had been putting off his death while awaiting his successor had instantly recognized him as the new master.

Having studied intensely with his revered and elderly Chinese for the few months he had left, Kobo Daishi was anointed as the new master of this order. Then, after a few years' stay in China, he took his knowledge back to Japan where with time his reputation grew. He became a beloved man of all people, trusted by the emperor, sought after by the daimyo, the barons and counts and lords, and a hero and friend to the common folk. He tapped his staff and brought forth springs of water during droughts.

He built a dam that still exists to irrigate the northern part of his home island. He taught that all—rich, poor, male, and even female—can achieve enlightenment in this lifetime. He started schools for the poor and refused to eat at one temple until females were given entry to the grounds (because they would not let his mother visit him). By the time he died, from his base at the temple on the holy mountain of Koya, he had ordained hundreds of priests.

Even during his life, there was also a growing number of non-ordained "holy men." These were relatively uneducated and untrained men who called themselves monks and were, at least originally, pure in their pursuit of what the Daishi offered. This all took place during the Daishi's years in his body, beginning in 774 AD and ending on the day he had foreseen in the spring of 835.

The Admiral interrupts, "Did you say Kaya Mountain?"

"No, Sir. Koya. I have noted the similarity in names to our holy mountain, too."

He nods and takes a sip of his wine, which I take as the signal to continue. "The Daishi, of course, has been credited with many miracles since his death. Miraculous cures occur, sons come to women too old to have children, and dying people recover from hopeless illnesses, all thanks to the goodness of Kobo Daishi, and his having answered their prayers."

"I can see why you like this saint, Priest Wonho. But what of him and swordsmanship? How did this by all accounts kind, wise, and pure man come to be an inspiration to the samurai?"

"He isn't personally, Sir. Not directly."

The Admiral gets that "I know that you know that you had better explain this well" look. For a man who is so physically imposing and vital, he can sit still for long periods, but now he adjusts the position of his legs. There are some shouts barely discernible from down toward the harbor, but this is a frequent thing. We Koreans are not a quiet people.

"Sir, it is his teachings. I mentioned that they were esoteric."

"Yes."

"Some of his teachings are meant for the general populace, but others are for a special few. These are for priests who have gone through years of training at the teaching temples. These secret teachings are also for a few others who have gone through years of special training and study."

"Hmm … like swordsmanship."

"Yes, Sir. The founder of the school at which I stayed was Choisai Sensei. He had been a samurai and, by all accounts, a good one. Then, at the age of sixty, he detached himself from regular family life and went into seclusion in Katori Shrine. This was after the daimyo family, the Chiba, to whom he had been loyal his whole life had been defeated.

"Throughout his many combats and battlefield experiences, he had come to realize that the only sure thing that would occur if Japan continued in its present way was destruction of anything that really mattered, including one's family. He determined to find out if there were a better way. He had already heard about Kobo Daishi. Every Japanese, after all, has.

"Choisai Sensei believed the shrine to which he had retreated to be especially powerful, and when he retired from regular life pledged himself to special austere practices and severe martial training for 1,000 days. When he finished, he believed that he had indeed received divine instruction. Others believed it, too. He began to teach. That his teachings incorporated some parts of Kobo Daishi's teachings surprised no one. Very quickly his name became famous all over Japan, especially among the samurai. From the time he started to teach, it was said that warriors from all over Japan were drawn to him.

"Many came wanting to fight Choisai Sensei. They thought to achieve a type of self-aggrandizement by beating this very famous, almost legendary, swordsman. But the gods had revealed much to the old master. As he had suspected, the true essence of his martial techniques was not in fighting and killing, but in being able to do so and choosing otherwise. He taught that the best victory was the one that could be won without fighting and without violence, that the next best was the victory won while only injuring your opponent, and that the least desirable victory occurred when you killed your opponent. This is certainly as the Daishi would have explained these matters, too.

"Although many challenged Choisai Sensei, he showed each challenger a different way of looking at things, and it is said that those who came to visit him went away more stable and calm."

"How did he do this?" asks Admiral Yi. "How did he keep the Japanese swordsman who had come to duel from wanting to fight him?"

"'Kumazasa no oshie.'" I say it in Japanese, and then tell the meaning in Korean. "The teachings of the dwarf bamboo," I reply.

The Admiral eyes me, knowing that the explanation is coming. I notice how slowly and deeply he breathes. It is quiet outside now. I hear only the breeze and begin to feel the heat of the day mounting, beginning to creep in from outside.

"Sir, when he was challenged, Choisai Sensei would say something like, 'Of course, let us have a contest. But first, some tea.' As a traveler and a guest, the would-be opponent would naturally accept this offer. Then, Choisai Sensei would have an assistant from the dojo, the 'place of the way,' spread a thin straw mat on top of a stand of short miniature bamboo. The straw mat would be about knee high off the ground. Choisai Sensei would climb up and sit on the mat, which did not collapse to the ground beneath his weight. Then he would ask the challenger to join him, and, of course, the visiting samurai knew he had been beaten.

"After this demonstration, Choisai Sensei never had to fight a single opponent. All bowed to him, and called him Master.

"In fact, Choisai Sensei did not even like sparring, let alone true duels. To him the competitive contest, *shiai*, was the same as a duel to the death, *shiniai*."

"Was what Choisai Sensei did a trick?" asks the Admiral. "Or was he truly so special a person?"

"By all accounts, Sir, it was not a trick. During his 1,000 days of training and austerities in the inner precincts of Katori Shrine, he gained many insights and much power. He also came, based on all I was able to learn, to have reached a very full understanding to that which Kobo Daishi had actually taught."

"And this was …?"

"I only know part of it." There is a knock at the door. The Admiral says to enter, and a message is delivered. I know when to be quiet. Perhaps this will be the end of our time for the day. I sit still and breathe deeply and slowly. Again, I notice that the Admiral is breathing this way, too. Some carts can be heard bouncing along outside. The Admiral finishes reading the message, thinks for about three seconds, and puts it aside.

"You only know part of it. Tell me what it is you do know, and what it is you know you don't know."

I pause for a second to consider the phrasing of his request and then nod. "I do know that for anyone not highly trained and skilled to fight anyone from this school with a sword would likely be futile and foolish. They are as good as any sword fighters could be and are expert at using their razor sharp blades to cut their opponents in the vulnerable areas in their armor—the face, the undersides of the wrist, the insides of the biceps, the sides of the neck and waist, the groin, and the insides of the leg. They know exactly that a cut to the crotch causes death in up to twenty seconds, one to the armpits even more quickly, and that the jugular vein when severed will result in death in less than five seconds. And they know perfectly how to slice these places.

"They are also experts with the spear, the halberd, the staff, and, of course, the short sword. We know that every samurai carries the katana, the long sword, and the kodachi, the short sword.

"They train as hard with these weapons as my friend the Chinese priest trained in fighting at his temple—at least I think so. I say this because I cannot imagine any person training any harder and surviving."

I pause, because I never talk for so long without stopping, and because I especially do not want to babble in front of Admiral Yi. As a priest, silence for hours is nothing, for days or weeks is common, and some of us keep vows of silence for months or years. One winter I did not speak for months and saw no other person for weeks. And here I am, spewing words like an old woman to long-unseen grandchildren about something I had not even wanted to talk about a little while before. I take a deep breath, slowly.

"Something to drink, Priest Wonho?"

I admit the truth. "I feared I was over-speaking, Sir."

"Never worry about that with me. I will let you know if that happens." The way he said it made it very clear this was true. It also reaffirmed that I never wanted him to have to tell me that. "Please go on, Priest Wonho. You were describing their training in swordsmanship."

"Of course, Sir," I begin. "Almost all of their training is with kata. That is, they learn and practice set forms. They practice the same movements over and over again until they are automatic. It is said that once you have mastered these forms for any weapon, you are virtually unbeatable in a real combat situation."

"Do you believe this?" The question is quiet but potent.

"Sir, I cannot believe any swordsmen anywhere would have anything but the most difficult of times defeating someone who has studied for a period of years at that school."

The Admiral nodded. "Thank goodness for cannon and arrows."

I remember that the Admiral is renowned as having been one of the top archers in the kingdom, and I know that our archers are unsurpassable. There are some good Japanese archers, but none that are better than ours. Also, I know that Admiral Yi has personally overseen the improvements in our own cannon: Heaven, Earth, Black, and Yellow. He has also found ways for our most powerful cannons to be mounted on and fired from our ships without capsizing them. But even he could not produce trained swordsmen so quickly. And the Korean land forces are behind the Japanese in musketry.

Thank goodness for cannon and for arrows, indeed. Not to mention the kobukson.

I pause for a drink here. Suddenly I am very thirsty. And no wonder. Even now during the war, I often go for days without saying as much as I do to Admiral Yi in a few hours. For me, talking is hard work. (Now, as my old wrist cramps up, and my fingers ache, I know writing can be, too.)

However, I know that it is my task to speak of what I know, and that if I become tired in so doing, so what? My voice will recover, and sleep and meditation both refresh. The Admiral has taken a sip while I gulped. Now he asks, "Is this school, the type of training they do and the great swordsmen they produce—is this typical in Japan?"

"Typical, Sir?" I reflect before answering. "Not all samurai are this well-trained, Sir. That is why this dojo is so well known. But, there are many good schools. I believe that it could be said that the Japanese with the sword are like the Koreans with the bow."

He nods, and then asks, "What about these secrets? What about this esoteric Buddhism of Kobo Daishi and how it helps them to be great warriors?"

"Admiral, the most I know about in any detail is the *kuji no in*, the nine hand gestures." I show them to the Admiral while I repeat the words that go with them. "These hand gestures have a variety of uses. Especially when melded with the tenth sign, which is secret and, I think, situational, they are said to have much power."

"Situational?" interjects the Admiral.

"Yes, Sir. I believe they use a different tenth sign based upon what their purpose is at this moment. The sign they use depends upon whether they are preparing to go into individual or group combat, whether they are trying to find or force their way into an enemy's castle or stronghold or to protect their own, whether they are doing work toward healing injuries or curing an illness, or …"

"Healing? They are healers, too?"

"It is a perfect example of Choisai Sensei's beliefs that they are supposed to be as good at doctoring wounds as they are at giving them. And that they do this both physically and with other methods, such as the use of the nine signs."

"And these nine signs come from your hero, Kobo Daishi?"

"They come from the Mikkyo sect of Kobo Daishi's Shingon school of Buddhism, yes, Sir. Priests of the Mikkyo sect would claim that the Daishi was the one who either invented them, or who learned them in China and then passed them along. At the very least he inspired them."

He hears my words, and a look of concentration, of intense focus, appears on his face. He looks up, as if to this day's beautiful sky through the roof of his headquarters' building. After a few minutes, his expression changes.

"The weather is still excellent, Priest Wonho?"

"It was wonderful while I was coming here, Sir. It looked unlikely to change soon."

He nods. "I will fire arrows later today." He calls out to his attendant. Kim Taejin is on duty. The Admiral instructs that the officers with whom he usually shoots should be informed of his wish that those who can may join him in the afternoon for an archery session. Kim Taejin gives his usual polite bow and is gone. For a big man, he moves very lightly. And we know that the word will be given promptly. He is an excellent aide. Then the Admiral's attention is back on me.

"So, every samurai trained at Tenshin Shoden Katori Shinto Ryu ends up an excellent warrior, highly proficient with every bladed weapon, and very knowledgeable of the most lethal areas to be struck on his opponents.

But he would prefer not to kill. He uses secret Buddhist methods to prepare for fighting, to protect himself and his fortress, and more. He is also an excellent healer of the sick and the wounded. All of this is due to the excellent and divinely inspired teachings of the school's founder, Choisai Sensei, who himself in his teachings incorporated at least some of the esoteric knowledge handed down by the great Buddhist saint Kobo Daishi. This knowledge includes the kuji no in, the nine signs, which are hand gestures that have much power, especially when the secret tenth is added, this tenth being situational."

I begin to say that this was an excellent summary, but the Admiral continues.

"So what did you not learn? What secrets do you not know?"

Before speaking, I make a mental list of things I want to remember to mention. More shouts can be heard from near the port, but again these are not of a worrisome type. I turn my thoughts away from the voices outside and the beautiful weather. I refocus, check my mental list, and say, "They heal some wounds and illnesses by touching the patient with their hands. It is called *te-ate*. I do not know how this works.

"They incorporate the study of yin and yang and the five elements into their training. It might be in a way different than we do. Plus, I have not mentioned this before, but I have heard that not just the great swordsman use these Mikkyo practices. Many of the great Japanese generals and strategists also use them. The meditation practices of Son, which is called Zen in Japanese, are very popular with some fighters, but by using Zen, it can take years to reach the place of fighting for one's life while perfectly at ease and detached. The concrete practices of Mikkyo are held to be much faster and just as effective.

'Many of the Japanese now are also claiming that they are believers in another religion brought to their land by the red devils with the big noses. These people come from a land far away and on huge ships, and they claim that their god is the best and only. Yet they have three of them, some others say. I don't know much more about that belief, but have not heard anything about it helping the swordsmanship of the samurai in any way."

Admiral Yi said, "That is good, perhaps. Maybe these big-nosed red devils will cause problems for the Japanese, and if their faith is not as much use for swordsman and fighters, so much the better." He paused. "If you hear any more about this, let me know."

"I will, Sir."

Admiral Yi nodded, and then, "Back to what you don't know about the swordsmanship, Priest Wonho."

I bow a nod and continue. "At Tenshin Shoden Katori Shinto Ryu, they also have fighting techniques I was not allowed to witness. These include some from nin-jitsu, the arts of the assassin. I know that some of the things include throwing deadly objects noiselessly and maintaining invisibility even while within the sight of your opponent or victim, but I never saw these or any of the other arts of the ninja performed.

"Also, I did hear of, but did not see, methods that are taught which allow an unarmed opponent to conquer the armed. They teach their most advanced students ways to beat a trained samurai who has both swords ready, even while they themselves are barehanded. There are other secret arts and techniques, I believe, about which I was not even able to hear a single word."

"I see why they keep these secret, Priest Wonho."

"Sir?"

"It could only work by surprise. If all the swordsmen were allowed to see this technique, it would cease to work."

I consider this. "That makes sense, Sir."

"Same with those ninja secrets. If they did not stay secrets, they would have a much harder time using these techniques successfully." He pauses for a moment. I know him well enough by now to guess that he might be about to change topics on me. Then he says, "Priest Wonho, do you remember hearing of the Battle of Tangpo?"

I almost blush. "How could I not, Sir. That was when the musket shot went through you and you kept fighting!"

"Yes, that was the week. Did you hear about what happened to Captain Lee on the Seventh Day of the Sixth Moon when his ships ambushed the enemy outside of the outer entrance of Tanghangpo?"

Thinking hard, all I can remember is that there had been hard fighting that whole week when the Admiral was shot, and that the Korean navy beat the Japanese numerous times. I also know that Captain Lee Sun-Shin, the commander of Pangtap harbor, is acknowledged to be one of the best commanders the Admiral has. And, that Captain Lee is often noted for having a name so similar to the Admiral's own. His name can actually be pronounced the same way as the Admiral's, although the Chinese characters for each of the names are different. Captain Lee Sun-Shin, it is said, makes Admiral Yi Sun-Sin very proud. But I cannot remember having heard of the exact incident the Admiral seems to want me to recall.

"No, Sir, I either didn't hear or don't remember what happened to Captain Lee there."

"Priest Wonho, listen to this story and tell me if you think it sounds like the way one of your samurai from Tenshin Shoden Katori Shinto Ryu might have fought."

I am fully attentive. The Admiral is going to tell me a story! This is in itself noteworthy, and I am certain it will be memorable. He is not a person who enjoys wasting time.

"Captain Lee had set up his ships in ambush outside of the port of Tanghangpo before daybreak, guessing the defeated Japanese would try to escape to Pusan in the morning. He was right. At dawn, one ship tried to slip away. Captain Lee attacked it straight away with his ships firing from all sides out of the darkness. Over a hundred of the enemy were on board, and to our Earth and Black cannon, our firebombs, bullets, and long arrows, they fell like heavy flies into the sea.

"Soon there was only their commander and eight men left. The commander, a young man of impressive physique, stood fearlessly. He was wearing fantastic armor and swinging a long, beautiful sword. He directed the few survivors expertly until he was the only Japanese still alive. And yet, he did not hesitate fighting. To come within range of his sword was to meet death. Then, Captain Lee, from short range, fired an arrow through the enemy's chest armor. Even this did not seem to slow him down. The Japanese kept battling. Captain Lee reported that it was not until the tenth arrow had penetrated the chest armor of this Japanese that he finally let out a loud shout and fell. Only then were we able to claim his head.

"I have thought about this Japanese ever since having heard about him. I have wished that this one, of all the Japanese I have heard of, could have been spared." The Admiral paused for a few seconds before quietly concluding, "Perhaps he was too brave to have been killed." Then he looks at me, and I remember his query.

I say, "Yes, Sir. It could well be, yes, it could be that this Japanese commander had received training at Tenshin Shoden Katori Shinto Ryu or similar training at a different place. The use of the kuji no in, and who knows what other secret techniques, might have helped him to fight so valiantly and to survive for so long despite those wounds."

The Admiral nods and, for a few moments, there is silence. Again, I note his deep, slow breathing, and that he breathes with his stomach as well as his chest. This is a well-known meditation technique said to promote health, equilibrium, and long life. I wonder if he learned this or just breathes this way naturally. But I have something to say.

"Sir, what happened to Captain Lee with that Japanese reminds me of one of the most famous stories in all of Japanese history." His eyes are on me. I can see that he is interested.

"The first shogun of Japan was Minamoto Yoritomo. He lived over four hundred years ago. He was a great military commander. He had to be to conquer and unify all of that country."

"You said that he, Oda Nobunaga, and the Taiko were the three Japanese leaders most respected by the Japanese themselves," said the Admiral.

Of course he would remember my having told him that when I had let it slip my own mind. Nodding, I go on.

"While he was in the process of unifying the country there were many problems, including treacherous lords and traitorous vassals." Now the Admiral nods. These are problems everywhere and always. I continue, "Minamoto Yoritomo came even to suspect his own younger brother, Minamoto Yoshitsune, who was very popular. Some were said to favor Yoshitsune in becoming the true ruler of Japan. This scared Yoritomo enough that he ordered his brother's arrest. Knowing that this order was in truth a death warrant, Minamoto Yoshitsune fled. He attempted to escape accompanied by a loyal band of samurai who were led by the strongest warrior of the land, Benkei.

"Benkei was impossible to defeat one on one. Everyone knew this. No one had come even close. He was incredibly strong and brave. When his lord became an outlaw, he became an outlaw, too. They traveled in disguise, experiencing many adventures and, time after time, escaping sure death by a hair's breadth. Finally, there was only Benkei left alive along with his lord, Yoshitsune, and the woman who loved Yoshitsune more than life. She had chosen to stay with him and die rather than live without him.

"Finally, the three of them were cornered in a house in Oshu. The forces of Minamoto Yoritomo had caught up with them. Benkei told his master to flee out the back, and he would go out the front to hold off the enemy. Fire arrows were hitting the house and it was starting to burn.

"In the yard outside the house, there was a stir as Benkei emerged and was recognized. The troops hesitated, and the commander did not want to waste men. He knew that any who went after Benkei with a sword would die. 'Archers,' he called. One arrow hit Benkei, then another. Finally, he was riddled with arrows. He stopped walking, but he continued to stand. Everyone looked on, amazed.

"There is one story that Benkei had a pleased expression on his face, as if glad that his act had given his lord time to escape. In fact, though, Yoshitsune and his lover knew there was no hope of getting away and were still in the house, burning to death, even as Benkei was in the front being struck by arrows.

"Outside, there was a hush. Benkei did not move, but was still standing. No one could believe any man could still be on his feet after having been hit by so many arrows. Finally, an officer dared to ride his horse by where Benkei stood. The vibrations on the ground from the horse's weight caused the standing body to sway and then fall."

Stopping, I realize that I have likely just set a record for uninterrupted words while speaking with Admiral Yi, but as I look at him, I realize it is all right. He is as impressed with the story of Benkei as I was the first time I heard it.

This story has always been one that attracted me. It is one of those that from the first telling I knew that I would never forget. Except, Benkei is a figure of legend, with the exact truth hard to really know. He lived four centuries ago. What Admiral Yi has told me actually occurred, and very recently. The valiant death of the Japanese commander at Tanghangpo is the first time I have heard of anything happening in my lifetime that even remotely resembles the fate of Benkei. Yet this story, this battle, had truly happened here, in Choson, in this war.

Somehow I hoped that the spirit of this one Japanese would know that at least two persons alive on earth had compared his death with that of the legendary samurai, and that one of these two was himself a warrior as grand as Benkei. I cannot imagine that any samurai or daimyo could hope for anything more than that.

Part III

▼

First Moon, 1597–Seventh Moon, 1597

Includes:

- *A series of terrible personal tragedies for Admiral Yi, including treachery, demotion, trial for treason, and the death of someone held to be most dear.*
- *The Priest Wonho makes a new friend.*
- *An old friend surveys the Priest Wonho's past.*
- *Disaster for the Korean Navy.*

The second of the monstrous swords that Admiral Yi is said to have kept near him is also inscribed with his words. This sword, and the inscription upon it, can also be viewed today at Hyonchungsa. As with the first, this sword is dedicated to his fight against all enemies of his land and people. In English, his words on this sword could be read:

Once this sword is brandished,
the country will run with blood.

Chapter 21

The Arrest

Of the First and Second Moon, 1597

It is the saddest thing I have ever seen.

It is the most horrible thing I have ever heard of.

It is unjust beyond anything that I could ever have imagined.

Admiral Yi arrested and his command taken away. This ridiculousness spawns from a royal decree.

Admiral Yi tied with the red rope of the criminal and no longer an Admiral, but, instead, a prisoner accused of treason. This travesty is said to be ordered by the royal court.

Admiral Yi bound in a cart in a cage, hauled through towns in the public view for the purpose of humiliation and disgrace.

Admiral Yi, being transported north to Seoul for trial and possible execution. Can the King truly agree with this? Is there no sense anywhere, no brains, no understanding of the reality of what this will likely mean?

And worse, if there can be worse. Won Kyun has been given Admiral Yi's command. This is a good thing? He has lost every battle in which he has held the command. He does not follow orders well and gives them even more poorly and injudiciously. He fights heartily only when he sees things are going to our advantage, and otherwise, tries not to be around.

Who is laughing harder, the Japanese or the demons of hell that will soon have so many more Korean souls to torment due to this decision? Is Won Kyun happy now that he and his Western Confucianists have won the day? Now that he actually is in Admiral Yi's shoes, does he believe he can come close to filling them?

I cannot meditate. I am lost as a priest, for now. The world's doings have ensnared me, and it is as the Buddha said. Desire is the root of all pain and misery, and my desire for what is correct and for what is just is causing me more anguish than I could have imagined. Admiral Yi is the most admirable and honorable man I have ever met, and also likely the smartest and the most courageous. To see him treated this way is unbearable.

* * * *

I do not want to write of this. It is thirty years since it happened, and it still is painful. Yet, I need to. The abbot has reviewed my writings and has noticed a gap. He correctly noted that I had written nothing about the time of the Admiral's arrest.

Regarding this, the abbot has correctly stated that what has happened is what has happened, and that to be attached to it is not correct. He said that he believed the only point to remembering the past is to help us live a better "Now," and, of course, he is correct. He also said to me, for the first time, that one of the reasons he wanted me to write my memories of Admiral Yi is that often the lives of those who are considered to be great are more meaningful as examples to those who are just starting to learn. Once further along the path one sees that what humankind judges to be great is actually irrelevant. But, in the beginning, many new monks and priests pay attention more closely to the lives of the heroes than to those of the nondescript.

I was impressed that the abbot thought that Admiral Yi, a Confucianist, was at least in some ways a suitable role model for aspiring Buddhist monks and priests. I agree with him certainly. Now I see at least part of why he has me writing. Perhaps my writings will be of use some day.

Except, right now, while remembering the Admiral's arrest, while reliving his being transported north to Seoul, and then the cold days and icy nights waiting for news while being fed mostly fear by the rumors while he was being judged.... Feeling all of this again does not make the writing of it any easier.

Chapter 22

The Accusation
Of the First and Second Moon, 1597

The abbot has also asked me to make sure to write what I know of the accusation against Admiral Yi. He knows by the look on my face how distasteful this is, but he seems to feel it is significant. Of course, it is important, but …

I was well known and trusted by many of Admiral Yi's associates by the time of his arrest. They told me what they could about what had happened and why. Plus, there was no other topic of conversation in the whole province anyway. There were many wild stories flying about. However, even the wildest of the rumors were not as stupid or as bizarre as the actual accusation.

It was when I heard the charge that I remembered the story about Oda Nobunaga I had told Admiral Yi five years before. Suddenly, I saw the similarity. The Japanese had used their dead leader's trick. They had made up a story to be used against an important enemy commander, and the enemy had swallowed the lie. Now the Japanese tricksters could sit back and let the Korean people kill their own greatest military leader.

Ever since, I have wondered if the Admiral saw the similarity. I will never know. From the time of his arrest until his death, he was certainly too busy to talk about it.

"May Yojiro rot in Hell," are the kindest words I hear about the spy. Yojiro's ridiculous story had tricked a Korean general, an otherwise good man named Kim Ung-so. The spy, Yojiro, professing to be a loyal Korean who had sneaked away from Japanese controlled territory, had told General Kim Ung-so a most wonderful tale. From what I learned it went something like this:

"General Kim, I am a humble man, Yojiro, a loyal Korean who has been forced to work for the Japanese. I have been employed in the headquarters of the Japanese commander Yukinaga. This Yukinaga is a typical Japanese military commander. He is arrogant, loud, and generally disdainful of all things Korean. However, this has had a good result in one way. Yukinaga hates Korea and wants to go home. He wants Hideyoshi to give up and call the troops home. Yukinaga says this is now a futile war.

"Except, Hideyoshi was angered by what he thought was duplicity on the part of the Chinese envoy Shen Wei-ching. Hideyoshi now wants to teach the Chinese a hard lesson, and of course to do that, he must attack them by land through our country, Korea. Therefore, the Taiko has ordered another Japanese Commander, Kato Kiyomasa, to assemble another huge army and with it to sail to Korea to renew the war.

"Although nothing in myself, I have been forced to work around the Japanese for so long that I know very well that my old commander, Yukinaga, hates Kato Kiyomasa. One time, a Japanese even gave me a kick and said, "You are lucky you are only a Korean. If you were Kato Kiyomasa and without rank, you would suffer worse in this camp.' Yukinaga hates Kato, and it seems that Kato returns the feeling.

"I have thought about this a lot. Yukinaga, the arrogant Japanese bastard for whom I have been forced to work, hates Korea and wants to go home. He also hates Kato, who is coming to Korea with more troops, which means Yukinaga will have to stay here longer. Unless …

"I was delivering items to the command tent when I heard words to the effect of 'Wouldn't it be a shame if a typhoon hit Kato's fleet as it sailed to Korea. Then Kato would be gone, and the Taiko would have to call the rest of us home.'

"I almost believe, General, that Yukinaga meant for me to hear these words. I also was 'accidentally' able to overhear the dates upon which the fleet is supposed to arrive."

General Kim was not held to be a stupid man. However, he believed Yojiro. Excitedly, he sent word of this important information to the Supreme Korean Military Commander, Field Marshal Kwon Yul, the hero of Haengju. Kwon Yul had been promoted to the number one military post in the land. He was even the superior of Admiral Yi. In his message, General Kim recommended that the Korean naval forces be apprised of the situation, and that Admiral Yi could be the leader of the military "typhoon" which would sink Kato and his army before they reached Korea.

So I began to summarize the ridiculousness. The plot started with the Japanese. Yukinaga, likely with his "enemy" Kato's knowledge, coaching their agent Yojiro on what to say and do. Yojiro was very convincing when he spoke with General Kim. General Kim then went to Field Marshal Kwon Yul, the hero of horse washing at Haengju. And Kwon Yul, great man though he was, fell for it, too. On the 21st day of the first moon of 1597, Field Marshal Kwon Yul actually visited Admiral Yi in person to advise that the Korean fleet should use this intelligence by sailing out and destroying Kato and his army soon to be arriving in a huge, well-protected convoy from Japan.

I was not a member of Admiral Yi's staff. All I knew was that Field Marshal Kwon Yul had come to camp to talk with Admiral Yi. I, of course, never heard the things said in private by them. I did note great concern among the staff after the meeting, which had happened on the 21st. Happily, I also noticed a great sense of relief in the officers of Admiral Yi the next day, the 22nd. I did not speak to the Admiral himself at all on these days.

It was a few days after that I heard what had happened. The matters discussed in the meeting between the Field Marshal and the Admiral on the 21st had been military secrets, but everything had changed with a message from our outpost on Ungchon the next day. The message from our observers at Ungchon is what had brought the relief I had sensed.

Over wine one night, an officer who knew me felt safe to talk about it. "The Admiral had been ordered by the Field Marshal to attack the Japanese Fleet as it passed near the island of Tsushima. The Field Marshal believed the story which had been told him regarding a rivalry between two of the Japanese leaders and how one of them, Yukinaga, had let slip the other's date of arrival with thousands of troops.

"Admiral Yi knew this would be a terrible place for our outnumbered ships to fight, and that the huge Japanese numbers would give them a virtually insurmountable advantage in such a location. The Admiral also suspected that the whole thing was a trick and didn't want to carry out the attack for that reason, too.

"Except, he had been told to go by Kwon Yul, the Field Marshal, the man appointed as our Supreme Military Commander by the King. What a mess! As commander of the fleets, he did not wish to order his ships into what was likely a trap, and even if it was not, we would likely lose. The whole thing could prove to be a hopeless and suicidal mission either way. However, not to sail as ordered would place him in a state of insubordination, and we know how much his enemies at the royal court would love to hear about that."

We both made a face. By now, the goings-on at court were less and less a secret. We knew of Admiral Yi's enemies, or at least of some of them. We still would never have foreseen how stupidly they could act. Or how soon we would find out.

The navy man concluded, "We are happy now because a message came in from Ungchon that Kato Kiyomasa, the Japanese commander we had been ordered out to intercept, actually had already arrived at Changmunpo on the 15th. The Japanese bastard we were supposed to intercept this week was actually already here a week ago! There's no way to follow that order now." He smiled wryly. "A dispatch with this information was, of course, sent immediately to Field Marshal Kwon Yul. No one could expect us to attack Kato at sea while he is coming here when, in fact, he has already arrived, could they?"

I was relieved to hear of this happy outcome to what could have been a terrible development. The wine tasted better after hearing this news.

Then it turned out that yes, someone could. They could expect Admiral Yi to have caught Kato at sea even though Kato had actually arrived at least six days before the order to ambush the Japanese reinforcements had been given.

The Admiral's enemies at the royal court convinced the King that the Admiral had missed a wonderful opportunity to crush the Japanese and to kill one of their top commanders. Remonstrators of the Court insisted that Admiral Yi needed to be punished. From far away in Seoul, the details of who had done what and when were at best fuzzy. The King, who certainly could not have known what had actually happened, eventually agreed with them. After years of all the haranguing and lying intrigues at court, he was worn down. He gave the order. Admiral Yi was officially accused of having been disloyal and insubordinate. He was to be arrested and brought to Seoul for interrogation and to be judged.

Horrified, none of us could believe that this was happening. Of course, we knew that the charges were nonsense. We could not believe that any sane person would believe any of it. It was like a nightmare, except that we were not asleep and waking could not save us.

We all knew the outcome for Admiral Yi if he were to be found guilty. It was death.

Chapter 23

Transport

Of the Second and Third Moon, 1597

I had no real home. I had only the loosest of affiliations with my home temple. This was enough to permit me to go along my way when the authorities chose to check me. In fact, I was virtually an unaffiliated priest, free to roam at will. I had not joined a guerilla band, having been ordered not to. I was in Hansando because the Admiral had asked me to be there, and he was not there when the news came.

When the arresting party arrived, Admiral Yi was at sea with the fleet off of Kadok. Upon receiving the news, he returned to Hansando immediately and dutifully turned over everything to his successor, Won Kyun. The items he signed over included over 50,000 bushels of rice and other grains, two tons of gunpowder, and 300 cannon and various guns besides those on the ships. The Admiral maintained a quiet demeanor and did everything calmly and thoroughly. He did not call for me at this time, and I could say nothing to him. I could only watch from a distance and listen to the tidal wave of rumors about what was happening.

I was able to be nearby on the day that he left on the journey north to judgment in Seoul. I nearly fainted when I saw the red rope and that they intended to put it on the Admiral. I became dizzy. I saw that Kim Taejin had to be held back from attacking the functionary who had produced it and was moving toward the Admiral.

I was just near enough to hear the Admiral's strong voice ask, "Was this ordered by the King?"

The man with the rope must have said yes.

Then I heard the Admiral say, "This has been ordered by His Majesty. Let no person gainsay it!"

I believe some of his men wept at these words.

And then the Admiral was taken away toward Seoul, on the 26th of the Second Moon of the year 1597. Part of the journey was by land, and part by sea. He was, for much of the journey, kept in a cage pulled along on an oxcart. A heavy guard was necessary, especially in towns and cities.

The heavy guard had been ordered by Admiral Yi's enemies as protection from a dangerous criminal and any treasonous plots he might hatch when he realized he was finally being brought to justice for his terrible crimes. Instead, it turned out the heavy guard was needed more because the common people along the road so vigorously protested the arrest and taking away of the one man, the only man, they trusted to save them from the Japanese.

I had to answer to no temple, and I was a member of no guerrilla band. Admiral Yi had never made me an official member of the navy. I had no fixed home and was, for those years, amazingly able to travel about freely. I even had a small travel pass from southern naval headquarters attesting to my loyal, and not to be questioned, status.

I could, therefore, go where I wished. I chose to go toward Seoul.

I would follow the Admiral, keeping him in my view whenever possible. When he was pulled through a town, I would be in the crowd. When he was traveling through the countryside, I would be just ahead or just behind the party transporting the prisoner to Seoul.

It was painful to hear the cries of the crowds of common people. "Admiral, you cannot go! Now we will all die!" There were also angry protests at the guards and functionaries. These members of the arresting party quickly learned that just about the only safe response was something like, "We follow the exact instructions of our King in this matter."

Early in the journey there had been a cry, "Where are you taking our Admiral?" and one of the guards had gruffly replied, "We take a traitor to justice." The guard was rewarded for his brilliant response by a stone that hit him in the head and knocked him to the ground. There had almost been a riot. I was surprised that no one ended up dead in the melee. Yet, through it all, Admiral Yi sat still.

Before his arrest, he could have and would have stopped the whole mess with a few loud words in his commanding voice. Now, though, he said nothing. I wondered if it was because he was officially a prisoner. Keeping order was no longer his duty. He was no longer a trusted officer of the King. From beyond the crowd, the shouts, and the fighting, I watched him. He sat impassively in the cage on the ox cart. He never said a word.

It was in this town that I noticed another person. He also seemed to be keeping pace with the Admiral's party. He was big, strong, and I knew him immediately. It was Kim Taejin. He saw me, too. On that day, we simply nodded at each other, knowing that at night the party would stop, and we could talk then. Better not to be too conspicuous.

"What are you doing here, Taejin?" I ask him. It is very cold, being wintertime. He was dressed the same as me, in thick woolen robes. Of course, his were not the gray robes of a priest.

"Same as you, Priest Wonho, I am sure."

"How did you get away?" I mean that he is a member of the navy, and he is not free to travel at will, as am I.

"Orders." He has never been a man of many words, and he often enjoys making others, or at least me certainly, dig for the information desired.

"Orders? I doubt Won Kyun sent you along to Seoul to watch out for Admiral Yi."

"Hardly. Neither did Captain Yi Ok-ki." Taejin took out a piece of paper. I could barely read it in the poor light, but I was able to see that Kim Taejin had been granted an official leave of absence due to serious personal family problems by Yi Ok-ki, Naval Commander for a period of up to three months. The leave of absence began—I look hard to read the date—the 20th of the month.

For a moment, I think of Captain Yi Ok-ki. He is, all in all, a good man. The more he came to trust Admiral Yi, the better a commander he himself had become. I know that he has been commended for bravery in battle by Admiral Yi and promoted to his present high rank as a result. He is no doubt as joyful as I am about this turn of events. How horrible it must be for him to be under the command of Won Kyun. I realize that it would be just like Captain Ok-ki to want Kim Taejin close to Admiral Yi as much as possible at this time. I wonder for a moment whether it had been Kim Taejin's idea or Captain Ok-ki's? I decide on the former with the captain agreeing to it instantly.

I look again at the paper in my hand. "Hmmm.... This is dated by Captain Ok-ki just before Won Kyun took command."

"Yes. A coincidence, I am sure."

The way he says it makes me smile. Then I say, "But I noticed you were still in camp on the 26th...." I do not say that I also noticed that he was ready to tear the head off of the man with the red rope headed towards the Admiral.

"Yes. My departure was … delayed." This time it is my eyes that smile.

"But now that you are at last able to make your way to take care of these 'serious personal family problems,' it just happens that the road …"

"Yes," he nods. "The serious personal matters just happen to take me towards Seoul." He maintains an expressionless face. "I take it you have business in Seoul, too, Priest Wonho?"

I looked at him silently for a moment, do not even bother to nod, and then reach up with one hand and grab a big shoulder. "I am very glad you are here."

"I, too, am glad there are two of us, Wonho."

It is the first time he has used my name. Before it has always been Priest Wonho or Priest. And he said "us."

Of course, Kim Taejin sensed it in me. He knew as soon as he saw me this afternoon. There was nowhere else I could be. There was no other place he could be either. It would have been awful beyond words to be at Hansando thinking of Admiral Yi as a prisoner and possibly being mistreated. It would have been impossible to have been back at Hansando watching Won Kyun in the Admiral's headquarters.

I had been at Hansando because that was where Admiral Yi was. I was there to serve Admiral Yi, and only to serve Admiral Yi. And I know Kim Taejin felt the same way. He likely would have headed toward Seoul with or without orders, even though without orders he would have been, technically, a deserter, and himself subject to execution. I was very thankful for Captain Yi Ok-ki's wisdom in giving him the leave papers.

We decided that night to alternate. One day, one of us would precede the party, and the other follow it. The next day, we would reverse our positions. If the party went by boat or ship for part of the journey, whichever of us was in the lead that day would arrange the best transportation possible in order to stay near them. Each night, we would meet near where the party was spending the night. One of us would walk a perimeter just beyond a long arrow shot from wherever the Admiral was staying while the other slept nearby. We were correct in assuming that the heavy guard around the Admiral during the day would not be so diligent at night. We would each, by turns, patrol and sleep. We would do what we could to make sure everyone and everything was as it should be near the Admiral.

We were both highly suspicious by this time. The fact that the Admiral had been arrested and might be facing execution was bad enough. However, his enemies at court had to realize that the King might eventually recognize the truth. And if he did come to understand the facts, he would certainly not execute Admiral Yi. Therefore, his enemies might try to arrange an accident. Admiral Yi, after all, was a prisoner. He was constrained and unable to maneuver. (Oh, how every military part of him must have hated this! Thank goodness he was also a philosopher.) He was in a relatively helpless and defenseless position. He was certainly much too vulnerable to an "assassination by a Japanese agent," or to some tainted food, or … There were too many unspeakable possibilities. Plus, it was not just his enemies at court who wanted him out of the way. It might be that the Japanese themselves would actually try to get a suicidal spy close enough to Admiral Yi to make sure he would never return.

We were probably correct to have been suspicious. It was a good idea to do what we could to protect the Admiral at this time. However, during the journey, Taejin and I uncovered no new major conspiracies or problems. We discovered no actual would-be assassins. It is likely that what we did had no significance at all, except perhaps in one way that I never would have guessed and did not find out about until months later. But, together we did what we could to escort the Admiral to Seoul and to insure his safe arrival.

In actuality, what we did was little, but at least we felt we were doing something. When we arrived, and the Admiral was shut up in the royal prisons, we felt fully how horribly helpless we were. We felt absolutely futile. We could do little or nothing for him, except pray. That I did.

But I would have been nowhere else, and I know Kim Taejin felt exactly the same way.

It was on the 4th day of the Third Moon of 1597 that we arrived in Seoul. Taejin was in front and me behind. We watched as Admiral Yi was taken inside the walls. We imagined his being put into a prison cell. At least on the road, we could see him. Now we could not do even that.

His time before the King and the smooth snake-tongued talkers of the court was at hand. It was now time for the interrogations, the arguments, and then for the King's judgment.

All we could really do now was to wait.

Chapter 24

Waiting for the King
Of the Third Moon, 1597

Admiral Yi is behind the walls where we can no longer precede or follow. He is a prisoner in Seoul. All we can do is try to be patient. It could be weeks, or even months.

Kim Taejin and I have discussed what he should do. He is of the military, but he is on leave. It is best for him to stay unnoticed as much as possible. Therefore, he comes with me to a temple very close to Seoul. Sad to say, in these Confucianist times no Buddhist temples are allowed within the walls of Seoul itself. However, this temple, Bong-whan, is just a kilometer outside to the west. That it was not destroyed by the Japanese might simply have been an oversight on their part, or the fact that they were too busy pillaging other places. Plus, Bong-whan temple is not rich.

Abbot Park, the head of this temple, is an old friend. I have known him for over forty years, since we were children. He greets me with warmth and glad feelings. He looks much older than when I last saw him, and while he used to run to roundness, now his short body is very thin. His head is shaved completely, but he looks like he would be very gray if he had hair.

He used to have only lines from smiling and laughter. The last years have been difficult for him—no wonder.

As youths, Park and I were close, but then we chose different paths. As I have remained on the road, with only the loosest of affiliations, he has found a temple to call his home, and then his own. Now my old friend Park is this temple's leader. This is not surprising. He always seemed to be headed in such a way. In fact, many of the friends and acquaintances of my youth have become abbots or other persons of note.

On the journey north accompanying the Admiral, I had thought about where to go, and the temple of the Abbot Park stood out as the best choice. For one, I heard that it had at least partially survived the occupation of the Japanese. Most temples hadn't. Plus, he was an old friend. Except, for the past few decades Park and I have seen each other only infrequently. In fact, as I put the dates together I was very surprised to realize that we have not seen each other for almost seven years.

Over the formalities of tea and greetings, he says that he is glad that I am alive, and that too many of us aren't, thanks to the war. He tells us what things had been like with the Japanese, how, in fact, our allies, the Chinese, had not been much better, and of the specific happenings regarding his temple. Nobody has had it easy. On the positive side, most of this temple's members are still alive, and the temple itself has not been totally destroyed, though another one, in particular, that had been is painful to hear about.

"The Japanese were not kind in Soraksan," he says. He is looking at me intently as he says this. He knows how I feel about this area and these temples.

"No! Not Hyangsongsa!" I read his face. Can it be true? "Why? It is the oldest Son temple in Asia! The Japanese have Zen temples of their own! Why would they destroy it?"

Memories come to me. There are many great temples, and some of them are small, the ones we never hear of, like Kaesimsa. But this one, big and ancient as it was, deserved its reputation. The area of Soraksan ("snow-covered peaks") in which Hyangsongsa resided is one of the most beautiful mountain places in all of Korea. The peaks are fantastic. The morning mists, like spirits, come to visit, and in the autumn the changing leaves give a view unmatched this side of paradise.

Not only was the temple itself wonderful, but its hermitages were, to me, unsurpassable. These wonderful smaller places for solitude and meditation were, as with most temples, within an hour or two of walking distance, except possibly in midwinter. Then they might be unreachable for weeks. I remember especially the paradise of Kyejo-am, and the diamond cave, Kumgang-gul. Memories ...

Kumgang-gul—is there any place in the world as perfect for meditation as that wonderful cave on the cliff face of the rocky pyramid peak? It is so difficult to climb you wonder how even the great sage Wonhyo did it the first time.

Perhaps, I once surmised, he had made it only because he was inspired by the name. The rocky peak he climbed above the beautiful icy pools of Pison-dae is named Miruk-bong ("Buddha of the Future Peak"). Perhaps the name helped him to float the last stage of the ascent. I know that I could never have made it without the ropes, and I am not a poor climber.

Wonhyo, the priest of priests. I have always wondered if my abbot gave me the Buddhist name of Wonho in tribute to this legendary Buddhist. Certainly, my particular admiration for him was well known. If this were so, I have wondered if he gave me this name to encourage me in my attempts to emulate him, or whether it was to keep me from pride, since Wonhyo was unmatchable, at least by me certainly.

Wonhyo had founded the hermitage of Kumgang-gul. He had also meditated at Kyejo-am, the hermitage called "paradise" next to the rocking boulder. Hundul-bawi. A new thought strikes!

"Hundul-bawi! The rocking boulder. It is all right, isn't it?"

Abbot Park just looks at me. He has said nothing while I was remembering. "If they tried to knock over the rocking boulder, they failed. As to everything else at Kyejo-am and Kungang-gul—the caves are still there, anyway." He says quietly, "And buildings can be rebuilt."

His answer stills me. I realize that the spirit of these places has not been lost. It is too strong. It cannot be killed. And even what the Japanese have destroyed of the buildings can be replaced. Hyangsongsa is more than the buildings, after all. And the caves where Chajang, Wonhyo, and Ulsang lived and meditated are still there. And Buddha would ask that even when those mountains someday crumble, what difference would even this make? And not just Buddha. The abbot has asked me in his own way just now.

"You are right, of course," I say. He sees the change in my energy, and nods. We both reach for our cups of tea at the same time. Then, for a while, we talk of the fates of mutual acquaintances and of other temples and places, and then, finally, it is my turn. He has been very polite in not asking what I have been doing, where I have been, or why I am there. He also has not directed any inquiries at all toward my travel companion, Kim Taejin.

I remember part way through all of this that Abbot Park is one of the men who is aware that I have some Japanese ancestry. He also is aware that I have spent years in Japan and that I know that language and people well. Yet he says nothing of it. He knows I will have to talk, and that then he will know how to handle us. We have been the best of friends, but these are strange times, and now I have not seen him for seven years. I have Japanese blood and, for five of the last seven years, Choson has been at war with Japan where I have ancestors and where I have lived for a long time. He knows this. Does he suspect I have become a spy for the Japanese, or that I have mixed loyalties? I might wonder if I were in his position.

Abbot Park stops talking and asks if I would like more tea. Actually, I would as the tea is hot and the day is freezing outside. I take a sip of tea, knowing it is my time. I begin directly.

"You must know the full truth. I was in the south just before the war started, and a naval commander named Yi wanted someone who spoke Japanese and knew of the island country's ways and history. I met this commander. He put me through various types of tests, including some of language, of knowledge, and of loyalty. It seems I passed his examinations for he then decided to avail himself of my unworthy services. I have been attached to his service since before the war began and still consider myself to be at his disposal.

"My friend here," I nod toward Kim Taejin, "is also in the service of this naval commander." The abbot's eyebrows have already risen when I mention the Naval Commander Yi in the south. I had specifically not said 'Yi Sun-sin,' but knew that I did not need to. Now Abbot Park seems about to ask the obvious question regarding Kim Taejin, so I quickly continue, "although currently Kim Taejin is here in Seoul on a properly issued leave of absence to take care of 'urgent personal matters.'"

The abbot's eyes show much, but I do not know what it is he is feeling. I can tell the abbot needs time to think. He nods toward Kim Taejin and says politely that he honors those who fight for Choson and that he trusts that the urgent personal matters turn out well for him, to which Kim Taejin responds with the appropriate thanks. But Park's true thoughts are not on that dialogue. That is obvious.

It is probably only a few moments before he says anything else, but it seems a long time. I wonder how much our old friendship counts and if he is thinking about how to throw us out of his temple unnoticed since we are associated with a prisoner accused of treason. Then he begins softly speaking.

"You had been in the south …"

I nod.

"And just before the war started, you were called to assist a naval commander …"

I agree again.

"And this naval commander finds your background in Japan and with that other language useful …"

"Yes."

"And attaches you to his retinue …"

I need to clarify. "Well, not officially. He just ordered me to stay nearby, and …"

Kim Taejin interjects, "And not to join any of the fighting Buddhist guerilla bands. The Admiral wanted Wonho near him. Plus, the Admiral sent Wonho on missions. He …"

At the same time Abbot Park and I both raise our hands to ask Kim Taejin to stop. The abbot likely does not wish to know too much, at least not yet. And I do not want to be made to sound important, for I am not. There is a part of me that does appreciate Kim Taejin's words, though.

I continue, "… and I have been with this Admiral in some capacity ever since."

It is Abbot Park's turn to nod. He breathes deeply, and sighs. "We are doomed, it seems, to live in interesting times." He says it in a way that brings the full feeling of the Chinese saying to life. Indeed, the last five years have been very interesting.

Then the abbot speaks, but more quickly. "The whole capitol is abuzz with word of the great warrior from the south. This Admiral has beaten the Japanese fleets repeatedly and convincingly. He is the man who stopped the Japanese ships from sailing around to the west and bringing supplies to the enemy armies that had occupied Seoul and all of the north. This man is said to have welcomed all loyal subjects of Choson to fight for Korea against the Japanese and to have inspired Buddhist monks and priests to join him. He is said to have looked for those among the Buddhists who showed courage and leadership and to have given them commands of troops and of ships. He is also said to have cared for the poor and the refugees, to have given them aid, and to have found them land to farm."

His voice changes. "The whole capitol is talking of this man, who likely saved us all with his courage and leadership. They are all discussing how this hero is now accused by his enemies at court of horrible things. There are those who say that this man is guilty of insubordination, cowardice, malice towards the throne, and, to listen to them, likely also the burning of live babies over a fire."

There is another tone now. "Still others say that the man was once great, but now has lost himself to intrigue—that he was once loyal, but now he has become dangerous, a threat to the throne itself."

His voice is not loud, but the question is huge. "What is the truth, Wonho?"

In my reply, I have no need to lie, and I know that Park will sense this. I put as much feeling into my words as he had in his question, though I, too, speak calmly.

"Admiral Yi Sun-sin is the greatest warrior who lives. He is the most loyal, intelligent, and worthy man I have ever known. He has done all he can to help our people while leading our fighting in the war and is totally devoted to the expulsion of the Japanese from the Kingdom of Choson. Anyone who says anything different is making the most horrible of mistakes or is the most dastardly of liars."

The abbot continues to look at me, and then his eyes change. I notice what could almost be a tiny, wry grin. His words are quiet. "I thought so."

He takes a sip of tea, and then puts it down firmly. It is obvious he has decided. Then he says firmly, "As abbot of this humble temple I hereby offer a place to sleep and a sharing of our meager meals to a wandering priest and to his travel companion. This invitation shall extend for as long as their various missions keep them here. I wish them well and will pray that things turn out as they would have them."

I begin to bow and speak my thanks, thinking that he is done, but he surprises me. He turns to Kim Taejin and says in a quieter voice, "I have known Wonho since before he was a priest. He was not even named

Wonho then." Then he told Kim Taejin my pre-Buddhist name, the one my parents had given me. "We were novices together. And even then, he had a way of getting into the thick of things." Kim Taejin says nothing, but is obviously interested. The abbot goes on.

"As a teen he managed somehow to get assigned as a menial on a trip to many of the most famous temples of China. He was gone for a few years and had some incredible experiences. He also learned a lot."

"I am aware of some of what he learned," said Taejin. At these words, I remember Kim Taejin's part in my judgment the day in Yosu after I dealt with the two drunken sailors who were assaulting the woman, and then with their three rescuers. I do not think the abbot knows I ever learned anything of the martial arts. I hope that he will assume Kim Taejin is talking of my Chinese language ability.

The abbot simply goes on. "Then he went to Japan, as you also know." The big man nods as the abbot continues, "And now I meet him again only to find he is somehow connected to our kingdom's greatest warrior and has even gone on missions for him."

He inclines his head to the side. "And we Buddhist priests, perhaps our biggest quest is for peace, for the meditative life, for time to become that which is the true part of us, that which is part of the all-and-the-not-all. We know that all here is illusion, and that to be attached to this illusion, to have desires for parts of it, causes the illusion called pain and fear. That is why some of us retreat to temples, and others roam the mountains and hills.

"My friend Wonho makes me wonder, Mr. Kim," he continues. "How does a priest seeking non-attachment and looking for peace and enlightenment go from adventures in China to surviving the civil wars and persecution of Buddhists in Japan to becoming a semiofficial assistant to the great Admiral who is now the most dangerous man in the kingdom to be associated with?"

Abbot Park is looking at Kim Taejin, and when he asks this question, I watch the big warrior, too. Kim Taejin is obviously hoping he is not expected to answer, and remains silent as we both look at him. He hesitates and then says, "Some men are just lucky, I guess." At this, the abbot laughs and I smile.

When Abbot Park glances over at me, all I can say is, "I am not so sure I would call a lot of those times 'lucky,'" which makes him laugh harder.

When he stops laughing, he says, "I have not laughed like that for many months." He smiled for a few more moments. "Thank goodness, I as the simple abbot of this temple have merely let an old friend, a fellow Buddhist priest, and his quiet travel companion stay here for a while...." He sighs.

"Wonho." He is speaking very seriously now. "We will have much to speak of, when the time is right." He pauses and I receive the full strength of his powerful gaze. "Until the time is right, a low profile, please."

He has given us as much as I could have hoped for. Food, warmth, shelter in the winter, and, even better, warm friendship even though we have come in connection with a man arrested and on trial for treason. I bow and say, "Most certainly. Our thanks for your gracious hospitality." I add the correct Buddhist words and phrases and bow again, sincerely and deeply, as does Kim Taejin.

The abbot blesses us and calls for his assistant. The young priest comes in with a rush of cold air and is told to take us to a certain room. The abbot also informs him that our stay could be for some days, and that we will be joining in the temple meals whenever we wish. The young priest's face betrays nothing.

It is a cold walk to the room the abbot has given us. If anything, the northern wind has picked up. But upon arriving there, we find the small room to be dry and warm. The young priest tells us that the underfloor heating will be attended to periodically, mentions the times for chanting and ceremonies to me, gives us the meal times, and then is gone.

"Wonho," says Kim Taejin. "I am glad this abbot is your friend." I nod. Then Kim Taejin surprises me. "Someday, if we are stuck here for awhile, perhaps you could tell me what it was like for you in Japan."

Each day that we waited at the temple, I prayed for a just resolution to the matter of Admiral Yi at the court. I had prayed each day throughout the journey, too, either at a temple we were near or, if one were not available, by myself.

But waiting in Seoul for those weeks, I prayed more, and I worked in the temple. I wanted to keep busy. If I did not keep busy, I would think too much. I would ponder and worry about what was happening. All I knew for sure was that the Admiral had many enemies, that these enemies had the ear of the King, and that they were sure to be attacking Admiral Yi as strongly as they could. However, as I heard from a few people, he also had supporters and friends.

Kim Taejin worked with me many of the days. Of course, he kept up with the news of what was happening with the Admiral as best he could. He made contact with the proven allies of the Admiral that he knew of in the city. He did this both to request information and to let them know he was present and available to be of service as soon as the Admiral was released. From these sources, he got nothing solid. From them and from everyone else, all we heard were rumors. Most were bad, and we did not want to believe them.

It was cold working outside in the Seoul winter, but Kim Taejin was a strong and active man and sitting quietly inside was not his way. So, when he was not out making contacts and trying to find out what was going on with the Admiral, he helped me with the work. Staying active helped him not to worry, too. We talked about many things during these hours. Not so much at any one time, for neither of us was garrulous. However, over the many days and tasks there was much time, so I did as Kim Taejin had asked and told him of my years in Japan. He was very interested, especially regarding anything to do with their military.

Partly in return, Kim Taejin talked to me of the Admiral's family. What he said was largely new to me. Until then I had only seen his sons as they went around the camp. There was often one or two of them around, and I knew what they looked like. But the Admiral had never talked to me in front of them. And, of course, when the Admiral did call for me, it was certainly not to discuss personal matters.

The husky attendant, of course, knew them quite well. He told me of the sons by his wife, who from oldest to youngest were Hoe, Yol, and Myon. At that time, Hoe was about 31, Yol 27, and the youngest, Myon, was barely 20. Taejin also mentioned that the Admiral had two other sons by his concubine, and that their names were Hun and Sin.

Kim Taejin told me that Admiral Yi was generally pleased and proud of his sons. (He, of course, never mentioned the Admiral's wife, and I maintained propriety and never asked of her. Confucinaist wives stay out of worldly matters. I did ask specifically of daughters, though, and it turned out that the Admiral had three of them, one by his wife, and two by his concubine.) He also told me that the Admiral had instructed his sons to stay at a distance while he was a prisoner. His words to his sons, said to one of them in front of the silent, ever-present attendant, had been clear.

Admiral Yi had reviewed the situation, saying that he believed that he had acted properly at all times. Then he said that his own belief regarding his actions was meaningless, that the King was certainly the only correct judge of a subject's behavior. Then he said in conclusion that as subjects of the King, his sons were to maintain proper decorum and behavior at all times. The last thing Admiral Yi did was to deliver careful instructions to take care of their mother and of their grandmother, for both had experienced poor health recently.

The loyal attendant said that this son, and likely all of them when they received his instructions, had not been happy about this, but that they knew they had to obey their father. Of course, the sons would do all they could for him, knew him to be innocent, and loved him as sons should love their father. But the message from their father had been clear. In essence, what he had said was that if what happened to him was bad, he would like to limit the penalties to himself, and not to have further punishments enacted upon his family. So, stay at home in Asan, take care of the women, and do or say nothing untoward.

I was not surprised, though, to hear that the family had followed his instructions regarding his sons, but had interpreted his injunction to mean that at least some of the nephews might just happen to be in Seoul to quietly keep an eye on how things went.

It was probably while working during a snowfall that Kim Taejin told me of the Admiral's nephews. There were six of them, the sons of Admiral Yi's older brothers. (One of these nephews, Wan, as well as the Admiral's oldest son, Hoe, I would later come to know quite well.) Admiral Yi's older brothers had both died while their children were young, and Admiral Yi had taken responsibility for their families. When he was away, the children lived with their grandmother, Admiral Yi's beloved mother. Sometimes, they could be with him, or he visited his family home in Asan and then he was like the father each of them no longer had.

Snowing ... it seemed that most of the time when we were working out in the temple yard, clearing paths and walkways of snow, the skies were letting go upon us with their infinite supply of frozen white crystals. It became our joke. "Have to move faster than the gods of the sky, Taejin." "Right, Wonho, we can out-sweep and out-shovel the gods ..." It was during these times I heard of the Admiral's family matters.

On one windy frozen-nose of a day, Taejin said, "The nephew, Wan, once mentioned a time when the Admiral had all of his family with him. Before the war when the Admiral was the magistrate at Chong-up, he received criticism due to feeding so many dependents and relatives at the public yamen house near the gate of the fortress. Under the Sok-Taejon law, this was definitely not appropriate. In response to this criticism, the Admiral waited until he knew that many of the complainers were around and said loudly, 'The extra mouths I have heard complained about are those of the families of my elder brothers who have died. Would any person prefer I leave these youngsters homeless and without food? I would rather be punished for feeding so many then to leave them in such a terrible condition.'"

Taejin stopped talking and kept shoveling. I had to ask, "Well, what happened?"

The big man looked at me and said, "What do you think? Who could argue with that? No more complaints were heard, that is for sure." He shoveled a bit more. "There were tears in the eyes, stirred by his compassion and by his words."

I kept moving snow as I thought about how Admiral Yi was a person who could bring tears over the plight of orphans or change an untrained crowd into fighters who could beat the best armies in the world. I wondered if I would ever see him again and dug especially hard into the snow.

"There was another story that his nephew Wan told me," said Taejin.

"Unfortunately, it is one that relates too closely to the Admiral's own situation now." Now he hit at the snow. "Years ago, before the war, Admiral Yi went to the royal prison to wish well to Chong On-sin, who had been the State Councilor of the Right. Chong On-sin had been charged with something terrible, and no one knew what would become of him, but the Admiral didn't care about things like that. To him, Chong On-sin was a good old man who had fallen upon hard times. While the Admiral was there, some of the jail officers came in drunk and were singing and laughing. Admiral Yi gave them that horrible look he can get and shouted, 'How can you play music and drink here? Whether guilty or not, one of the three State Councilors is here in this terrible place charged with a crime. Do you not feel anything—no pity, no sorrow?'"

In one of those strange coincidences, as Taejin had been speaking, the sound of music drifted into the temple grounds during a temporary easing of the winter wind. He heard it and shook his head. "I hope that now someone is there to tell them the same thing, if it is needed. I hope no one is stupid enough to have a loud and happy party while Admiral Yi is in a cell there."

I considered Taejin's words. I agreed with him, of course. But I was also thinking about how sad everything was. It was horribly sad that the Admiral had been arrested in the first place. It was also terrible that some idiotic jailers could even think of having a boisterous time of it in the vicinity of the Admiral's cell. Perhaps, even worse, it would probably take another person to shut them up. Based upon how Admiral Yi had remained silent in his cage in the oxcart during the near riot when the guard had called him a traitor, he would probably say nothing himself if the jailers should be so unfeeling. He would just sit there and listen.

Chapter 25

▼

All Right, For Now
Of the Fourth Moon, 1597

Admiral Yi was released from custody yesterday, and I am at the temple waiting for Kim Taejin to return. The news of his release was of course fantastic. He received a "Special Pardon" from the King. This, I understand by rumor, is in part due to the intercessions of the Prince Kyong-nim and of the Minister Chong Tak. If this is so, let them receive both blessings and praise.

However, not all the tidings are so good, but which is rumor and which is true I will not know until I hear from Taejin. He, of course, went to Admiral Yi as soon as he heard of his release. When Taejin returns, I will know the facts.

I wish I could have gone with him. I wanted to. But it seemed better not to go, and Taejin had understood my reasoning, having discussed it at length in our conversations about what to do should this day come. For me, I believe it to be more appropriate to wait. The Admiral is safe and certainly has no need of my protection now, if he ever did. Certainly there will be many around him, friends, family members, and military and government folk happy that their best commander is still alive. And I am but a Buddhist priest, after all, with no official duties.

As I wait, I summarize what I do know in my mind. With the coming of spring goes Admiral Yi from his cell. The Japanese cannot be happy. Especially since he is going to be moving south, towards them. And certainly his enemies at court did not get what they wanted.

That the Japanese and his own homegrown enemies are unhappy—these are good things. That he is alive is wonderful.

All of this is true, and I am glad of it. There are rumors I do not like, though.

I have already heard that the Admiral has not regained his rank. He is now the lowest in the forces, a simple private and is being sent south as the humblest of soldiers to the command of Field Marshal Kwon Yul. He is not under arrest, but officers of the court will escort him the whole way. Plus, Won Kyun is still the commander of the naval forces in the south.

Knowing this, but nothing else, I wait for word from the Admiral. Yesterday after Taejin left, I worked at the temple until dark and then meditated, and when he still had not returned when it was very late, I tried to get some sleep. I did not get much. I kept thinking about Admiral Yi and, also, about myself.

What I should do now is very unclear. Admiral Yi is no longer an Admiral. This could mean he would no longer feel it appropriate for me to be around in his unofficial service. He might not want me around at all any more, anyway. (And then what should I do? Join the bands of guerilla priests?)

When Kim Taejin heard of the Admiral's release, he believed he knew where the Admiral would go and wanted to get there immediately. Now, while very glad that the Admiral is alive and out of custody, I am wondering about me, the future, and what to do next, even though I know that this is not correct Buddhist thinking. We Buddhists know that in Truth there is only the now, the eternal moment in which we all reside, that time actually does not exist. I consider the words and intended meanings of my friend Abbot Park and whether I have been living a good life for a Buddhist priest. And as far as the right thing to do goes, the whole concept of "right" is … footsteps!

Kim Taejin bursts in. "Wonho! The Admiral looks so tired! He seems older! But I believe he will, sooner rather than later, be himself again. He is too much the warrior to stay down for long. His friends and many of his family were already at the house of Yun Kan's servant, near the South Gate, when he arrived. They kept on trying to cheer him up, and every new arrival kept offering him wine with which to celebrate. Everyone ended up quite drunk!

"But this morning the Admiral said to me—you know how he wakes up earlier than almost anyone else even if he has been drinking—the Admiral says, 'You and the Priest Wonho were like shadows around me on my journey north.' I said nothing, and he said, 'Where is Wonho now?' I told him.

"The Admiral nodded and asked me to tell you this: He says that he is no longer even an officer and that he has no business engaging the services of such a well-traveled and well-educated priest at this time. However, things in the south could change very quickly, and, if they do, your services would then again be much appreciated—that is, if they are still available."

I have never seen Kim Taejin like this. He is talking a mile a minute. He did not even hesitate to keep me in suspense before telling me what the Admiral had said. He goes on.

"What I think the Admiral means is that, unfortunately, there are rumors that not all is going well with Won Kyun as supreme naval commander in the south. The men are unhappy, the officers worried and uninspired by his leadership, and a great disaster could be forthcoming. Of course, we hope this doesn't happen, but even Captain Yi Ok-ki has predicted it! I heard this last night!"

I think again of how horrible it must be to be in the navy in the south right now. Virtually any commander would have had a hard time replacing Admiral Yi. He is unsurpassable. But to have to serve under Won Kyun, who is better at plotting and stabbing in the back than at command, and who has never been better than mediocre even on his best days, would be loathsome at the best of times. My heart goes out to Captain Yi Ok-ki, and the others there. There are many brave men at Hansando, and, unfortunately, the one man best fit to lead them can't, at least for now.

"Can you imagine being led by Won Kyun against a large Japanese fleet?" asks Taejin. "Admiral Yi can do it—he can find a way to win while horribly outnumbered, but can Won Kyun? Will he?"

The answer is horribly obvious. I look down, my expression probably too sad for me to want to be seen. But Taejin keeps going. Nothing can stop him right now.

"Wonho, the Admiral cannot order you to do anything, but, I hope that you will find a way to keep yourself free to join us, should the time come."

This is the first time Taejin has asked me anything of importance. To talk of Japan had helped to pass the time, but this is significant. I am touched by his words. My answer comes quickly, for I have long considered what I would do if the Admiral's message was like this.

"Tell the Admiral that to me he still is, and always will be, the Admiral. I will find a way to be fed and fit and free for when the time comes for him to again be doing what he should be doing, which is leading our navy against the Taiko's pirates."

Taejin beams at my words. Again I am surprised by his open display of feelings. The stress of the last weeks is showing on him. He cannot stop talking and otherwise expressing himself. Finally, he can breathe again.

Then he says that, before going back, he must find Abbot Park to share his thanks for his hospitality for the past weeks. I decide to share some of my feelings with him, too, before he goes.

"Taejin, I must say that there is part of me that envies you."

"What do you mean?"

"You are again to be with the Admiral daily, and me, not yet, and even in the days to come, only sometimes."

Taejin takes in my words. His eyes close for a moment, and when he opens them, I see the truth of someone who has seen the future.

"Your time will come, Wonho." He pauses. "Until it does, stay healthy, friend."

He stands up to find and bid thanks and goodbye to Abbot Park and then to hurry back to Admiral Yi.

Chapter 26

"How Could the Sun in Heaven Be So Dark?"

Of the Fourth Moon to the Seventh Moon, 1597

Sometimes life is too hard.

Admiral Yi's beloved mother died. The Admiral found out twelve days after he was released from prison. He got the news on the day on which they were supposed to meet. Despite her weak and sickly condition, she had been traveling by boat to meet her beloved and newly-released-from-prison son.

I heard later that when he got the news, Admiral Yi collapsed to the ground and said, "How could the sun in heaven be so dark?"

I can only imagine how difficult this must have been for him. He was a Confucianist, and to them the bond between parent and child is particularly strong. For a true Confucianist it is as natural to honor one's parents as it is for a Buddhist priest to meditate or for a mudang to play music and to dance.

It was his mother who had told him words that somehow all of us have come to know. While visiting her in the Eleventh Moon of 1593 when she was already very old, sickly, and feared to be near death, she had said to her son, the great Admiral, her country's fiercest and most feared warrior, "Fight gallantly and wipe out the disgrace to the kingdom." Although already old, she had helped raise her many grandchildren while Admiral Yi was gone on military duty. To the offspring of the Admiral and his deceased brothers, she had been like an angel.

The death of such a woman had to be a terrible loss. However, I knew that her passing was not the signal I was waiting for. This was not the event that would trigger me to report to Admiral Yi. Instead, for him this was a personal thing, and he had his sons and his nephews for this time.

I was not of the family. I was not for personal events and times, especially family ones. Rather, I was of the war. I remember Abbot Park's words about how we Buddhist priests seek calm and peace, and what a strange type of Buddhist priest I seem to be. Then I think about Admiral Yi and how things worked out that, through him, I have become involved with this series of slaughters and battles. It seems unusual that without the invasion by the Japanese it is unlikely that I would ever have met him. It seems even more bizarre that without the invasion, I probably would never have heard of him.

Strange to muse upon. Of course, Admiral Yi would have been just as great a man had the Japanese never attacked. He would have been as honest and intelligent, as brave and stalwart. However, it is only because Hideyoshi ordered the invasion that people came to know and remember Admiral Yi. Had he not displayed his wonderful qualities as a warrior and leader against the invaders from the islands, he would probably never have become noticed. It is likely that only his family would remember him. They would bow to his memory each year at their private chusa ceremony, and that would be that. Perhaps he would even still be alive. Maybe he would be a very old retired military man living at his family's rural home near Asan.

But Admiral Yi has been gone for 30 years, and now I have been asked by the abbot of Sudoksa to write my memories of him. The abbot is a Buddhist, dedicated to moving beyond this world in the highest of ways. And he asks me, another dedicated Buddhist, to share his memories of times with a man we remember as being great. I am asked to share my recollections of a person we recall as a superb hero worthy of emulation. Yet he is considered so largely because of how wonderful he was at killing other human beings.

I write as requested. Perhaps there is some worth to doing so. But it does bring up many questions. But, then again, perhaps these questions are part of the reason the abbot has asked me to write.

So, back then, thirty-one years ago, I had become a man of war. I spent some more time with the Abbot Park at his temple near Seoul after the Admiral and his entourage, which was absurdly large for a mere private, had left. Then I, too, began to move south, which is what I was doing when I heard about the passing of the Admiral's mother. But I knew this was not yet my signal, so I continued my wanderings.

As I moved south, I mainly checked on my old places and friends of many years. I checked the temples where I had stayed on and off for the decades of my wanderings. I stopped by the farms where the families had given me a meal. I went to the villages that had made sure a wandering priest got a place to sleep.

Devastation reigned. Many of the temples were in ruins. Some I was sure would never be rebuilt. The majority of farms were empty, burned, gone. At these I could only bow my head and pray for the families I had known. Things had not gone much better for the villages.

The survivors told me that it had been even worse a few years before. In 1592 and 1593, the Japanese had come through first, and then, chasing them south, the Chinese. The Chinese had not treated the Koreans much better than had the Japanese. Most people still alive were hoping that neither of these armies would ever come back. When most of those survivors heard that I had been in Seoul, they asked about the King and what he was doing, and what was being done to finish the war and was there any hope? Hope for peace? Hope for a regular crop harvest? Hope for fairer taxes once everything was normal again?

These were many of the same questions I had been hearing my whole life. But I was now hearing them even more strongly. The people were worse off than ever.

I would say what I always said as a priest. Sometimes this didn't seem like very much, but it helped some of those I talked to, or seemed to. At least this was something.

Admiral Yi had been released in the Fourth Moon, and as time does, it went by both slowly and very quickly. Then, slowly, suddenly, time had moved to the Seventh Moon.

Then the signal came. For me, the war was to begin again.

The news that was the signal was even worse than I had imagined.

The Japanese squadrons had combined in a massive early morning attack against the Korean fleet at Hansando. Reports were that Won Kyun had fled, beached his ship, and run off into the woods to hide almost before the battle had started. There, the Japanese had found him and taken his head. The fleet, leaderless and dispirited, was almost totally wiped out. Some said that there were only ten or twelve Korean ships left.

I did not hear of this disaster, which came to be called the Second Battle of Hansando, until a week after it had happened. This was late in the Seventh Moon. I listened to the rest of the tidings, which confirmed that for me it was time to go. As I had promised, I was on my way south as soon as I could.

There had been other news along with that of the disaster. The better information had caught up with the horrible.

Field Marshal Kwon Yul had decided that there was only one man to salvage the situation. This man had recently been in serious trouble, and, at the moment, was only a private attached to his camp. But Kwon Yul was no fool.

His orders were for this man, on the Field Marshal's authority, to take command of any ships and crews that were left. This man was to do all he could against the Japanese fleets with the surviving elements of the Korean navy, and with whatever he could add to it. This man would be expecting my arrival. I had promised.

Admiral Yi was back.

Part IV

▼

Seventh Moon, 1597—Eleventh Moon, 1598

Includes:

- *The Miracle of Myongnyang—one of the greatest military feats in all of history.*

- *The Priest Wonho in battle for the first time.*

- *The Death of a Son.*

- *The Chinese Allies—Arrogance, Enemy Bribes, and Will They Fight?*

- *The Defeat of Japan—The Final Campaign.*

- *The Death of Admiral Yi.*

After the almost total annihilation of the Korean naval forces under the command of Won Kyun at the second battle of Hansando in the Seventh Moon of 1597, the King had an idea. He openly wondered about whether it would be good for Admiral Yi to give up attempts to rebuild the navy and to concentrate on land battles instead. In response, Admiral Yi memorialized the throne. He wrote that since the war had begun that the navy had been Korea's only steady winner. Korea's naval forces had beaten back the Japanese fleets from being able to get around Yosu and Mokpo to where they could sail to Inchon and send their cargoes up the Han River to supply their armies. He also stated that, even with only twelve major warships with which to fight, with a desperate effort he could drive the hundreds of Japanese ships back. Words which are perhaps one of the greatest understatements in military history were included in his writings to the King and might have been pivotal in keeping the navy afloat:

"As long as I live, the enemy must respect us."

Chapter 27

Time to Fight
The Eighth Moon, 1597

"Wonho!"

The voice coming out of the rain is one that I am very happy to hear.

"Taejin! You have led me a merry chase!"

He looks at me. I stand soaked to the skin, as I have been for days. Illness and floods from long and terrible rains have delayed my getting to Admiral Yi, and the Admiral also has been hard to find. He has been switching locations along and near the southern coast a few times a week. The Admiral has discovered that there is even more to do than trying to put our navy back together. He has also found himself needing to reorganize local governments and put some discipline back into the land forces, whose immediate leadership is in a shambles. He has found a horrible mess in all too many towns in place of consistent and just authority.

The Admiral had arrived with his party at the town of Puyu only to find that the local army commander had burned down his own headquarters and headed for the hills because he thought the Japanese were coming close. In the town of Nagan, the same army commander, Lee Pok-nam, also burnt down the Korean government warehouse, which had been full of supplies. In both cases, Admiral Yi had shown up soon after the fires.

I have finally caught up with the Admiral and his people in Chosong, where they had finally found a government warehouse intact. Here they have stopped for a time. As I recollect the journey past the panic and the ruins in the rain, I realize that I have finally gotten to my destination; the Admiral is nearby and Kim Taejin is talking to me.

"You must change into something dry and get cleaned up. The Admiral asked just yesterday about you." He pauses. "It took you long enough to get here."

I just look at him. For a second he has gotten to me, and then I see the humor in his eyes. "Taejin, you are a rat sometimes! I had the fevers for almost a week. If not for a poor farmer's kindness, I might have died. Then I had to deal with floods, Japanese patrols, a gang of robbers, bands of refugees, some of our own army patrols asking, 'What are you doing here, Priest?' and, once I got close, the Admiral 'has just left Kurye on his way to Amnokkangwon' or 'he is now on his way to Okkwa.'"

Taejin smiles. "I knew you would get here as soon as you could. Come. Let us get you cleaned up and find some warm food."

I am taken to what turns out to be the officers' facilities. By this stage of the war, just the presence of Kim Taejin was like a pass to this otherwise off-limits area. Everyone knew he would do nothing that was not as Admiral Yi would have it. I receive a warm bath and my robes are cleaned, and the meal I eat is simple but wonderful.

"You just came in from a mission, Wonho, so you deserve this treatment," is all Taejin says about it.

"A mission?"

"To report here. Many men are trying hard to evade service, to hide from the officials looking for soldiers and sailors for the military, and yet you report to Admiral Yi despite many hardships and obstacles."

I can say nothing for a moment. Then, "I told him I would come when it was time."

"I know. And I knew that for you, that would be enough. When the Admiral mentioned you yesterday, I said that I was sure that only your death would keep you from finding us." He pauses. "Based on that assumption, it is especially nice to see you."

Again I can find nothing to say. Kim Taejin's words are the kindest I have heard in many weeks. The farmer who nursed me back to health was not a talker. However, even better words are coming this day. These occur only an hour or two later, when Taejin accompanies me to the room of Admiral Yi.

He tells me that Admiral Yi has been sick and so has stayed an extra day in Chosong at the house of Kim Ando. "That is the reason you were finally able to catch up with us," smiles Taejin. "We have been moving around a lot." Then his face grows serious. "The arrest. You heard about the death of the Admiral's mother?" I nod, so he goes on. "The ridiculousness of being a private, not an Admiral, along with the sadness regarding his mother. The Admiral's health has suffered, and then, Won Kyun …

"He fled. The fight had barely started when he ran away to land. The Japanese found him there by the end of the day and took his head, or, by now, the people would have. So, of course, Field Marshal Kwon Yul sent for the Admiral right away, and now, for over a week, the Admiral has again been officially the Admiral." The story continues. Taejin tells me that Yang Ho, the Royal Communications Emissary, had visited the Admiral on the Third Day of the Eighth Moon. The Royal Emissary had brought the royal decree officially reappointing Yi Sun-sin as Fleet Admiral of the Three Provinces and concurrently as Commander of the Cholla Left Naval Station.

"First they did all they could to break him, and then his mother dies," summarizes Taejin. "And now, he has to save them again. The weight of the war against the island dwarfs is again on his shoulders. It is no wonder his health has been affected."

His health! I have to ask. "Is it serious, Taejin?"

"For anyone else it would be potentially lethal. But for him, I believe only a bullet or an arrow to the heart could kill him before he knows the Japanese have left Choson for good."

Then I am surprised. "The Admiral has asked to see you. Commandant Pae is also sharing the house of Kim Ando, but he is ill disposed and will have retired by now. The Admiral, though he stayed put today because of his illness, still has more energy than two ordinary men. He wants to see you now."

The Admiral does look older. I see this immediately. However, he brightens upon seeing me. I have never seen this before. Usually he has kept things to himself, maintaining the proper reserve of a senior and high-ranking Confucianist military commander.

I begin the usual courtesies upon entering the presence of one of his rank, but he cuts me off. "Priest Wonho!" His voice is as strong as ever.

"Sir!"

"You are here!" It is not a question or a statement of the obvious, but an appraisal of the fact and, perhaps, a question.

"Yes, Sir."

He looks at me for a moment and then several moments. His gaze is somehow even deeper now then it had been before. This is saying a lot.

"Priest Wonho, I have a message for you."

"Sir?" I wonder what this could mean. The look on my face must be amusing, for he shows a small smile. I notice that Kim Taejin is smiling, too. He is the only other person in the room, which is, thankfully, warm and dry despite the rain.

"It is a private message, meant only for you, though Kim Taejin may hear it, also, if this will be allowable to you."

Allowable to me? Words from the Admiral? By now I must look ridiculously confused. I try to compose myself but can only manage to stutter, "Sir, please, please, certainly you should, please say whatever you wish, and … and Kim Taejin may stay, of course."

The Admiral nods. Then he says, "I would speak of private things. I would speak of personal matters as once a good man told me secret things about himself."

He pauses in case I wish to say anything. I don't, so he goes on.

"A man was of high rank. He had many people in his command. But this man came to be accused of crimes, and his rank was removed. He was arrested and taken in the most dishonorable of ways to the court of his king for judgment."

The Admiral is speaking so only those of us in the room can hear. Even someone in the hallway outside would not be able to distinguish his words. Yet, his voice is as clear and resonant as ever. A part of my consciousness notes that Kim Taejin has knelt down to the side, and that he is unmoving, his eyes lowered. The Admiral continues.

"This man was disgraced and had no right to call upon any person for assistance. He was powerless and likely to die.

"Yet, some persons remained loyal to him. They were not family or kin. They were not relatives with an obligation. Nor could they expect a financial or career reward for their loyalty. Instead, if anything, their steadfastness could have endangered them." He pauses, and takes a deep breath. I note that, despite everything, he still breathes very slowly and deeply. Then he goes on. "But, despite this, they stayed near him when he was arrested and imprisoned. They also did their best to keep him safe while they could.

"Whenever this man who was then a prisoner was tempted to feel sorry for himself, he found himself heartened by a few people who made their loyalty apparent. On his way to Seoul, this man, this prisoner, could look out from his cage and see friends."

I catch my breath at these words. I had never hoped to be considered in this way by the Admiral.

"The man in the cage made himself a promise. He said that no matter what happened, he would talk to these men if he could. If at all possible, he would mention his gratitude to these men who stayed loyal. Whether he would be sent to execution, reinstated to command, or something else, he swore an oath to himself to tell each of these men what their loyalty and service had meant to him."

He pauses, but not for me to speak.

"The man in the cage is grateful to be able to give this message in person."

I am fighting back tears. All I can say is, "I could have done nothing else, Sir."

He smiles. It is the most beautiful smile I have ever seen. "That is what makes you such a good man, Wonho."

Looking down, I fight for composure. I cannot speak.

Time passes. I know I will never forget these moments. Then he speaks again, and his voice has changed subtly. "Thank you for hearing my message. It is a pleasure to help a promise to be kept, even if it is the promise of a lowly prisoner."

Then his voice alters again. "However, now, I am again, though through a sad event, the Commanding Admiral of the Three Provinces." Now his voice is again the Admiral's. "And I have only a dozen ships and a bunch of fishing boats and ferries with which to fight the Japanese, whose fleet is as strong as, or stronger than, ever.

"I do not have enough ships, Priest Wonho." I note that he is calling me Priest Wonho again, as he continues, "And I have not enough men." His voice emphasizes the word 'men.'

He pauses and looks at me. As so often happens, the Admiral has switched gears too quickly for me to keep up. One moment he is thanking me, and the next he is telling me about too few ships and not enough men.

Then I understand what he is saying. Later I will be surprised by how quickly I speak.

"Sir, if I may be so bold, I could man an oar."

The Admiral's gaze is firmly upon me. I notice that Kim Taejin has looked up. The Admiral has said nothing yet.

"And, Sir, if you agree to let me do so, I would be greatly honored to serve on the ship which you personally command."

Still he studies me. Then a pleased expression crosses the Admiral's face. He says, "So be it." He breathes deeply, and says, "It gives me great pleasure to assign you to an oar on my flagship."

Then he looks at Kim Taejin. "Our new sailor needs to know what is expected of him. He is to live as before, except that he may draw what rations there are in camp as a sailor, and during training and, of course, on missions, he will be expected to be at his post on board. Make sure that he knows of his duties while at sea. He is your trainee."

I have never seen Kim Taejin betray any hint of feeling to the Admiral, but now he smiles. "Yes, Sir."

Admiral Yi turns back to me, and says, "Welcome to official duty in the military of His Majesty, Priest Wonho."

All I can say is, "Thank you, Sir."

There is a brief moment, and then, "And now, I would like to be alone." Suddenly, the Admiral again looks tired and older.

We part from him with our usual courtesies. Outside, Taejin claps me so hard on the shoulder that it jars my bones.

"Welcome to the navy, shipmate," he says.

A lot has happened quickly. A few hours ago I was soaking wet and alone on the road, and now I have been welcomed by Kim Taejin, fed and bathed, and then, unbelievably, thanked in person by Admiral Yi, who actually called me a friend, and now I am in the military. I am to row for Admiral Yi on his flagship.

"You are going to be a busy man," Taejin continues. "The Japanese won't wait forever before coming at us again. Thank the gods we have the Admiral, because they will want to finish us for good this time."

Chapter 28

▼

The Miracle of Myongnyang

The Sixteenth Day of the Ninth Moon, 1597

I am going to die.

There are thousands of them in hundreds of ships. The huge fleet and fierce samurai of the most feared military in Asia are coming right at me. They want my head. They want my ears for their trophy pile back in Kyoto. But a thousand times more than me, they want the head of the man who stands a few meters away. Admiral Yi commands this ship, the one on which I, and all of us here, are about to meet the next world. Whichever Japanese gets the Admiral's head is sure to get a huge reward. I am frozen, petrified.

My bowels feel loose. I am about to soil myself on the deck inside the kobukson. I cannot allow this to happen even though I am about to have a bullet or sword enter my body, or to find myself wounded and sinking in the water, unable to get air.

The Japanese are coming down the channel right at us. They are at sail and rowing, and the tidal current is pulling them, adding to their speed. And we are all alone. Admiral Yi has anchored our ship in the middle of the narrow channel. The other Korean ships, all eleven of them, are hanging back, even as, or is it because they can see, the whole Japanese fleet is bearing down upon us.

We are doomed. This is impossible. I wonder again how it will be, to actually die. Will an arrow get me? A musket ball? Will I fall wounded into the sea and drown before I hemorrhage to death? How will it feel? How painful will it be?

There seem to be a thousand Japanese ships. They fill the channel and go back farther than I can see.

A man in front of me begins to move his oar. He is trying to back our ship away from the overwhelming numbers of Japanese. Admiral Yi sees him, and with the roar of a tiger, has his sword at the sailor's throat. "One more move like that, and I shall hoist your head to the top of the mast!" His voice is fierce beyond the human. "Have no fear! Though the island robbers have a thousand ships, they shall not defeat us. Shoot the enemy with all your might!"

A thought forms inside me. My mind, or is it my spirit, says that he wishes the Japanese knew that Hachiman, the god of war, was on our side. Somehow this encourages me. I start breathing again.

"Fire!" Shots. Smoke. Screams. Smells. Gunpowder. Shouts. Piss. Excrement. The sea. Our cannon firing, our fire arrows being launched. Explosions. Shrieks. I can see nothing. Dim shapes. We fire at all of them. The only ships near us are Japanese. We fire, and our ship lurches.

Someone shouts, "Some of them have run into our anchor chain!"

Admiral Yi tells some gunners, "Hit them below the waterline as they roll to the side after hitting our chain!"

There is more noise, more smoke. The ship shudders. Unless we are ordered to row, I am free of a single duty station. I know nothing about firing the cannon or arrows. There has been no time to be trained on these. I am also not an archer who can poke out the top, fire, and duck back inside. I find myself carrying gunpowder to a cannon, then arrows to a launcher. Some men are shouting for water, and I bring it to them. These things I can do.

Admiral Yi is everywhere. He is encouraging, ordering, picking targets. Yet he is also always there in front, solid, leading us, daring the Japanese to try to get past him.

There is a lull. I see the Admiral scanning the seas. He has a more terrible look on his face when he looks astern than he does when he looks out at the Japanese to our front. He commands, "Hoist the command flag! Raise the call sign to the other ships! Sound the call trumpet!"

Immediately the flags go up and the trumpet sounds. One of our ships responds quickly, coming up alongside. This ship is that commanded by An Wi, the Magistrate of Koje Island. Admiral Yi roars, "Do you wish to be hanged? Do you seek to be court martialed for deserting your Admiral in battle? How do you come by falling astern as the Japanese fleet comes near?"

I cannot see An Wi, but I can see the reaction the Admiral's words have. An Wi's ship charges forward toward the Japanese, guns blazing, and the archers hard at work.

Then a second Korean ship comes up. Admiral Yi is shouting again. His words are similar, and so is the result. "Kim Ung-ham, you are the Commander of the Central Squadron, and yet you leave me alone to be slaughtered! You fell far astern and did nothing when my ship was surrounded by a hornet's nest of the enemy! But I live, Kim Ung-ham, and if you wish to survive the week, SHOW ME NOW how you wish to escape your guilt!" Admiral Yi was pointing at the Japanese fleet, which was again coming at us.

It is like Kim Ung-ham's ship has been pushed forward at full speed by Admiral Yi's arm. This time I hear the shout from that ship. It has to be Kim Ung-ham himself, "Forward! Attack! Death to the Invaders!"

The Admiral turns to the front. It has only taken minutes for An Wi in his first ship to embroil himself amidst a number of the enemy. Two small boats can be seen moving from the enemy's flagship, filled with troops. They latch onto the side of An Wi's ship, which is not fully outfitted as a kobukson and does not have a full complement of rooftop spikes. The shapes of the enemy horde look like deadly black ants scuttling up the sides of the Korean vessel. An Wi's men can be seen repelling the boarders desperately. They use sharp-edged clubs, long spears to stab the marauders, and even stones to knock them into the sea. For the Japanese, if they have any armor on at all, falling into water can only be a journey down to death.

"Release the anchor chain! Forward! Full speed ahead!" shouts Admiral Yi. "Cannons, and fire arrows. Go after the Japanese boats and ships around that of An Wi!"

I jump to my oar. Together, we propel ourselves forward. We arrive at the rescue like the hounds of hell crying for blood. The Japanese in the three attacking boats turn to see where the arrows and cannon fire have come from only to find themselves being rammed and capsized by Admiral Yi's flagship. We keep firing at all the Japanese we can find, which is easy, for they are everywhere. An Wi's men cheer and, with new energy, enjoy finishing off the few Japanese still alive on their decks.

Kim Ung-ham's ship is raising havoc among the Japanese ships and boats nearby. Then I see arrows and shots landing from behind, into, and amongst the enemy. Inspired by the example of Admiral Yi, the other Korean ships look to be finally joining the fray.

We are still horribly outnumbered, but our few ships have as best as possible been outfitted as turtle ships. This makes us hard to attack, let alone sink. Plus, we have the better cannon, since Admiral Yi personally oversaw their design and testing. This makes it very dangerous for the enemy when they come close. Most important, though, we have Admiral Yi himself. Their huge numbers alone should flood over us, but he will not let this happen. He will not permit us to allow it.

Behind the walls of our vessels, we are difficult even to see, let alone shoot with arrows or muskets. All of our ships have at least some of the protruding spikes of the kobukson on the sides and roof. An Wi's has the fewest, yet some of the Japanese who had attacked his ship lie impaled. Each of our ships soon becomes decorated with red-stained Japanese who have tried to board them. For a passing moment, as I watch one bloody figure squirm as he lies with a spike through his lower abdomen, I wonder if those who have attempted to board one of our more fully-equipped ships were brave or stupid. How could you hope to succeed, climbing a ship with wet sides in a rolling sea through the forest of deadly spikes while we, the enemy, wait for you with sharpened blades and clubs, if you get past the arrows and cannon in the first place?

The battle rides in the wind. It is hundreds against a few, and the few are doing well, but the hundreds are still coming, and most of them are fresh. There is a shout. I recognize the man whose cry I have heard. He is a surrendered Japanese who has come over to the Korean side. He had come to hate his commander and to prefer the Korean cause to his own. This man is saying that a figure floating in the water is the Japanese commander in Angol.

Admiral Yi orders this Japanese to be fished out of the water. He is still barely alive, and there is jubilation from the man who has recognized him. "Yes, it is him! He ordered me whipped like a dog! Now look who is beaten!"

Admiral Yi gestures at the almost drowned commander and says, "Take this Japanese to the top of the deck where all can see. Display him. Then, cut off his head."

It is done.

A wonderful cheer goes up among the Koreans, and a groan of anguish comes from the Japanese. They have all recognized the bright red brocade uniform of their commander and seen his fate. The Korean ships that have been only modestly engaged charge forward to attack. The Japanese are dispirited. Now they only want to escape.

There is no doubt. We have won. Admiral Yi has triumphed again.

By the end of the battle, over thirty Japanese ships have been captured, capsized, or sunk, while we have lost none. Hundreds, perhaps thousands, of the island robbers float dead, or lie on the bottom of the sea feeding the crabs and the fish.

I hear someone say, "It is a miracle!" Another voices the obvious, "We have won." Still another, "Look, over there, more ships!" A sailor is pointing to the west, out to sea.

We all turn. Could there be more Japanese coming in to attack? No one breathes.

A voice says, "You are reacting like I hoped the Japanese would, and, like I think they did." It is Admiral Yi. He has never looked better. He explains, "Those are the refugee boats. They wanted to stay close to me. They said they only felt safe near where I was. So I told them to stay back, near the horizon. They would be safer there, and I knew the Japanese would know that they were not their own ships. I wanted the Japanese to see our strong vessels down here at the bottom of the channel waiting for them, all outfitted like kobukson. Plus, I wanted them to see in the distance many 'reinforcements' coming to help us against them."

We are all beyond words. Not only are we exhausted, but we are also in deep admiration of Admiral Yi. The way he does things to help us to win battles never ceases to amaze.

The battle is over. I am alive. I breathe. I smell the sea air. I hear a voice, barely. My ears are pounding after all the cannon fire. It is Kim Taejin. "You are a veteran now, Wonho."

As I look back at the battle, his artillery piece was among the most active. He had been moving incredibly fast and had been handling his huge Heaven cannon as if it were a toy. Kim Taejin is soaked, dripping with sweat. I hand him some water, which he takes gratefully.

Then he says, "The Admiral knew their numbers and ours. He knew that we still matched them ship for ship, but that they outnumbered us horribly. So he met them here," he gestures towards the narrow channel, "where they could not maneuver, and where their numbers would get in their own way." He drinks the last of the water I have given him.

"Did you see their ships colliding with each other, some trying to get away, and others trying to attack all at the same time? And then, boom! We would ram them from the side and over they would go. And with so many targets jammed together, how could our cannon and fire arrows miss?"

Thinking about his words, I realize that everything he has said is true. Except, in my mind it was all a confusing jumble. Now, the horrible, deadly confusion makes a kind of sense.

Then there is another voice, louder and talking to all of us. It is Admiral Yi. He looks unfazed, and of all the people on the ship, seems the least affected by the battle. Has he taken a moment to clean up? All the rest of us are dirty and sweaty. Our faces are black. He looks fresh in comparison. I conclude that he feels that the commanding officer must always be the highest example, and that he must have taken a few moments to wipe off his face and to clean his armor and clothing. I get the feeling that he has begun to calculate what move the whipped Japanese might dare to make next, and he already looks ready to checkmate it.

The Admiral says, "Signal the fleet. Proceed to Tangsado. We shall spend the night there."

As I move to my oar, I look at my surroundings, not just for enemy ships or survivors. I realize the wind has picked up and that the sea is getting rough. To stay out tonight would not be wise, and the sun is already low in the sky.

Time. Again I feel how strange it is. Just a moment ago we were doomed. The enemy was coming at us, and we were outnumbered at least one hundred to one. It was hopeless. And now, just a few memories later, it is sunset, and I am becoming aware that it is getting cold, and that my body needs some food. I am a veteran now, and I am so very tired. I know that sleep will never be so nice to awake from as that which I will have tonight.

Chapter 29

Dreams and the Death of a Son

Tenth Moon, 1597

The abbot of Sudok Temple just asked my old bones about dreams.

Dreams. Yes. Admiral Yi had dreams. He believed that they could be powerful messages, and that they sometimes could be accurate warnings or prophecies. Plus, just as with everything else in his life, if he thought something could help him in his goal of defeating the Japanese, he wanted to use it. He used everything and everyone he could in this way and made no pretense about it.

Perhaps it was regarding dreams that the Admiral was the most personal he ever got with me. (I talk of the Admiral, not of the prisoner who made a promise. That was very special, and very different.) I was a priest so he thought I might know about them. Once, he shared his thoughts about dreams with me. I was called to the Admiral in the midday.

"Wonho, I was napping and I had a dream. It was one I wish to have interpreted."

"Yes, Sir. I hope that I can be of some assistance."

"It was a dream about my son."

I had no doubt which one the Admiral was talking about. His third son, Myon, who was barely twenty years old, was known as especially spirited and skillful. It was said that his talent in arrow shooting might even rival that of his father. As befit a member of the Yi family and particularly a son of the renowned Admiral, Myon had ridden out to defend the environs of his family estate from Japanese raiders. A samurai sword had cut him down. There were strong and, it was felt, likely rumors that the Japanese raiders had been especially targeting Admiral Yi's family and estate.

Admiral Yi had gotten the word of Myon's death on the 14th of the 10th Moon. The whole camp had mourned with him and for him. It was a few weeks later that he called me to his headquarters regarding his dream.

"I hope I can help with it, Sir," I said.

The Admiral nodded and explained, "I was taking a nap and, in my sleep, Myon came to me bitterly weeping. He said to me, 'My Father, my father, slay the Japanese who has killed me!' I replied, 'Myon, you were a strong, young man. Can't you kill this man yourself?' Myon replied, 'He killed me in life, and now I am wary of him, even in death.'

"Then I woke up, and I could not understand this dream. Of course, I would kill the slayer of my son in a second, but our ancestral home is many days away, and there are tens of thousands of the Japanese robbers infesting our land. How can I find this one?"

I wonder how to help the Admiral. There are many instances where dreams have proven to be accurate prophecies and to have been true messages or warnings, even regarding countries and wars. In one well-known case from the three kingdoms era, the ruler of Silla interpreted a dream correctly and, as a result, routed a surprise Paekche invasion force. But this dream?

Perhaps more information would help me. I asked, "Sir, if I may, it might help me to know if you have had other important dreams that had significant meanings?"

The Admiral paused. The attendant in the room was perfectly still. It was not my friend Taejin. It only seemed he was always at the Admiral's side. "Yes," came the Admiral's reply. "At least twice. The first was the morning of the battle of Sachon, near Noryang."

"When you were shot?" I ask.

"Yes, the same day. Early that morning I was asleep, and I dreamed of an extremely old, white-haired man who shouted to me, 'Get up! Get up! The enemy approaches!' Immediately I woke up, called the alert, and ordered the fleet to set sail for Noryang."

"Did the old man tell you the danger was from Noryang?"

"No, but if the Japanese were coming, it almost had to be from that direction."

Normally I would never ask questions of the Admiral like this, but this is a very special occasion. I hesitate and remind myself that I am only asking because the Admiral wants me to help him, and these questions might be the way I can do so.

"What was the second dream, Sir?"

"It was during the end of the two plague years, 1593 and 1594. I had finished preparing my second elegy for the ashes of the many dead to be honored at the second grand funeral. The night before the funeral, I heard crying and voices. I asked these voices what the problem was. The answer was that I had forgotten them in both of the funerals, and their spirits needed solace, too. I asked who they were, and they said, 'We are the ghosts of the drowned. You have only included those killed in battle or who died of the plague in your elegy.'

"When I woke up, I checked and found this to be true. I then had special ceremonies carried out for these spirits."

His voice stops, and there is silence inside the room. Outside, the camp carries on its business, and, in the distance, the sound of the sea, the waves hitting; the eternal sea, ever changing and ever present. The eternal sea—at least it is so compared to my short-lived, tiny speck of human form. The Buddha would say that even the sea is ephemeral, and that nothing of this world is forever.

How can I help the Admiral? A memory comes.

"Sir, I once heard that if a person wants to achieve clarity regarding a dream, he could resume the same position as he had been sleeping before and just let his mind be clear. Let sleep come again, if it will. Sometimes, things become understandable then."

Admiral Yi looks at me, obviously considering this. Then he turns to his attendant, "I desire to be alone for awhile. Let nothing save a message from the King or Field Marshal Kwon Yul, or news regarding an imminent attack, disturb me." The attendant bows his understanding while the Admiral says to me, "Please wait in the outer chambers." I, too, signal acknowledgment and leave him, if all goes well, to his message from the spirit of his son.

The attendant offers me food and drink, which I accept. I eat and drink slowly and hope that somehow my idea might help the Admiral. I try to recall when, where, and from whom I had heard of this method, but the details escape me. Only the memory of the practice itself has stayed with me. It always seemed to make sense. Less than an hour later Admiral Yi loudly emerges from his inner quarters.

"Staff, to me!" He sees me and nods to stay nearby. I bow my understanding.

His on-duty officers and staff rush to his presence. "Sir!" "Yes, Admiral!"

"Have we taken any new prisoners in the last day or two?"

"Yes, Sir. One, an officer, brought in yesterday."

"This officer, I want him questioned. Thoroughly questioned." The way he says "thoroughly" makes me wince. Our interrogators are not subtle. Of course, neither are those of the Japanese. He continues, "Find out where he was on duty for the invaders since the Ninth Moon. And find out what battles and skirmishes he has fought in, and how many Koreans he has killed, and where, since then."

"Yes, Sir."

"Immediately!"

The officers almost sprint from the room. Abruptly, there is again only the Admiral, the same attendant, a just-arrived Kim Taejin, and me present. The Admiral turns to me.

"It worked, Priest Wonho."

Later that day, near sunset, the screams of the prisoner could be heard all over the island. He had confessed. As the spirit of Myon had told his father in his second visit, the gods had willed it that his murderer be delivered to his father. The Admiral listened to the confession, apparently heard details that only a visitor to his home area could have known, and ordered the punishment.

To the Admiral, this raid by the Japanese had not been an act of war. It had been a spiteful and personal slap at him, their greatest enemy. He would slap back in similar fashion. A son had died because of the Japanese desire for revenge, and the Admiral had the perpetrator in his power. That was enough.

The orders were to kill the Japanese slowly by cutting him to pieces. There was no hesitation in carrying them out.

* * * *

In the thirty years since his death, other things have been heard about Admiral Yi regarding dreams, visions, and prophecies. In one of these tales, an astrologer is said to have predicted that the newly born child would be a fantastic military leader around the age of fifty. In another story now well known, the Admiral's mother received a message from the spirit of her father while she was in confinement waiting for her third son to be born.

Her father, Admiral Yi's grandfather, was known in life as Paeknok. Posthumously, he would be named Champankong, indicating honors worthy of the rank of Vice-Minister of the Treasury. In her dream, which happened when she was in confinement pending the birth, she heard a voice from heaven. She recognized it as that of her father. He told her that the boy would achieve noble successes, and that, therefore, he should be named Sun-sin. This was an honored name. The original Sun-sin had been a person of great merit and a loyal vassal of a sage Chinese King.

She shared the tidings of the dream with her husband and soon it was agreed. The voice of the grandfather was to be respected. Because of this dream, her third son was named Yi Sun-sin.

There had been another dream about Admiral Yi that had occurred just as the Imjin War was beginning. Admiral Yi had not yet fought in a battle. Kim Taejin told me of this dream during that horrible winter shoveling snow at Abbot Park's temple in Seoul while we waited for news of the imprisoned Admiral.

"In the dream," Taejin had said, "there was a huge tree spanning the sky. Its branches and leaves went from the earth to the heavens and across the sea. Masses of people climbed onto this tree for safety and placed their backs against it. However, it was going to fall. Doom was imminent. Then, a giant figure approached and used his own strength to hold the tree in place. It did not fall, thanks to him. Of course, the giant figure was Admiral Yi."

I asked, "And this happened before a single battle?"

"Yes. And this was not from a dreamy, romantic type person, I can assure you."

Kim Taejin had stopped shoveling for a second, and considered. "You are a priest, Wonho, so this probably occurs more often to you, hearing about such things, than it does to me. But I must admit, I have often remembered hearing of this dream as triumph has followed victory ever since, at least until now." He hit the snow hard with his shovel. Whenever he thought of Admiral Yi in prison his shovel would gather enough force that just with its impact it might open up the earth to one of the lesser hells.

He still had a few more words, though. "Someone said that this dream reminded him of that one from China."

"The legend of Wen Tien-shung of Sung in China who held up the heavens when they fell?"

"Yes." He gave me a wise look. "I knew you would know about it."

Chapter 30

▼

The Recruit

Of the Eighth Moon of 1597

The Young Captain was feeling good. He was in a mood to reminisce, which was usually the case when I was with him, and we had been drinking, which often quickly became the case when he found out that I was around.

"Did I ever tell you how I came to fight for Admiral Yi?"

"No," I said. I had assumed he had just shown up and offered his services. He had never seemed one that had to have been forced to join.

"I had to fight my way in!"

"What?" This didn't make sense. I knew that the Young Captain had joined sometime in 1597 after Admiral Yi had been reinstated, but to fight his way in? Admiral Yi was desperate for sailors. The countryside was depleted of able-bodied fellows after years of war, and most of his veterans had died under the (lack of) command of Won Kyun at the Second Battle of Hansando. "What do you mean, fight your way in? They were desperate for people. That is why the Admiral finally let me join."

"But you were a fully grown man. I was a scrawny, semi-starved, frail-looking 14-year-old who probably looked 11 or 12."

I look at the athletic man sitting next to me. He must have appeared very different as a youth after years of growing up destitute because of the war. He wants me to ask, so I do. "So what happened?"

"I had more desire than brains. It was simple. I heard that the great Admiral was stopped for lunch at a nearby inn, and I knew that this was my chance to join him. I ran to the place, arriving just as he and his small party came out to their horses. I shouted out, 'Heroic Admiral, let me fight with you against the Japanese!' The Admiral stopped, turned around, looked down at my puny self, and said, 'What is this? So many of our men run away from service, and now a little boy wants to fight?'"

The Young Captain keeps talking, but my mind wanders. I remember something from over two decades before. I remember that it was very hot and humid. It was like the nearby sea was invading the air and there was not a cloud in the sky. I saw Taejin in the camp with a few of his friends. They were laughing with and at him, but I knew that Taejin was usually not the laughing type. When his friends left I greeted him. As I came closer, I saw that he had a few scratches on his face and neck and a slightly swollen eye. I mentioned that, based on the condition of his face and neck, I did not see why he had been laughing.

He smiled. "Today, the Admiral had ridden out to check things on some of the farms. We stopped for lunch at an inn, and when we came out, a little urchin shouted out that he wanted to join up with the great Admiral and fight the Japanese. He was tiny, and looked starved. He claimed to be fourteen, but we did not believe him.

"The Admiral said that he appreciated his spirit and, indeed, that he needed men with his spirit, but that, unfortunately, the boy had a few years to go before his body could do what his spirit rightly yearned to do."

Yes, I thought, that is just how the Admiral would have put it. The only time Taejin sounds eloquent and not just simple and direct is when he is quoting the Admiral.

"The boy said, 'I can fight, Admiral' and we all laughed. Even the Admiral had a big smile. The boy said again, 'I can fight. Please let me fight!' And we laughed some more. The boy was very funny, even though he didn't mean to be. Our laughter just made the little guy more angry and determined. 'Let me prove it, Admiral,' he said. 'Let me fight one of your men, right now!'

"Wonho, that made me laugh even harder. I must have been the loudest, because the little kid pointed at me and said, 'Let me fight him, the big loud one there!' The other men started guffawing and told me not to tremble too much, and that perhaps I should surrender to the child without being hurt. But the boy said it again. Then I noticed that the Admiral was not laughing or smiling anymore.

"The Admiral began to speak, and everyone shut up immediately. 'In order to fight for me and risk your life against the Japanese, you would fight this big man?' 'Yes!' the little guy replied. The Admiral gave the boy that look, and the boy withstood it. Then the Admiral turned to me. 'Are you willing, Kim Taejin?'"

"This surprised me. I did not wish to hurt the boy. I told the Admiral that I would of course do as ordered, but added that I had no wish to harm a child. To that the Admiral said, 'Your only instruction is to hold your ground and stay on your feet. You will not strike out to injure, and no one will use weapons.'

"Now everyone was really paying attention. The Admiral said to the boy, 'The man you have challenged has stood firm against the Japanese in many major battles. The armored barbarians of Hideyoshi have never knocked him to his knees. If you can bring him to the ground, you may join us.'"

"'Good!' said the boy.

"The Admiral said, 'To clarify, no weapons. And for Kim Taejin, only defense. Your job is to hold your ground and remain standing, and yours, boy, is to bring him down. Is this understood?' I said yes, and so did the boy. The Admiral added, 'This shall continue until the boy gives up, or until Kim Taejin is on the ground.' The men around me moved back. 'Are you ready?' We both said yes, and the Admiral said, 'Begin.'

"Wonho, the nasty little bugger hit me like a small typhoon. I had been looking at the Admiral, but the boy was charging me before the Admiral had even finished saying the word. He almost won right there, but he was so light I was able to maintain my balance. Then I was trying to hold him away, and he was clawing and scratching and hitting at me, and, finally, I simply threw him back onto the ground. It was not meant to hurt him, but only to get him away from me.

"He was back on me in a second."

I imagine this scene. It is like an enraged raccoon attacking a non-aggressive bear, or a mad magpie attacking a passive eagle. I smile at the thought of Kim Taejin being assaulted by this ragamuffin. I laugh.

He smiles, too. "Yes, it must have looked funny, and all of my friends were hooting at me, but they were not the ones with a little wild animal clawing at their eyes and trying to box their ears. All I was trying to do was to keep from being seriously injured before he got too tired to keep going.

"I must have thrown him away from me five times, and he kept coming back, charging me again and again. Finally, he seemed to be tiring, and I held him out in front of me, and said, '"This should end!' He replied, 'You are right! Are you surrendering?' And then he kicked me full strength in the groin."

As every man would, I grimaced and said, 'Oh, no!'

"I dropped him and doubled over in pain, but I stayed on my feet. I was seeing stars and was ready to vomit, though." Taejin winces with the memory.

"Can you guess what the little varmint did then?"

"No."

"He rolled behind me and threw his shoulder into the back of my knee."

"Damn."

"I went down then."

We are both silent for a moment. Then he goes on, "The Admiral said, 'The trial is completed. Boy, you have succeeded in enlisting. May you continue to bring honor to yourself with such valor.' Some of the men applauded him then, and the boy looked about three times his real size for a minute. 'Boy, you may join us as soon as we have notified your family of your having volunteered.' Then he asked the boy his name and guess what?"

"His family name is Yi. One of my friends said, 'No wonder you lost, Taejin. You were fighting a Yi. No one beats a Yi in these parts!' At that everyone laughed, and we headed back to camp. The Admiral sent one man off with the boy to let his family know what had happened. Before leaving, the Admiral said to the man, 'Tell the boy's father that his spirit today has earned him a place manning an oar on my flagship. This boy will go forth to battle with me.'"

All of this memory has taken my concentration away from the words of the Young Captain. I had only been partly listening to him as I remembered the scene from the hot summer over twenty years before.

I interrupt him. "It was you!"

"What?"

"Let me tell you how it ended. You kicked the big man in the groin, and he dropped you, and then you tackled him in the back of the knee, and he went down. Then Admiral Yi accepted you and sent word to your family that you were to row on his flagship."

"Yes. Exactly. How did you …?"

"The man you fought. He was a friend of mine. I talked to him later that afternoon. His friends were laughing with him regarding his defeat.

You had scratched him all over his face and neck. He told me what had happened." I shake my head. "I have not thought of that story in years. I probably should have guessed that that was you!"

I raise my glass in salute. "To you, as the child warrior, and to my friend, Kim Taejin, who was a good man."

"And strong as an ox. To him," the Young Captain raises his glass, too. He takes a healthy swallow and asks, "What ever happened to him?"

I tell him, and the Young Captain looks down. There is silence for a moment. Then he says, "He was indeed a good man."

Chapter 31

Arrogance and Disdain—The Ming

Seventh to the Eleventh Moon, 1598

I have come to have very mixed feelings about the Chinese.

I admire their culture, their advanced ways, and some of their people. Certainly the priest who taught me to fight is one of the finest men I have ever met. However, at the same time, I hate how many of them treated us. During the war, many of the Ming thought of the people of Choson as lesser human beings and treated us as such. Particularly early in the war, raping our village women was generally held by Ming soldiers to be great fun. For the Chinese army to take all the supplies from a town or village to glut themselves, even if it left the people likely to starve during the winter, was just fine with the soldiers.

And these were our "friends" and "allies" against Japan.

Much as I felt ambivalence regarding the Chinese, the Young Captain loathed them. He could speak of little regarding the Ming without anger.

"It is amazing the bastards fought with us at all with all the bribes they took from the Japanese!"

Usually I reply to this with, "Yes, but thankfully, they did."

"True," the Young Captain replies. "But they almost were not worth the bother. When they first arrived at Admiral Yi's headquarters on Kongmun Island, they were plundering houses. No woman was safe! It took Admiral Yi threatening to leave, even beginning to dismantle our base, before Commodore Chen Lien put things in order."

I respond, "He did more than that. He gave Admiral Yi the authority to discipline Chinese sailors. After that, there were very few problems."

This brought a grin from the Young Captain. "Yes. They came to fear Admiral Yi more than their own commodore."

"And the commodore always respected Admiral Yi," I add. "He called him Li-Yeh, meaning His Excellency, and more than once said that the Admiral was too great a man for a small country like ours and should come back to China with him, where he would be a Mandarin."

"That's the problem with the Chinese! Admiral Yi was a wonderful commander, so he was 'too good' for Choson. Since he was a super man, he would be better off in China with others like himself." The Young Captain is quite drunk by this part of our conversation. I am always glad there are no Chinese merchants around when we, or he, get this way. "But did any Chinese you ever met match up to Admiral Yi?"

"Not as a war commander," I say honestly. And I think of the fighting Chinese priest, the only other Chinese I had met who was even close to the Admiral as a man. "Even Commodore Chen Lien bowed to Admiral Yi in battle, and followed his orders."

"One of the few good things about that commodore …" says the Young Captain.

The Chinese could do nothing right according to the Young Captain. Once and only once, he revealed the deeper, hidden cause of his hatred. He was deep in his cups and said something that revealed much more than he wished. "My cousin was little then. He was young and looked younger. And some of those Chinese were like the samurai." He blinked and started, as if unaware he had been talking out loud. I pretended to have heard nothing and moved the conversation on.

"Once the commodore even threatened to pull his sword on the Admiral!"

I remember this. I had heard about it directly from Kim Taejin, who I am sure would have stepped in had the commodore actually drawn his sword. As Kim Taejin told it, the commodore had come to the Admiral with a plan for the Chinese to go to Namhae to mop up the enemy there.

"But there is no enemy worth attacking there. Mostly, there are only Korean prisoners who have been forced to work for the Japanese," responded Admiral Yi.

The commodore said, "But they are collaborating with the enemy, so they can be considered as the enemy, too. By going there, we can collect many heads!"

"These are Korean heads you would be collecting, Commodore! Some of the Koreans who have been made to work there are actually sending us information at the risk of their lives even while being used as slaves.

"And meanwhile, while you were gone on a mission to kill Koreans, the Japanese commander Yukinaga and his fleet could use your absence as a most fortunate time to choose to depart for home!"

"You accuse me!" Here the commodore was correct. Everyone was suspicious about whether the bribes the Japanese had been sending would buy off the Chinese fleet. It was anyone's guess whether the Chinese would fight or not. However, the Ming commander did not appreciate having this accusation even be hinted at out loud.

The commodore shouted, "I am here to do the emperor's will and my emperor gave me a long sword!" He grabbed the hilt of his sword threateningly.

The Admiral just looked at him. "Only you know your heart, and I can die but once. However, as a field commander, it is my job to be here, fighting the Japanese. I cannot leave this place now, especially to do something I would not do anyway, which is to kill my own people."

The commodore cooled off, but the big question remained until the final battle. Of course, in the end, the Chinese did fight, as I experienced perhaps too well. I never did tell the Young Captain the full story of my involvement in that. He might not have forgiven me.

"The Japanese tried to buy off Admiral Yi with gifts, too." The Young Captain was continuing his list. "Fat chance …"

This event I had seen and heard myself. I believe Admiral Yi wanted us all to hear it.

Yukinaga sent an envoy with guns and swords as gifts to the Admiral. Their intent was obvious. We will give you much if you let us go in peace. The Admiral's answer was also plain, loud, and public, though he addressed it to the Japanese envoy and his party.

"Since you attacked us for no reason in 1592, we have captured and killed countless numbers of your soldiers and sailors. Your women weep for loneliness back home. We have piled up mountains of your guns and swords as trophies. What use have I for more? And for this trespass of the enemy into our camp?"

The Japanese had no answer for this, and left. They were skilled at keeping their faces expressionless, but you could certainly detect no joy in them as they departed.

The Japanese tried to influence Admiral Yi only one other time. They were obviously happier the farther away Admiral Yi and his fleet were from them. They also seemed to correctly assume that the Chinese would be easier to bribe into not fighting them when they left if Admiral Yi were not so close by. With this in mind, another envoy had come and asked why the Korean fleet camped so close to the Ming, as if to say that farther away might be better.

To this, the Admiral simply said, again loudly and publicly, "In our land, we camp where we wish. It is no matter to you."

Chapter 32

▼

Victory and Death

The Nineteenth Day of the Eleventh Moon, 1598

"It was the saddest moment of my life. Only his arrest could match it."

I spoke these words a while ago now. The abbot had again been checking my writings. It seems to be my unfortunate gift that I have always been able to sense unhappy questions coming to me. As I feared and knew he would, the abbot has asked me about the only thing left.

"What about the death of Admiral Yi?"

I had not been able to look at the abbot for a moment. Then I told him how I felt about it.

"Where were you when it happened? Were you rowing on his flagship?"

"No." I shake my head. "I was on the Chinese flagship."

"You?" The abbot is surprised. No wonder. He has just read about the behavior of the Chinese during this war.

"Yes. I believe the Admiral had planned it that way long before, but he made it seem like a chance occurrence."

"What happened?"

"As you know, the Chinese had been acting, at best, questionably. They had been very friendly with the Japanese emissaries to their camp and had accepted many gifts from them. Obvious bribes not to fight, we thought.

"With this in mind, it is not surprising that Admiral Yi kept some things from them. A Chinese spy, paid off by the Japanese, could easily have slipped the enemy the details of our plans."

I take a sip of tea. Not wine, I reflect. I am certainly not with the Admiral or the Young Captain. I am at a temple, and it is cold, even inside where it is heated. Could it seem cold to me only because I am so old? I think so much of being elderly these days. But perhaps it is not the age that bothers me. It is being feeble. Without the temple, I no longer can support myself. My thoughts wander. I need to continue speaking.

"Or, at the very least, a spy might have been able to inform the Japanese of the exact meanings of all of our flag or trumpet signals.

"That is where I became involved and why I am suspicious that my presence on the Chinese flagship was planned by Admiral Yi well in advance."

The abbot's expression urges me to continue. I know he will read this, but it is not untoward perhaps to mention that he has very intelligent eyes which, when he chooses, can communicate very well.

"My friend Kim Taejin took especial care to teach me all of our fleet flag and trumpet signals. He drilled me on these until I saw them clearly in my sleep. I could not figure out why, as a lowly oarsman, I needed such knowledge, and, of course, my taciturn friend gave no explanation. He might not have known himself. He could likely just have been following the simple instruction, 'Make the priest an expert on our battle communications.'

"However, when the day came to attack the Japanese for one last time, Admiral Yi turned to me and said, as if on the spur of the moment, 'Priest Wonho, you know Chinese, and you know our ship-to-ship signals. Somehow, the Chinese have not been informed of all of the recent changes in them. Please report immediately to Commodore Chen Lien's flagship. You will serve as his eyes to read my intentions during the battle."

The abbot looks surprised. However, thirty years ago, I was too busy to be stunned. At the time, I had just acknowledged the Admiral's order and left for the mooring place of the Chinese flagship. But now, thirty years later, it could be that the abbot believes that such an important mission was beyond my humble station, that being the eyes of the commanding Chinese commodore to the orders of the Admiral was more than he thought I would have been assigned or entrusted with. Perhaps, at that time, I would have agreed with him that it was too much of a job for unimportant me, but only if I had had time to consider the matter. Back then there was too much going on to think of such things. Besides, after six years of war, the unusual had become the ordinary, and the commonplace somewhat rare.

My mind again wanders. I focus on the abbot who still has said nothing and decide it best to go on. To talk of these things makes the writing of them easier.

"So I reported to the Chinese commodore, Chen Lien. I had seen him many times, but had never spoken to him. I greeted him as befitted his status and explained my mission. He said the obvious thing. 'Your presence here seems necessary.' Then he added words that were in keeping with his reputation. 'Stay out of harm's way for I need you, but also stay out of my way until I do need you. Just keep your eyes on the Admiral's ship, and let me know of developments.'

"Of course, I said, 'Yes, sir' to that. Quickly we were on our way out to sea. The combined fleets of Ming and Choson were a sight indeed. For once, we had significant numbers of ships and men. There was enough of a moon that night, and the sky was clear enough that we could see a long way. The Japanese were trying to escape in the darkness, and Admiral Yi would have none of it."

"Moon? Night?" The abbot seemed surprised.

"Yes. The combined fleets of Choson and Ming set sail around 10 PM. We were at the straits of Noryang by 2 AM. The Japanese had been caught. We had gotten word from our observers in time. They were trying to slip away unseen, but in this they had failed. And the Chinese were fighting after all, despite all the bribes.

"I must admit this. The men of Choson who had to deal with him often called Commodore Chen Lien 'a son of a bitch.' He was haughty and arrogant, angry and full of himself, and he had worried us with his accepting of so many 'presents' from the Japanese. But he did respect Admiral Yi and let people know it. And, when it came down to it, he fought. He and his men, in the final battle, fought pretty well. Some Koreans complained of how part of the Chinese fleet behaved during the battle, but I know for sure that the ship I was on did not shirk the attack.

"I will never know what happened and the words that were said, but on the eighth day of the Eleventh Moon, Admiral Yi had attended a banquet at the commodore's headquarters. This was exactly ten days before we sailed out for the final battle. From this night onward, there was a shift in the commodore's behavior. He still accepted gifts from the Japanese, but he was also quite a bit more enthusiastic about fighting them.'"

I again search my memory. Nothing stands out. There were no rumors of wild words between the commanders that night. I can remember the weather, which was wonderful, and the fact that we were all eating well and that everyone was healthy. These things I can remember about the days leading up to the last battle, but nothing else. But something had to have happened at that dinner.

"A coincidence? I think there are no coincidences. Something happened then. I wonder what it was the Admiral did or said there." Pausing, I realize I am not conversing with the abbot, but am just storytelling. This is not generally correct behavior. I look at him, and know that is all right. The abbot seems to be interested in my words and to want me to continue. Indeed, I am remembering more and more as I speak. Plus, I do not feel so cold now. Is my own hot air warming up the room? It is good to keep talking.

"The actual battle plan was simple. As far as I could tell, the plan was simply to sink as many ships and kill as many Japanese as possible without undue risk, but also without being overly cautious. Admiral Yi wanted the Japanese to suffer such a disastrous defeat that they would never want to come back. He wanted the survivors who managed to escape to know they were lucky to have made it back to their homeland and to say so.

"And, of course, his plan succeeded."

I stop talking and for a while there is silence. The wind is whistling outside now. The night before a similar wind had made a big tree fall in the courtyard. All day priests and helpers have been busy cutting it up and clearing it away. Thankfully, it fell missing the pagodas, the buildings, and our bells and drum shelters. "A blessing of the Buddha," were the words said about the way the tree had fallen.

But I looked at the tree, and I knew that it was my same age and that now it was on its side, dead and gone. And I feel that soon I will be joining it.

The abbot breaks the silence. "Yes, as always, the Admiral won a great victory."

I look at him again. "Yes, Choson and Ming, Korea and China, together, mauled the Japanese as they left. And we only had a few dead compared to them." My voice is betraying me. "But, of course, one of these dead was the Admiral. And that made this victory virtually worthless to me. I would have preferred the Japanese had been left to sail home without an assault being launched, without an arrow or cannon having been fired."

The big dead tree comes to mind. Blown over by the wind. The Admiral had been blown over, too. Knocked down and sent away by what the Japanese would call a lucky shot, a musket ball from across the water. It hit him around the left armpit and from the side. It went into at least one lung and likely touched his heart.

Thousands of these shots had been fired at him by the Japanese in the dozens of major battles and skirmishes he had been in during the last six years. Only one had previously struck home. And it had gone through him and left him standing, able to lead us to victory in the war. And then, with the war ending, he was killed. One shot.

His drawn sword was in his right hand, and he had lifted his left hand to point, to accentuate a command, the call to attack the enemy, and the small piece of metal moving too fast to be seen hit him underneath the arm where there was no armor. He fell, with only enough words left to order the battle to continue and not to reveal his death until victory had been attained.

I remember the battle. My mind moves back in time and I forget about the abbot.

Cannons are firing all around, muskets banging, arrows thudding. There are screams and shouts in three languages. I hear parts of death shouts of men from Korea, China, and Japan.

The commodore's ship has been too aggressive and has been surrounded by Japanese who recognized it as a great prize. Some of the Japanese ships pause in their flight to come after the Chinese flagship, and they come after it with a vengeance. We are in danger of being overrun, looking to be engulfed by the enemy. The Japanese have tied onto our sides and are coming on board.

In the middle distance, I can see that Admiral Yi's flagship has noticed our distress. It signals for others to help us and moves to do the same. The Japanese see the Korean ships change course and know they have to kill all of the Chinese quickly (and one Korean, but the Japanese do not know that). The commodore stands and shouts on the foredeck, bravely rallying his crew. The commodore is not a coward, but he does not see the enemy boarder. No one does, except me.

A Japanese has come in from behind him. The battle has swelled to the lee side of the ship, but this Japanese has climbed aboard from windward. Plus, it is still not fully light out. The sun has barely risen. I hold a spear in my hand, picked up when a wounded Chinese dropped it. I move behind the commodore, feeling strangely invisible and moving with the speed of the Chinese priest who taught me martial arts. This is only the second time I have felt it. The first was the night with the woman and the five attackers in Yosu.

No one sees me move. My gray robes must blend in with the morning twilight. The Chinese have their backs turned, busily shooting and hacking at the enemy who are trying to get on board. And the lone Japanese, coming in from the other side, only has eyes for the commodore whose uniform, bright, shiny, colorful, and rich, stands out. To take his head will certainly win this Japanese a huge prize.

He doesn't know I am there until his own momentum has caused the point of my spear to run into his guts. Then he looks down, surprised. He had just begun to spring, sword in hand, at the commodore's back. A cry of pain comes from the attacker. The commodore spins around to see me, a grey-robed priest, only meters way, holding a spear in the stomach of a death-intending Japanese.

I know this man is dying. He looks into my eyes, his suffering evident. My hands feel a tingle in the spear. It is as if the man's life is running through it. His expression changes, and I understand. I do as Kim Taejin had drilled me to do.

I turn the spear, making the sharp edge cut a huge hole and then rip up into the heart and lungs by pushing the back end of the spear down, and thus moving the blade up at the front. It moves easily until it hits his ribs. This spear was very well sharpened. The man gasps, inhaling for the last time. Then blood flows out of his mouth and nose, his eyes glaze over, and there is suddenly dead weight dragging down my spear. His weapon has fallen onto the deck from his stilled hand.

I just stand there. I have killed. This I have never wanted to do. I had moved instinctively.

How did I do this? Why? My mind says that he would have slain the commodore, who is the Admiral's ally, and who is a commander leading his forces in a battle to kill the Japanese, the enemies of Choson. It had been one death or another. But part of me wonders, no, knows, that for us puny humans to make such decisions is futile. For a quick moment I reflect on this, but then there are shouts, Chinese shouts.

"Well done, priest!"

"He saved the commodore!"

The Japanese have been beaten back, and the reinforcements ordered by the Korean flagship have arrived. The Chinese sailors have time to congratulate me, at least for a few moments.

My eyes meet those of the commodore. He says, "Your actions are appreciated. You shall be commended to your Admiral for what you have done." He looks at the body and back at me. "The man's head is yours." He does not maintain eye contact long. It might be he is wishing that it had been a Chinese who had saved him. He turns to his men, "I shall commend the priest to his Admiral after we sink and kill some more Japanese. Let us move to the attack!"

His men, heartened at their rescue, and perhaps also at their good fortune in not having lost their leader, respond with a cheer. But now, for us the battle is mostly over. The main part of the huge Japanese convoy is past us, and they are more interested in escape than fighting.

It is obvious that we have been victorious. Any Japanese who gets to his homeland will feel lucky to have done so. Their last memory of Choson will be a fierce one indeed. Almost like after Myongnyang, it is good to be breathing fresh air again, to feel the sway of the ship in the water, to feel the sun on my face. Now it is no longer night, but fully day.

Admiral Yi's ship comes close.

"Admiral Yi, your Excellency, let us talk," shouts the commodore.

There is no sign of him.

"Admiral Yi, please come out quickly!"

I see one of the Admiral's nephews, Yi Wan. He looks to have been weeping. He says, just loud enough for us to hear, "My uncle is dead."

The commodore falls to his knees. Then he says, "You must be mistaken!" He stands up.

Then the eldest son, Yi Hoe, comes into sight. He says, "It is no mistake, Commodore. A musket ball ..." and he can speak no more.

Again the commodore falls to his knees. "When?"

"Early in the main battle. His last orders were to keep attacking and to keep his death a secret until we had won."

The commodore has stood again in order to hear the answer. Then back on his knees, he cries out, "Great Admiral, even after your death you have saved me." He weeps openly.

Upon returning to port, all members of Chen Lien's fleet forbade themselves beef and showed the other traditional signs of mourning. In fact, Chen Lien went further than he needed in honoring the Admiral's departed spirit. He and some of his subordinates composed elegies to Admiral Yi, and, as the last of the Ming squadrons left for their return to China, the commodore entered a temple and said that he would offer sacrifices in honor of Admiral Yi. Still later, Commodore Chen Lien went on record stating his desire for the Korean King to honor Admiral Yi more fully and more quickly. He said that in China such a great hero upon his death would have been much more recognized and much faster.

If not before, at least the commodore and the other Chinese acknowledged the Admiral appropriately after death.

If the Chinese were sad, the grief of the Koreans was immeasurable. There was no joy at our victory. It would have seemed to a newcomer that we had lost as badly as at the second battle of Hansando when Won Kyun ran away and the fleet was annihilated. Word came that a few Japanese ships had not left with the main fleet, and there was no thought of going after them. They would not stay long we knew, and our Admiral was dead. It was as if we were all numb, as if we had all lost our hearts. And, indeed, in a way we had.

It was only hours after our return to land that I thought of my friend. With a start, the thought came, *What about Taejin?* I had not seen him and in my selfishness had not thought of him at all after hearing the news of the Admiral's death. It is shameful to admit, but I was so downcast at the Admiral's death that I thought of nothing except my own sadness for all those hours. I went to look for Taejin.

I was too late.

The other attendant told me that, on hearing the news, Taejin had frozen showing no feelings except for unending tears. When he moved, it was to the Admiral's body. He made a deep, low bow of abeyance to the Admiral. He was frozen on his knees, his head on the floor, and his hands outstretched towards the earthly remains of Admiral Yi. Suddenly, not long before I had come looking, Taejin sat up. He was heard only to say words which started with "Yes," then some which were not understood, and then, "Admiral." He bowed deeply again and was gone.

He had left purposefully, as if with a destination and a task. By then it was late afternoon. I wondered where he could be going. By nightfall, I had not found him, and it was only the next morning that I heard.

The story came in from a woman, a war refugee and oyster picker, who was out on a lonely beach about half an hour boat ride from camp. She had seen a boat coming toward the beach. Times being what they were, she had hidden herself. (Later, it came out that she had been with two other women refugees, but she was the one with the courage to come forward. The others wanted nothing to do with telling the strange and sad tale.)

The woman said that the boat had landed, and six ugly Waenom (she used the derogatory word for Japanese) had gotten out, supervised by one big Korean military man. The Korean man had a big bag with him, and she had thought it carried tools. She thought that she was looking at a work party and was just about to reveal herself when she heard the Korean man speak.

"Six years! Six years you island robbers have stayed here in Korea! You stayed to kill, to rape, to steal, and because your monkey bastard Hideyoshi made you stay even after my Admiral beat you again and again!"

The Japanese prisoners looked around at each other. They did not know what to make of this, but it was obvious that they understood his words. The woman said that it was near sunset, and she noticed that the tide had changed.

The big man continued, "And now, the war is over. Your monkey-faced Taiko is dead. Your navy has again suffered a great defeat. Just a few of your ships are left in our ports, and they will leave at any time."

At this, there was a reaction among the Japanese. This was likely confirmation of rumors that they had heard, but what would become of them? They had to be very concerned.

"But, today, this morning, you killed my Admiral."

The way the man said this made them freeze.

"And the dying is almost over."

They did not move. The big man was armed, they weren't, and he looked very capable.

He spoke a bit more softly. It was hard for the woman to hear him over the waves and the birds. "Six of you. Six. One for each year you have been here."

The big man opened the bag and poured its contents on the sand. It had been full of swords, samurai swords. They were some of those that Admiral Yi had spoken of when he told the emissary that he had no need for any more Japanese weapons.

"Tonight you have your chance. If you can get by me to the boat, you will have a chance to row to where the few of your countrymen are left and from there to sail back to your homes.

"And if you fail to get by me, the crabs and roaches and birds will be picking your bones clean by morning."

The Japanese did not move. The big man stepped back from the pile of swords towards the boat. He moved back slowly, warily, and stopped only when he was a few steps farther away from the pile of weapons than were the Japanese.

"What are you waiting for? Should I just slaughter you while you are unarmed?"

Two Japanese rushed the pile. Taejin charged. One of the Japanese stood up with a weapon just in time to have his throat sliced open by the Korean. The second was smarter and more skillful. He sprinted to the pile slightly behind and to the side of the first person, and dove, grabbed, rolled away, and came up slicing. The Korean was after him and in the seconds it took to dispatch the wilier of the first two, the other four Japanese had gotten to the pile and armed themselves.

Now it was four against one. The Japanese fanned out, trying to get the Korean cornered, encircled, or otherwise unable to move freely. They had seen his speed and his strength. The Korean, meanwhile, used their numbers against them, keeping one of them between himself and most of the others as best he could. He knew they would break for the boat if they could and moved to keep this from happening. All of this moving and shifting took only seconds, and we only had the oyster picker's account from which to glean the details.

He killed all of them. He won his last victory. Just as had his Admiral, he in his own way single-handedly defeated Japan.

However, he also followed his Admiral in another way. His sword caught in the ribs of the third of the four as he withdrew it, and this split-second gave the last of the enemy the chance to step in hard and to stab from behind. The sword went through Kim Taejin back to front. His last act was to stab backward underneath his left arm into the body of his slayer.

Ironically, the last Japanese to die, the killer of the Korean, and the Korean, the killer of the Japanese, ended up dead almost arm in arm, their blood shared in a pool beneath them, as the sun set gold, orange, and red over the once-again all-Korean land of Choson.

It was also ironic, I realized, that Kim Taejin's last act was to kill an invader of his land, a member of the forces that had killed his Admiral, with a sword thrust backward past his own left arm pit. A musket ball had killed his Admiral entering here, and, then in his own last moment, Taejin had put a sword past the same place on his own body into one of their enemies.

I happened to be nearby when the oyster gatherer came in with the news. I had been searching for my friend since first light. As soon as I heard her story, I knew that it was Taejin. He probably felt that in spirit form he could go on serving the Admiral and could think of no more appropriate way to achieve this than with the assistance of some Japanese. If he had killed all six and survived, I am certain that he would have gone back to our camp and picked up seven more and tried again.

I went with the party to identify and to collect his body. With more respect than many commoners often show, the three refugee women had covered Kim Taejin's body so that the worst of the scavengers had not been able to get to it. The Japanese, of course, had been left to the vermin.

I made sure that my friend received a fine burial, and I have conducted the rituals for him every year since his death. It is the least I can do, and I do not know what more I could.

Part V

Epilogue
Following the death of Admiral Yi

Admiral Yi and Admiral Nelson are the two greatest admirals ever to have lived. This is almost unarguable. The question among armchair admirals is who was the greater?

In the West, the glorious 19th century victories of Admiral Nelson against Napoleon's French and Spanish fleets are certainly better known than are the superb triumphs of Admiral Yi against the Japanese over two centuries earlier. However, some questions might be worthwhile considering.

Admiral Yi's tactics, strategy, courage, and genius are virtually beyond reproach. He mastered the best teachings of the ancients and simultaneously designed, introduced, and improved weapons not matched by the modern Western navies of the world until over 250 years later. Many American schoolchildren have been taught that the United States (and the Confederacy) in the Civil War were the first to use ironclad ships. While there is still debate as to whether the kobukson were totally iron-plated or whether they were armored only in especially vital areas, it is quite possible that Admiral Yi and his kobukson shot almost as many holes in that American claim as they did into Japanese squadrons.

In comparing Admiral Yi to Admiral Nelson, the following questions should be considered:

Which of the two did not start out with the best fleet in the world at his disposal?

Which of the two needed to supervise the design and building of his own major type of battleship as well as the weapons for it?

Which of the two had to survive against the treachery of members of his own government and his own military and being put on trial for his life?

Which of the two had to organize agriculture, handle refugees, and send supplies to the royal court while serving as commander in chief of his country's main fleets?

Perhaps these questions are slanted, but the answers are telling.

In Korea, there are still numerous shrines and monuments to Admiral Yi. Many of these were built soon after his death. They were spontaneous responses from rich and poor, from Buddhist and Confucianist, and from the weak and the powerful alike. His subordinate officers proposed to the King that a shrine be dedicated to Admiral Yi and the King agreed. "The Shrine of Loyal Grief, Chungminsa," was built on a hill above Yi's old naval station in Yosu. Royal proclamations ensured that appropriate rites and sacrifices would take place there twice a year, once in the spring and once in the autumn.

One of Admiral Yi's Buddhist Monk Captains, Chaun, prepared bountiful food for sacrificial rites at Chungminsa. This was after he had contributed two thousand bushels of rice to a grand mass in Noryang in honor of Admiral Yi. It would have been someone like the Monk Captain Chaun who was prevented by Admiral Yi from recruiting the Priest Wonho as a guerilla monk early in the war.

Admiral Yi's sailors and the common people he had never stopped caring about wanted to do something for him, too. They contributed donations to the "Monument To Tears For Admiral Yi, Chungmu-kong Tarubi." The six Chinese characters' message was carved in stone and situated above his old naval station at Yosu. This memorial was on the easternmost peak overlooking Yosu. Possibly it was beneath this peak and next to the shore where the Priest Wonho was meditating when he saw the dragon, the kobukson returning to port at sunset. Perhaps the written message on the monument points east toward Japan deliberately.

The coastal inhabitants of Chaknyang, which is located just across the water from Hansando, built a grass-roofed shrine called "Shrine of the Loyal Heart, Chungnyol-sa," dedicated to Admiral Yi. They offered sacrifices there whenever they were departing for a long journey.

At the wish of the local people, Yi Un-yong built a shrine to Admiral Yi on the island of Kojedo. He was not a relative of the Admiral, Yi being a very common last name in Korea. Now it is usually Lee when it comes into English, and, once in awhile, it is even Ri. But Yi Un-yong was similar to the Admiral, having risen through the ranks to command the navy. Whenever his warships were to leave the island, Yi Un-yong visited this shrine to honor the spirit of the Admiral.

Hyonchungsa was created in 1709 at the Admiral's family home near Asan by order of King Sukjong. Today, it is perhaps the grandest of the shrines to Admiral Yi. At Hyonchungsa, one finds his ceremonial swords, draft copies of his war reports and the memorials to court of the early war years, his diaries and letters, a bomb shell, a grappling hook, firearms and cannon that the Admiral designed and improved upon, paintings and diagrams of some of his greatest victories, and a one-sixth sized replica of his most famous weapon, the kobukson. Fittingly, as the Priest Wonho would have it, there is also a set of wine cups.

Seeing his writings at Hyonchungsa, I have heightened my intent to do further research regarding the fate of the *Memorials to Court* that Admiral Yi sent after early 1594. I would also like to find out more about the missing dates in his diaries.

In 1910, Japan took over Korea. One can imagine how Japan felt about shrines to Admiral Yi. Hyonchungsa fell into a sad state of disrepair. However, in a very brave and classic "in your face" campaign, a major Korean newspaper, *Dong A-Ibo*, successfully led a restoration drive for Hyonchungsa which concluded in 1932. Later in the 20th century, President Park of Korea made Admiral Yi's courage and loyalty a constant focal point of his speeches and pronouncements. In 1966 (on April 28, Admiral Yi's birthday), Park attended a ceremony denoting Hyonchungsa as a national shrine and officially detailed its expansion and renovation, which was completed in 1974. Here, each year on his birthday, there is a ceremony to honor Admiral Yi.

Koreans visit Hyonchungsa and the other shrines to Admiral Yi by the hundreds of thousands each year. He is the ultimate hero to many.

However, having become westernized, modern Korean historians have tried to find flaws in him. They cannot believe anyone could have been so good. Also, for some Koreans, any person liked so much by President Park must have had something wrong with him. Park, after all, was a dictator who had taken power in a military coup and had as many enemies as friends. Those who do not like Park have had more reason to find flaws in Admiral Yi because the Admiral was Park's own special hero.

The Admiral's disparagers have had little success. His enemies had tried to besmirch him while he was still alive and had failed. Fortunately, it is still as difficult to assail this great hero and good man centuries later.

Even the Japanese do not criticize him. During my October 2001 interview of Mr. Yi Tae-Hwang, one of the Admiral's 15th generation descendants, on the grounds of Admiral Yi's tomb, I was told that the descendants of Admiral Yi had never experienced any persecution from the Japanese because of their heritage. Instead, the Japanese seemed to hold a strong respect, albeit grudgingly, for the Yi family's legendary ancestor. The Japanese consensus seemed to be that "Anyone who could beat Hideyoshi's samurai had to be special."

The words of one very important Japanese probably helped this attitude. This was Admiral Togo, the Japanese naval hero of the 1905 Russo-Japanese War, whose ships had sunk the Russian Baltic Fleet in a matter of minutes just after they arrived at their new battlegrounds in the Pacific. The Japanese hero had gone on record that what he had done was fine, but it was not much compared to what Admiral Yi or Admiral Nelson had accomplished. As far as Admiral Togo was concerned, Admiral Yi was one of the top two admirals who ever lived. And Togo's opinion went far with other Japanese.

Although this book's main character is Admiral Yi, it is actually the writings of a wandering Korean Buddhist priest who experienced a most full and interesting life. It is of his memories of Admiral Yi. Therefore, it is only fitting that we shall leave the last words in it to the Priest Wonho.

* * * *

Spring 1628
Birthdays, and Remembering

The people remember Admiral Yi. They have put up shrines for him. There are at least two in Yosu and others all around the country, especially in the south where he won so many battles.

As I have wandered during the thirty years since his death, I have been glad that the Admiral is being remembered and honored as I believe he deserves to be. Some revere him almost as a deity. I met a man named Pak Ki-so. His parents had both been killed by the Japanese, and he had yearned to fight, but he was lame and couldn't. When he heard of the Admiral's victories, he thanked the gods for this wondrous being who could do that of which he could only dream. Pak Ki-so donned mourning clothes on hearing of the Admiral's death and still offers sacrifices on the anniversary days.

I was a friend of Okhyong, a fellow Buddhist priest. He loved the Admiral and almost literally took over Chungminsa in Yosu. He swept, polished, and guarded the shrine from any disrespect as diligently as the Admiral himself had protected Korea. I said this to Okhyong once, and he was horrified, "Never compare me to the Admiral, even as a joke."

It was this same priest who, on a cool night in Yosu near the shrine from which he never went far, proposed to me that Admiral Yi was the Boddhisatva of warriors. This shocked even me.

"Are you saying Boddhisatva kill?" I asked. "Boddhisatvas are exalted; they have attained enlightenment, reached nirvana. They have completed their time here and have come back only to show others the way to completion, to fulfillment, to ending their cycle of lives in this world of suffering."

"Did not Admiral Yi show others the way to live?" replies Okhyong. "Was any one more wise, more honest, or more brave than he? Was any one less attached to life or attainments for personal aggrandizement than he? Did he ever kill unnecessarily, unjustly?"

"He wasn't even Buddhist," I counter.

"Buddha never claimed to be a Buddhist either," says Okhyong.

I heard of Okhyong's death with a pang. All of my old friends have left for their next birth. That is, unless they reached enlightenment here before dying. As the great Japanese saint Kobo Daishi said, it can be done in one life, this life. I believe he is correct. This can always be hoped for.

So far, however, I seem to be the one who is the rememberer and the observer. If I have reached enlightenment, I have not realized it. But soon my days of remembering a lot and maybe seeing too much will have ended. Perhaps I will soon walk the hills toward Haemi, to the hilltops of Kaya around Daekok. This is where I have found the place I would prefer to sit for the last time.

But I wonder at it all. I am still here in this body, and the great Admiral has been gone for thirty years. Why was it he who died? Why, in the final battle, did the bullet not hit his son Hoe or his nephew Wan instead? They stood near him. Better yet, why did it not travel two feet higher? What if he had not raised his arms to exhort and inspire his men, and the bullet had not snuck into his chest from the side through his unarmored armpit?

Why is he gone and not me?

The eighth day of the third moon in the first year of the reign of King Injong.... We had the same date of birth. He never knew it, but, of course, I did. His officers and staff celebrated his birthday every year. Meanwhile, mine was known by nobody and cared about by no one. But we were the same age, to the day. Had he lived, he, too, would have just passed that date for the eighty-third time.

Sometimes, in the years after the war, I have wished he could see what I have seen. As I wandered through the sturdy hills and gentle valleys from bustling town to quiet village, from silent monastery to busy temple, from blue port to green mountain pass; I have sometimes wished his spirit could borrow my eyes, my eyes which opened on the same day as his. I wanted him to see his country doing better, the land at peace, the people he had saved, and their offspring, laughing and raising crops and children.

For twenty-nine years after his death, no country dared attack us. Last year, however, the Manchu did. They occupied the north. So far, though, they have stayed away from the south. Some have said that they heard in the markets that the Manchu are scared of Cholla, of the southeast. An old man, perhaps even as old as me, once said that they fear to tread where the Japanese failed. His elderly wife said that it is the spirit of Admiral Yi that keeps them away from the south, and that, thanks to him, it will be hundreds of years before the Japanese dare to bother us again.

Maybe. But I know if he had lived as long as I have, he would have been busy now figuring how to expel the Manchu from the northern part of our country. And he would probably have found the way to do it. His only unhappiness would be that he was too old to lead our fighters in the decisive battle.

Except, he is gone, long gone. And soon I shall follow his path.

I always have felt it right to die on the trail, since I have lived on it. Soon I will stop writing. I am done. In a day or two, or in a week, I will open my eyes before sunrise, pray at the main hall, and then take a walk. I often do this. This time I will not return. The birds and the bugs and the little creatures will eat my remains. I am too scrawny to interest one of the giant cats, most likely, though perhaps a tiger as old for a tiger as I am for a human being might be interested in such a weak and gnarly target.

I have finished. My memories of Admiral Yi and of Japan have been written, as I promised the abbot they would be. Soon it will be time to walk to the hilltop above the pretty valley with the sea glistening in the distance and to meditate until I am in the next world. Will I see the dragon? Will the firebird come for me? Will my last moments in this body be the ones in which I attain enlightenment?

Have I seen, learned, come to know, any more now than I had already known that day in Yosu when I saw the kobukson at sunset? Will I, could I, feel more than I did with the music and the mudang in the forest almost thirty-five years ago? Have I gained more from the glimpses and hints that my practice has provided than I realize? Am I closer to oneness with the great all-that-is-and-is-not than I know?

I hope so. But it is the hope of a tired, old man. This shell is worn. Time to move on. Time, perhaps, for a new husk.

Any fear of death I have ever had has been almost surpassed by the pain of getting by each day. The aches and fatigue to be beaten off by sheer will power each morning are almost too much for me now. Even now, in the late spring, when it is warm, I know the time has come. To wait for another winter, pointless.

I go to join many I have known. Priests, farmers, innkeepers, old friends, to join the Japanese I helped to kill, and, possibly, my mother and father. I hope they can be friendly again in the other world. I hope the bad feelings here did not move with them. Maybe, too, I will again be with

Admiral Yi. This would be wonderful. I would not be surprised if he is as high ranking a spirit as he was a human being if ranks occur for spirits. But I think I could talk with him. And if I do find Admiral Yi is there, I know that Kim Taejin will be close by.

Rank, hierarchy for spirits? Is that even a Buddhist concept? There is so much Taoist and Mudang Shamanism and even Confucianism mixed up in my Korean self. Can I not even die a simple Buddhist priest?

There is so much I do not know. I understand this better than ever now.

Perhaps, in a few days or a week, as my spirit has left behind my bony form on a Kaya hilltop (as the sun is rising, for this is my best time), I hope that when I enter the next world, I will know, or remember, much more.

Compiler's Notes

Although a search of all surviving records has been ongoing since the 365-year-old manuscripts were found in the cave at Sudok Temple, no actual document has been verified as referring to the historical Priest Wonho. Both amateur and professional scholars and researchers continue the attempt to find proof that the Priest Wonho is a historical figure. In the meantime, it is left to us to attempt to verify the names, dates, events, and details contained in his scrolls by using other sources. Fortunately, since the main topic is Admiral Yi Sun-sin, this is easier than it would be with almost any other person from that time in Korean history.

Even initially suspicious scholars and authorities have now come to believe in the authenticity of the manuscripts. These Compiler's Notes will illustrate the reasons why.

Two books, containing three primary sources, were of key importance in validating the accounts of the Priest Wonho. These were the highly regarded translations by Ha Tae Hung of *Nanjung Ilgi War Diary of Admiral Yi Sun-Sin* and *Imjin Changch'o Admiral Yi Sun-Sin's Memorials to Court,* which were published by Yonsei University Press in 1977 and 1981. In the second book, there was also a translation of the *Biography of Admiral Yi* by Yi Pun, his nephew. In my chapter-by-chapter notes, these sources will be mentioned frequently. They will be identified as the *Diary*, the *Memorials*, and the *Biography*. I cannot give the works of Ha Tae Hung any but the highest praise in having helped to make this book possible.

Part One

Chapter One
My First Meeting with Admiral Yi

"Know yourself and know the enemy; this is the surest way to be victorious in a hundred battles," is a saying known by every Korean.

The surprise is not that Admiral Yi used a person such as the Priest Wonho as a source of information to help to know the enemy. The startling fact is that the Priest Wonho was previously unknown to history. If not for a child lifting one rock and then another on the hill behind the Main Hall of Sudok Temple in November of 1993, the manuscript, which had been hidden away for 365 years, would still be unknown.

Many had believed that Admiral Yi's extensive writings revealed almost everything about his life. *The Complete Works of Yi Sin-Sin* was compiled and published by order of King Chongjo in 1795. This was a fourteen-volume work with the second, third, and fourth volumes being the Admiral's own writings.

However, the Priest Wonho was not mentioned in any of these works. This alone made the find at Sudoksa suspect. Among the most pronounced expressions of disbelief were those of the *Scientific Journal of Asian Historical Studies*, which in December 1995 devoted almost an entire issue to attacking the validity of what we now know as *The Priest Wonho's Memories of Admiral Yi*.

Nevertheless, over the last few years, every type of expert analysis has confirmed the validity of the Memories of Admiral Yi. The ink, the paper, the wording, or perhaps symbols is more accurate, that were used, the style of calligraphy, and the other items found near the manuscript all seem to prove beyond any doubt the authenticity of the Priest Wonho's work.

Thus, another historical debate ensued. Was the Priest Wonho one of a network of quiet, almost invisible agents that Admiral Yi had working for him or was he the only one? At least until other documents are discovered (and there is now a search going on for any that might still exist), the consensus seems to be that we must assume the Priest Wonho to have been the only one of his kind.

However, in at least one other way, the use of the services of the Buddhist Priest Wonho by Admiral Yi should not be a surprise at all. Along with his professed belief in the saying, "Know yourself and know the enemy is the surest way to secure success in a hundred battles," Admiral Yi has also been credited with having written:

> *The four obligations are to provide national security with minimal cost; to lead others unselfishly; to suffer adversity without fear; to offer solutions without laying blame.*

Certainly, using the services of the Priest Wonho fits with the first of these. He was the least costly addition to national security. He required only food to eat and a place to sleep. And as a Buddhist priest, he did not expect these from Admiral Yi. His only possessions seem to have been his robes of which he likely had only one set. From what we can now see from almost four centuries away, the priest also contributed a wonderful mind, an able body, and a loyal, kind, and brave spirit.

Admiral Yi was not always blessed by the people he needed to work with. But with the priest, he had found a person of the highest quality. The Admiral most probably thought of Wonho as a wonderful bonus, as a valuable tool to provide for the national security, and as a good man. And, had he survived, Admiral Yi would likely have rewarded the priest's loyal service. As was noted a few times by the Priest Wonho himself, Admiral Yi made sure those who deserved credit received it. Wonho's notes on this aspect of Admiral Yi come later in the book.

Unlike some of the chapters, this one was exactly dated. Based on the activities that are described by Admiral Yi in his *Diary*, the non-verified (by any other source) events regarding the Priest's first meeting with Admiral Yi likely had to have taken place on the 13th, or possibly the 14th, day of the 4th moon of the year of Imjin (1592).

Chapter Two
Who are the Japanese?

Admiral Yi's *Diary* verifies the location and dates for Admiral Yi given in this chapter.

The information that the Priest Wonho (according to his manuscripts) gave to Admiral Yi is, as best as can be confirmed, totally accurate. The only surprising thing about his words is the depth of his knowledge on the matter, but given his ancestry and travels, perhaps this is understandable.

Everything regarding the origins of Imperial Japan as having been founded by the Korean kingdom of Paekche (although some recent scholars say it was actually done by the kingdom of Kaya, with Paekche help) in the 4th century has been backed up by many sources, including, most interestingly, the present Emperor of Japan who admitted a few years ago that the blood of Korean Kings ran through him. However, for one book to answer many questions in this regard, *Paekkche of Korea and the Origin of Yamato Japan* by Wontack Hong (Kudara International, Seoul, 1994) is an excellent choice.

Chapter Three
The First Victory at Sea—Okpo

The location, dates, and victories given in this chapter are verified in Admiral Yi's *Diary*. The perspective about them seems the same in modern times as it was when the Priest Wonho wrote thirty years after the war had ended.

Chapter Four
Tell Me of Their Leaders

There still is a Buddhist temple sited high above the port of Yosu, located exactly where the writer of the manuscripts would have it, but since the Priest Wonho never wrote its name, this is only the probable temple identified in his writings. And, though all archives have been searched there, there is no mention of him.

The Priest Wonho's stories of Japan, as told to Admiral Yi, exactly match those recounted in Japan today. The details given here about Minamoto Yoritomo, the first shogun, Oda Nobunaga, the first of the three great unifiers, and Hideyoshi Toyotomi, the Taiko, are to be found in most general histories of Japan, and, of course, in their many biographies.

Egami Kojin, descendant of samurai, Director of Ideas United Institute in Omuta, Fukuoka Prefecture, Japan, and a lay Shingon Buddhist priest, first told me of the destruction of the Enryakuji Monastery by order of Oda. His method of telling the story was better than any book I have yet to read. He also was very interested in the story of Oda, the young wife, and the two generals. "Exactly the Oda way," was his comment. The actions of King Taejong of Korea and his antipathy and harsh actions toward Buddhism and the Buddhist Temples of Korea are verified in any general Korean history.

Kabuki theater fans have Takeda Shingen, the enemy of Oda mentioned by the Priest Wonho, as the subject of many plays. The wars between Oda (and Hideyoshi) against the Takeda clan are also the subject of the Akira Kurosawa film, *Kagemusha the Shadow Warrior*. In the climactic scenes of this movie, the type of musket-shooting army that the arrow-wielding Koreans would soon be facing is seen in stunning and terrifying fashion. In the Priest Wonho's writings, cannon, arrows, and swords are the weapons most frequently mentioned, but the Japanese were also the most proficient users of muzzle-loading muskets in all of East Asia at the time of the Imjin War.

Chapter Five
"The Bullet Went Through Me"

Wonho's recounting of the bullet that hit the Admiral at Sachon makes sense. Before there had been two versions of the shot which hit him. One came from Admiral Yi's *Memorial to Court #8*, dated 14th of Sixth Moon, 20th Year of Wan-li, {Imjin, 1592}, which states:

> *During the fierce battle, a bullet went through my left shoulder and passed out through my back, but the wound was not serious.*

The second version comes from the *Biography of Admiral Yi* by Yi Pun, his nephew. Of this incident, Yi Pun wrote:

> *... he was struck by an enemy bullet in the left shoulder that stuck in his back. He stood commanding his men to fight with his bow in hand even as blood flowed down to his feet. After the battle had ended with our victory, he had his wound cut open and the bullet removed. It had been lodged two inches deep. Admiral Yi smiled and talked as if this were a usual daily occurrence despite the great surprise of all his officers and men about what had happened.*

Although I call him Admiral Yi in this English rendition of Yi Pun's work, in his *Biography*, Yi Pun always wrote of Admiral Yi as Chungmu-kong. Chungmu-kong is the posthumous name and title awarded to Admiral Yi by King Injo in 1643. This title can be translated as Lord (or Minister) of Loyal Valor.

Chapter Six
The Young Captain—Scholar Captain

Some researchers claim to have found records to show that Captain Yi Woo-si actually is a historical figure and might indeed have been the Port Captain of Yodo at the time the Priest Wonho says he was. Others dispute these findings, saying that the Chinese figures used to write his name are very rarely read Woo-si and, while this is intriguing, unfortunately, it does not bring us any closer to the Priest Wonho. (Certainly there will be no snapshot found anytime soon of the two arm in arm with wine cups raised.)

However, there can be no doubting the accuracy of the historical, scholarly, and military facts and points they make in the conversation as recorded. As usual, the main verifications for this are the frequently cited translations by Ha Tae-hung, but, in this case, another source is also helpful. This is a 1997 paper for Professor Milan Hejtmanek, then of Harvard University, by Woo C. Lee entitled *Admiral Yi Sun-sin and the Art of War—Application of the Seven Military Classics of Ancient China in the Imjin War.*

Chapter Seven
"Why Call It a Turtle Ship?"

This conversation is likely the least verifiable section of the whole book regarding the people involved, but the facts as recounted by the Priest Wonho are very accurate. The Koreans did and do hold the turtle in very high esteem. Based on my experience, there is not a Buddhist temple in Korea that does not have the statue of a turtle somewhere on its grounds. The primary source used to verify the Priest Wonho's conclusions in this chapter was *Korea's Cultural Roots* by Dr. Jon Carter Covell, Seoul, Hallym Press, 1981.

Chapter Eight
"Tell Me About What Happened With the Languages"

The primary source used to verify the Priest Wonho's statements regarding the Korean and the Japanese language was Wontack Hong in *Paekche of Korea and the Origin of Yamato Japan*, (Kudara International Press, Seoul, 1994, pp. 160-164) and Dr. Kim Wonho, Professor of English and Linguistics at Hanseo University. Professor Kim mentioned that not all linguists agree on this interpretation, and that some do maintain that Japanese could be a hybrid of various Pacific islands, Ainu, and Chinese-based languages with a strong smattering of Korean influence. However, given the tide of recent research, geographical reality, and the archaeological evidence, the Priest Wonho's conclusions do seem the most likely.

The excerpt of *Memorial to Court #8* was based on the previously noted original translation of the *Memorials to Court* by Ha Tae-hung. Dr. Kim Wonho, Professor of English and Linguistics at Hanseo University verified this version.

This chapter contains one of the few instances where the Priest Wonho's memory seems to have played a serious trick on him. There is no doubt that the Mound of Ears was created in Kyoto, and that it numbered tens of thousands of ears of slain Koreans and Chinese. However, this horrible monument to the war had not yet been created in 1592. In this instance, it seems the Priest Wonho has put part of a later conversation together with one from a few years earlier.

Chapter Nine "He Bettered Them"

Regarding verification of the Young Captain's praise of Admiral Yi and his exemplary use of the wisdom of the Chinese military classics as written of by the Priest Wonho, again the 1997 paper for Prof. Milan Hejtmanek of Harvard University by Woo C. Lee was very useful and much appreciated.

Chapter Ten
The Priest Wonho, Suspected Criminal

In modern Korea, Tae Kwan Doe is absolutely the primary martial art. However, Tae Kwan Doe did not exist in Korea until after World War II when it was developed based on older ways. The Priest Wonho could not have been trained in its use. Plus, he mentions he was assessed as not being good at high kicks, which are a trademark of Tae Kwon Doe.

Based upon the techniques used, the style of teaching of the Chinese priest, and the number of techniques mentioned, it appears that the martial art used by the Priest Wonho against the five sailors appears to be an early version of what is now called Kenpo in the United States and around the world. In particular, the evidence points toward the style presently taught by Tracy's Kenpo.

Tracy's Kenpo is the truest version presently known of what was being taught in the 13th century Shaolin Temple. According to the founder of Tracy's Kenpo, Al Tracy, what we now call Kenpo came from China to Japan in 1232 via a Shaolin priest. In Japan, a few clans kept Kenpo to themselves for centuries, but finally took it to Hawaii when both samurai swords and Kenpo (considered too dangerous) were outlawed in Japan in the late 1800s. (Ironically, the martial art that made Japan the most famous, karate, did not actually come from Okinawa to Japan itself until the early 20th century.) It was not until World War II that James Mitose, the equivalent of the Grand Master of Kenpo, a Hawaiian of Japanese descent, agreed to teach the art to non-Japanese. Of the early non-Japanese students of Kenpo, Ed Parker, who was Al Tracy's teacher, is acclaimed for having brought Kenpo to the continental United States.

There are now many types of Kenpo, many of which are doubtless worthy martial arts. But, shortly before his death, Mitose himself declared Tracy's style to be closest to what he himself taught.

Kenpo Master Jerry Samuelson of Redmond, Washington, a loyal student of Al Tracy, recognized the techniques used by the Priest Wonho. He called the twisting technique used on the first person to be, in Tracy's Kenpo terminology, a technique called "Turning the Key." The technique used against "Broken Nose," confirmed Samuelson, was a textbook use of "Clawing Panther." "When you use Clawing Panther against a charging opponent, it is just like what happened here," asserted Samuelson. "After the forearm has impacted their face, the second half of the move is not even needed."

Regarding the taking away of the stick from opponent number five, Samuelson said, "It could have been a variety of techniques. We have many for taking sticks or clubs away from opponents. It might have been 'Spinning From the Sun.'"

Samuelson and all of Tracy's instructors teach situational self-defense, as did the Chinese priest to the priest Wonho. "We teach that way from day one with each student," said the Kenpo Master. "Every day, each student is shown at least a few new ways to deal with certain attacks, like an opponent punching from the front, or an opponent approaching and grabbing from behind.

"It is interesting the Chinese priest chose twenty techniques to teach the young Korean," said Samuelson. "And about the 264 techniques the Chinese priest said he had to learn to move beyond beginner's status. To get a Black Belt in Tracy's Kenpo, you need to know 250 techniques, and at my school, anyway, as part of the Black Belt Test, each candidate needs to use twenty of these techniques against experienced Black Belts, repeatedly." Samuelson smiles.

Regarding the need to practice emphasized by the Chinese priest, Samuelson said, "Al Tracy says you need to do a move or form two thousand times to really get it. He says that then you can do it properly and automatically." Based on this, if the Priest Wonho practiced each technique daily for six years, he would have been well versed in these twenty techniques. He would and could have performed them automatically. And

Wonho had apparently learned from the Chinese priest at least twenty years before the incident in Yosu.

Upon being asked why he chose a certain 20 of the 250 techniques learned for the Black Belt test in modern-day Tracy's Kenpo, Samuelson asserted, "Probably for the same reason the Chinese priest did. Certain techniques contain principles which can be adapted to many situations, and twenty gives you enough to cover most opponent situations, including some with knife, club, stick, and handgun."

Chapter Eleven
Of Warrior Monks and Refugees

Ha Tae-hung first translated the excerpts of two actual *Memorials to Court* summarized here to English in the previously cited book. Professor Kim Wonho of Hanseo University verified this version as being accurate.

Chapter Twelve
The Best Month of the War

The Battle of Haengju, along with the first battle of Chinju and Hansando, is one of the crucial victories for Korea in the Imjin War.

Thanks to Jeong Sehoon of Seoul National University for his recounting of the story about washing the horses with rice, which verified what was told by the courier to the Priest Wonho and the crowd in the inn.

The belated attempt by the Japanese to conquer the only part of Korea they had skipped in their early campaigns was very similar to the strategy of Alexander the Great against the Persian Empire. Alexander chose to fight the Persians on land and to eliminate the significant threat of the Persian navy by taking away their ports. To do this, he would have to go around the Mediterranean all the way from Greece to Egypt while taking every port and harbor along the way. Tyre, in what is now Lebanon, gave him rough work, but he succeeded.

In Korea during the Imjin War, the Japanese never did.

Chapter Thirteen
Carelessness

The allusions by the Young Captain to the bet between captains are confirmation of something that is only vaguely hinted at in the three primary sources. Everything else is verified almost exactly by these sources.

Chapter Fourteen
The Second Battle of Chinju

The mission of the Priest Wonho cannot be exactly confirmed. However, the subsequent events at Chinju are recounted exactly as in the history books. Wonho's account of the interview with Hwang Chin does reflect an accurate summary of the situation prior to the battle.

The heroic death of the girl Nongae has taken on legendary aspects in Korean history, but is factual. Cheong Sehoon of Seoul National University confirmed the use of the interlocking rings to help her ensure the death of Kiyamura.

Admiral Yi's assessment of the girl's act showed a strong similarity to words written almost exactly 350 years later by a man who would win the Nobel Prize for Literature. Albert Camus wrote for the French Resistance against the Nazis in World War II. In one article, part of a series called *Letters to a German Friend*, he sent a public message to his pre-war German friend. Camus told the German that the French had lost in the beginning in part because they were not sure of themselves, but that now, after some time observing the German occupiers and their behavior, the French people had realized something. They had come to understand that though they themselves were not by any means perfect, they were still much better than the Germans.

Camus' conclusion then, similar to Admiral Yi's centuries before, was that, sooner or later, the occupation of the land by the invaders was doomed since the people, as a whole, had decided against them.

Part Two

Chapter Fifteen.
"They Were Terrified Of Him"

The actual identity of the young naval officer called the Fresh Lieutenant by the Priest Wonho is even more a mystery than is that of the Young Captain. Besides possibly having given many ladies a happy memory, his name for now is lost to history.

All three of the usual primary sources were of help with verifying this chapter. Total verification was found for the allegations the Young Captain believed Admiral Yi's father-in-law held regarding corruption within the Choson dynasty administration, especially regarding the collection of tribute (taxes). An excellent source for this was *Confucian Statecraft and Korean Institutions: Yu Hyongwon and the Late Choson Dynasty* by James Palais, University of Washington Press, Seattle.

Verification that the father-in-law recommended a military career for the Admiral came from Mr. Yi Jae-Wang, a sixteenth generation Yi family descendant, in an interview at the grounds of the Admiral's tomb in October 2001.

The belief that the respected and heroic Kwon Yul was a master of defensive tactics and strategy, but not as confident regarding offensive actions, seems to be shown by the events of the war. However, this belief was not explicitly stated in the sources that I used to confirm the Priest Wonho's account.

Of course, it could be argued that Kwon Yul's method of generalship really was the best way given his ways and means at the time, much as his respected comrade Admiral Yi would have wished differently.

For the sake of the Western reader, I wish that the respected Field Marshal Kwon Yul's name did not somewhat resemble that of the dubious admiral Won Kyun. The *won* and the prominent *k* in both names have confused me enough that once in awhile I say one name when I mean the other. I hope that the huge difference between the two men has been made clear in the Priest Wonho's phrasing in their English translation.

Chapter Sixteen
The Escaped Prisoner

In this chapter, the bad feelings the Priest Wonho has towards Admiral Won Kyun, the ill-fated opponent of Admiral Yi, become even more pronounced. It factors repeatedly into his writings. In the original Korean, the Priest Wonho mentions his antipathy towards Won Kyun even more often than has been put into the English version. Despite having been partially filtered out, the priest's feelings are still very evident in the English.

It almost seems as if the otherwise detached from worldly affairs priest has one thing he cannot let go of. It seems he cannot rid himself of anger over the unhappy doings of Won Kyun in his plots against Admiral Yi and their horrible results. His feelings regarding the arrest of Admiral Yi and the disaster that befell the Korean navy at the second battle of Hansando are the strongest negative words he put to ink in the manuscripts. (These are found in Part Three of this book.)

The full original English translation of the testimony of the escaped prisoner to Admiral Yi may be found in the *Memorials to Court* translated by Ha Tae-hung.

Chapter Seventeen
Assigned to a Second Mission

I first heard confirmation of the difference in the treatment of women under Confucianism and Buddhism in Kagoshima, Japan, in 1984 from George Brooks who was then a recent graduate of the University of California at Santa Cruz. Brooks also was the first person to tell me of Admiral Yi. I will never forget how he spoke about this "great Admiral" who "developed an unbeatable armored ship" and "kicked the Japanese' butts at sea as bad as the Japanese beat up the Koreans on land." To my mind, it is one of the tragedies of recent United States academic history that George did not become a history professor. His enthusiasm for these topics could inspire a comatose turnip.

It is thanks to George that I jumped as fast as a person can when given the opportunity to become the compiler of these translations. The result, of course, has become *The Priest Wonho's Memories of Admiral Yi*. Due to George, I had been interested in Admiral Yi for almost nine years before the manuscripts were found in the forgotten storage cave at Sudok Temple in 1993, and had already visited Yosu, Mokpo, Pusan, and some of the islands where the Admiral had lived and fought.

The fact that it has taken over a dozen years since 1993 for these manuscripts to have been translated into English and compiled has been driving George (and others) to howling. However, accuracy was paramount, and there were debates among the translators themselves. Plus, then I had to put the translations into some sort of coherent order, which meant correlating with the three major sources and….

The details of the court intrigues, which ended so sadly with Admiral Yi's arrest in 1597, are, of course, covered to some extent in all Korean histories. They are definitely mentioned in the translations by Ha Tae-hung and are strongly highlighted in the *Biography* by Yi Pun.

It was in the fall of 2001, with the highly valued and appreciated interpreting assistance of Professor Kim Wonho of Hanseo University, that I interviewed Mr. Yi Jae-Wang, Admiral Yi's 16th generation grandson. Mr. Yi was the caretaker of the Admiral's tomb, which is about a nine kilometer drive from Hyonchungsa, the greatest shrine to Admiral Yi in Korea (there is more about Hyonchungsa in the Epilogue).

Mr. Yi kindly gave detailed information regarding the plot at court and spoke warmly of the Minister of the Left, Ryu Seong-Ryong, of the Eastern group, and of the worthy general Kwon Yul. He mentioned that there has even been intermarriage between the families of Admiral Yi and General Kwon Yul in the interceding centuries. (With perhaps a bit of the dry wit of his great ancestor, Mr. Yi paused, looked at me with a straight face, and said that there had been no intermarriage of the families of Admiral Yi and the descendants of Won Kyun.)

During the interview with Admiral Yi's descendant, the closeness with which the words of the Priest Wonho are supported by the best and highest of sources became even clearer.

Chapter Eighteen
The Love of the Goddess

The English version of the romantic sexual encounter between the Priest Wonho and the Mudang Sugyong contains more detail than he himself wrote. However, I do believe that the Priest Wonho stated everything written by me. Except, in the style of his time and as appropriate to a priest, he did not write as explicitly as modern readers are used to or, often, prefer.

His words could also in part be translated, "As I played a flute in the forest during a rest on my journey, what I thought to be a beautiful goddess appeared and danced. We were both in a heightened state of awareness. Caught up in the moment, we joined as man to woman. Later, she told me she was Sugyong, a mudang, and that …" He goes on to mention the shepherd's hut she knew of "in which to spend the night."

The case of the mudang named Sugyong follows the classic example of the "Charismatic Mudang" as detailed by Dr. Yang Jongsung, Senior Curator and Shamanism Specialist at the National Folk Museum of Korea, in Jongno-gu in Seoul. On June 23, 2001, Dr Yang presented "Korean Shamanism: The Training Process of Charismatic Mudang" to KUCES, the Korean National Commission for UNESCO. During his presentation and in the accompanying booklet, Dr. Yang asserted that normally in the Yosu area the mudang are hereditary, not charismatic. The Priest Wonho confirmed this indirectly. Sugyong indicated to him that she might not have been sought for training had her spirit mother's own young child not died.

Sugyong's illnesses upon reaching puberty are a classic description of those that fall upon someone who is said to be touched by the spirit world. Based on Dr. Yang's research, her training seems to have included all the areas of which "Great Mudang" then and now are supposed to be proficient. The exact training methods used by the spirit mother to train Sugyong were not detailed, but according to Dr. Yang, it would be surprising if they were and also would be largely meaningless to prove the authenticity of the Priest Wonho's words. The training techniques of new mudang vary widely from mudang to mudang.

Again, the original English translations of Admiral Yi's *Memorials to Court 53* and *54* may be found in Ha Tae-hung's frequently cited work.

Chapter Nineteen
The Test

The officer's examination occurred on the dates and location given by the Priest Wonho. These and other details regarding these examinations and some of the related facts mentioned by the Priest Wonho and the Young Captain may be found in all three of the translations by Ha Tae-hung.

Some details given in the Priest Wonho's manuscripts were not mentioned in the usual sources. These included the types of arrows used, the exact distances normally targeted, and the banging of a drum for a successful hit. Yang Bong-hwan and Yu Hyeuk-ju of Hanseo University, acting as research assistants and translators, verified these facts.

Chapter Twenty
The Saint and the Sword

In this chapter, the Priest Wonho talks to Admiral Yi about two main subjects. The first is the Buddhist saint Kobo Daishi, who is one of the most important religious figures in Japanese history. The second is the history and some of the teachings of Tenshin Shoden Katori Shinto Ryu, which was then and happily still is one of the premier martial arts centers in Japan and arguably one of the top schools of swordsmanship in the world.

In this instance, the words of the Priest Wonho are perfectly verifiable by two excellent books. *Japanese Pilgrimage* by Oliver Statler, William Murrow and Company, New York, 1983, is, in my view, one of the three best books ever written about Japan by a non-Japanese. The book is about Kobo Daishi and verifies everything said by the Priest Wonho. I cannot recommend it highly enough. Regarding its author, James Michener was quoted as saying that he believed Oliver Statler knew more about Japan than any other western man alive.

The Priest Wonho's words are the only ones I have ever found that show that Admiral Yi might even have heard anything at all about the strange foreign belief called Christianity. That there were tens of thousands of Christians at this time in Japan is historical fact, and some of the Japanese daimyo who came to Korea as generals for the Taiko were known Christians. It was only a few years later, though, that Christianity was proscribed in Japan.

One of Hideyoshis's best generals was not assigned to Korea. This was the daimyo Tokugawa Ieyqsu, who would eventually follow him as ruler of Japan as a true Shogun. It was this man whom Clavell made immortal in his book. The Shogun, whose descendants would rule Japan for over 250 years, outlawed Christianity. It was felt that a religion which gave power to a foreign man (the pope) and that was too often followed by enemy occupiers (the closest example to Japan at that time was in the Philippines) was unsafe. Shusaku Endo wrote two superb books about the fate of Christians in Japan, *Silence* and *The Samurai*. Both of Endo's books are set in the years when the Priest Wonho was meeting the Young Captain.

Regarding samurai swordsmanship, for any person with even a moderate interest in the world of martial arts, *The Way of the Warrior*, by Howard Reid and Michael Croucher, Century Publishing Co. Ltd, London, 1983, is a must read. This book focuses on the whole history of martial arts, from their beginnings in myth and history with Bodhidharma, the Indian Buddhist Monk, who seemed to travel across and have an impact on all of Asia, to the late 20th Century. Fortunately, a whole section of this book (Chapter Six, "The Classic Weapons Schools of Japan") focuses on Tenshin Shoden Katori Shinto Ryu, and the information given by the Priest Wonho to Admiral Yi is closely verified by this source.

Also, I have personally experienced verification of the words of the Priest Wonho. In Omuta, Japan, lives Mr. Egami Kojin, who is one of my live sources as mentioned in the Compiler's Notes for Chapter Five, and who is a lay Shingon Buddhist Priest. As his guest, and even before I became the compiler for this book, I was able to participate in some special Shingon ceremonies designed to heal or bless the participant or someone whom the participant represents, or to answer another type of prayer.

Mr. Egami knows the Kuji No In, the nine letters or signs of Shingon, which are the same as those of the Mikkyo sect (Mikkyo being a sub-sect of Shingon). He taught them to me in their verbal form and demonstrated them in the hand version mentioned by the Priest Wonho. For the waterfall ceremony, in which I participated in Fukuoka Prefecture in February 1993 (about nine months before the lost texts of the Priest Wonho's *Memories of Admiral Yi* were found at Sudoksa), I was also taught one of the tenth words. The tenth word that I learned is probably different from that used by the swordsmen of Tenshin Shoden Katori Shinto Ryu.

I believe it is wonderful that in modern Japan the teachings of Kobo Daishi and of Tenshin Shoden Katori Shinto Ryu are still alive and real. So, too, are tales of Benkei. The story of Benkei can be found in the Kabuki theaters of Japan, and there are many versions of it in the movies and on the television stations. Where the facts regarding this great hero end and legend begins are now hard to discern.

However, the story of the young Japanese commander killed by Captain Lee Sun-Shin (so spelled to prevent confusion with the name of

Admiral Yi) is verified in the *Memorial to Court #8* and can be read in the translation by Ha Tae-hung.

Part Three

Chapter Twenty-One
The Arrest

The account of the Admiral's arrest seems to be totally accurate. It combines details from the accounts of the event that have come down to us and adds none which do not fit or that are unlikely. The usual three sources were important in verifying the information given in this chapter.

Another source for verifying this account was Admiral Yi's 16th generation descendant, Mr. Yi Jae-wang, in the October 2001 interview. The Priest Wonho's account is also verified by the "Editor's Note" by Professor Sohn Pow-key of Yonsei University in the translation of the *Diary* by Ha Tae-hung. Dr. Sohn, Director of the Yonsei University Museum, Professor of History and Pre-History, and editor of the book, writes of the arrest and subsequent related events to explain the interruption in Admiral Yi's writing of his personal war diary from the 11th day of the 10th moon, 1596, until the 1st day of the 4th moon, 1597.

Chapter Twenty-Two
The Accusation

The Priest Wonho's account is again solidly in line with the information given by the three primary sources.

Chapter Twenty-Three
Transport

All of the sources given in the notes for Chapter Twenty One above agree that the Admiral was transported to Seoul while under arrest. One source, the *Biography* by Yi Pun, specifically states he was kept in a cage loaded on an oxcart and under heavy guard, and that he was bound for at least part of the time with the red rope of the criminal.

Mr. Yi Jae-wang also mentioned the red rope during the October 2001 interview. A depiction of the caged Admiral Yi in an oxcart with the red rope tied around him is commonly featured in all popular accounts of his career. At Hyonchungsa a picture of him in this state that also shows crowds of lamenting common people is included in a series of paintings that tell the story of his life.

Admiral Yi as a prisoner in the oxcart is a familiar scene in all spheres of Korean life. That even the great can fall or that even good people can be unappreciated seems to strike a major chord with the Korean people. Even today, there is a general understanding that the law is provisional and conditional and that justice is arbitrary, although certainly to a much lesser extent than during the Choson era.

Regarding the Priest Wonho and the loyal attendant Kim Taejin escorting Admiral Yi to Seoul, there is no word in the official histories. It would seem highly unlikely that at least a few of Admiral Yi's retinue would not have been nearby during this time, but there is no document I have yet found that verifies this.

Chapter Twenty-Four
Waiting for the King

The date given by the Priest Wonho for Admiral Yi's arrival at Seoul is verified as the 4th of the Third Moon by both Ha Tae-hung in the Preface to his translation of the *Diary* and by Yi Pun in his *Biography*.

It makes sense that the Priest Wonho and his travel companion would find shelter in a temple during the Seoul winter while awaiting a decision at court regarding the Admiral. It also makes sense that the abbot of the temple would check them out carefully before letting them stay there. For the second time, the Priest Wonho names the dates he was staying at an actual temple and even names the abbot.

Bong-whan Temple still exists. It is now within Seoul, the city limits having expanded greatly. The prohibition about temples in the city was rescinded around the time of the fall of the last Confucianist monarch, the final King of Choson, when the Japanese occupied Korea in 1910.

This temple used to be located on the grounds of what is now Yonsei University (interestingly, the place which was the home of Ha Tae-hung, who translated Admiral Yi's *War Diary* and *Memorials to Court* into English) but was moved up the hill to make way for the growing campus.

Records from the Imjin War period are largely nonexistent. The Japanese had destroyed parts of the temple, so it is possible that it was a rebuilt section or one of the few surviving buildings in which Abbot Park met his old friend and Kim Taejin. Here is the closest we come to finding out his pre-Buddhist family name. The Abbot Park says it, but the Priest Wonho chooses not to write it. The fate of Buddhism under Confucianism was mixed in the Choson era. There were not many temples close to Seoul at that time, and some of these have disappeared in the ensuing centuries or were not rebuilt after their destruction by the Japanese.

The words of the Abbot Park regarding Hyangsongsa were accurate, as were the Priest Wonho's accounts of its history and hermitages. In Soraksan, the Japanese destroyed the temple of Hyangsongsa during the Imjin War. However, in 1645, forty-seven years after the war had ended and forty-eight after the arrest of Admiral Yi, the temple was rebuilt and renamed Shinhungsa.

Today, the old temple of Shinhungsa and its two hermitages, Kyejo-am and Kumgang-gul, are highlights of Soraksan National Park, which is a renowned destination for all Koreans and visitors to Korea. As Korea entered the 21st century, over five million visitors a year visited Soraksan. During the summer vacation weeks and the leaf-changing times in the fall, the paths of the park are as crowded as the streets of Seoul on a Saturday night.

The information passed on by the Priest Wonho regarding the names, identities, and ages of Admiral Yi's family members is verified exactly by the texts and notes from the translations of Ha Tae-hung. Not surprisingly, Yi Pun relates the episode about Admiral Yi insisting on feeding his nephews despite complaints. Yi Pun, after all, is one of those nephews. It is also Yi Pun who verifies the story of the Admiral silencing the partying jailers when he had gone to visit Chong On-sin.

However, there is no word in these sources of the exact words given by the Admiral to his sons and nephews about what to do while he was under arrest. The words of Kim Taejin in this regard can therefore only be called likely, not totally verified. Evidence for their accuracy is only circumstantial. Admiral Yi's *Diary* does state that when he was released, two of his nephews were with him the first night, but apparently none of his sons was there that quickly.

Chapter Twenty-Five
All Right, For Now

Admiral Yi was released with a special pardon on the first day of the Fourth Moon of 1597, the verifier, in this case, being the Admiral's nephew Yi Pun in his *Biography*. In his *Diary* (as translated by Ha Tae-hung), Admiral Yi mentions getting drunk that night with family members and friends and identifies his nephew Yi Pun as having been there.

Chapter Twenty-Six
"How Could the Sun in Heaven Be So Dark?"

Except for the writings of the Priest Wonho, we do not have other sources verifying that he spoke these words out loud. However, Admiral Yi did write, "How could the sun in heaven be so dark?" in his personal diary entry of the 13th day of the Fourth Moon of 1597. He also notes that on hearing of his mother's death he jumped up and then fell over.

Compiler's Notes   293

This translation also verifies the mother's words to Admiral Yi regarding "Fight gallantly and erase our disgrace," which are well known to all Koreans even in the present day. They were likely remembered especially strongly during the Japanese occupation of Korea from 1910–1945. Whether her message was so well known in 1597 is less clear, though, of course, the Priest Wonho was most likely actually writing in early 1628.

The condition of the Korean countryside after five years of war as described by the Priest Wonho is confirmed by all sources.

Part Four

Chapter Twenty-Seven
Time to Fight

Everything except for Admiral Yi's interactions with the Priest Wonho and Kim Taejin is verified by the three primary sources. Based on these translations by Ha Tae-hung, the locations, dates, events, many of the names, and even the weather are accurately depicted.

While it will probably never be proven, the incident in which Admiral Yi "as a private person" thanks the Priest Wonho for his loyalty seems to be true to the way Admiral Yi did things. The great man we have come to know would have arranged such a meeting. It was quiet, private, dignified, and led straight into matters regarding what he knew to be his primary duty—defeating the Japanese in the next battles or to die trying.

Chapter Twenty-Eight
The Miracle of Myongnyang

The Priest Wonho's depiction of the Battle of Myongnyang is in exact accordance with those given in the Ha Tae-hung translations.

The version of events regarding the Japanese ships overturning themselves when they hit the anchor chains of Admiral Yi's flagship resolves the mystery of the chain. When people with whom I worked at Hanseo University first heard that I had been chosen to compile the English translations of the Priest Wonho's manuscripts into a comprehensible book, almost every person came to me with their favorite Admiral Yi story. Some of them were truly fantastic, though a few of these tales were not mentioned by the Priest Wonho nor in any sources I could find and are thus not included in this book.

One thing that I was told a few times is that there is now a bridge over the site of the Battle of Myongnyang. In fact that strait is so narrow between the mainland and island that you can now cross it by car in less than a minute. (A great place for an ambush. The perfect spot, rather than in the open sea, for 12 powerful ships to go up against 150 of the enemy. Yet this important site is so commonplace now that it reminds me of Thermopylae in Greece. The site of the epic battle between the Spartans and the Persians is now just a place on the highway.)

Another favorite story of many Koreans had been that "At the Battle of Myongnyang Admiral Yi was so smart that he stretched a huge chain across the strait to catch the Japanese ships." This made a nice tale, and I looked forward to reading about it in the translations by Ha Tae-hung. However, the story is not there. Neither Admiral Yi nor his nephew (whose approach to his uncle's life, written within a few years of the Admiral's death, seems as mythological as historical at times) mentions a chain crossing the strait.

How had that story started? Admiral Yi was not a person to leave such a thing out nor was his nephew. The Priest Wonho's account, in which some of the Japanese ships are damaged or sunk after colliding with the anchor chain of the Admiral's flagship, describes the myth of the chain and why Admiral Yi didn't write of it. It was a happy incident that hurt the Japanese, but it was also not considered a big thing at the time. Or, perhaps, since it was not planned, he did not want to take credit for what was simply a fortunate accident.

Or, perhaps, this story was told years later by an old grandfather, who had been a sailor on one of the twelve Korean ships at Myongnyang when he was young. Things were no doubt said over the fire at night, stories told and retold, and, perhaps, exaggerated.

Chapter Twenty-Nine
Dreams and the Death of a Son

The three translations by Ha Tae-hung verify everything regarding Admiral Yi in this chapter except for his interactions with a certain Priest Wonho.

Chapter Thirty
The Recruit

That Admiral Yi would have been impressed by the fighting spirit of such a boy is very likely, and the fact that he needed more personnel for his ships cannot be doubted. However, as discussed in the Compiler's Notes for Chapter Six about a Yi Woo-si being a Captain in the Korean Navy around the years 1617 and 1618, there is no mention of this event in any source yet to be found.

Chapter Thirty-One
Arrogance and Disdain—The Ming

The three primary sources (as well as others) verify the actions, attitudes, and behaviors of the Korean's Ming Chinese allies while in Korea. They also confirm Admiral Yi's reactions to the bribery attempts and manipulative proposals made by the Japanese.

Chapter Thirty-Two
Victory and Death

The final victory and the death of Admiral Yi as recounted by the Priest Wonho are very much in accordance with the three primary sources.

However, the role of the Priest as the decoder of Admiral Yi's battle flags and his saving of the Chinese commodore is nowhere mentioned. It is clear that, had he lived, the Admiral would have listed the Priest Wonho as a hero in his next *Memorial to Court*. The Admiral never tired of mentioning the good, the positive, and the heroic that he found in others. It was likely that the shock of Admiral Yi's death (his nephew in the biography specifically mentions the commodore collapsing to his knees three times at the news, and the words regarding "even while dead he saves me") kept word of the Priest Wonho's action from becoming well known.

However, having gotten to know the Priest Wonho from his writings, very likely he never mentioned it to anyone during the rest of his life. We know he didn't tell the Young Captain. Maybe he only wrote about it because he thought there was a chance the abbot of Sudok temple would not read it until after he had taken his final walk.

Part Five

Epilogue

I have visited many of the shrines for Admiral Yi; have been fortunate enough to attend the ceremony commemorating his birthday at Hyonchungsa, the shrine at his family home near Asan; and have had the privilege to meet and to interview some of his descendants. Replicas of the kobukson are in many places all over Korea. His giant statue stands in the middle of the street near the heart of Seoul and near the ancient palaces. (It is a picture of this statue which graces the back cover of this book.) It is close to one of the city gates and the site of the city's walls and near the modern parliament. The Blue House of the Korean President is only a few kilometers away.

The Korean people's responses to their great fallen hero as recounted here were detailed in his nephew's *Biography*. The fact that there is a manuscript that is apparently accurate and made of paper and ink from the period they claim it to be provides the only proof that the Priest Wonho actually lived.

The abbot of Sudoksa did all of us a big favor when he asked the Priest Wonho to write. Neither of them could have guessed the academic stir that their project would cause close to four centuries later. If they had been able to, I hope they would have laughed. However, also they would both, I believe, smile sincerely at the idea that their work had helped non-academic and non-Korean people gain knowledge and understanding of a man who stands out as a beacon of courage, honor, leadership, integrity, and genius on a planet where such traits are in short supply.

It is not only the Buddhists or Confucianists of our world who can appreciate him.

Appendix A

Regarding Japan and Korea

As was mentioned in the Compiler's Notes, everything that the Priest Wonho said regarding the history of Korea and Japan seems to be proven. In December 2001 while this book was being translated into English and compiled for publication, the Emperor of Japan publicly affirmed that the blood of Korean kings ran in his veins. To the amazement of many, the Emperor confirmed what had been considered to be treasonous heresy in his country only sixty years before.

What the Priest Wonho said of the founding of a unified Japan, Yamato Wa, by a group of horse-riding Paekche soldiers, led at times by a strong princess, her son, the young prince, and their generals, is factual. The records indicate that it was in or about the year 369 AD that these Paekche Koreans took control of a port in southern Korea, which was one of the cities of Kaya, also called Mimana or Imna, and sailed with the winter winds to Kyushu.

Today, the voyage from Korea to Kyushu is an overnight ferry ride, or a few hours on a hydrofoil. It was a more dangerous journey back then, even though the journey from Korea to the island of Kyushu in Japan is not a long one. At the shortest point, it is barely 170 kilometers. Now, if typhoons are coming, sailing is canceled for the day, as has happened to me twice. However even in the fourth century if one sailed with the seasonal winds (winter to Japan, summer to Korea) and skipped typhoon season (usually later in the summer and in the early fall) one could generally depend upon making it to the desired landfall.

And Homuda-wake, Prince Chin, Jimmu, O-Jin (these were apparently names for the same person) and the horse-riding warriors of Paekche did just that. They made it to the islands of Wa that they would make into Japan. By early in the fifth century they ruled those islands.

Archaeological records prove this. Every royal tomb opened (though the Japanese prevent this on every pretext possible) proves more completely that the royalty of Japan were Paekche. The tombs in Japan changed at the time of the Paekche arrival. All of a sudden, the rulers' tombs are similar to those of the Paekche, and the items inside are identical to the invaders'. The evidence in King Muryong's tomb in Kong-ju in 1971 provided certain proof of the relationship. Japanese temples and their ancient treasures prove this, too, as the Priest Wonho saw in his journeys.

The written records of China and Korea show that Japan, as it came to be known, was formed at this time. As Wonho pointed out, the Japanese records tell the truth even as they distort and create myths about the line of emperors. Some modern Japanese historians admit, or come close to admitting, this truth. One was even arrested for doing so during the dark years leading to World War II. (Nothing good came from Korea, let alone the Imperial family.)

There are too many facts and documents to detail here, but scholarly works which detail the archaeological and written records summarized here have been detailed in the Compiler's Notes. Especially helpful were the works of Wong Hontack and of Covell. A must read on this area, as mentioned previously, is *Paekche of Korea and the Origin of Yamato Japan* by Wontack Hong, Kudara International, Seoul, 1994.

Two aspects of this historical situation should be mentioned. These are matters of which the Priest Wonho could have known nothing.

First, given the realities of the geography and climate, the Paekche had to sail to Japan from the south of the Korean Peninsula. In the fourth century AD, the southeastern end of the Korean peninsula was governed by a confederation of walled city-states, each with their own port. This confederation has been called Kaya or Imna or Mimana.

Kaya had two monstrously powerful neighbors on its borders, Paekche to the northwest, and Silla directly north. Eventually, in the sixth century, Kaya would be gobbled up by Silla, and, in the seventh, Paekche, itself. However, in the fourth century, when Homuda-Wake, a Prince of Paekche, wished to travel to Japan, one of the cities of Kaya needed to make itself available as a port of egress and ingress. In reality, any individual city-state of Kaya would have been helpless to say no.

Once founded, the new island kingdom, then called Wa, or Yamato Wa, would remain in steady communication with its cousins in Paekche as long as the latter existed. Indeed, the emperors of Yamato Wa are recorded as having married Paekche princesses, and members of both royal families were almost perpetually in attendance at the other's court.

There was also a large traffic to Japan in goods and people, including the first Buddhist, who went with an introduction from the King of Paekche to the royal court in Japan.

Yamato Wa, quite naturally, ended up with what we would call a consulate or a customs house at a port in Kaya. (It can also be concluded that the Paekche would have had a similar office in Japan, likely at the port of Hakata in Kyushu.) This port in Korea is called Imna. The *Nihon Shoki* writes of the Japanese government entity in Imna attempting to settle "disputes between the people of Japan and the people of Imna," which is exactly what a consulate/customs house would do.

It was natural that there would be an embassy, consulate, customs house, or trading station, whatever it was called, given the political, geographic, and trade dynamics at work at that time. Plus, this customs house was for Japanese, who to the Koreans of the 5th, 6th, and 7th centuries were basically just expatriate Koreans. They were like Canadians coming home to visit England. Or possibly, the Koreans of Kaya would have viewed the Japanese as a Scotsman in Edinburgh in the 1850s would have looked at an Australian born of two émigré Scottish parents. They were not really foreigners, but …

Sadly, the way this "Imna Japanese Government" was written up in the *Nihon Shoki* (and not the *Kojiki* or in any other Asian historical document) ended up being sadly misused by the manufacturers of State Shinto in the 19th and early 20th century. These were the same people who instituted Japanese Emperor worship. These makers of modern Japanese nationalism made the *Nihon Shoki* (which is also sometimes called the *Nihongi*) and the *Kojiki* to be the literal unquestionable truth. It was to be considered by all good Japanese the way the Bible was by the medieval Inquisition—true in all ways, not to be questioned. These right wing nationalists also pointed out that Japan was superior since only it had a line of emperors over 2,000 years old who are descended from the gods. These Japanese used the *Nihon Shoki* to justify the "re-colonization" of Korea.

Their "Colony of Imna" was used as a reason for "reasserting their historical right" to rule Korea, which they did from 1910 until 1945, in a strong, one-sided, and often-murderous way. The Priest Wonho could not have guessed that the *Nihon Shoki* could ever be used to support this program.

Korean researcher Hong Wontack points out an interesting comparison. There was a Japanese customs house/consulate at a Korean port for over 200 years. Similarly, there was a Dutch trading station in Japan in the port of Nagasaki, on the little island of Dejima, for a similar amount of time during the times of the Tokugawa Shogunate. Following the line of reasoning of some Japanese, the Dutch should now be entitled to colonize Japan. And, we might add, the Dutch were in Nagasaki with their trading station from the 1600s until the middle of the nineteenth-century, which gives them a much more recent claim than that of the Japanese over a thousand years before.

The second sad misuse of the *Nihon Shoki,* which the Priest Wonho could never have guessed, relates to Western historians. Certainly until the 1950s, and to a large extent since then, Japan has been a major focus of study and interest. It was the first Asian country to industrialize, and it gained respect by beating China, and then, surprisingly, Russia, in major wars.

Western countries, including the United States, largely approved of the colonization of Korea by Japan. This was in part because it was felt that it was better for Japan to have Korea than for Russia to have it, especially after Russia became the Communist Soviet Union. However, this feeling was also partly because Korea was a small, seemingly backward country, and it was easy to believe the Japanese when they said they were "helping a poor neighbor." The United States, Great Britain, Spain, the Netherlands, France, and Germany had been "helping out" many more people than Japan, after all, and not just lands that were close by.

By the Western powers, Korea was not considered worthy of independence until Japan attacked Pearl Harbor. With this act, Japan disqualified itself as an approved imperialist nation. Even then, though, Korea was not considered of any significance (as was shown by Dean Acheson's now infamous speech, in which Korea was not mentioned as being important to the sphere of American defense) until the Soviet-sponsored North Koreans attacked South Korea in 1950. It was actually a matter of which side would attack first, the Japanese-trained south or the Communist Chinese-trained north. The latter had been reinforced by thousands of veterans who had fought in China for Mao but were no longer needed after the victory in 1949.

This is not often mentioned in the official histories. Bruce Cummings is generally accurate and honest in his books on these subjects, which has made him a bit controversial in South Korea. Since the end of the 1800s, most Western historians visited Japan when they came to Asia, read the Japanese books, and ended up (Japan was more advanced, after all) accepting Imna as having been a Japanese colony in the 5th and 6th centuries. They and political leaders accepted Korea's subjugation by Japan, at least until World War II partly as a result of this mistake.

Shockingly, even since the 1950s, some seem not to have reexamined this matter. There are still historians who defend Korea's colonization by Japan in the early 20th century. Starr of Chicago might be excused for thinking this one hundred years ago, but what of historians now? Academic writings that matter of factly mention "Japan's colony in Korea in the 5th to 7th century" are still to be found.

It seems that some western historians still need to wake up regarding the truth about Japan's and Korea's histories and interactions. It is to be hoped that the words of the Emperor of Japan will have started this process.

In the long run, the Japanese people would also benefit from acknowledging the truth. Almost predictably, some Japanese responded to their Emperor's words with disbelief, affirming, "Our Imperial line descends directly from the gods" (no matter what the present Emperor himself says, it would seem).

However, even as the writings of the Priest Wonho were being translated and this book compiled and after the Emperor's words, Koreans are still angered by the Japanese Ministry of Education's approval of middle school history textbooks that are full of historical inaccuracies and half-truths regarding Japan's historical interactions with Korea. Among these incorrect "facts" which will be taught to another generation of Japanese schoolchildren is the mention of a Japanese colony called Inma in Korea from the 5th to 7th Century AD.

In the early 21st century a best-selling novel in Korea told that it was Kaya, not Paekche, that led the civilizing of the previously primitive, and in part Polynesian, older cultures of Wa. Certainly the huge mass of evidence I have found shows that it was actually Paekche, but Kaya (Imna or Minama) is certainly a far cry closer than the *Nihon Shoki's* version, or that of some Japanese textbooks.

Appendix B

Facts are Facts or …?

Facts are facts except when they are written by someone who is not a major in a particular field of study. Then some academics will discount whatever is said no matter how accurate the information. In Korea, this seems to be what has happened to Hong Wontack.

Dr. Hong is a noted economist with many publications in his field and a professor at one of Korea's top universities. His works on the history of Japan and Korea are extensively footnoted and seem to be well researched. The English language versions are not perfect, but the English is very good, particularly in the cited book. The instances where the intended meaning is ambiguous are relatively few.

When asked to write an article for the Hanseo University newspaper, I mentioned my past experience in Japan, which had been largely created by Paekche during the Three Kingdoms Period of Korea. To my surprise, this information was cut from the article when it was published. The reason given was that "it would upset the Japanese," and "the Japanese do not like to hear of this." I found this amazing since most Koreans are not overly sensitive about the feelings of the Japanese, and I was only speaking the facts as I have found them to be after working and living in both countries.

Then I remembered that when I was asked my source for the historical information about Japan and Korea in the fourth century, I mentioned Hong Wontack, and the editor made a face. "Oh. I have heard about him," was the answer. A doctoral student at Ewha Woman's University, one of Korea's most venerable places of higher learning, told me, "I would not want to mention Hong in any of my classes. Since he got his PhD in Economics, my professors think he is an interloper writing in 'their' field."

Of course I replied, "But he's right! Don't the facts matter?"

"Not until one of the approved brains writes the book," was the sad answer.

Final Note

This book is as accurate as I could make it. All sources, including books, interview sources, lecturers, and other authorities have been noted as best I could. Any mistakes are my own.

One excellent source, however, was a book by James G. Underwood II, the son of the founder of Yonsei University and its second President. Called *Korean Ships and Boats,* the book was written early in the 20th Century. (As I write, I have yet to get the exact bibliographical information from the worldwide web, and a friend has "borrowed" my only copy, but it is guaranteed to be in the Yonsei University Library in Seoul.)

Underwood gave the best description of a kobukson up to his time, and one that has probably not been improved on since. His book helped me immensely in describing this special type of ship. He fairly conclusively states that the kobukson may well have had iron plating in parts and functioned as did the ironclads of the American Civil War. They were impregnable to all of the enemy's weapons. However, it is doubtful that in fact they were 100 percent "iron-clad." He correctly points out that Admiral Yi himself never wrote or is recorded as having said that they were.

All agree upon the fact that these ships were an essential part of Admiral Yi's strategy to defeat the Japanese at sea. One can only wonder how Admiral Yi would look at modern weaponry and what he would think of our wars now. However, the Priest Wonho would say that mind games of this type are just that, frivolous ways to stay out of the "Now."

The Priest Wonho would likely conclude that it is enough that Admiral Yi set an example for all of us with a life of honor, integrity, leadership, and courage. I for one would never argue with that.

Other Books by M. F. Sawyer

More about M. F. Sawyer's books cand be found at:
www.mfsawyer.com

Married to Islam
by Dalia Shah and M. F. Sawyer

M. F. Sawyer helped Dalia Shah put her unusual and illustrative life story into English. "Dalia Shah" is the pseudonym of a European woman who converted to Islam and married a Euro-Arab Islamic man. At first, she was quite happy. She had four children in her first eight years of marriage. The pseudonym is needed because the man she married could never stand to have his identity and doings revealed in public. Therefore, everything is true, but some things have been disguised.

Things changed. What had started off well began to show the stress of religious, cultural, political, familial, social, and other factors. The relationship with her husband became troubled, as did many parts of her life. This book is about this, and more.

Married To Islam has four main themes. First and second it is about Dalia's life and personal experiences, and how she came to convert to a beautiful Islam that she found does not in reality exist. She loved and still loves Islam in its pure form, which is Islam as the Prophet, peace be upon him, transmitted it, and as it is written in the Koran. Sadly, she found that this was very different from what most Moslems practice today, including her husband. As part of her life story, she explores how and why Islam has lost its way.

Dalia also emphasizes the importance of the Islamic marriage contract for any non-Moslem person thinking of marrying an Islamic person. This contract is the best protection a spouse can have, and yet many Westerners know nothing about it. In a related emphasis, she tells the prospective husband or wife to absolutely meet the prospective in-laws before moving ahead.

This is part of her message about Islam. She believes that originally it was very generous towards women, unlike how it is practiced in many places in modern times. She maintains that for his time Mohammed was very progressive and a friend to and for women, but that this has been skewed; that for a variety of reasons (and she tells us many of them) Islam is not how it was intended to be.

In *Married to Islam,* Dalia also gives her perspectives on world events and on late 20th and early 21st century politics from her somewhat unusual Swiss-Islamic perspective. She chooses "the third way," asserting that Bush was not correct to say, "You are either with me or against me." She affirms that one can be against many of his policies while opposing the so-called Islamic terrorists at the same time. She believes that most Moslems are in this third group.

Dalia also writes of the depression that gradually began to affect her husband. He was a man brought up between two very different and conflicting worlds, of which even he in a light moment said, "It's enough to make a person schizophrenic." The political events centered around 9/11 did not help him feel more at ease. Add these stresses to the guilt he felt for his children not growing up in a way his in-laws in the Middle East would have felt proper, along with the judging eyes of the ghost of his father always peering over his shoulder, and the cause of a heightening bipolar condition can be seen.

The effects of his depression and its strange symptomology are still being weighed. The children are now coming to adulthood, and their choices will show a lot. Methods on how to recognize that a spouse is suffering from depression and how to deal with it are another story within the tale of Dalia's very eventful life.

The effects of the problems caused by the conflicts regarding raising children as Moslems in the West, the stresses of West versus Islam caused by 9/11 and the ensuing wars, and the depression suffered by her husband along with his bizarre symptomology were enough to imperil any marriage. Dalia's tale is both simple and profound. Her unending quest to be a good mother is inspirational. Her patience with her husband borders on the miraculous. The insights she can give her readers, both non-Moslem and Moslem, are wonderful.

Married to Islam is a worthwhile book to read in many ways.

Preview

of

Temple Cook's Guide to (Almost) Enlightenment by Mark Sawyer

Temple Cook's Guide to (Almost) Enlightenment is about an American man, raised as a Christian, who came to explore the spiritual places and teachings of Asia. Mark went from the islands of Japan across to Korea, south to Thailand, to the Himalayas of Nepal, to the rich, wonderful, divine, loving madness of India, and even to Israel and Palestine.

As seen through eyes of one brought up Christian, it is a tale of gurus and masters, teachers and fakes, temples and ashrams, of yoga and meditation, of Buddha, the Hindu gods, of Sufism, of the best and the worst, of dangers, detours, tricks, and traps of the spiritual path, of the zaniness of the New Age, and more.

In India, Thailand, and Nepal many strange persons tell or experience even more unworldly a set of tales. A sexy survivor of the debacle at the Osho ranch in Oregon tells the truth about everything. Old, gnarly, beloved Papa-Ji unloads on a false teacher and anoints a true successor. A holy woman attacked by a knife-wielding madman says not to hurt him. A tantric swami encourages and stars in orgies and is deported, but keeps going. A kind foreign woman, who goes on to marry a "mad mountain monk," rescues a little bearded man by the holy river from the police. Teenage Hindus chant "Om" in an ancient Buddhist temple with a deep-voiced foreigner. Young Swedes shag Thais, giving the temples a bye. New Agers emulate their beloved teacher and end up in prison. A gentle teacher speaks of love for all while the dying holy river spends its last years flowing past her beloved teachers ashram. Foreigners shave their heads, give up money and sex, and become monks and nuns in Buddhist temples....

Mark is careful to make no exalted claims for himself. However, he does express great gladness at having met and studied the works of some wonderful teachers. In the concluding chapters, and sneaking in throughout the book, Mark shares ideas, teachings, ways, and information about those who have actually helped people to reach Nirvana, to attain sattori, to become enlightened, to get there in whatever terms one wishes to use.

978-0-595-42326-2
0-595-42326-4